A KNIGHT'S
ENCHANTMENT

Also by Lindsay Townsend

A Knight's Captive

A Knight's Vow

Published by Zebra Books

A KNIGHT'S ENCHANTMENT

LINDSAY TOWNSEND

ZEBRA BOOKS
KENSINGTON PUBLISHING CORP.
http://www.kensingtonbooks.com

ZEBRA BOOKS are published by

Kensington Publishing Corp.
119 West 40th Street
New York, NY 10018

All Kensington titles, imprints, and distributed lines are available
at special quantity discounts for bulk purchases for sales promo-
tion, premiums, fund-raising, educational, or institutional use.

Special book excerpts or customized printings can also be cre-
ated to fit specific needs. For details, write or phone the office
of the Kensington Special Sales Manager: Attn.: Special Sales
Department. Kensington Publishing Corp., 119 West 40th
Street, New York, NY 10018. Phone: 1-800-221-2647.

Zebra and the Z logo Reg. U.S. Pat. & TM Off.

ISBN-13: 978-1-4201-0697-8
ISBN-10: 1-4201-0697-X

First Printing: June 2010
10 9 8 7 6 5 4 3 2 1

Printed in the United States of America

Chapter 1

April 1210, England

"You come now," said the steward Richard Parvus, his blue-robed bulk filling the doorway.

Joanna tried to reason with him. "Sir, this distillation is almost complete and I should not leave it. I will come soon."

"Come now," the steward repeated, staring at a point in the windowless chamber somewhere above her head and refusing to look at her or the room full of stills, glass and earthenware vessels, star charts, and burning candles. He could not stop breathing, however, and his wide nose wrinkled in distaste at the heady scent of rose petals.

"My lord loves rose water," Joanna reminded him, but Parvus merely snapped his fingers at her as if she was a hunting dog.

"Now, girl! Leave this—*wreck* and make haste! Our lord would have you as a scribe in his audience chamber now, and none of your puffer's nonsense will delay him!"

"I am no—" Joanna stopped, refusing to dignify the insult of "puffer"—meaning a fake alchemist—with a reply. As for the rest, she could leave it. The fire and

candlelight were safe now. It was a small risk, and making
rose water was scarcely part of the great work of alchemy,
but she disliked obeying the steward, who was forever
trying to peer up her skirts and bullied everyone in this
grand, unhappy household, even its priests.

And where was her lord's regular scribe?

She slipped round him, closing the door after her, and
ran down the spiral staircase. Reaching the landing of the
first floor of the tower, she stopped, listening for the slightest sound in the room beyond that strong oak door. To her
dread, she could hear nothing.

"Boo!" said Parvus behind her, laughing as she flicked
up her skirts and sped on, rushing down the second spiral
flight of the great stone donjon. She did not stop to remon-
strate with the steward. Knowing always what was at stake,
she was suddenly desperate for fresh air and natural light,
for the freedom to leave her workbench and walk with her
father by the river and in the city.

*Oh, my father! Will I ever see you delivered from these
terrible men?*

She ran down the rest of the stairs, deliberately not looking at the weighted trapdoor set in the flags of the ground
floor. She ran straight past a guard and out into the yard,
into a day of misty sun and drizzling rain.

Shouts and catcalls at once assailed her as the rowdy
prisoners in the three wooden cages in the center of the
yard roared out what they wanted to do to her. After two
days of this, their lewd persistence wearied her and their
imprisonment was another dread. What if her lord decided
to place her father in with these rough rogues? How long
would he survive in their company, in cages open to the
rain and cold? And what of her lord's other "special" prisoners, held captive with her father in the stone tower of the
donjon? If they were moved to these outdoor cages, how
would they fare?

"Good nature, protect them," Joanna chanted breathlessly, taking the outdoor wooden steps to the great hall two at a time. Inside again, she mounted another stairway leading to the private audience chamber on the second floor and prepared to run again, then stopped.

Ahead of her were five guards surrounding a stranger who topped them all by half a head. Even as they marched away the stranger glanced back, gave her a curt nod, and addressed the captain leading him.

"Your men will be returned once I leave through the main gate."

"As agreed," the captain replied, "though our lord will not be pleased by your plucking them off the streets of West Sarum like so many fallen apples."

"That is no grief to me," said the stranger. "How much farther?"

He was a rude fellow, Joanna decided, coming up behind the troop. Trying to slip by again, as she had with the steward, she saw him closer and liked him less.

He looked a thing of fire to her. Dressed in a long red tunic, he was as high colored and as lean as a single flame, moving with the swift agility of a salamander. His hewn features were as sharp as freshly forged metal, his charcoal-black hair was ruthlessly hacked short, and, even at this early hour of terce, his jaw prickled with fresh black stubble.

He was hot and dangerous, Joanna decided, wishing to be past him. If he had snatched hostages from her lord's entourage before this meeting, that did not bode well. Now she was about to be admitted into her master's presence, she had hoped to plead with him, to ask for more than a month to complete her sublimations. True alchemy was the secret work of years, not days. But her lord was impatient and, thanks to this bad-mannered, fiery stranger, he would be in an ill temper.

Gliding by the first guard, she was making progress overtaking the troop when the door at the top of the staircase crashed open and two of her lord's unruly hunting dogs bounded toward them, tails up and teeth bared.

Not again! Joanna reached into the purse belted to her waist and plucked out a handful of her handmade sweets, which the hounds, though bred to attack the boar and stag, adored. About to cast them to the noisy beasts, she heard the stranger shout "No!" and then whistle: three loud, sharp blasts. At once the great white alaunts became almost comically docile, lowering their heads and whining softly, their claws scratching softly against the floorboards as they milled close to the nervous, stiffened guards and the striding stranger.

Without breaking step he bent, scratched both their ears and throats, and scolded her. "Sweets spoil them, girl, do you not know that yet?"

"Better than the teeth of an alaunt in her throat," muttered a nearby guard.

Joanna silently agreed with the guard but for courtesy she raised her head and looked into the stranger's cold blue eyes. "Thank you," she said, still smarting at the *do you not know that yet?*

"No grief to me," came the arrogant reply as he swept round her.

For a moment, Joanna was so aggrieved she stopped on the final step and a dog lumbered into her, almost knocking her off her feet. At once the stranger somehow lunged past his guards and put out an arm to steady her. It was like being supported by a bar of iron.

"I am grateful, sir," Joanna said, sweet as her honey drops, although her face ached from forcing her mouth into a thankful smile.

He was about to say "No grief," but instead did less, flicking his eyes over her slim figure and tanned face and clearly finding her wanting. He turned soundlessly and marched away, leaving the guards bobbing like flotsam in his wake and Joanna furious at his dismissal of her.

Hugh Manhill of Castle Manhill cursed himself as he strode away. What kind of bully was he to get pleasure from taunting such a slip of a creature? She was not even pretty: too tanned and long-nosed, and her hair was not blond. But her eyes were the warmest, brightest brown he had yet seen and her mouth reddened to a lush cherry when she was indignant. Would her kiss be cherry sweet, or sour? Still, she was nothing but a distraction, one of the bishop's hangers-on and so his enemy.

And where was David in this wretched place? How was he? Since learning the news that David had been captured by Bishop Thomas, Hugh had heard nothing more. He had been on the trail for a month, following the cleric from London to Oxford to West Sarum itself, before he had even discovered where David was being kept. Now that he knew for certain, he had already acted, taking prisoners of his own so as to compel Bishop Thomas to see him.

I will save you, brother, and bring you out of your captivity, he vowed, sweeping into the audience chamber. The girl was there, too, hurrying to a desk close to the dais in the middle of the room. Intrigued by her role—was she a scribe, or a confidante?—Hugh turned his attention to the figure enthroned on the dais.

Bishop Thomas was a small, neat man with a pale, ageless, pleasant face, unremarkable gray-brown hair, and a body only slightly softened by years of good meals and little exercise. Certainly, he did not have the look of a devilcleric, a gluttonous lord of the church, rumored to be rank in murder, sexual intrigue, high politics, and witchcraft, but, as Hugh knew from his own sour personal experience, appearances were often deceptive.

As if to compensate for his very ordinary aspect, the bishop was robed not in the cloth of the clergy, but in a brilliant blue and scarlet two-colored silken tunic, with hanging sleeves of yellow, a cloak of pure white ermine, and gloves embroidered with gold thread. Perhaps he genuinely believed this show of colors and fabrics proclaimed the richness of his see, but to Hugh it put the bishop just a little higher than a performing player: all spectacle and no substance.

As the guard captain stepped up to the dais and whispered in the ear of this gaudy manikin, Hugh mentally ran through his own plans.

Think of this as a tourney and be as you are in battle, doing what you must to survive, he reminded himself. *Do not lose your temper.* Faced at last with the gaoler of his beloved brother, that was almost impossible, but grimly Hugh determined to try.

"By kidnapping my scribe, you have committed outrage against our person and the holy church," Bishop Thomas remarked, in a surprisingly deep voice, as the captain stepped back. "I demand that you return him and the rest of my men at once, unharmed, and that you make payment for your assault."

"You will have your people when I have returned to my men," Hugh replied. "Until that time, they are my honored guests within my camp."

"Let us not play games with each other," snapped Bishop Thomas, his pale face darkening. "Your camp, as you term it, does not exist. Your men have gone to ground and my people are your hostages."

So Thomas's men were seeking his, thought Hugh, gratified at the bishop's irritation. But he had to be careful.

While Thomas held David, he dared not goad the churchman too much.

"I come in peace," he said, tapping his empty scabbard as proof. "I seek news of one of your 'guests' and bring an offer of a ransom for him."

The bishop's look of anger was replaced by one of calculation.

"What did you say your name was?" He slid forward on his chair.

"I did not give it," Hugh answered. "I will say nothing more until I have seen the inmates of your donjon. I can pay a suitable ransom," he added, "but I will see these men for myself. I know that such a great lord as yourself will have kept them in conditions appropriate to their standing."

This was a risk, Hugh knew, but he had to be sure that David was indeed held captive here, and he gambled that Bishop Thomas's greed and vanity would prick him to agree.

And so it did. Bishop Thomas snapped his fingers, rapped out orders, and stepped down from the dais with an escort of priests and soldiers, the fighting men and unarmed dark-robed priests huddling urgently about their lord. Passing Hugh, the cleric directed a single glance not at him but at the tanned girl in the drab robe, jerking his head. At once she snatched quill and parchment from the desk and hastened to join her master.

Shortening his stride to march behind them, his mouth drying with hope even as his gut tightened with anxiety, Hugh tightened one hand into a fist. *At last, I will see you, brother.*

They crossed the yard, soldiers, clerics, and even the dogs, the bishop paying no more heed to the groveling pleas of his caged prisoners than to the dust under his boots as they all entered the sturdy tower.

This must have cost Bishop Thomas almost a thousand pounds, Hugh thought, stubbing his toes on the narrow spiral steps in his eagerness to climb them. *I and my men cannot storm this, but I will find another way to breach it.*

As if in answer he heard the girl, her clear, warm voice rising sweetly above the panting priests and scraping metal as the soldiers toiled with swords and armor up the stairs.

"Your rose water is now finished, my lord. I have made much progress with the other matter and will make more if I am allowed to visit my father when I wish. Please, may I do so? Please, my gracious lord?"

The gracious lord's answer to this heartfelt request was lost as the door to the tower's first-floor chamber was struck by a mailed fist and noisily unbarred. Straining to see ahead of the rest, Hugh saw a large, square room with a comfortable fireplace and, sitting on a bench by a small fire, the person he had searched for and longed to save for over a month.

"David," he breathed, and as if his brother could hear him, David Manhill, once of Castle Manhill, now of Outremer and the Knights Templar, turned on his seat to face his captor.

To Hugh it was as if he looked into a transforming mirror. David was fair where he was dark, open and expressive in features where he knew himself to be stark and grim, easy and merry in manner where he was so often wary and aggrieved. Even now, imprisoned by the worst bishop in England, David rose to his feet and bowed as if greeting honored guests.

"How do you fare, my lord bishop?" he asked, not yet having noticed his brother, a loss which gave Hugh a stab of hot, sickening guilt in his belly. David did not expect to find any of his family here, striving for his release—how could he, when their own father's castle was scarcely forty leagues away and yet no word or succor had come from there? Hugh himself had already called there.

But David was speaking still. "I am healthy in the care of your guards, although I regret my loss of liberty. There is no word yet from my order, I presume? No one to vouch for my good faith?"

"I am here," Hugh answered, buffeting the guards aside as he forced his way into the chamber. "Here, David, and ready to take you home."

He turned and faced Bishop Thomas. "I am Sir Hugh of Manhill," he said, finally giving his title and his name. "No man is my lord, for I make my own way, but I am this man's brother."

"Soft, Sir Hugh," said the bishop, his bright, avaricious eyes darting between the two wall warriors. "Lordless as you are, I doubt you have wealth or wit enough to free your kinsman."

Temper surged in Hugh but he checked it, reminded by the girl's sharp intake of breath just what was at stake here. "I have goods enough for any ransom," he said mildly. "But on what charge is he here? My brother is but lately returned from fighting in the East, a most Christian enterprise, and—"

The rest of Hugh's question was lost as another, smaller man stepped from behind a curtained-off part of the room and approached, speaking urgently in French. Dark as a troubadour, with pale blue eyes showing very startling against his deeply tanned face and shaggy black hair, he was garbed in silks as bright as the bishop's. His accent and language was of southern France, the Languedoc, and Hugh could not understand him.

"Mercury asks if he may have fish again for lunch," David translated, beckoning to the stranger to sit beside him. "His memory is still lost to him, my lord bishop, but he has told me that his head aches less than it did from the battle wounds that he presumes he received when he was taken, together with the brigands in the yard, and brought here."

If the bishop was disconcerted by any of these claims he did not show it, although Hugh wondered at the name "Mercury" and was puzzled, too, by the man's claim to be injured—he could see no mark on him.

Hugh's silent question regarding the nickname was answered by Bishop Thomas himself, who sighed, grumbling, "It will be a mercy for all of us when that young man's memory returns, for I tire of that foolish title."

Unabashed, the Frenchman launched into another speech. Whoever he was, it was obvious from his dress and bearing that he was rich and accustomed to power. He was charming, too, bowing to the company before he sat beside David and smiling at Bishop Thomas as if the man were keeping him in the donjon as a favor. Clearly, Bishop Thomas did not know what to make of him, and did not want to admit that he could not understand him. Again, he was waiting for David to translate.

Others were less comfortable. Standing apart from the crush of guards and clerics, under a thin arrow slit, the girl scowled, then schooled her face into placidity. Hugh had not noticed her move to there but he marked how she looked at the stranger nicknamed Mercury and then at a sallow-skinned, balding man who had joined her by the doñjon wall.

A relative surely, he surmised, thinking them both small and skinny. He wanted to dismiss the pair of them, especially the girl, who was already tainted as part of the bishop's entourage. She had made the fellow rose water, no less! Why should he care if she was on edge, all color stripped from her face and her eyes wide and bright with fear? It was no concern of his if her father or uncle had fetched up in this prison: David should be his sole interest.

David spoke now. "Mercury asks if Joanna may stay to soothe his spirits with her company."

Around him, Hugh noticed many quickly suppressed smiles but the girl—Joanna—was talking, saying something in Latin that had David nodding and the bishop frowning. As the bishop drew in breath to doubtless refuse whatever urgent plea Joanna had made, Hugh stalked across to his brother and clasped him firmly by the shoulders.

"Not so well met, in very truth, eh, David?" he asked softly, startled and alarmed by how thin his brother was. He could feel all his ribs. Turning swiftly before Bishop Thomas could frame a protest, he said, "Name your ransom."

Mercury said something—a witty pleasantry, perhaps, topped off by an elegant wave of a finger. Staring at the man more closely than before, Hugh could see no mark anywhere on Mercury's narrow face or wiry body and decided that the man would be much improved by some. "My lord bishop?" he prompted, before the Frenchman could interrupt afresh.

"What price a man's soul, Hugh de Manhill?" Bishop Thomas answered, pointing at him with a gloved, ring-studded hand. "There are many who speak against the Knights Templar. Word has reached me that your brother has committed many deadly sins of witchcraft and blasphemy."

Hugh laughed. "My brother is the most holy man I have ever known."

"Then your knowledge is sadly lacking," snapped the bishop, "and you are either a fool or a blasphemer yourself. Who else would dare to lay hands upon my own people in my own city?"

You would not have granted me an audience without

such persuasion, Hugh thought, but this was too obvious to speak. "How may I make amends for David?"

"Bring me the relics he has stolen! The treasure he has kept from me!"

Hugh had no idea what the bishop was talking about. Keeping his face very still, he tried a second time. "I have gold in abundance."

"And have you also the blood of Saint George? The swaddling cloths of our lord Jesus Christ?" Thomas looked directly at the girl Joanna: a hot and at the same time reptilian glance. "Have you the secret book of the Jews?"

Hugh narrowed his eyes. "On what specific charge do you hold my brother?"

Bishop Thomas flicked a long sleeve at one of the milling dogs, catching the beast across its nose. "Such things as an honest Christian would dread to whisper. *He* knows."

"Hugh, enough," said David, but Hugh ignored him. David was his elder by scarce two years and they were equal in arms.

"Why do you claim he has such relics?" he persisted, just as Mercury bounced to his feet with another beaming smile and another mellifluous, incomprehensible inquiry.

"The relics. How?" Hugh asked again.

At his brusque demand, the bishop hissed like a disturbed adder and drew back in a swirl of brilliant silk. "It is not for you to interrogate me!" In his sudden fury, his pallid face became even more corpse-like. "Take him!"

But he spoke to air. Hugh had already anticipated the order and reacted. In an explosive series of movements he barged through the guards, hurtled to the eastern wall, and grabbed the girl. Whistling to the barking dogs, he slid a dagger from his boot with the speed of a snake's tongue and flicked it to and fro before the bishop's seething face.

"God's blood, he has a killing knife!" shouted one man.

"'Gainst all courtesy and honor!" wailed a priest, crossing himself over and over.

"The hounds blocked us, my lord—"

"Can no one silence those blessed dogs?" roared Thomas, glowering at Hugh as if he wanted to cast him into the lowest reaches of hell.

Hugh whistled and at once the yammering dogs fell silent, turning trusting faces to him. Other faces, blank with shock, also stared.

"I am leaving now," he said, ignoring David's murmured disapproval and hauling Joanna off with him as if she were a squirming puppy. "I shall return tomorrow, with my brother's weight in gold and, possibly, this girl. Then we negotiate."

Still brandishing the killing knife and with his back always to the wall, Hugh moved to the door. No one spoke as he motioned the two guards outside the chamber to step within it—although they were two against one, neither was keen to tackle him, even with an armful of girl. No one seemed to breathe as he motioned to the dogs and set them at point in the doorway.

He had hauled Joanna, panting and furiously protesting, halfway down the stairs before a new tumult erupted above their heads, shouts and bodies colliding and pounding feet while Thomas's voice was raised in loud complaint.

"Get those dogs away! Get after him! Away!"

Carried off under Hugh Manhill's brawny arm like a parcel of clothes, Joanna struggled fiercely and silently. There was no point in appealing to the donjon guards, who rightly feared this brigand, but who also distrusted her, her father, and their alchemy.

But it was humiliating to be so trapped and helpless! Wasting no breath or energy on pleas, she kicked back at her kidnapper, blow after blow on his shins that made her heels ache. Speeding down the staircase at a dizzying clip that was turning her sick, she coiled about in his brazen, hairy arm, trying to break free of his rib-smashing embrace.

Sensing his head lowering toward her, she tossed back her own, seeking to crush his nose. He avoided her attack easily and blew a squelching kiss against the back of her neck.

"No grief to me, Joanna, if I drop you on these steps, but your backside will smart."

"Release me!"

"No."

His husky voice close to her ear vibrated up and down her spine, making her even more aware of his greater power and strength. Skimming above the stones, flailing out uselessly with her arms as she scrabbled against the tight spiral stair for any purchase, Joanna was tempted for an instant to give in, to twist and rest her aching, bouncing head against his shoulder.

Appalled at her own useless girlishness, Joanna kicked out harder. Manhill merely grunted, stopped on top of the trapdoor on the ground floor, dropped her, and then tossed her over his shoulder. He was striding even faster now, and the half-light of the donjon gave way to sudden, brilliant sunlight.

"You shall not take me!" Joanna bawled, pummeling his back with her fists as her stomach hurt from being squashed against his shoulder blade and her chin smacked painfully against his spine. There were surely other men in the yard, men whose wives and children she knew, whom she had helped in the past. Surely they would not leave her lolling over this man's back!

"Help mmmm—"

Her cry was stifled as Manhill swept her off his shoulder into his arms, bearing her into a shadowed corner beneath some scaffolding that had not yet been taken down from the base of the donjon. There, amidst benches, and planks of wood, workmen's tools, and a ripped and dusty old cloak, he set her down, tipped back her head, and engulfed her mouth with a massive hand.

"You will listen!" he said urgently.

She tried to knee him in the groin. He shifted too quickly and took the blow on his thigh, without any obvious discomfort.

"Now you will listen," he growled, giving her a teeth-rattling shake. "I have no interest in harming you."

"As say all kidnappers!" Joanna rasped out behind his hand.

He smiled at that, a brief softening of his lean, tanned face. "If I take my hand away, will you scream? Yes, I think you will," he went on, answering his own question. "A bucking little mare like you will always rattle the rafters with your complaint. So I will leave you here, Joanna, to cry for your loathsome lord, who even now has sent his men to the main gate when I am leaving by the postern. His guards are slack: too much wine and food and easy duty."

Speaking, he manacled her wrists in his other hand, released his numbing grip on her jaw, and thrust a woolen glove past her gasping lips. She gagged afresh and he pushed her down onto her knees.

"Until tomorrow."

He left her amidst the scaffolding, sprinting for the postern gate while she clawed the glove from her mouth. She tried to yell but her coughing, muted alarm was lost in the greater whirl of rushing bodies as Bishop Thomas's men pounded futilely after their quarry and Hugh Manhill escaped.

Chapter 2

Losing the bishop's men in the narrow, crowded streets of West Sarum was nothing, the work of moments, but afterward Hugh felt guilty. He wished he had not gagged Joanna with his glove, nor handled her so roughly. She was half his weight, an unarmed, untrained girl.

Very brave, man, to take on such an enemy. Why not terrorize the little dogs, too?

David would be ashamed of him, and he would be right. He should not have done it. He ought not to have pushed that old woolly mitten into her mouth. A mouth made for talk and laughter and kisses—

"He let you go," said Bishop Thomas. He and a guard Joanna did not know, a new one, had climbed the donjon steps with her to her chamber in the tower. Between scratching his stubble and acne, the skinny young guard kept peering at her star charts and distillation vessels and crossing himself. Joanna longed to tell him to stop, but she dared say nothing. The bishop was already in a foul mood.

"He released you," Thomas repeated. He stripped off a glove and stirred a finger in the cooled rose water, his neat face as impassive as on those rare times when he read scripture. "Why should he do that?"

Joanna felt a rush of inner heat singe her cheeks and ears. To admit the likely truth—that she was too much trouble and too worthless for a man like Manhill to drag off with him—was too mortifying and too revealing.

"No, my lord. I escaped him," she lied, her voice firm enough to disguise her inward trembling. Accustomed to respect from alchemists and scholars, she was still shocked by the ease with which she had been taken by Manhill. Truly in matters of brute strength, it was a man's world. "When your guards came, he fled," she added. "And he is returning tomorrow."

"So he claims. With gold." Bishop Thomas flicked one of her glass flasks, making it ring. "Gold. Which I do not see here."

"On your instruction, I am working on other elixirs, my lord," Joanna swiftly reminded him. "I have great hopes for several, and my father agrees. If he could rejoin me, my work here would be done in twice the time."

The bishop smiled and shook his head. "Solomon has his uses where he is."

Joanna bit her lip to stop herself from crying out, *What uses in prison?* For that was where her father was: in the donjon, with David Manhill and the mysterious Mercury, whom she herself had named for his quicksilver charm and dazzling smile. "Should I see Mercury again today? If I can help his headaches, he may recover his memory more quickly."

Thomas gave a snort of laughter. "And you see your father also, and that blasphemer Manhill. What do you find to talk about with him? I know you do so. The guards tell me you always have your heads together."

"Of learning from the Arabs," Joanna said, and left it at that. She was too seasoned in dealing with the bishop to question his assessment of David, whom in truth she admired and who was easy to talk to. Trying to help him, she did venture, "Tomorrow, though, if his unruly brother brings a fine ransom—"

"It will make no difference. That Templar is mine and he has things of mine, things I want."

"But what if it is as David claims? What if he has nothing from Outremer but a few more battle scars? Would it not be a mercy, or prudent, to release him? The Templars are a mighty order."

Bishop Thomas slammed both hands on her workbench, causing the glasses to ring out afresh in shrill protest. "Manhill has my relics! He carried them back from the Holy Land, relics and treasure, and he has stubbornly hidden them! You should look to your own concerns, girl, before you take his side!" A leer glinted across the man's pallid face like a flash of lightning. "Or are you now in league with that big brute, Manhill's brother? If so, you have lost your way! Hugh Manhill has no lord or lands: he is a tourney knight, intent on winning prizes, jousting from tournament to tournament. I know his type, the kind who brings a killing knife to a sacred negotiation!"

"My sole interest, my lord, is with the red work and your well-being," replied Joanna, hating to refer to the search for gold, the "red work" of all serious alchemists, but desperate to remind the man that she was still useful to him. "Both my father and I—"

"Will be together, in the lowest part of the donjon unless I see some results before the end of this month! Before the rising of the next new moon, Joanna!"

Bishop Thomas turned on his heel, knocking an earthenware bowl of sulphur onto the floor timbers with a trailing sleeve. On her hands and knees, urgently sweeping up the precious material before the slouching guard could tread in everything or it was further corrupted, Joanna heard the lord of the church leave. The door slammed after him and she was alone again, with her father, Solomon, still a prisoner, David still unfree, and Mercury still a living mystery.

And now she had less than eight and twenty days to find the secret of producing gold.

After that, she tried to work but her hands shook too much for the exacting measurements required. As the day drew on she pottered about her workshop, cleaning, recording, and desperately thinking. When the bells of West Sarum cathedral pealed out and she knew her lord would soon be at his lunch table, she ran to the kitchens. In the hubbub of preparations she was able to gather a basket of fresh manchet bread, cheese, green salad and verjuice, beer, and a whole baked trout on a platter for Mercury, keeping fish and cheese separated by the jug of ale. The chief cook saw and nodded to her—they had an understanding, she and Walter. Last winter, Joanna had nursed Walter's wife and twins through the greater pox when no one else had dared go near lest it was the small-pox. Now all were thriving, but the cook had never forgotten. He even sent a spit boy with her, with a second basket for food for the guards, to clear a passage through the kitchen smoke and crowds and, later, to announce, "Victuals for the prisoners!" within the donjon.

Crossing the trapdoor on the ground floor of the tower, Joanna paused and, when the guards were marching elsewhere, she pushed some of the bread through a small gap. It was not much, but it was all she could do for the poor wretches beneath her feet, whose names and crimes were unknown to her. She thought she heard a wild scrabbling somewhere in that fetid dark, but now the guards were marching back and she sped swiftly up the staircase, following the spit boy.

Within the first-floor chamber, Mercury was playing

dice on his bed, but he came quickly, seeing the platter of fish. Sweeping it from her with a grin of thanks, he returned to his bed to eat.

While the guards crouched and rummaged in their own basket, Joanna and Solomon had a moment in private. David tactfully hung back as Solomon approached the table where she was setting out the food.

"*Shalom,* daughter," he said softly in Hebrew. Neither of them knew much of the tongue of their forebears, but what they knew they kept alive.

"Are you well?" Joanna whispered, passing him a chunk of bread and clasping his hand—the only contact they could smuggle for themselves without the guards manhandling them apart.

"I could be far worse, my daughter." To prove his point, Solomon took a healthy bite of the bread, his dark brown eyes lively and twinkling at her. Starry eyes, Joanna had always thought them. She could stare at his tanned, mobile, jaunty face all day.

"How goes the work?" he asked, prodding the dish of salad toward her.

"I will eat later," Joanna lied. She wanted Solomon to eat as much as possible. She wanted to be hopeful, to give her father respite from care, but she could not lie about alchemy: it was a sacred task. "It goes slowly," she admitted.

"Our lord still desires gold?"

"Amongst other things." Joanna glanced at David, who was standing with his back to them, slowly pouring himself a beaker of ale.

"You fear for David against our own Goliath?" Solomon asked. "David and Solomon. It is apt we are together, is it not?"

Joanna nodded, trying not to smile. Her father said this at least once each time she was with him. But then he was very old: at least sixty.

"We spoke of the temple today. He has seen it, Joanna! He has touched its living walls! But something has happened." Solomon scanned her face and sighed, the straight set of his wiry shoulders drooping for an instant. "You are in greater fear than yesterday."

"No, Father."

"I say you are. You are as taut now as wise King David's lyre string."

She would not tell him of the terrible deadline. To speak instead of the Goliath of Manhill, of Hugh, who had bested lord Thomas's alaunts and stood against the bishop like a living tower of stone, was a strange relief. She liked talking about him, Joanna discovered. She wanted to talk about him—without mentioning the matter of the glove.

He will apologize for that, she vowed.

As if sensing the content of their conversation, David turned and beckoned to her. "A beaker of beer for your father?" he asked.

The question was nothing the guards could object to, and it was natural for Joanna and her father to join David. Leaning over the table as he poured two beers gave them all a chance to put their heads together.

"You are in good health?" he asked Joanna.

"I know all about my daughter's abduction, my boy," murmured Solomon, wiping his long black mustache with his fingers, a habit of his when nervous. "There is no requirement to dissemble."

"I am in perfect health." Joanna smiled at both men, thinking how bright and fair David was beside his dark, looming brother. Aware that David might report this to Hugh, she was gratified to add, "I have known worse roughhousing from Giles the spit boy."

Solomon raised his fine dark eyebrows and took a long drink of beer. David gave her a measuring glance, then nodded.

"Hugh is the very best of brothers. I know he has a temper worse than fire, but I swear on my soul that he would never harm a woman."

"Amen," said Joanna, thinking of the glove. Aside from her pride she was unhurt, but what is injured pride but a blow to the spirit? Would Hugh or David have liked a gauge thrust into their mouths to silence them?

"But the hounds this morning?" Solomon asked. "I know those alaunts of old, and they are not cheerful beasts. Big as donkeys, too. Large, white donkeys with huge teeth."

"How did he persuade them to obey him? That I do not know. It is Hugh's peculiar skill, and he has had that uncanny gift since boyhood. He is the same with horses. In the Arab kingdoms he would be much sought after, I warrant, as a keeper of hawks."

"Or women," remarked Solomon unexpectedly, an interjection which Joanna found less than amusing. She raised a hand, wanting to distract her father, but David was already answering.

"Ah, not women, my friend! My younger brother is a confirmed bachelor. Or, I should say, no woman has caught his heart yet."

Listening, Joanna found her own heart beating faster, although she told herself it was because of Bishop Thomas's earlier threat. "You think he will return tomorrow?"

"As certain as the rising sun. His word is as strong as Saladin's."

Even in West Sarum they had heard of the famous, chivalrous Saladin, scourge of King Richard while that great warrior king was on crusade. Another time and Joanna might have prompted David for a tale of Saladin, or of the wise men of Saladin's court, for David knew many such stories and was well versed besides in the learning of the Arabs. He knew a little of her work and they had spoken together of it. He had read the famous

texts of Jabir and had even heard of Joanna's own heroine
of alchemy, Maria the Jewess. Today, though, her interest
was in the Templar's younger brother.

"Is he learned? Cultured?"

"My brother? I doubt it. He cannot read and his signa-
ture sprawls like a spider's web. He knows nothing of
music and less of mathematics."

"You cannot pick his brains for the red work, then," said
Solomon, chewing now on a lump of cheese.

"As if I would!" Joanna told herself it did not matter.
She already knew that Hugh Manhill was a scoundrel, so
why should his lack of refinement disappoint her?

"He is no fool, my brother," David added quietly.
"Unlike some." He half turned to admit the smiling, sated
Mercury into their midst.

"If Mercury is slow-witted, then I am a bear," Joanna
whispered back.

"Surely a bear cub?"

"Hush!" She was never comfortable when the Templar
knight flirted with her. A donjon was no place for courtly
games, least of all when she and her father had been threatened with the underground prison and David himself held
as a blasphemer. "This is not the time!"

"Nor the place," David agreed. "Good meal?" he asked
Mercury in the tongue of the Languedoc. "I notice you ate
all the fish."

"But yes, it was so delicious and I was so hungry," Mercury replied, bowing over Joanna's hand as if she were
the lady of the bishop's palace. "Do not look so troubled,
Joanna, my heart! My memory will return"—he tapped
the side of his head and snapped his fingers—"and I will
bear you off to my manors and farms, to eat more fine
things and dress in cloth of gold."

"You have seen cloth of gold, then?" Joanna countered.
"You remember it?"

"But yes! Though when you smile I forget again. It is a shimmer of a thought, no more."

"Still, that is progress if you can recall anything, and know you have manors," Joanna remarked, charmed but not convinced by Mercury's boyish smile. "How is your head today?"

"It aches," came the predictable response, while he bethought himself to pat one side of his perfectly shaven cheek. "I think it aches a little less. But perhaps not. Who knows? Not I! I do not remember my own name!"

Joanna avoided David's quizzical eye. Over these last few days she had often wondered how much of Mercury's memory loss was real. He had been brought in a few days earlier, with the rabble of prisoners now caged in the yard. Those men were notorious brigands, well known in the district for mayhem and kidnapping, and although Mercury appeared to be of their party, he had been brought in unconscious and when he stirred, he swiftly denied being one of their "gang." He had denied everything: who he was, where he was, and what he was doing in woods close to West Sarum. His fine dress had attracted Thomas's greed and interest and the bishop had ordered him brought up here, to be kept safe with the other "special" prisoners.

Since then, Mercury had rapidly recovered his appetite while at the same time he continued to assert that he had no idea who he was. If that was true, Joanna wondered how he could be so carefree. But Mercury was clearly of a sanguine humor.

"Do you ever wonder what will happen if you never remember?" David asked, but Mercury merely shrugged.

"Someone will know who I am."

"Suppose no one comes?" David persisted.

"Like your order?" Mercury replied, with that quickness—slipperiness—that Joanna had named him for.

"That is enough," one of the guards warned, with uncanny timing, saving the young Frenchman the trouble of adding more. "The prisoners have eaten now and Joanna must go back to her studies." The guard spoke gently: Joanna had given him a tincture last summer that had eased the aches and pains of his grandmother.

There was nothing else for Joanna to say or do but gather up the baskets and leave. This guard at least allowed her to embrace her father, and as she did so Solomon whispered the ancient alchemical wisdom: "One becomes two, two becomes three. Mark it well, my daughter!"

"Out of the egg comes gold," Joanna replied, speaking this secret of "red work" to give him heart and to encourage herself.

But how would she find gold in less than a month? And if she did not, what would happen to Solomon?

Leaving the baskets with the spit boy, she climbed the stairs back to her chamber workshop with an uneasy mind and an aching heart.

Chapter 3

She lost herself in work, spending hours refining an elixir that Bishop Thomas had demanded of her to give him more "manly vigor." Joanna dared not suggest that such potions were unseemly for a man of God. She could only pray that if her lord was thinking of using the mixture *with* someone, that the person he desired also wanted him.

Calling it a love elixir made her hands more nimble as she pounded together dill, thyme, garlic, and yarrow for vigor, adding mint for good digestion and marigold for the couple's hearts. Simmering and distilling what remained, drawing off impurities, testing its color by candle flame, Joanna tried to focus on excellence.

Toward midnight, opening the narrow door to her chamber and allowing the moonlight from the arrow slits to clothe her workshop all in silver, she found herself thinking not of the work, or gold, but of love. When would she know love? When would her essence mingle with another's?

She remained standing at an arrow slit for so long that she fell into a curious dreaming state: a daydream at night. She was walking beside a shallow, sparkling river with a long-stemmed red rose in her hand. A man strolled with her, his arm threaded through hers, his face in shadow from the overarching trees. He pointed to an alaunt, splashing in the water, and they both laughed at the dog's play. Then he turned to ask her something and she saw his face.

It was Hugh Manhill.

It means nothing, Joanna told herself for the hundredth time the following morning. *A daydream of Hugh Manhill is just that, a dream.*

Still, she could not shake off feelings of excitement and anticipation. Her heart kept racing and her breath shortened each time she thought she heard horses outside. The very palms of her hands tingled as she sped about her workbench, endlessly checking, endlessly devising reasons why she had to leave the corbel-roofed chamber and peer out through the arrow slits into the yard.

If I am looking out for him, she told herself, *it is only as a favor to David. I can call out to David when Hugh returns.*

She did not consider for a heartbeat that Hugh would not come back.

Even so, she could not forget the threat looming over herself and her father. That, and professional pride, ensured that she made the bishop's "love" potion with the utmost care and skill.

She was pouring the sweet-scented elixir carefully into a very pretty blue glass bottle when Richard Parvus reappeared in her doorway.

"Bring your toys," he ordered her brusquely, hovering on the threshold in a miasma of pursed-lipped disapproval. "That Manhill pestilence is back and our master wants a show."

"He is here? Already?" Unconsciously, Joanna put her

hand up to her lips as her heart stampeded within her body. She was about to see Hugh Manhill again. Would he speak to her? Had he dreamed of her, too?

"A show, girl! Or is even that beyond you?"

"Will it be here? I can assay gold here in my furnace and test Manhill's coin to see if it is pure gold."

"My lord hold an audience in this poky, stinking chamber? I think not."

"But still a show?" she asked, disappointed that Hugh Manhill would not see her workspace or her greater skill. Attempting alchemy in the audience chamber would be almost impossible: the fire there would not be hot enough to drive off impurities from the materials she used. But she could do one thing, she thought, dipping beneath her bench to find a large carrying basket and sling. "Naturally, I can do that."

This was not the first time she had been compelled to corrupt her work. And she would have to give Thomas his potion some time in her "performance": the bishop would expect it. The thought of handing over that pretty blue bottle while Hugh Manhill watched made her want to crawl into her furnace and shrivel away into ashes—yet what did Manhill's opinion matter?

She began placing candles, cinnabar, and other ingredients in the basket. "I will exceed all wishes and expectations," she added as her heart felt to plummet somewhere deep into her belly and then instantly began to rise, like a skylark, in a sweet blaze of excitement. "But I shall need more supplies afterward. I will need to go into the city to fetch them. Please tell my lord bishop this."

"If it were up to me, you would not go."

"But it is not, sir, and the bishop will allow it."

"Foolishness!" grumbled Richard Parvus, starting back down the stairs.

Joanna ignored him as she rapidly gathered the rest of

her equipment. A visit to the city would give her a chance to visit other scholars and alchemists within West Sarum, and she did not intend to waste it.

Yet, as she carried her things down from the tower, step after step, taking care not to spill anything or jostle the volatile substances, her main thought was of Hugh.

I am about to see him again.

Hugh had brought the bishop's scribe with him, returning the hostage as a sign of his good faith. To reinforce his argument, he had also brought along half his men, treasure, plate, coin, and Beowulf, who would show the alaunts how to behave. Beowulf growled as they entered Thomas's audience chamber, hung today with silks and tapestries, and Hugh touched the wolfhound lightly on the neck.

"I dislike it here, also," he said softly, "but we must do this for David."

His brother was already waiting in the chamber, unchained, standing pale but steady between two heavily armored guards. Hugh's spirits leapt to see him—today, they would walk out of Thomas's palace and ride at full tilt as they used to as boys. Today they would drink a lake of ale in every ale-house they found, and wink at every tavern wench, and—

Joanna is here.

Hugh straightened, conscious of the single glove at his belt. For a foolish moment he tried to make himself smaller, hunching over Beowulf as his face and body sweated, as hot as if he had run a mile in armor. She was not even turned to him but he would know her anywhere: that bright riot of waving brown hair, monk-brown robe, and trim figure.

She had her back to him and he saw the supple arch of her body as she leaned over a low table, busy with bowls and cloths. She crouched lower, bending to pour something, and the pert roundness of her bottom was instantly suggested by the curving pleats of her skirts. It would be a lush pleasure for her sweetheart to throw up her gown and have her there, facedown across the table, amidst the shimmering bowls.

Hugh felt himself immediately aroused by the image and the idea. Trying to disguise his state he crouched and fiddled with his boot ties, glad of the distraction when Beowulf attempted to lick his ear. "Down!" he muttered, both to the dog and to himself.

Somehow, Joanna heard him and now she twisted about to face him, her robe slapping against the table leg as her head snapped upward. He braced himself for a glare, for her to jab her own lips, for her to protest to her lord. Instead, she nodded at David, as if silently saying, "Here is your brother. Do your best for him."

I will, he thought, glad of the reminder, gladder still that she was there. He did not wonder at the reason why: to see her again and realize that she did not consider him lower than a worm was sufficient. Still kneeling, he smiled at her, while the bishop's steward cleared his fat throat and called for quiet.

He was grinning at her, the arrogant pig. No, Hugh Manhill was no pig: he was too large and fast. A modern Goliath, Joanna decided, thinking she had wasted her silent warning on him. If he gained his brother she would be overjoyed, but if he failed today, David would be the loser. She sent up a swift prayer for Manhill's calm success as Bishop Thomas settled more comfortably on his chair and resumed "negotiations."

"I have seen better silver cups in a common tavern," he started, smirking at his steward, "and more gold under a peasant's mattress. Do you think such paltry offerings will redeem your brother, Hugh de Manhill?"

Joanna glanced anxiously at Hugh, whose color and countenance had not changed as he rose slowly to his feet. Only his trim, well-brushed wolfhound, glowering at the cowering alaunts, revealed any tension.

"This is for his lodgings only." Hugh swept a negligent arm in the direction of the treasure chest and bags of coins. "I have more in readiness for his release."

Thomas raised his eyebrows. "And the relics? My relics?"

"You have your scribe," Hugh reminded him, nodding to the man, "and it is no grief to me to speak to the Templars." He ignored David's slight head shake and spread his hands, inviting a response.

Instead of which there was silence, broken only by Parvus's harsh nasal breathing and the cheeping of sparrows nesting in the roof.

"How now, my lord bishop?" Hugh asked softly, as the silence drew on. "Or shall I speak of the rumors I have heard concerning the lascivious corruption present in this see?"

Watching with lowered head through half-closed eyelids, Joanna felt herself becoming more uneasy. So far, her lord had not asked Hugh to approach or be seated on one of the benches lining the walls of the audience chamber. He was even sucking a sweet—no doubt one of her peppermint pastilles, which Thomas insisted that she make. In a dragging, clammy realization, she recognized that he was merely toying with Hugh. A quick look at David's tense, unhappy face told her that he thought so, too.

But I cannot help!

"Idle gossip," Thomas observed, refusing to be drawn on the murky matter of his own morals. "I am waiting to be amazed."

That was an omen to her, and a cue she could use. Before she thought herself out of it, or became too afraid, Joanna acted.

"My lords!" Calling out, she stepped away from the low table, unfurling the huge circular sheepskin she had brought down with her as she swept a deep curtsy to her lord and everyone in the room. Briefly as she bowed she saw Hugh's deep blue eyes, darker than the lapis lazuli she used in her work, fix upon her and stay with her. He was frowning, whether at her or for her she could not tell.

There was no time to tell: she must be swift and fault-less and win the attention she had commanded.

"Look, my lords. Witness and observe." She whirled the sheepskin about her where it draped across her narrow shoulders in folds of shimmering gold. She moved to catch the light from the half-open shutters and heard the muted gasps at her sparkle.

"My fleece of gold, my masterwork," she intoned, feel-ing the men in the room *sublimate* to her—be ignited and changed by her—a heady feeling, if she allowed it to take hold. She raised her arms, holding the pose for an instant.

The fleece shimmered about her, seeming to draw the day and candlelight to it. It was a real golden fleece, its wool drenched in gold that Joanna had painstakingly gath-ered from many streams in a bare, treeless land far to the southwest of here, where she and her father had spent a joyous free summer between patrons. Following the advice of an ancient copper miner for whom she had made a pain-relieving salve, Joanna had taken a sheepskin and pegged it in a stream. The following day she had lifted out the dripping fleece and found it had snagged small nuggets of gold.

There had been many other strips of fleece and other streams since then and now this cloak was the result: heavy with gold and iron pyrites—fool's gold—and painted over by Joanna herself with liquid gold. It gave her presence and weight and wearing it always gave her confidence, as if some of the spirit of that great female alchemist, Maria the Jewess, had passed into her.

She knew Bishop Thomas was already entranced—he always was, at the sight of her cloak. Breathing out with relief that her intervention had indeed been well timed, she glided quickly to the first small bowl on the low table, arranged five candles in a tight circle, and lit them.

"See the first sublimation." She placed a tripod over the candles, then a metal sheet. She placed a glove over her hand—Hugh's glove, she realized, astonished at herself for bringing it with her, instead of her own. His glove was loose on her fingers, the wool warm and dry, much as his fingers were.

But she needed her wits about her now. Resisting the temptation to glance at Hugh Manhill to see if he recognized the glove, she found the red dye cinnabar in her carrying basket.

"Behold." She disliked that word, thought it too showy, but her father always used it in his demonstrations. For Solomon's sake she added the flourish but it was Hugh who watched her now: she could sense his dark eyes on her, tracking her every move.

Raising her gloved hand high and using a golden spoon, she poured some volatile oils onto the warmed metal plate. Instantly the oils burned off in a rich perfume and, when she brought a lit candle close, green flames.

Now she sprinkled the cinnabar onto the plate, hearing gasps as the powdered red dye melted and changed, becoming silver, becoming a perfect round sphere of—

"Mercury," she intoned, lifting the plate from the tripod and tilting it for her lord and the others to see. "One of the two elements that makes our world. It looks fluid, does it not? Yet, it is dry to touch."

"Jabir calls it the beautiful element," remarked David, an observation which although accurate Joanna wished he had not made: it broke the mood. Indeed, her lord was on to his remark like one of his hunting dogs after game.

"Jabir? An Arab scholar?" he demanded, beckoning Joanna to approach for him to study the new mercury more closely. "One of those Arabs who even now pollute our holy places?"

"A learned man, who lived long ago but whose work on alchemy is much revered in Outremer," David persisted, in that quiet, stubborn way he had. Joanna longed to tell him to be silent: Bishop Thomas was looking his way now and his glance was not kind.

Crossing the sweet rushes on the floor, she brought out Thomas's potion for "manly vigor" and handed it to him with a bow, relieved when he received it with a tiny smile. Convinced she had succeeded in distracting him, she returned to her place and raised her hands. "For my second sublimation—"

"Alchemy and what other secret arts?" Thomas cut across her. "What dark arts, Templar? You know a great deal of magic for a simple knight."

Magic! Hugh had heard enough. Amazed at David's own academic idiocy—when would his brother learn to keep silent?—he pulled out the roll of parchment at his belt, presenting it seal first to the bishop.

"These are the names and pedigrees of the horses I will exchange for the release of my brother. If you look, there are some famous chargers. And this"—Hugh pulled out another parchment from his jerkin—"is a letter from the prelate of all England, the Archbishop of Canterbury, in which he vouches for my brother and gives me his support."

That final piece of paper with its heavy seal made the bishop pause; Hugh saw his hesitation and rejoiced.

The audience chamber was silent except for the small crackling of the candles. The girl Joanna had flitted back into the shadowed part of the chamber and shed her sparkling cloak. She already knew the show was over for today, although she still wore his glove. When he had seen that first, Hugh felt as guilty as when his father first told him that he had caused his mother's death. Seeing his glove again, on Joanna, he was mortified afresh, his victory over Thomas damped down in shame.

"I will need to study this," said Thomas at last.

"Of course," Hugh agreed. "Keep both: I have copies. I shall come again tomorrow."

He knew it was the right time to go. Leaving the treasure to emphasize his wealth and pique Thomas's interest and greed, he turned on his heel. With Beowulf shadowing and his men trailing behind, he strode away without looking back, thinking of the girl, the wonder-worker, Joanna.

Tomorrow I will seek her out and apologize.

Chapter 4

Her lord bishop was pleased with her for the moment and, when she reminded him that she needed more supplies, he graciously allowed her to leave the household and go out into the city. Now, accompanied by two guards—a further sign of favor—Joanna almost ran through the main gate of Thomas's palace. The day was bright, the sun was shining, she was out and free—

But for how long?

Hugh prowled about West Sarum, returning often to the high-walled stone enclosure that marked the bishop's palace. He had sent his men and Beowulf on, into the dense oak woodland outside the city, while he lingered. He was, he admitted, watching the place, spying it out, looking for a weakness he could exploit. He had little faith in tomorrow's meeting: he wanted a backup plan.

He marked the comings and goings. A fish seller with a handcart; a sweeper pushing away piles of horse and pig dung from the streetside entrance; an old man with an armload of clothes to sell greeting the guards as he passed into the palace courtyard. The morning was drawing on and the early dawn crowds had slackened to a trickle as people hurried back to their homes for the midday meal. Hugh inhaled the scents of boiling pork and pottage and told his grumbling belly to be silent.

Directly outside the palace gate were the city stocks and pillory—no doubt erected there for the bishop's entertainment, Hugh thought grimly. He bought a venison tart from a passing pie seller and ale from a brewster selling it by the door of her freshly rethatched house and continued to stare.

Shooing away a browsing pig that seemed determined to befriend him, Hugh almost missed Joanna tripping through the palace gate. He saw the guards first, large, simple-looking fellows in their fathers' old mail and helmets, strutting over the deeply rutted main street with an air of nervous belligerence. One cackled at the moldering gray wretch in the stocks, stopping abruptly as if he had been admonished.

By whom? To see more clearly, Hugh crouched down under the roof eaves of the house where he was standing and smiled. His guess was right: it was Joanna.

Watching her, he forgot to watch the entrance. She was carrying a basket, swinging it along. She looked happy to be outside and she had dressed for the occasion. There was no grubby glove on her hand now and her gown was freshly brushed, with new sleeves attached in a rich, subtle scarlet. Her pretty brown hair was caught up in a golden net and her belt was new. Wound twice around her slender middle, it was still long, with golden tassels that drummed against her legs as she walked.

The old man with the secondhand clothes came beside Hugh and sat down on a house step.

"Pretty, is she not?" he observed, in a clear accent that revealed he had been more than a clothes seller once. He scratched at the sore on his arm and two others on his bare legs. "Been with the bishop now for a year."

Hugh gave the old man a coin. "What else do you know?"

"Of Joanna?" The old man tucked the coin into a ragged glove and leaned back against the wattle house wall. "Rumor says she's the bishop's leman. Some call her a necromancer." His voice dropped. "She visits houses no decent woman would go near.

"Not the stew," the old man added, following Hugh's glance at the public bathhouse at the top of West Sarum's main street, where even now off-duty guards cavorted outside with girls in soaking wet tunics. "She is no whore."

"So?" Hugh prompted.

"Do you not want that pie?"

Silently Hugh handed it across. His companion took a huge bite and spoke with his mouth full. "She reads books," he said with relish. "Strange books."

Hugh tracked the small graceful figure down the street. Joanna was going away from the bathhouse, walking down the slop-filled lane in the direction of the southern city gate and the river. As she moved he saw a sparkle on her right wrist: slim metal bracelets. Given to her by Thomas?

Nodding to the old man, who was intent on his pie, Hugh stepped out into the road. Seeing the girl again, learning about her place in the palace, had given him an idea—a nasty, furtive idea, one that went against all tenets of chivalry. Whether he would act on it depended on opportunity, but for the moment he would follow Joanna and see where she went.

Whether she was a necromancer or magic-worker, she was certainly no fool, he conceded, keeping close to the guards as they wound their way down the steep main street. She remained with the pair as they spent a long time trying their hands at the city's archery butts ranged on a pitch of spare ground by the square, squat Saxon cathedral—a place where Bishop Thomas never preached, Hugh wagered. She bought them both pies, but ate nothing herself and waited with seemingly endless patience as the thicker-set of the two haggled with a cobbler over the repair to a shoe.

Down the long street they went, Joanna scarcely looking at the many clothiers' stalls or the brightly colored puddles outside the dyers' workshops. She was obviously bent on leaving the city though the southern gate—to ford the river? Or to visit the small narrow settlement that had grown up just outside the walls?

Away to the south, beyond the meandering Avon, were hills green with woodland and beyond that, his father's castle. That thought gave Hugh no pleasure as he drew a shabby cloak over his tunic and draped a hood over his head, grunting an acknowledgment at the gatekeeper as he followed his quarry through the open entranceway.

Here the ground leveled off into water meadows grazed by horses and cattle. There were stables and a hamlet of tumbledown houses with long stripes of garden and more rooting pigs. Grubby children playing close to the river called after Hugh and a few bolder ones tossed pebbles in his direction. None cast stones at Joanna, he noticed, although they jeered at her guards in a dialect so thick he could not understand it.

He assumed she was making for the ford, so was startled when she swung away from the well-worn track into a mess of old gardens and derelict house plots. Weaving through brambles and patches of nettles and tall grass, she led the way and the guards trudged after, perhaps wondering, as he did, where she was headed. None looked back although he trailed them at a long distance, skulking through this old warren of former dwellings like a burglar.

She had a saucy walk, he decided, watching her sway over a wreck of fallen house beams with the poise of a dancer. They were coming to more recent and crowded habitation: the grass path became small cobbles, the houses larger and the gardens of greens well tended. Here were people, sitting out of doors on benches, some eating their lunches, others making baskets of reeds.

Suddenly, where the houses were packed closest together so that the very sky became a mass of jostling thatch and roof jetties, Joanna spun about.

"What is it you want, Hugh de Manhill?" she called out, pointing directly at him so that every householder in the district stopped what he or she was doing to stare. "Why are you following?"

The girl had spotted him! By all the light of heaven, how had she done that? Her own guards were standing blinking in the dabbled shade of the houses, fidgeting with their sword hilts. They had known nothing of his pursuit. How had she?

With so many witnesses, he was forced to dissemble. "If you see my brother again today, will you give him a message?"

"It is no grief for you that I speak to him then, Sir Hugh?"

She had not forgotten or forgiven the glove. More justice to her, Hugh thought, amused at her twist of his own words, while he answered, "I am most sorry for our earlier confusion. But for David's sake, I ask this favor."

His appeal worked. Joanna put her basket down on the cobbles and spread her hands.

"Will you tell him I never forget him? Not at any moment? That I love him?"

She raised her brows at that while her guards relaxed, smirking at each other. The onlookers were wiser, saying nothing as Hugh closed the gap between them.

"Anything else?" she asked.

He was near enough to her now to pluck her basket off the ground and hold it out. "Only this: what do you think of my brother's imprisonment, Mistress Joanna? Do you think it right?"

He had startled her afresh: a rush of color stormed into her eyes and face.

"I cannot speak for my lord—" she began.

"But you, yourself?" He wanted to know. If she was the bishop's mistress, he wanted to know if she agreed with his brother's captivity. "Do you truly think David is an evil man?" he asked softly. "A blasphemer?"

"I do not think so, but I am no expert."

"But you have spoken with him, eaten with him," Hugh continued relentlessly. "Do you consider him a witch?"

"No!"

Her denial was sharp, causing her guards to stop their gawping at a young woman outside one of the houses who was washing her long red hair in a pail, and glance at her instead.

Blushing deeply now, Joanna added swiftly, "No, what I mean, is—"

Hugh stepped forward, closing the last of the gap between them, and touched the narrow copper bracelets on her left wrist.

"How many of these has your master bought for you with the blood of innocent men?" he asked, speaking in French so only she would understand.

She snapped her arm out of his reach, putting it behind her back, as a child might. "You have no cause to say that to me," she said, also in French.

"Why not answer my question?"

She said nothing, merely shook her head and looked at him in pity.

Sympathy from the bishop's whore was too much— Hugh's already fragile hold on his temper severed.

"You will not use the Manhills this way," he said, through a clenched jaw, as the blood and his rage pounded in his head. For an instant he wanted to take on the guards, take on this whole settlement. But these folk he had no quarrel with, even the moon-faced guards he had no dispute with, but *her*, Joanna, the bishop's thing—

"I will have satisfaction." Making his words a promise, he tore off his brooch pin, tossing into the cobbles between them. "I will be back to redeem this, mistress, and when I do, you had best not be in my path."

For the second time that day he turned his back on her and left, his shoulder blades prickling in expectation of a stone or dagger that never came.

But he knew, now, what he would do. She would be his key that would turn the lock on David's prison and bring him out of the donjon. He would pick his moment, the time and place, and then he would kidnap Joanna, the mistress of Bishop Thomas. He would hold her and keep her as his prisoner, until Thomas agreed to a hostage exchange.

Smiling grimly at the thought, Hugh strode away.

Chapter 5

Joanna looked over her new supplies, bought or bartered from Joseph of West Sarum in the hamlet that morning. Joseph, a herbalist and secret alchemist, had no suggestions for her. He had looked at her with pity when she admitted that Solomon was still in the donjon. "That is why I live and work here," he said, "outside the city walls and the keen greedy eye of the bishop. But I know that is no comfort to you."

"No," agreed Joanna as she gathered up her things and left the cottage to find the guards watching a cockfight in the alleyway outside.

Sitting now at her workbench with her elbows braced amidst glasses and earthenware pots, she tried to concentrate on a parchment Joseph had loaned her. It was called "The Cure of Mercury," and claimed many things for that element, including the prolonging of life. The crabbed letters and symbols kept blurring on the scroll as she fought and failed to pay attention.

At length she went to the top of the staircase and sat down on the top step, listening out for David's voice from the floor below. What must it be like to have a brother like Hugh, so protective? So determined?

She glanced at Hugh's glove at her belt—she felt it to be hers now, although she did not know why she did not burn it in her furnace. He had handled her twice now, without her permission: once over the glove and then today, in the hamlet, a brief, disturbing caress of her arm as he brushed her bracelets. Even through her sleeve she had felt his fingers, warm and strong and steady. Her whole arm had been changed by his contact, tingling and feeling lighter, as if some inner dross had been burned off by his touch. She wished she could have answered him honestly when he asked her what she thought of David's imprisonment. Were her father not also captive, she would have said, roundly, that the holding of a man such as David was an abomination. Except for her father, he was the kindest, gentlest, most learned man she had ever known.

But it was not his fingers that her body remembered.

Joanna let the scroll roll up in her fingers and allowed herself to daydream. Hugh had challenged Bishop Thomas, called the man corrupt to his face. Even as she had goggled at that memory she had envied Hugh his free speech: he had said what she had longed to say and had never dared to.

Before Hugh, she had never seen a man with such blue eyes. Blazing blue eyes, sharp with feeling. He was passionate, easily angered, fiercely loyal. He would do much for those he loved.

Joanna sighed and tried to consider her work again. During her visit to Joseph, her fellow alchemist had mentioned a process of growing gold in the earth, seeding the ground with gold, cinnabar, mercury, silver, and lead. It must be special earth, purified by water and fire.

How often does Hugh bathe?

The question rose in her mind, insistent and magical as a salamander. He would be beautiful, nude, with his long, shapely limbs and toned muscles.

"Stop this," Joanna admonished herself, trying to plan where, in the palace, she might seed the ground for gold. All places were too public: too many guards and petitioners and heralds. Even its gardens, of which she was allowed a small corner where she grew a patchwork of herbs and marigolds for her work, was busy with strolling priests.

On the floor below she heard the door open and stiffened, listening closely as she leaned down into the dark stairwell.

". . . nor my daughter are privy to the bishop's mind, but yes, he desires gold. What man does not?"

It was her father. He must be speaking to David, Joanna surmised. Hoping to catch more, she leaned farther forward on the cold step.

"I would say my brother wants other things than gold. Hugh can be wantonly generous."

Ask him more, Joanna mentally pleaded with her father, hugging her knees. *Ask him what Hugh wants from his life. Ask if Hugh likes girls. Ask if Hugh has a sweetheart.*

"And you, a knight in a holy order, do not approve of his unworldliness?" Solomon teased. "You would prefer him to be a miser, perhaps?"

"I did not mean that, Solomon, and you know it. No, I—"

The rest of David's reply was lost as the chamber door closed. Joanna waited a moment, trying to hear, then slapped the staircase wall in frustration. From two floors lower she heard a sudden, piercing shriek, then a ghastly, broken sobbing.

She fled down the stairs and pounded on the first-floor door. Sometimes guards were within the first-floor chamber, sometimes absent; right now she prayed someone was there. A guard thrust his head out. "You cannot come in now. Today, you must wait until sunset." Always, her visits were strictly monitored and timed.

"But those men in the lower prison!" Joanna panted, just

stopping herself from wringing her hands in front of the impassive guard. "Please, let me take them food and water! Please, as an act of Christian mercy—"

"Not today, Joanna."

The door was shut and barred against her. She kicked it, violently, and yelped as her toes felt as if they had been nipped by red-hot pincers.

An image of Hugh stalking away, free, proud, powerful, inspired her to rebel. What use was it, hanging over her books and experiments, when her mind was so distracted, when her thoughts were full of a tall, strapping knight who would risk so much for love? She wanted to see him again. She wanted to tell him what she really thought about Bishop Thomas.

Of course it was not so easy. She could not leave on a whim. Permission must be sought. She found the steward and spun him a tale of river gold—such gold was rare, especially in these parts, but she made Richard Parvus blink and rub his palms together at the image of nuggets of gold as large as her fist. Later, she might have to explain why she had brought none back with her, but the excuse was sufficient to win her another release for the afternoon. She went off as she was, without cloak, or hat. Scarcely remembering her carrying basket, or the scraps of fleece which she needed to collect any river gold, she scampered so swiftly through the palace yard and then the streets of West Sarum that the guards with her grumbled at the pace she set.

Recalling her time spent far to the southwest, Joanna followed the river to a swifter tributary and then branched off to trace the stream to its source. She paid close attention as the vineyards, orchards, and open fields gave way to woodland, aware that the woods and all within them belonged to her lord bishop. At first she gathered herbs and bark there, then, as the land became steeper and the stream sparkled with a gurgling rush of water, she straddled the narrow banks to study the stream bed itself, paying close attention to the bends in the stream, where heavy gold might gather.

"How much longer?" asked a guard, leaning on his spear as he picked his nose. "Does your back not hurt, with you crooked over the water like that?"

"I am accustomed to it," Joanna answered, although in truth her back and thighs ached like toothache and her skirts were becoming damp and clinging with water and spray. "I am going as quickly as I can," she added, recalling that these men also worked in the donjon, where her father and Mercury and David were. Where Hugh would return some time tomorrow, probably early—

A piercing high-pitched scream, followed by a splash, drove all thoughts of Hugh and gold from her head. Tossing aside fleeces and carrying basket, she set off in the direction of the splash, forcing her numb legs to go faster as the screaming resumed.

"I'm coming!" she shouted, unable to see who had fallen into the stream as the woodland seemed to crowd in closer still and the ground rose almost vertically ahead of her. "Help me!" she yelled at the guards, dropping to her hands and knees to scramble through thick, lush grass and banks of flowering garlic and bluebells. Somewhere over the crown of this hill a woman or child was screaming, panicking, thrashing in the water.

"Hurry!" she urged herself and the guards, without wasting time in looking back. Snatching at a low-growing hazel branch, she pulled herself up the slope with it and finally reached a summit, where the ground leveled off for a space and the stream widened into a pool. Panting, her lungs feeling as if they were plastered against her ribs, Joanna anxiously scanned the ring of sparkling water—

—and saw the child, a dark tangle of flailing limbs and staring eyes. The boy was trying and failing to find a handhold on the bank while the swirling water battered his thin little body, threatening to drag him down beneath its bright, treacherous surface.

"Grab hold of this! Grab it!" Joanna untied her belt and cast one end into the stream. "Grab hold and I'll pull you out!"

She tossed the belt a second time, willing the child to catch it. The little lad made a brave dive for the belt and seized it. Joanna heaved on her end, praying that it would not break. Her arms shook with effort as she fought the churning water and supported the child's stiff, anxious weight, easing the belt through her numb fingers hand over hand as if she were climbing it. Each time she drew a little more of the belt closer, the boy dipped in the stream and seemed to drift farther away. And where were the guards? Was it their laughter and cheerful banter she could hear between her own spurting breaths? Joanna was not certain, but she dared not look round lest the boy disappeared under the water. Then she would be forced to dive into the pool, although in truth she was a poor swimmer.

"I have you now!" she called out, wishing she could be faster. Her teeth were chattering and her hands and feet felt to have sublimated into blocks of ice. If she felt this way, how must the little lad in the water be?

"You are safe now, but keep hold, and hold on tight!" she exhorted.

A shadow fell across her and she shook with relief, realizing that one of the guards had finally ambled up to the pool and had chosen to help. But the long, powerful arm that shot past her shoulder and caught the exhausted child was clothed in red, not serge.

"I have him." Hugh Manhill lifted the boy clear of the water and wrapped him in his own cloak, briskly rubbing at the child's arms and legs while speaking to him in a low monotone. Joanna heard some words but could no longer grasp what he was saying. Suddenly overwhelmed by weariness and a wave of rising heat and sickness, she sank down on the bank with her head hung over her knees.

"Thank you, sir," she said, when she could speak.

Hugh acknowledged her thanks with a terse nod. "No thanks to these two." He glowered at the guards, who were staring sheepishly into the trees. "They were laying bets on which of you would sink first."

Hugh set the boy down gently, bracing him against his own body so he would not fall. "What brings you here?" he asked, now proceeding to peel off his tunic. "The lad needs warm fresh clothes," he said, correctly interpreting Joanna's silent question. "So, girl, why are you here?"

"I am not required to answer you," Joanna replied stiffly, smarting afresh as his use of "girl." "But for the sake of good manners, I will say that I am in my lord's woods to seek herbs." She did not mention gold. Neither the guards nor Hugh should know that.

She was distracted, too, by his casual disrobing. *We are not animals,* she longed to say. *How dare you parade your body?* He would deny it, of course, turn it back against her, claim he was acting in the child's best interests—and how could she dispute that? Feigning disinterest, she raised her head, determined to look only at his face. "Why are you here, sir?"

"I happened to be in the district." Hugh ran both hands through his short yet tousled black hair, trying and failing to rake it into some order. He offered his tunic to the forest child, who shrugged it on over his own patched clothes and then proceeded to drape the warrior's massive cloak on top, seemingly delighted at how he was steaming in the dappled woodland sunlight.

"One happy outcome," Hugh remarked, ruffling the boy's hair and being rewarded by a gap-toothed grin from the child. "So, girl? Herbs with scraps of fleece?"

The brute was baiting her! Determined to show him exquisite courtesy, Joanna forced a smile. "Fleece is useful to collect seed heads," she lied. Suddenly, she could not resist a tease in return. "Not all of us carry our own fleece on our bodies."

Hugh gave a bark of laughter, and as he glanced at his hairy chest and arms, Joanna stole a glance herself. He was very handsome to look on, with his broad shoulders, lean muscled arms and flat, taut stomach. Between the dark swirls of jet-black hair over his torso and belly she glimpsed two long white tags: the drawstrings to his linen breeches, she guessed. Instantly, she imagined pulling on the strings, disrobing him further—

No! Stop this! Joanna felt the heat pound into her face and she closed her eyes, shutting Hugh out. There were other handsome men in the world and she had never been tempted to tease them, so why was this man so different? Why did she have this insistent wish, each time she encountered Hugh Manhill, to touch him? And did he feel the same tug, the same desire, or was this her shame alone? Confused and alarmed, she studied the child, who was now contentedly making knots in Hugh's cloak, and dipped her head lower to avoid encountering Manhill's knowing eyes.

And there in the water directly ahead she saw a dull yellow gleam—not in the curve of the stream, as she had expected, but in the shallows of the "pool" itself. Without explaining, she moved forward, plunged her arm into the water, and her hand came up with gold in it—fragments too tiny to be called nuggets, but valuable all the same.

She flicked her other hand into the pool as a distraction, lifting out a fistful of weed and holding it aloft like a trophy. "This is excellent for all manner of ills," she declared. "Would you bring me my carrying basket, please, Sir Hugh?"

If he was surprised at her request he showed and said nothing, slipping back from the stream into the woodland and returning with her basket. As Joanna swiftly deposited gold and weeds into the carrier, he paid more attention to the boy, asking the lad his name and if he did well now, and then remarked, "Here, I think, are Hacon's parents."

Joanna followed his pointing finger to a cluster of swaying elder and hazel bushes. The one nearest to her seemed to explode and then two small, crouching figures burst through the undergrowth and pelted up the grassy slope, stumbling often in sheer haste. Both were red-cheeked and at the same time haggard—with worry, Joanna guessed, her heart lifting as she saw the couple rush up to the child and snatch the boy up into furious hugs.

"Blessings on you, my lord!" the mother exclaimed, bobbing before Hugh. "We heard him call, but we were so far away—"

"Thank her," Hugh answered, nodding to Joanna.

At once Joanna felt herself enveloped by the older woman, who, although small and thin, could hug like a bear and would not let go. More praise and thanks spilled from her as Joanna tried to explain she had done no more than anyone would have done and the woman's husband pumped Hugh's hand.

"Keep the clothes," Hugh answered easily, refusing to admit to any part in the child's rescue. "I have plenty more. But now I must away."

"As must we," growled a guard, plainly bored and discomforted by the whole affair.

The party split up soon after, Joanna being promised a jar of honeycomb by the cottar's wife as she retrieved her scraps of fleece and prepared to return to West Sarum. Hugh had already turned and was striding away; the light caught on the points of his shoulder blades and the muscles down his back seemed to ripple.

I will see you again, Joanna almost called after him, before she realized what she was about to do and stopped herself. If Hugh was too bad-mannered to say farewell, why should she prompt him to speak? He might even think she wanted him to turn so she could look at him again. Stubbornly she kept silent and fell in between the guards.

They walked back down the steep slope, Joanna wondering how Hugh had gone away from them so quickly. Wrenching her thoughts away from him, she reflected bleakly that this trip had been almost a waste, apart from the fragments of gold. These were now safely tucked away in the small purse hidden inside her gown, and she should be directing her ideas as to how she might increase them.

I have less than a month to do so. So how may I do it?

Deep in thought, she did not know where her plodding feet were taking her until one of her guards muttered, "That is a very fancy nag," and the other one gave a long whistle. She raised her head to see what the commotion was about, not at all surprised to see Hugh again, although her heart beat a little faster.

He was standing on the main woodland path, gripping the reins to a truly magnificent black stallion: a big, long-legged, strong-necked, handsome brute, much like his master. His wolfhound lay close to his horse's feet and both were prick-eared and ready, waiting for a sign from Hugh.

Is he waiting for me?

Foolish one! Joanna remonstrated herself. Hugh doubtless

wished to talk to the men for some reason; it was nothing to do with her.

Now he patted the gleaming neck of his black horse and stepped away from stallion and hound, tapping his sword belt.

"Give me the girl and you may go free."

Wide-eyed, the guards stared at him and then at each other, plainly trying to spur themselves on to some reaction.

Hugh drew his sword and scraped a line in the dirt track with his boot. "I have no quarrel with you men, and I swear to you now that the girl will not be harmed. Walk away now, uninjured, your honor intact."

Genuinely angry, Joanna picked up a stone and hurled it at his feet. "Hey! Now I have your attention!" she yelled, planting both fists on her hips. "I am no parcel! You do not dare to fight over me! I am walking out of this wood and no man is going to stop me!"

She took a step forward, beside a cluster of hazel bushes and then sideways, neatly shielding her departure. Tossing away her basket a second time, she picked up her skirts and began to run, sprinting from one patch of cover to another.

Behind her she could hear shouting but no clash of arms—she had not expected it, nor did she blame the guards for not accepting Manhill's challenge. Even two against one was an uneven match when the one was a tourney knight, and Bishop Thomas's men knew that as well as she. But for him to call them out in her presence, to not even look at her—

Her face burned with indignation.

How could he? How dare he? Her thoughts pounded in her aching head as fast as her rushing feet. Again, as with the glove, Hugh Manhill had belittled her. She was sore in her aching legs and in her jolted stomach and there was a soreness, too, in her chest, that had nothing to do with physical hurt.

"He speaks of honor when he has none!" she burst out, almost spent as she crossed a small stream and began climbing up another tree-clad hill. The guards would be safe enough, she reckoned—those were not his target. She was—and why? "What have I ever done to you?" she panted aloud and missed her footing, stumbling against a holly bush that raked her arms.

And now she heard behind her the steady rumble of an approaching horse, ridden swiftly through this maze of trees, with great skill. She dropped and tried to crawl over the rough ground, trying to find some hiding place, but the wolfhound burst through the grass, bounding up close to her and, startled, she yelled.

No longer able to conceal herself, she tottered to her feet and lunged ahead, her vision blurring as she strained with the effort of running. Her blood was now banging so loudly in her ears she could no longer hear the horse, but then she sensed its looming shadow and jinked aside, swerving at the last moment. Above, she heard a muffled curse and almost laughed, but then a massive arm hooked her round her waist and off her feet.

Flung roughly over the neck of the stallion, with the pommel of the saddle grinding into her stomach and her arms and legs beating the air as she tried to break free, she was carried off by Hugh de Manhill.

Chapter 6

He had been following Joanna and her party at a distance ever since he spotted them leaving West Sarum. Coming late to the rescue of the cottar's child, Hugh had done what was needed to ensure the boy's safety and then had decided to take his leave. After seeing the girl's valiant efforts with the child—and her keepers' appalling lack of interest in the boy or Joanna—he had felt too ashamed to put his earlier plan into action.

How could he, in good conscience, seize Joanna as his hostage after he had found her risking her own neck to save a little peasant lad? Telling himself there had to be another way to grab Bishop Thomas's attention, Hugh walked away from the woodland pool, prepared to ride off.

Then, halfway down the long hillside to the main track, he thought of how she had ordered him, asking him to bring her carrying basket as if he was a maid, not a knight. And he remembered her staring at him. In truth he had stripped to the waist as a means of giving the lad warm clothes, but he had been glad to show himself off to her. Now, imagining how she would compare his fit, young frame to the bishop's soft, sagging body, Hugh found himself becoming angry again. How could she prefer a man like Thomas?

"She is the bishop's leman. If she does not like how I treat her next, she must take it up with him," he muttered under his breath, changing his mind in that instant and reverting to his original plan.

So he had challenged the guards. And she had cast stones and fury and hard looks at him. And now, even hauled across his horse, with the earth skimming less than a yard beneath her nose, she fought him still, squirming like an eel. He planted a hand in the middle of her back, pressing her tightly against the horse's powerful flanks.

"Yield, girl, and you may ride pillion."

He did not expect thanks and he only wanted her to stop struggling, but she jerked her shoulders free, hardly seeming to care if she fell. As he grabbed her waist to stop her plunging headfirst off the beast, she twisted her head, her face a single dark scowl.

"Or what, sir knight? Will you use your other glove to silence me?"

Still she remembered that! Hugh reined in the horse a little. "I told you, I am sorry for that. Be at peace! I do not abuse my captives."

"If you believe that, you are deluded. Look out!"

Hugh glanced forward, checking the horse, and Joanna pushed off with her arms. He was only just quick enough to seize her skirts as she tumbled toward the ground.

"Yield!" he yelled in French, in that instant transported to the combat ground and badly shaken as he tugged her back, seating her astride his horse, and wrapped both arms tightly round her. "Be not so reckless!"

She reared up again. "Why not, when I am now riding with you, without any promise?"

"Hell's teeth, girl! No man prisoner gave me so much trouble!"

"And I fight my way!"

Her hair, which had been loosened in their turmoil, now

spilled free of its gold net. The thick brown mass whipped Hugh's face and he could not answer for a moment: his mouth and eyes were full of hair. He could smell her, taste her: peppery and spicy. His mind reeled with the scent as his body reacted, stiffening and yielding at the same time. He was naked to the waist still and the feel of her against his naked skin made him burn up with desire. He still clasped her, but more gently, his fingers spreading in a semi-caress over her narrow waist.

Using his knees and thighs, he brought the snorting stallion to a stop.

"You are the bishop's woman," he said urgently when she moved restively against him and he could speak without the gag of her hair. "For you he will give much, including the release of my brother."

"Is that your justification?" she flung back, spiraling round in his arms to face him down. "If so, I do not think David would approve! But then he is thrice the man you are!"

"In that we are agreed," Hugh said, smarting at her easy use of his brother's name, "and it changes nothing."

"Were I the strumpet of the garrison, you should not treat me this way."

"No, you are more choice in the men you bed: raddled, decaying churchmen who can pay you gold."

She gasped, a blaze of color rushing into her face. Seeing the glint in her bright brown eyes, Hugh held himself taut. She marked that—she noticed everything—and her lip, from trembling, stiffened.

"You do me wrong. Again, you do me wrong," she said quietly. "What woman harmed you so, that you are this discourteous?"

He had braced himself for a blow. Her words, though less dramatic, stung the more. He had injured his mother first, fatally, and since then had seemed fated to do badly with women.

"'Tis not you," he admitted, wondering why he was troubling to explain. He was used to women thinking the worst of him. "If you swear not to dash your skull into the track, I will tell you the whole of it."

"You expect me to obey my own kidnapper? Besides, I know the whole already. You mean to instigate a hostage exchange. I should be in your 'care' for one, two days, no more, before you barter me for your brother. A most powerful plan."

She had pretty eyes, he thought, especially as she now was: flushed with battle. Her mouth was reddened by the ride and he was tempted again to kiss it. Instead, he drew his legs over hers, fixing her in place.

"You laugh at me, mistress."

"If my laughter means you stop calling me 'girl,' then why not?"

Abruptly, she twisted round again and faced forward.

"You are watching where we go to find your way back when you escape," he remarked, several moments later, when she was quiet.

"You can always blindfold me with a glove."

Hugh chuckled: doubtless he deserved that. And now she was no longer fighting him, it was oddly pleasant to have her sitting in front of him on his horse. Making his living in tournaments, he'd had little actual contact with women and being this close to Joanna made him feel light-headed, almost happy. The scent of her, the pliant, sweet feel of her—it was like sinking into a warm bath at the end of a grueling day's battle, one where he had won many prizes.

He had to remind himself that she had not yielded yet. She was turning her head this way and that, picking out landmarks. "Is this your first time out of West Sarum?" he asked as the round ramparts of the city stole into view from the woodland track they were on.

"It is not," she replied, triangulating with her fingers the course of the meandering river and the hill on which the city was built.

"See those walls?" He pointed ahead, above the flat, reed-filled landscape to the east and north and the tree-clad slopes of the city hill to the massive circular earth-works. "I think these must have been made by giants. What do you think?"

"I think if you have men in West Sarum you should get word to them, lest my lord take out his anger on them. Have you jousted in many places?"

"In Picardy, France, Italy—" A small sigh from her then prompted him to expand his answer. "In Italy the cities are amazing: so many people! And the markets there! You can buy pepper and spices and silks and books!"

"What do you like to read?"

Hugh cursed softly, then admitted, "I do not. I cannot."

She touched his arm—a gesture of pity?—then asked, "What do men call you at the tournaments? Do you have a nickname?"

Hugh felt himself going hot: this was becoming worse and worse. "Destroyer," he mumbled, then berated himself for being ashamed. Why should he be made to feel guilty by this scrap of a female? "Though men like your bishop decry it, the tourney is a good life for a man. Better that than being dragged into King John's wars with the King of France or his barons, where only the leaders gain."

"A life for a young man, certainly," Joanna answered, "and he is not my bishop."

She drew in a large breath that he felt through his own ribs. Alerted by that, he reined in the ambling horse, caught her shoulders, bent her back into the crook of his arm and kissed her—just as a shepherd appeared around a corner on the track in front of them with a small flock of sheep.

Her lips were hard under his, rigid. He nuzzled her

mouth with his, then thought, *If she dislikes this so much, let her make her appeal to the shepherd: he can only raise the alarm sooner.*

He withdrew slightly, then, when she did not cry out, he kissed her again, his lips now soft against hers. He eased her small, tense frame more comfortably against his shoulder and kissed her very lightly several times: tiny, swift embraces, as if he was burying his face into rose petals. Her mouth tasted of salt and a fresh sweetness that was her own perfume.

She sighed and then relaxed, allowing him to kiss her, even kissing him in return. Her hands brushed over his neck and shoulders as she lifted herself to him, plunging her tongue into his mouth.

Hugh reeled, heat pounding into him. He dropped the reins, forgot horse, shepherd, and sheep, and wrapped his arms about her, wanting their kiss to go on and on.

"Why?" he asked, when they finally broke apart. The shepherd was a distant speck, entering the city.

She did not pretend not to know what he meant. "I wanted to know what it was like," she answered. "And now I have my answer."

She shifted smoothly from the crook of his arm to face forward again. "Do we have far to go?"

"Ah." He shook a finger at her. "You must wait to discover that."

"I am used to waiting," she answered as he urged the horse into a steady trot.

They moved through the landscape of vineyards, hay fields, reed beds, and woods, Hugh watching her and watching out for the bishop's men or any hue and cry while most of his mind was racked by a single question.

Did Joanna like his kissing?

Chapter 7

Joanna kept watch but saw no one else all the time they traveled. It was not market day at West Sarum and folk were busy in the fields and vineyards, with no inclination to gawp at strangers—not even the bishop's mistress.

She had guessed the rumors, but hearing it from Hugh's lips was still a shock. Worse, she felt ashamed and actually alarmed by his clear disappointment, although why should his good opinion matter? She was the one wronged: he had kidnapped and manhandled her, kissing her to silence her. She wished now that she had not responded, but his lips had been so persuasive, so appealing.

Would he kiss her again? Would she respond?

He was a living wall, but there was a strange comfort in embracing him, in having him hold her. She and her father were not people who hugged or kissed much, so this feeling of safety, almost of peace, was new to her. Riding before him, feeling his naked chest warm and powerful against her back, his body hair tickling the back of her neck and her arms as his sinewy arms encircled her in a gentle yet unbreakable grip, was both exasperating and seductive. Trees and whole fields would slip by as she was lost in the sensation of being borne away. Her initial anger and panic had disappeared: she sensed he would not harm her.

Escape was different; it was her duty to do so, or at least to try. The nagging fear in her heart was that her lord would not care, or worse, that he would blame her for falling into Hugh Manhill's clutches. To ride on this smooth-stepping stallion might be a dream, but she needed her wits honed and sharp: she must snatch the chance to get away when she could.

First she must lull and gull him into thinking she was defeated, obedient. "Are you not cold?" she asked, flicking his arm. She dared do no more than the briefest contact: a full, lingering touch was too distracting to her; it made her want to do more. "I would be freezing," she added, trying not to stare at the whorls of black hair running over his forearms.

"I rarely feel the cold."

She waited, but he said no more.

"What is the name of your horse? He is a magnificent beast. Does he have a miraculous name?" she asked, waving to a lonely figure digging in a muddy, waterlogged field.

The figure took no notice, but Hugh tightened his grip around her waist, a warning squeeze, and said, "Behave there.

"His name is Lucifer," he went on. "I won him in a tourney when I captured Lord Stephen La Lude and won a worthy ransom. Before you ask, yes, you are my first girl hostage and far more trouble than any man."

"So you have already told me," Joanna replied, "and that is as it should be."

"You females do not like to be confined. Even in the garden of Eden, you were not content."

He sounded amused, so Joanna let it pass. *Lull him and gull him.* "What is the best prize you have won?"

"The freedom of a Jewish healer, Simon, who is now in my service."

She felt his laughter. "There. I knew that would surprise you. But I did not like his keeper, and Simon has since repaid any debt to me many times over. He is away at present, in France."

"Who oppressed him?" Joanna asked.

"One of Yves de Manhill's men, his lead knight, Roger Two-Blades. He had Simon in his entourage, but treated him poorly." Hugh's voice was clipped, his whole body taut. "It was my pleasure to win him."

"From your father's champion?" Joanna said softly.

"It was a fair challenge."

Making it clear he wanted no more talk, Hugh dug his heels into Lucifer's sides, spurring the horse into a gallop.

They stopped less than two leagues farther on the road, Hugh guiding the stallion behind a stand of oak trees into a narrow, high-banked road that was scarcely wider than a deer path. Deeper and deeper the horse plodded along the overgrown, reedy track, trees arching over their heads.

"Where are we?" Joanna whispered, feeling the pressure in her ears pop as they ventured down into this sunken land.

"A place I discovered as a lad," Hugh answered, "before I was sent away to train as a knight. There." He pointed ahead. "It has not changed."

Beyond a grove of alder trees a section of land rose into a small, perfect circle, round as an ancient grave mound. Hugh made for this and Joanna could now see a gaping black gap in the circle: the mouth to a cave. She had a vision of being swallowed by the earth itself, of being here where no one could hear or see her, and shivered.

"This is a safe place from footpads and animals," Hugh announced, as if he sensed her small withdrawal. "We shall sleep in the cave tonight: it is snug and dry."

Too snug, Joanna thought, fighting down a wave of sickly panic. "You have slept here before?" Her voice sounded calm enough.

"Many years ago, in different times. This should be more pleasant."

Why? Joanna clamored to ask, but she dared not.

"This time I have food and drink, sufficient for two."

"Naturally, because you planned this." Joanna tried to keep censure from her tongue but something must have leaked through, for Hugh took her hands in his and gently chafed her fingers.

"You are safe with me," he said, his chin so close to the top of her head that he could have rested it on her hair, had he so chosen. Joanna fought a sudden temptation to relax and trust him, to lean back against him, into his shielding arms.

"Safe, although I am the bishop's woman?" she tossed back, then wondered at her own folly. Why was she goading a man who had already kidnapped her, bringing her to Lord knew where?

"It is still an hour to sunset," she added quickly. "Do you not want to go farther?"

He twisted forward on the saddle to look at her, his eyes gleaming with amusement. "To escape our pursuit, you mean?"

He grinned as she said nothing and swung down from his mount, laughing outright as she scrambled down from the big horse without waiting for him to help her.

"Do you wish to help, or would you consider that treason to your master?" he asked.

Joanna spread her hands: let him make of that what he would.

He smiled again. "I will see to all, then. Why not go on inside and look? It is an interesting place. There are strange marks on one wall: runes, I think. Secret writing."

"Which you cannot read," Joanna shot back, then felt ashamed of the jibe. "I will look," she said, and hurried to climb the grassy mound to the entrance, musing that Hugh had already guessed her weakness for strange things and mysteries. Of all things he could have said to divert her from escape, *secret writing* was one of the most powerful. She was eager to see these runes and read their message for herself.

Hugh tethered and tended Lucifer, roughed a little with Beowulf, cut reeds for bedding, collected firewood, and kept a sharp eye on Joanna. She made no move to flee from the cave, which surprised him, and met him at the cave mouth with his armload of reeds, which astonished him.

"What is it?" he asked. Her eyes were wide and her color high, lighting up her tanned face, making her very pretty. This would be how she would look in lovemaking, he realized, and felt a mingled twist of desire and jealousy. "Well?" he demanded, now using a hated phrase of his father's, "Must I wait for doomsday before you speak?"

"I know what the runes say, and we must dig." She was clearly too excited to notice his rudeness. "There is treasure here! Viking gold! Look—"

She caught his hand in hers and fairly dragged him back with her, careless of whether he smacked his head on the low cave roof. Crook-backed, he let her guide him, enjoying the feel of her small fingers round his palm.

"Look!" She dropped to her knees beside the maze of marks he had found at the back of the cave years earlier. The setting sun blazed into the small dry space—had it always been this small?—turning rock and stone golden. The runes on one darker-hued stone close to the cave floor seemed faded to Hugh's eyes, but his eager companion read them easily.

"Orri's hoard is here. A mighty gift." She pointed to an X-shaped rune. "This rune, Gebo, means gift." She touched three straight lines with her foot. "Three, then dig, it goes on."

She stepped three paces from the cave wall and began to hack at the earth floor with her knife.

"Wait!" She was wilder than he was, in a fight, Hugh thought, astonished by this whirl of activity. "You will blunt your blade. I have something better."

He looked amongst his things and found the small hammer he used to drive in tent and baggage pegs and the metal file he used to sharpen his sword. He set to work, driving the file into the hard-packed soil where Joanna was laboring, and in a few moments struck something that rang out like a broken bell.

"Let me—" Joanna had her fingers probing and tearing at the loosened earth and now she sat back on her heels, a great smile of pleasure breaking on her face. "We have it!"

Down by her knees was a torn bag, gray-black and half rotten, no more than wisps of cloth. But through the tangle of fraying threads he saw the unmistakable gleam of gold.

"Orri's hoard," Joanna said softly. "He must have left it here for safety and never came back."

She moved but Hugh was swifter, scooping the coins and rings out of the dirt and onto his cloak.

"Hey!"

Fairness made him look at her and offer her a ring: a pretty one, he thought. "Thank you," he said. "That will be most useful."

Joanna stared at the ring without taking it. "You do not think we should share?"

He smiled at the question. "What use would you have for old coins? Your lord gives you all you need, but I must make my own way."

Her eyes narrowed. "You do not think I have expenses? Debts?"

"Take the ring, and this golden chain," he urged, shrugging off her questions, dismissing them as girlish folly. "Both would look well on you, I think. Were I your bishop, it would give me pleasure to see you wearing them."

"Thank you, my lord." She took them, almost a snatch, and retreated to the very back of the cave, leaving him to make up their rough reed mattresses and a fire.

"Will you leave scrabbling for more messages and condescend to help me a little?" he demanded, some time later, as the fire began to smoke. "Feed this while I find food to feed us."

"I thought you preferred to do all things yourself," she retorted. "Besides, you do not have enough kindling."

"If you can do better, do so." Hugh left her sulking over the crackling flames and stamped off outside again. When he returned, Joanna was nowhere to be seen and the fire was a glowing, growing mass of orange. Even as he stared in amazement, the whole mass exploded into more flames and gushed a fog-bank of purple smoke.

"Hell's teeth!" He began beating out the smoke and flames with the end of his travel-stained cloak, choking and half blind in the sulphurous fumes. "What in the devil's name—?"

He spoke to no one. Joanna was gone.

"Find her!" he bawled at his dog, but Beowulf was chewing something—doubtless dropped for him by the wretched girl—and merely sniffed his hand.

"Find her, boy!" Hugh exhorted, scanning the closely growing trees, the lane, and his horse, contentedly cropping turf. Where had she vanished?

Then he saw it: a blur of brown amidst green rushes. *Got you!*

A few strides down the round little hill and across the track was all it took. He found Joanna frozen like a painting against a wall of rushes, her face and hands tucked away from sight and she tried to keep hidden. Her hair had been her downfall: it was tangled into a briar.

"I slipped," she mumbled, hearing his approach. "Fell into this."

"Hold still. I will have you out."

Gently, he unwound the streamers, tress after tress.

"I should cut it," Joanna muttered, moving and stretching as he released her. "'Tis nothing but vanity."

"That would be a pity," Hugh remarked, teasing free the last clump. Her hair was soft and warm, scented with cinnamon. He held it between his fingers, wishing he could ask for a lock and knowing she would refuse.

"What did you put on the fire?" he asked instead.

"Cinnabar and other things."

"You keep such in your purse?"

"It is my trade." Joanna sighed. "And now I am your prisoner again."

"Indeed you are." Hugh savored the thought, adding, "And this time Beowulf will guard you."

She shrugged.

He held out a hand. "Come back to the fire and eat— before I decide to keep you close by stripping you naked."

Joanna gasped and whipped her hand away. "You would not!"

"I might if you pester me again, or interrupt my supper."

"You are no gentle knight! By this, you have just confirmed my low opinion of you!"

Hugh grinned, amused and discomforted in equal measures. Joanna seemed to have the knack of making him feel both ashamed and alive. He could not seem to stop goading her, nor she goading him. "And you are no castle lady, little wretch, so we are quit."

They returned to the cave in silence.

Chapter 8

The following day, Joanna vowed she would not speak to Hugh. Her opinions and wishes counted for nothing with him, so why should she share them?

Yet it was hard for her. She hated silence as a weapon, thinking it unworthy and a waste of time. Still, what else could she do? She would not beg for part of Orri's hoard, or her own freedom. Her captor had already shown what he thought: that she was a trinket of the bishop's, a girl with no worries except for pleasing her master. If she explained about her father's imprisonment, would Hugh care? If she told him how things really were between herself and Bishop Thomas, would he think even less of her? At least as the bishop's mistress she had some status.

I cannot tell him the truth, she thought. *I dare not.*

Sleeping in the cave with her back to Hugh, she had not expected to gain any rest. To her surprise she slept soundly, waking refreshed and unmolested in the dawn, where Hugh was already awake, dressed in a fresh tunic, and with more bread and cheese for her breakfast.

Already, though, he did not trust her, not a finger's-width. He sent the wolfhound with her when she slipped into the bushes, and when they rode together he actually tucked the end of her plait into his belt, fastening her hair into the belt clasp.

"The briar caught you so well yesterday, it gave me the idea to do the same," was all he said, when she twisted about as much as her bounds allowed to hurl him a glare of silent reproach. "We have a long way to go today, and I will not have you straying."

Straying where? Joanna almost asked, before she remembered she was not talking. Instead she kept quiet and marked every landmark as the stallion's hooves ate up league after league. Unused to riding, she was soon sore and the skin on her thighs felt both bruised and rubbed, but she kept her lips pressed tightly together. She would not complain. She would not ask for anything.

"You are very quiet," Hugh remarked as they cantered past an orchard where the apples were just coming into blossom.

Joanna said nothing. She was thinking of how bright the day was, and how pretty the apple blossoms, and how her father could not see either. Every day she was a hostage was a wasted day, one less off the dreadful deadline. She could not work. Even the gold she had found had been largely taken from her. She wet her lips, wondering if she should try to give an account.

Hugh took a swig of mead from a flask and offered it to her.

"Thinking of the bishop, no doubt," he said, which instantly extinguished any ideas Joanna had of trying to explain.

She look a large drink, half choking on the sweet, potent ale, jabbing her heel back into Hugh's shin as he chuckled.

"Not far now," he went on, revealing that he had noticed her discomfort. "You will be able to rest properly, on a bed, and bathe if you wish. Good! My men have set up our tents as I wanted."

He pointed ahead to something Joanna could not see and she nodded, the ache in her lower back and hips now burning like a furnace. For a bath she would do much— even delay her escape.

"Watch her closely," Hugh instructed Mary and the younger Mary, two of his men's wives. "She is of great worth to me, and vital for the release of my brother. She may dupe you into thinking she is doing nothing in that tent but bathing, but never leave her alone."

After yesterday he was taking no chance, Hugh thought, as the women bowed and hurried to obey him. Joanna had almost slipped away once but he would tame her. He had three men round the bathing tent and now two maids to spy—never mind turning base metal into gold, she would have to make herself invisible to escape this tourney ground.

And a hot bath would soothe her. She might even smile for him again, especially if he could find her a new gown to go with her new golden jewels.

Satisfied that he was doing all he should to keep his reluctant hostage safe and happy, Hugh whistled to Beowulf and went to look around the field of tents and horses, to learn who had come and whom he might be fighting.

She had always been the one hauling basins of hot water: it was luxury to be waited on, to sink into a barrel of delicious warm water. At first Joanna started at every sound in the camp, flinching each time she heard horses galloping, men shouting, blacksmiths working. For a camp that would soon witness men skirmishing and jousting it was a strangely happy place, with an excitement Joanna could sense.

The tent flap drew back and she reached for her eating knife, determined to stab Hugh with something more than words, but it was not her captor but the younger Mary, carrying towels and a gown.

"We are about a size, you and me, my lady, so I trust this will suit?" Mary unfurled the gown off her arm and spread it out over a chest, waiting for Joanna's approval. "My lord bought it for me and I have yet to wear it."

Joanna looked at the small, slim serving-woman with her frank, friendly eyes and smooth, unblemished skin and wondered how she could look so happy. The gown, she noted, was of scarlet linen, with darker red detachable sleeves: all very fine and better than the gowns she wore in the bishop's palace.

"Thank you," she said, astonished and touched by this gift. "But, please, it is your new robe—"

Mary smiled and shook her head. "My lord will get me another, very soon. He is generous, my lady."

"I am no one's lady."

Mary's pretty smile broadened. "You are my lord's, and he told us all to show you honor. Will you dress now?"

Mary would not allow her to step out of the tent until she had tied the gown and its sleeves to her satisfaction, lacing the waist far more tightly than Joanna would have done. After that, the maid dressed and covered her hair with a dark blue veil of some soft and luscious silk, and handed her the old gold necklace from Orri's hoard. Giving her shoes a final polish, Mary clapped her hands and at once a young page scrambled into the tent, bowing to both women and offering Joanna his arm.

"Go with Stephen," Mary said. "He will guide you."

She brushed aside Joanna's further thanks, turning back to the steaming bath with the air of a busy but contented woman.

Self-conscious in her tight new gown, Joanna walked with the page about the tourney ground, taking in everything. High on a level hilltop, surrounded by palisades and new ditches, the forthcoming field of battle was colorful with flags and fluttering pennants, beaded round with brightly hued tents and wagons. Squires and heralds went from tent to tent, delivering messages, issuing challenges. Horses stamped and snorted as they were groomed and prepared for battle. Traders walked about the hill, selling pies. Farther down the hill, beyond the field itself, were many campfires and men eating and drinking, comparing swords and maces.

"Should we not be returning to your lord's camp?" Joanna ventured at one point. They had walked the length of a bowshot seeing more tents, more carts, more men. No women, she noted, with alarm.

"This is all his company," Stephen replied, nodding a greeting to a passing minstrel. "See: my lord comes now."

Joanna decided it would be petty of her to ignore Hugh, but did so anyway, gazing off to the left. "Why are those men pointing at me?"

"Because damsels at a tourney ground are rare, leastways in England," Hugh answered for his page.

He was closing fast, still dressed in the leggings he had worn when he had kidnapped her, but he had found a patched rough tunic from somewhere and was handling some quilted linen body armor as he approached, seemingly checking it for holes and tears.

"They know you are my prize," he added.

Joanna stopped and took a step back. "You told them that?"

"No, but they have eyes. They will have guessed. Save your indignation, Joanna," he went on, frowning not at her but at a small hole in a quilted linen shirt. "You are my first prize demoiselle and today, at this joust, I will do battle in your honor."

His arrogance made her breathless with shock and then with anger. "I should thank you, then?" she said, when she could speak.

"It is but custom, the way of the tourney. In France, a damsel is proud to be a prize: she issues challenges to other knights to prove that her knight will keep her safe and protect her."

"That is a perversion of the knightly code," Joanna managed to say, through clenched teeth. "And were I a queen or noblewoman, you would not dare to treat me this way."

Finally, he looked at her fully, surprise showing in his tanned, handsome face. "Why do you seethe? It is but play."

"Tell that to the peasant whose lands these are and whose crops you have destroyed! I know! I have seen it before!"

Abruptly she was back in a dark past that she could recall only in terrible snatches: running with her father ahead of a troop of men; their clothes singed, their hair scorched and everywhere hay and corn stacks burning, burning. . . .

"Here, Joanna, take a drink. 'Tis good ale, nothing more."

Joanna accepted the cup of ale and sipped, memories playing beneath her eyelids as she remained standing with half-closed eyes, trying to force herself back to this day.

"Forgive me," she said, looking up at Hugh. "These old memories come over me at times: they are but shadows."

He clasped her hand. "Yet painful, nonetheless." He

looked at her solemnly, without malice or humor. "I understand. We should take a walk about."

Bitterness spurted in her at his compassion: what right had he to be sympathetic? "So you may show off your prize to the rest?"

He grinned: darkly and devilishly handsome. "To calm you down, as I might a skittish mare, but yes, to show you off, too."

He threaded his arm through hers and drew her along, pointing to birds' nests in the nearby trees and flowers blooming in distant fields as if they were strolling in a peaceful arbor, not a field of battle.

Who was she? Hugh wondered, guiding her to his own tent. He had to arm and prepare, but his mind was not on the coming jousts and skirmishes but on Joanna. Being out of doors in sunshine suited her, showed off her lightly tanned skin so that she looked like a little field maid: his nut-brown maid in a bright red dress. But then she had gone as pale as ice when she spoke of destroyed crops, reliving something.

Where had she been before she had fallen into the bishop's clutches? And why should her past matter to him?

"Hey, Destroyer! I will have you this day!"

The nickname startled Hugh, although he claimed it, lazily raising an arm in mocking salute of a fellow knight, bantering without thought. Never before had he considered what a destroyer might be like to those beneath the knightly class, to those left behind once the mêlées were gone.

Their lords will see them right, he told himself, but he knew that was too easy. What if their lords were like Bishop Thomas?

"I must arm," he said to Joanna, glad to see her stepping

out more smoothly and the color returned to her clear, inquisitive face. "Stephen will attend you."

He ducked into his own small tent. Normally he armed on the field, but with Joanna present he felt awkward: it was nothing to be stripped to the waist, but to be stripped completely? What if she was less than impressed?

"What do you care?" he muttered, checking back, all the same, that Joanna was being cared for; that the page was bringing a stool for her comfort, and more ale.

He was in his linen body armor and struggling with the mail coat when a scrape on the tent door-hanging had him reaching for his sword, in case a riot of knights had decided to start early. Flinging back the cloth flap, braced for a rush of burly squires and men-at-arms, he found his own squire Henri, stocky and round-faced, looking as proud and puffed-out as a highland capercaillie.

"My lord! I found your lady here wandering in the lists. I brought her safely back and warned her that it is not wise for so heavenly a damsel to stroll alone."

"My thanks, Henri," Hugh replied, giving the lad his due without glancing too closely at the heavenly demoiselle. "Bring the lady in; you may both help me to arm."

Henri bowed his way in and then nipped out immediately to find Hugh's surcoat, leaving Hugh alone with Joanna.

"That is a less than angelic expression, squirrel," he remarked, seeing her glowering round the tent. "I suppose you were trying to sneak away?"

She glowered at him. "It seemed a good plan. An experiment, to see how far I could go. Squirrel?"

"It seems fitting for you. Bright-eyed, busy, always vanishing from sight in a second."

"And I might vanish again—"

"And be caught again."

"I may try the experiment again."

"With the same result." Hugh stretched his arms above his head and shook the mail shirt into place, its cumbersome weight seeming far less than usual because he was on his mettle with Joanna. "Will you pass me my helmet?" He pointed to the closed-in helm on top of the single clothes chest—that chest, and two stools, were the only furniture in this tent. He was intrigued as to what she would do.

She crossed to the chest but did not touch the metal helm. "Why should I help you kill people?"

He almost laughed out loud at her folly, but remembered her pale, stricken face and answered more gently.

"In a joust or skirmish we do not seek to kill, merely capture."

The corners of her mouth turned down. "You should have good practice, then," she snapped back, but then she picked up the helmet and stalked across to him. "Here." She thrust it at him.

"No honeyed words of encouragement, oh heavenly damsel?"

"My tongue is vinegar for oafs such as—oof!"

The exclamation burst from her as he snatched her into his arms.

"A kiss first, sweet lady?" he asked, dropping the helm behind him, trapping her legs between his before she could injure his shins. He blew a stray lock of hair away from her flushed face. "You seemed to like my kiss."

He lowered his head toward her, chuckling as she sucked her lips inward. "No? Not even when I ride out for you?"

"Do not delude yourself, knight. You wage war for yourself."

Ignoring that, he flicked the old gold chain around her

throat, thinking again how pretty her mouth looked when reddened. "This suits you well. I will seek to win you more today."

"I make my own way." She was as stiff as a shield in his arms and twice as unyielding. The few women he had known had all told him bluntly that he was a one-night stand-in for their absent spouses: they had fought his clothes, not him, and afterward were keen for him to leave. Joanna was different: to win her would be the challenge of months, and to keep her the challenge of years. He smiled at the thought, not in the slightest daunted.

"What?" She scowled. "Are you devising new ways to humiliate me?"

"Are you humiliated now?" he asked mildly.

"You keep me against my will."

Hugh dropped his hands from her narrow waist and clasped them behind his back. "Now I do not." To prove this, he unthreaded his leg from hers.

Joanna instantly drew back—spurted back, she moved so fast. Hugh waited, as he might with a nervous hawk or hound, and she leaped forward.

She tugged at the chain around her throat. "I am not a thing like this! How can you call me a prize? How dare you? God made me, not man!"

"You are a true wonder of creation," Hugh agreed, wondering where his squire was and if he had time to kiss Joanna thoroughly before Henri dashed back into the tent.

"I am that," she said, and, standing up on her toes, she kissed him directly on the mouth, a lingering, ripe kiss that was over far too quickly.

"It worked," she said, when she withdrew, brushing some small speck off the bodice of her new gown. "I had a mind it would."

"What?" He echoed her and she smiled.

"I thought that I could kiss you to silence, and so I

have." She gave him a mocking half-bow. "God be with you, sir knight."

She sashayed from the tent before Hugh could speak, just as his squire Henri darted back into the space with his crumpled surcoat.

Chapter 9

Escape, while he is distracted. He has put you in this ignominious place, but you do not have to stay in it. Escape!

She hurried away from the small, patched tent, marking how inconspicuous it was when set against the gaudy wagons and tents of the other knights. Hugh, it seemed, spent his tourney money on other things—horses, for one, Joanna thought, recalling the fiery, splendid Lucifer.

Could she steal a horse from the picket lines and gallop away? Escape and then sell the horse later for gold: more ransom cash for her father? As a daydream the idea was as beguiling, but her sore back and thighs protested at the thought and her sense said no, she had not the riding skill. Yet, if she could find a drab bit of cloth to cover this red gown she might do well enough on foot. This place was filled with men, yet so far she had to admit that she had been treated with respect.

Because of who you are with.

Almost as if her head was on an invisible string, she found herself looking back, wondering how Hugh looked in armor. Yet what did that matter? She was seeking a way to remove herself from him.

"Lost are you, lovely?"

The woman's voice was a surprise; the nipping hand on her shoulder a shock. She swung round, finding herself confronting a matron of middle age, dressed in a gown that was unlaced to her stout middle and carrying a spindle with a hank of red dyed wool on its end—a parody of a spinster, Joanna realized.

"Not I, madam." Joanna shifted sideways but the woman waved her spindle and instantly a group of girls streamed from a nearby tent and surrounded her. Joanna eyed them warily: with their loose hair and skimpy, almost see-through gowns, these were true tourney girls, she guessed, women who followed the jousters for love or favor.

"I must be away," she said, but a tall girl with unbound blond hair and white make-up covering a rash of pimples held up a warning fist. Silently, the troop closed in.

"I am with Destroyer," Joanna added, despising herself for mentioning Hugh but hoping his nickname would prove useful.

At once, the madam snapped her fingers and her girls spilled back in clouds of rose perfume. She prodded Joanna with her spindle.

"Should have told me, lovely, though I could guess. Brown as hazel nuts, the pair of you." The madam continued to assess her, her eyes sharp as flints. "Keeps you nesh enough, I see, spoiled and soft, but then as I say to my girls: Destroyer's a devil in bed but he will not stint a woman. You had better return to him. He has a temper on him, as I am sure you know."

Under the older woman's beady eyes Joanna felt compelled to turn about on the trampled-down thread of a track that ran between the tents and stalk back toward the fluttering pennants of a black bear against a red field—Hugh's personal flag. Below this bare field were lines of horses and a further camp of farriers and smiths where she could have hidden, but the madam was still watching her.

Behind her, along the path where she had lately tried to flee, she felt the ground shuddering. That, and within seconds the drumming of hooves, alerted her to the horseman's approach. She stepped smartly toward a hawthorn bush with hacked and broken branches—it would provide some small protection if the horse happened to miss its footing.

The beast did not. Instead it slowed and its rider, a man in mail but without the tall closed-in helm worn by knights in combat, called out to her.

"My lady! My lady in red! Will you grant me a favor?"

He was young, fresh-faced with scarcely any stubble, and clearly a knight who had only lately won his spurs. As he cantered toward her his face and sword shone, as if newly minted. Joanna sensed his excitement and heady pride and despite her own plight she was touched.

"Here then." She handed him one of the trinkets off her own girdle—she would give nothing that had once belonged to Hugh. Quite apart from the fact she did not want to cause this young knight trouble, she did not want to alert Hugh or his men by granting anything distinctive, anything Hugh would recognize. This tiny golden tassel she thought safe enough: Hugh would not have noticed it swinging at the end of her girdle. "Wear this for me, in honor of my father."

Flushed with pleasure, the knight reached down from his horse, taking the tassel between finger and thumb, holding it as reverently as if he was handling a holy relic. "Lady, I will treasure it forever. Your gift will inspire me to great feats of arms this today: I shall challenge all comers and best all knights—"

"And I am most grateful." Joanna interrupted this flow of knightly enthusiasm, wondering how she might slip away. If the knight engaged her for much longer, she would be spotted by one of Hugh's men, or worse, by Hugh himself. "I must now return to my father," she lied. "May I know your name, Sir—?"

"Sir Tancred of Kenilworth." He lifted his lithe slim body, standing up on his stirrups prior to dismounting. "May I escort you?"

"'Tis only a little way," Joanna lied. Spotting a place where she could go and the horse and the young knight could not, she sped across the grass toward a cart and wagon drawn side by side, with no more than a hand-span between them. "Farewell, Sir Tancred," she called back hastily over her shoulder, blushing as she saw the young knight pinning her small token to his surcoat, as if she was a true noblewoman. "Do well for me!"

Ashamed at her deception, she did not look round again and squeezed between the carts, praying that no servant would protest or stop her.

Hugh was armed and checking his warhorse and weapons when two of his men-at-arms for whom he had yet to provide badges appeared with Joanna strolling between them.

He took off his helmet, so he would be less of a stranger, although it was obvious from the way she was frowning that she knew who he was.

"How far this time?" he asked her, nodding appreciation to his men, who busied themselves with looking over his charger.

"I had reached the outer palisade of the field." Joanna's eyes were bright and feral, her face hard and pinched with displeasure. "How could I know they were yours? They wear no caps, badges, or anything!"

The men hid their faces behind the charger's massive flanks.

"You cannot blame them." Hugh wondered at his lack of temper—by rights he should be furious at Joanna's folly where instead he rather admired her stubbornness. "You must understand this tourney field is no place for a young woman to be wandering alone."

Her eyes narrowed. "You brought me here. You allowed the world to believe that I am your prize."

"And I will take you away again, as soon as I may," Hugh replied. "Though that will not be—"

A single piercing horn blast sounded over the hilltop, the signal, Hugh knew, that the jousts would soon begin. He almost said as much to Joanna when he noticed one of the gold tassels on her girdle was missing. His heart racing, he looked her over, head to heel.

"She was unharmed, unmolested?" he demanded in French to his men.

"No one accosted me," Joanna answered in the same language. "And you can ask me."

Then where is the end of your girdle?

Hugh bit down hard on his tongue. She might have lost it on the field somewhere, or in a bush. What did it matter? It was a piece of womanly foolishness, the kind of decoration that holier clerics than Bishop Thomas were fond of railing against.

He pointed at the remaining golden tassel. "Will you give me that as a favor? I know you do not have your gloves with you," he added quickly, before she could remind him of that fact.

"Take my headrail," she said steadily, cool and smooth as the blue silk veil she wore as she unpinned it with nimble fingers. "It is yours to begin with."

She held it out, giving a nod and a fleeting smile as he

took the long streamer of cloth and knotted it round his surcoat.

"Take her to sit with the womenfolk—the ladies, not the others." Hugh snapped his fingers at the wolfhound. "Guard her, Beowulf."

As the dog attached himself close to Joanna's heel, Hugh slammed the helmet back over his head, making his skull ring as his face settled into a grim frown. Joanna's tiny smile had convinced him—she was up to something. What, he was not certain of yet, but he had his suspicions and he would be on the lookout.

Certain that the hound at least would not let him down, Hugh mounted his horse and rode off to the lists without looking back.

There were five noblewomen who had followed their lords to this tourney, all seated in a covered wagon close to where the knights would joust and surrounded by hounds and lapdogs and men-at-arms. The five had a look of each other, Joanna decided, as she climbed the wagon steps. Grudgingly they admitted her to sit upon a cushion but did not offer wine or honey-cakes. All were tall, narrow-featured, pale-skinned, and richly dressed, and all stared at her hands as if her fingers were stained in blood, not sulphurs. Joanna sat on her palms and watched the ladies make more of a fuss of the wolfhound than her. She longed to explain that she scrubbed her hands daily, but the stains remained; that she must work for her bread and her fingers showed the badge of her craft. She wanted to ask these long-nosed, haughty females if they were any knight's prize.

When Hugh galloped onto the field, the noblewomen praised his horse, his riding, the weight and grip of his lance and the length and power of his long, lean legs. Joanna was tempted to point to the blue gossamer streaming across his brawny shoulders but as he drew rein, waiting for his first opponent to emerge clearly from the mass of horses and knights already gathered on the field, her favor had already been noticed.

"Destroyer is wearing a favor, but I do not recognize the lady's colors. Did you give it to him, Eleanor?"

"Never in this millennium. I would not dare, though as God is my judge, I have often wished for the courage to do so. Did you, Matilde? He has smiled at you before."

"I would not give that handsome devil a token in case he challenged my husband, and then I would not know which of them to cheer."

"It would not matter, Matilde. We know who would win."

"And my husband left weaponless and horseless."

"How many chargers has he won now?"

"Too many to count. . . . Was it you, Berengaria?"

"No, but I wish I had. He is, as you say, so very handsome."

"That he is . . ."

The chatter ran on and Joanna hid her smile behind her stained hand as the speculation washed round her. None of the noblewomen deigned to ask her, but that did not matter: their nervous envy soothed her in a most un-Christian manner.

Hugh turned his head and for an instant Joanna sensed him looking at her. She wondered if he was smiling or solemn behind the helm and shocked herself by actually waving back to him, swiftly sending out a prayer for his safety.

Why have I done that? He needs no help or acknowledgment from me! In all, he inspires fear, not love!

Joanna knew that was not the whole truth. And how could she complain when that very fear was keeping her safe in this place?

"He should not have brought me here," she muttered under her breath. "He delays my work and puts me and my father in danger." She wrenched her eyes from him and saw his challenger cantering toward him, shouting threats and insults in French.

It cannot be!

Her heart cantered in turn as she recognized the slim, youthful figure and his big, bony chestnut stallion. It was the worst match possible: Sir Tancred of Kenilworth.

Joanna realized she was wringing her hands and quickly hid them again, in case Hugh or his young adversary had seen. This would be a horribly unequal contest, she guessed, and both wore her tokens!

Please do not let Hugh see the tassel. Please let Sir Tancred have hidden it away, in a glove, under his armor—

Her hopes and wishes were useless. There was the golden tassel, still pinned to the young knight's shoulder, swinging to and fro as he received his lance from a squire and yelled another insult. Inexorably, Joanna felt her eyes drawn to it and she sensed, without knowing how, that Hugh had also spotted it and now knew who had given Sir Tancred the favor.

She wanted to shout a warning, but dared not in case it made Hugh angry. Frustrated, her nerves on edge, wanting to close her eyes, sick in the pit of her stomach and longing to stop this folly somehow, Joanna knew she was compelled to watch. Helpless, she saw the knights raise their shields to each other in acknowledgment before they joined in battle.

The noise as they charged each other was incredible and then it was over. Suddenly and brutally, in an explosion of snorting horses and clashing arms, Hugh and his charge rammed into Tancred and his horse. Joanna winced as some poor creature, horse or rider, screamed. In a dreadful pall of dust and splattered gobbets, a horse and rider were down, rolling on the churned earth less than a bowshot's length away from the wagon. Joanna lunged for the wagon steps as the unearthly shriek went on but the noblewomen Matilde seized her arm and dug in, her nails like claws.

"Do not shame them more! Stay!" Matilde hissed, her face bright and her eyes wide as she instantly returned to watching.

She is enjoying this.

Appalled, Joanna tore her arm out of the older woman's grip and tumbled down the steps, almost falling headlong out of the wagon. Choking on the standing swirl of dust she saw a massive figure hauling his smaller opponent out of the wreck of a broken lance and a shattered, buckled shield. She screamed as Hugh tore her golden favor from the sagging knight's shoulder and took it between his teeth, gripping it as a dog might a bone.

"Enough! I yield!" she yelled, terrified Hugh would not hear her.

Incredibly, it seemed he did. Even as she drew in breath to plead again, she watched in ghastly slowness, the world about her gray and grainy, sluggish as moving ditch water, as Hugh set Tancred back on his feet.

He said something to the young knight, then turned and caught the rearing chestnut, smoothing the beast's quivering flanks with an ungloved hand while his own horse snorted and stamped. Another word from Hugh and the charger became quiet, shaking its head and flicking its long tail. Hugh himself remained where he was as squires streamed onto the field to help Tancred remove his helmet and guide him back to his tent.

Joanna felt herself go clammy with relief as she saw the young man's pale face and blinking, clearing eyes. He was in shock, but relatively whole: Hugh had not mauled him.

Beowulf whined softly by her side and she rubbed the

space between his ears, wishing for a moment to use the hound as a barrier as Hugh approached.

"We are leaving," he said. He had not yet removed his helm.

He held out his gloved hand and opened his fist. In it, resting on his huge palm like some exotic butterfly, lay her golden tassel.

Silently, she took it.

Silently, he now offered her his arm to lead her away.

"What did you say to him?" she asked, her voice low.

"I told him that his horse was whole, scratched but whole."

Hugh's voice was muffled by the helmet, she could not tell if he was yet angry, but then he added, in softer tones still, "The lad has a broken finger but no more. I will not take his horse or armor: he needs both more than I."

Joanna knew she should thank him, for by custom he could have taken all, but her tongue failed her in that endeavor. "Is it always this way?" she croaked at last.

"Worse," came the laconic reply. "Now let us go. This skirmish has brought no honor to anyone."

Joanna nodded. She wanted to say she was sorry, but she would not apologize for the favor: such tokens were part of the courtly game and Hugh knew it.

Still, she wished Hugh and Tancred had not met as they had. . . .

Walking away with her captor, her limbs stiff as she tried to prevent herself from shaking, Joanna heard the fussing behind her.

"She is Destroyer's woman! She never told us!"

"Jealous! I have never seen him so!"

"Do you mark how dark and tanned she is? Has she been living in a field?"

Trying to ignore the titters of laughter, Joanna moved on.

Chapter 10

"I like Tancred," Hugh remarked, after he and Joanna had ridden together in flinty silence for more than a mile. "Why did you give him your favor?"

"Because he asked me for it."

Hugh could only see the back of Joanna's head but he could sense the tension rolling off her, like waves of heat. He knew he was being unfair and unjust but, like his wolfhound scratching at a scab, he could not leave it alone.

"Then you should have refused. You should have known I would fight him, that I would have to fight him, once I saw it."

"How would I know anything? I have never been at a tourney before today."

It irked him that she was right, and that she would not twist round a little, to look at him.

"The customs are well known. You gave that young lad a token to defy me. I hope the outcome is to your satisfaction."

"Nothing is to my liking. Do not blame me for your jealous conscience."

They were riding up to a ditch that the horse would have

to jump or go round, but Hugh drew rein, determined to look Joanna in the eye.

"I gave up rich prizes today for you."

"I am your hostage, so that was your choice," she answered coolly, still without looking at him. "Besides, you have Orri's gold. Will he be able to joust again today?"

Hugh felt his belly boil at the lilt in her voice. "Why not?" he snarled through tight lips. "I have ridden again in jousts with two fingers misplaced."

"Dislocated?" She touched the hand that was always hovering near her waist. "Which fingers?"

Her fingers were soft and warm against his, making him briefly wish that they were dislocated now, so she might tend them. Dismissing such folly as worthy of Tancred, he raised his right hand.

"The first two here. A surgeon yanked them back and they hurt like the devil when he did it, but they give me no trouble now."

"Did you leave the field today for shame?" she asked quietly, adding, "I am ashamed."

"Why?" Already he knew it was not for handing Tancred any favor.

Her narrow shoulders tensed. "I am a scholar, a seeker after rare knowledge. Your world of war should not be for me."

"Because your world is better?"

"I did not say that. But I should be for peace. A wise man is always for peace. Yet today, at the tourney, I felt excitement." She turned now in the saddle, her legs brushing his as she moved. "I should not be moved by *glamour.*" She spat the word, as if it were a curse.

Hugh could hardly believe his ears. "Did you compliment me, then?"

In profile he saw her wet her lips with her tongue, a nervous gesture. "Perhaps I did. Your world is strange to me,

Hugh. Terrible and strange. Yet . . ." She sighed, rubbing her eyes like a little child does when tired. "Yet it is a true world, with its own honors. I saw that, too."

She tugged at the scrap of veil still trailing off his surcoat. "Do you feel you fought well today, my knight?"

The question pierced him like a lance and now he admitted the dismal truth. "It was a carnage. We were not well matched, and yes, damn all to hell, I am ashamed."

Wanting no more of this, he spurred the horse. Where they were going gave him no joy, but it would be better lodgings for Joanna than a tourney ground.

If—and this was a large if—his father admitted them.

Hugh rode hard and fast, counting off remembered landmarks under his breath. His men and baggage were following behind and he would send the wolfhound back to them if all went wrong and his father would not have them through the bailey gates. To return at all, after a gap of more than a year, was to swallow his pride, but he would have the satisfaction of asking his father face-to-face what he intended to do to help his son David. *It would be good to see the old man squirm.*

Before him, straddling the long saddle of his palfrey with its pommel driving into her stomach and her skirts in a swirl about her knees, Joanna rode in silence, her fingers white as she clutched the rough mane of the horse. Taking pity on her, he checked Lucifer, came to a stop, and gave her the mead flask.

She drank, nodding her thanks.

"Do you see that ridge of hills to the south? We shall reach them before twilight and find rest and shelter."

"In the strong new keep of your father," Joanna said.

"David told you." *Damn him.* Hugh took a drink so quickly that he began to choke.

"We have spoken of many things. He said your father's lands were nearby."

Feeling mead trickle down his nose, Hugh coughed and tried to snatch breath enough to answer. "You must wonder why my father does not parley with your lord the bishop."

"It seems to me you are wondering that yourself," Joanna replied, pulling a windblown apple blossom from her hair. Hugh wanted to tell her to leave it there, but the old bitterness against his father won through.

"Oh, he will do nothing for us, the lesser sons. We must make our own way. I prefer that," he added swiftly, lest she think he was moaning. "I would not be beholden to him for as much as a penny."

"Nigel is the eldest, is he not?"

Did David give out our entire lineage? "He is, and we have no sisters; no mother, either, thanks to me. Can you ride on now? We have a way to go before twilight."

Joanna ached in places she did not know she had, but she would not beg for another break. Sore and uncomfortable, she tried to recall the language of birds, the secret language of alchemy, in order to distract herself, but the pain in her hips and thighs from riding made it impossible. How did heralds and messengers bear this? she wondered. The ease of her earlier bath had long since vanished.

Behind her, as solid yet fluid as molten lava and as warm, Hugh rode with the horse, moving with a grace she could only envy. What had he meant by his *No mother, either, thanks to me*? She tried to recall if David had ever mentioned his mother in their talks, but nothing came to her. Instead, she tried to imagine Hugh's father. Would he be dark, like his son, and as stubborn? Would he be grim or gay, like David and Mercury? Grim, she thought, especially as he and Hugh were clearly estranged.

And Hugh was taking them to his father's castle for the night.

"Madness," she breathed, biting her lip as the palfrey stumbled on a stony part of the road and her soft and tender thigh scraped along the horse's flank.

They reached Castle Manhill an hour after sunset. Framed by hills and woods, it was possibly a handsome place by day but by the slender curve of a new moon it looked oppressive. The bailey loomed over Joanna's head as the palfrey began to canter up the final track to the main gate, and the stone keep within towered over the raised enclosure of the bailey. As she and Hugh rode closer, she could hear guards on the palisade and walkway calling out.

"Will we be shot at by a bow or sling?" she hissed, too tired now to slump around in the saddle to face her captor.

"The men know my banners, " Hugh replied. "See: they are opening the gate."

There was another rush of darkness under pounding hooves, a blaze of torches, more shouting, and then they were through the gate and into the bailey, riding briskly for the keep. As Hugh stopped by a narrow stone staircase leading out of the first floor of the keep, a door at the top of the stairs opened and a man came out.

"What is your father's name?" Joanna whispered. She knew someone had told her, David or even Hugh himself, but she was so worn down with travel that she had forgotten.

"Sir Yves." Hugh swung down from Lucifer, half catching her as she began to slide off the saddle. "Stay there. I will get you down in a moment."

"How many times must I say I am no parcel?" Joanna protested, but Hugh was striding up the stairs and embracing a stocky, bearded man dressed in a long mantle of some dark color—she could not say what hue, with the moon so new and dim. At a head shorter than his son and as broad as a barrel, Sir Yves was a surprise, and his reception of his prodigal youngest was far quieter and more subdued than she had expected. He gave no true kiss of greeting, but no harsh, loud words, either.

Because it was easier to stay where she was, Joanna forced herself to stretch protesting muscles and slither off the horse. A groom was now holding its head, so the task was simple enough except she went the wrong way and finished on the cobbles of the bailey, with the horse between her and the approaching Manhills, coming side by side down the steps. She grabbed the pommel to keep herself upright and waited.

Sir Yves stopped on the final step.

"Will you introduce your lady, so that I may greet her?" he demanded, his voice lighter and less gruff than Hugh's as his hooded blue eyes coolly assessed her smut-smeared face and wind-wrecked hair.

"I am Joanna of West Sarum, sir," she replied quickly, before Hugh could crassly recount she was his hostage, or worse, that she was the bishop's mistress. "I am of Bishop Thomas's household."

"The same place which holds David," Hugh put in.

Sir Yves still did not move off the step. "I am aware of that."

"Yet you do nothing," his son answered.

Yves's light blue eyes darkened to the color of his son's. "The Templars are his kin now. They should deal with it."

"And if they do not?"

"Be not so proud and stiff-necked!" his father roared out. "You come here after months, without word, greeting, or gift, without a by your leave—"

"Forgive me!" Joanna pitched her voice to rise above the

scuffle as Hugh looked ready to grab his father by his dark red mantle and hurl him off the stair. "I have your gift."

Both men turned and stared at her unexpected interjection, expectation lighting Yves's narrow features while Hugh was frowning. In truth, Joanna wondered at herself and why she had troubled to intervene, but then she thought of her own father, patient and uncomplaining, asking for nothing even while in prison, and her temper sharpened.

"But I am sure you have no wish to conduct our affairs on the doorstep?" she went on, with deadly sweetness.

Hugh's broad shoulders tightened as he stifled a chuckle. His father, mastering himself with a visible scowl, refused to smile.

"You must enter," he said, speaking without offering her his arm. "Tell me, what place have you, a spinster, in Lord Thomas's house?"

Marking both titles, Joanna spoke as Hugh did.

"I am alchemist to the bishop."

"She is with me, Father, and in my care."

"A fine care, that is, sir!" Sir Yves exclaimed, showing some bad teeth as he grinned. "The wench is exhausted. Bring her inside before she falls asleep over your horse's neck!"

With that sparse welcome, Joanna found herself ushered inside.

Chapter 11

Sir Yves, Joanna swiftly discovered, was a glutton, and Hugh was embarrassed by this. Yves's greed showed in the supper table she was led to within the great hall of the stone keep. On the dais was a table with enough food piled upon its boards to feed several families for a week, and the servers were bringing in more pies and trenchers.

Sitting down beside her at this massive table, Hugh murmured, "You shall sleep in your own chamber tonight. I will clear out the clerks' room."

"They will not object?"

"They will bed down with me in the corridor and like it," Hugh answered. "Now, can you sit through a dozen courses, or shall I make your excuses and have a bite brought to your room?"

She looked at him steadily. With his tanned good looks it was hard to tell, but she thought she saw a blush across his cheekbones, and discomfort in his dark blue eyes.

"Still ashamed?" she almost said, but then checked that meanness. "Thank you for not contradicting me earlier," she said softly.

He smiled and shook his head. "You are shy for a lord's mistress. Have you—?" He stopped. "I will say nothing unless you do of that matter," he went on gruffly. "Will you have some wine?"

Pouring her a goblet instead of waiting for one of the many swarming servers meant that Hugh leaned toward her. As he did so, he whispered, "Be careful of my father. He craves gold. In truth, I am surprised you told him you were an alchemist."

Only because I feared you would tell him I was the bishop's mistress, Joanna thought, sipping her wine to disguise her expression. "I should have said I was a cook, or laundress or farrier, I know!" she hissed back. "But had you not brought me here, against my will, I would not need to lie!"

"You are too slight for a farrier, and too disagreeable for a lady," Hugh said, tapping his own goblet as if they were discussing the wine. "And you know why I took you. But heed me. Watch if my father offers you a place to stay and study here. He will expect results."

A stay meant more time away from her father, more days slipping away of her own deadline. Suddenly more scared than she had ever been since the start of her strange captivity, Joanna ignored her clammy hands and dry mouth and fought to make a cool, considered answer. "So do all men. Have you no faith in me, Hugh?"

"I have less in my father," he growled, in a way that had Joanna anxiously glancing along the table to the central chair where Sir Yves was bent over a mutton pie. He was chewing with half-closed eyes, intent on nothing but his trencher. There were crumbs in his beard. The sight quenched what small appetite she had, and she was already light-headed with the toil of the ride and the shocks of the day.

"He will be at table for hours yet, and I will have to stay, else he will accuse me of being a poor son," Hugh remarked.

He beckoned to a page. "Escort the lady Joanna to her bed-chamber," he said. "It should be ready now."

The following morning, Joanna woke to the news that Sir Yves had allowed Hugh to send one of his messengers to Bishop Thomas, demanding a hostage exchange—herself for David.

The herald also told her that Sir Yves was eager for her to begin her experiments in finding gold, and that her sleeping chamber would now also be her workplace.

"Whatever you require shall be brought here," the herald intoned, which had Joanna hurrying to recite a list of her basic needs.

She was moving her pallet to the wall in the darkest place of the chamber—for she, unlike her experiments, did not need the light—when Hugh knocked on the open door. For an instant she was reminded of Richard Parvus, the bishop's steward, but Hugh was far taller and broader and younger. More disturbing, too, as he filled the doorway.

"You have heard, then," he remarked, entering the chamber and picking up a sturdy chest as if it weighed no more than a feather. "This—arrangement—is my father's price for sending a messenger from here to the bishop on behalf of David. Else he would have done nothing."

Say nothing, Joanna told herself, torn between anger and pity.

"He would have done nothing. For his own son. Where do you want this?"

"The chest? Under the pallet, please," Joanna answered, hating herself for blushing as she spoke of a bed to him. "I would applaud your concern for your brother," she went on, "were it not that what you plan is at my expense."

"He will want you back." Hugh straightened from lowering the chest and folded his arms. "I know you are right.

David will scold me forever, once he is free and you are safe again with the bishop."

Safe? Joanna started to laugh. *When have we ever been safe, Father and I?* She was laughing still as Hugh backed from the chamber, saying he would find her some breakfast.

While he was away and tables were brought in and Joanna spoke with the seneschal of the castle over supplies, she was thinking. It was clear from the seneschal's answers that Sir Yves understood that he would need to spend gold in order to beget more. This was a vast relief to her. If she could continue her work that must surely help her father: there was an elixir she was seeking to purify and a few more days would see that complete. It was not *the* elixir, the substance that would create gold, but Bishop Thomas would surely appreciate its virtue and value.

As for Hugh and his father . . . Joanna sighed, nodding thanks to a servant who had carried in a huge earthenware pot, the first of many. As she quickly relayed a list of herbs and minerals and glassware to the seneschal—after being told she could not leave the castle to scour the markets of the closest town for such items—she was working out, in her mind, how to deal with Yves and Hugh. And by the time Hugh returned with a slice of bread and soft cheese and a cup of ale, she was smiling.

Over the next few days, waiting for the messenger to return from Bishop Thomas, Hugh knew that Joanna was up to something. From being harsh and critical—*"Can you do no better than that? Is this what you call a horse? Your sword is too heavy. That helm is out of shape."*—his father was growing smooth. Not sanguine, that would be too great a transformation, but lively. The old man went about the castle rubbing his hands, asking after others, staring every evening at the heavens, something he had never glanced at before Joanna had been held up in the clerks' chamber.

"She says she will have something for me by the half-moon," Sir Yves confessed one night, and Hugh, aching from a poor tourney practice—his squire had been able to whack him hard on the helm because he had been trying to see if smoke was rising from Joanna's room—thought it wise to agree with him.

After he had doused his head in a water butt, he strode up the keep staircase to the tiny side chamber off Sir Yves's that Joanna had made her own. Greeting the guard outside, he ignored the man's protests, knocked, and entered.

She was not there. He had hoped to find her, busy among her distilling glasses, or whatever those curiously shaped items were called, with her clever fingers flying over bowls and candles and her brown fringe escaping its net and curling slightly over her forehead, damp with the steam.

Hugh blinked and the vivid picture vanished. The room was empty. The dull pounding in his head sickened to a sharper ache as he turned.

"She is in the bailey garden," the guard said. "I did try to tell you."

"Aye, man, you did. I was not paying attention," Hugh agreed. These days he was often distracted.

A walk outside would clear his head, he decided. A stroll in the garden . . .

He found her crouched by a rosemary bush, brushing her hands over its green spines.

"Do the same," she suggested, without looking up. "The scent will help your head."

"Did your spies tell you about my encounter with Henri's mace?" In less than a week, Joanna had pages and

maids talking with her as they never spoke with him. He
envied her that ease of making friends.

"I saw it myself." She looked up and beckoned. "It truly
will help, Hugh."

He knelt, and when she held out her fingers, he sniffed.
He did not want her scolding. She was damnably right,
though: the pungent scent cleared his head a little.

"You did take quite a knock. Follow my finger." Joanna
moved her hand before his eyes, her narrow face solemn
as she concentrated. "How many fingers am I showing
you?"

"One."

"And now?"

"Three—Joanna, I have taken far worse in practice and
in tourneys."

"You are not seeing double? Feeling sick?"

He shook his head, then wished he had not.

She laid a cool hand across the back of his neck, devilishly soothing. "Have you ever drunk sage tisane?"

"No. Will you make me some?"

"For my knight? Gladly." She smiled and the furnace
in his head cooled more. "I have finished here."

She rose and picked up a basket, balancing it on her hip.
"I have a powder, too, in my chamber: I make it and purify
it myself. My father and I use it when our heads ache or we
are feverish. The same should help you."

She took his block of a fist between her slender fingers
and raised him. "A drink and a sleep. That is what you
need, Hugh."

I am going soft, Hugh thought, as he allowed her to lead
him away. And what did she mean, calling him her knight?

He did not care. Sage tisane and some strange alchemist
powder, however filthy, had never seemed more appealing.

* * *

Within the castle he drank what she prepared for him, swallowed what she told him to take. After that, she suggested he lie on her bed and close his eyes.

Had his wits been less mazed he would have joked about sprawling on her pallet, but somehow the words would not come and he was already too comfortable. A warm languor was sweeping through him and he buried his head under the pillow, hearing her pad about the room. She was singing softly to herself, in words he could not understand, but her voice was sweet and true. Imagining Joanna singing to a babe in a crib, Hugh relaxed and fell asleep.

He woke to find a blanket over him and his father in the room, sitting at a table while Joanna pounded something with a mortar and pestle.

"I can wash bandages and make salves and make more of the white powder," she was saying.

"That is a wonder, that powder," his father said, more animated than Hugh had known him, except when Yves was speaking of a new food. "Now, do you need any help? That maid under the blanket: will she be of any use?"

"Of course, Sir Yves," Joanna answered, as Hugh had to bite on the pillow to stop him laughing. "Once her sick day is over."

"Very good!" There was the scrape of a stool as Yves clambered to his feet. "I shall leave you now and see you at dinner."

"My lord."

After she had bowed him out, Joanna came to the bedside. "I told your father you were a lass sickened with her monthly course. I knew he would let you bide there, then. How are you?"

"Very well." Hugh emerged from the blanket and stretched both arms above his head; he did feel very well indeed and he wondered how he might conjure Joanna onto the bed with him. He wanted to ask how long he had slept, for how long his father had been chatting so easily with her, but began with an uncontroversial question. "How did you guess I was awake?"

"I have sharper ears than Sir Yves." She stopped grinding and pointed her mortar at him. "You should leave now, my knight, or find us a chaperone. Tongues will wag, and you cannot rip them all out."

"Nor would I!" Hugh answered, stung by the image. Did she truly think so little of him?

She laughed, a merry, generous sound that made him want to kiss her.

"Ah, you are so easy to tease, my knight."

Hugh had flung off the blanket and was rolling off the low pallet, the better to catch her in his arms and claim, he hoped, a forfeit kiss. Now her use of that title twice in as many moments was a disconcerting reminder of his less than knightly conduct.

I keep her because of David. Hugh shrugged off his guilt again and made a play of folding the blanket. Anything so Joanna would not see him looking thoughtful, soft as a cleric.

"You are safe here. My father would never harm a guest."

"You say Sir Yves adores gold, expects results, yet will never harm me? That is a strange mixture, is it not? Were I to put such essences into a flask, I think they would explode."

Joanna resumed grinding with the mortar. The scraping seemed to scratch along the insides of his ears. He spotted the wolfhound slinking out of the door and was tempted to do the same.

"Why do you call me 'my knight'?" Anything to stop that scratching.

"You are mine, are you not?" She pointed the mortar

again. "You must be, since you have taken me from the bishop's household and bed. And did you not wear my token?"

I have it still. That, and the golden tassel. . . .

Hugh coiled the blanket into a messy ball, his insides coiling, too. The idea of Joanna with that loathsome slug Thomas made his eyes burn and teeth ache. "I suppose you expect me to quest for you?"

She stopped her work. A scent of fire and wax and cinnabar swirled in the air between them, like a demon's kiss. Hugh shook himself to rid his head of the fanciful image. "We have no time for games of courtly love," he said. "Tomorrow, you should be on your way back to the bishop's bed."

"The messenger will take longer than that." She held out the mortar and pestle. "If you truly wish to quest for me, as you put it, then you can help. I want this ground down to a fine powder, please."

Hugh stared at the tools, affronted at the very notion. "I am a knight in arms—"

"Then you will be strong enough to do it quickly." She tilted her head to one side, her eyes bright and knowing.

"How fine?" Hugh rapped back, almost snatching the mortar from her.

"As fine as good salt," Joanna replied, turning back to her worktable. "Then we have some bandages to wash, you and I. I promised your father I would clean them well, and I like to keep my vows."

Somehow, the matter of the chaperone had been forgotten, but Hugh decided not to mention it.

Chapter 12

Three days had passed. Her father was three days closer to being cast down into the prison pit. Surely the bishop would not expect her to keep the deadline now, while she was a hostage? How long would it be before the messenger returned? What would he say?

Joanna rolled over and sat up in her bed. She was alone in the chamber, with the shutters on the small window opened to their widest, to admit fresh air. Earlier in the day, Hugh had complained of the stink in the room and she did not want him moaning tomorrow. The chamber was more pleasant, she was forced to admit. She had become used to the scent of sulphur and had not noticed, until Hugh pointed it out.

Hugh had come every day after his practice to help her. He had even washed bandages, a job she secretly disliked because she did not care for the sight of blood. He seemed determined to prove he was a good knight.

His father, Yves, she noted, treated him with cool formality, speaking to his son only when necessary. Once, rushing to the garderobe, she had overheard Yves spit at Hugh, "Do not speak to me of David! He made his choice! You gave your mother none!"

Listening to the servants, she had learned that Hugh's mother had died soon after giving birth to him. His father had disliked him ever since.

"Called him a devil when he was but a young lad, scarce able to toddle about," the laundress Bertha told Joanna, over a cup of ale when Bertha came to collect Joanna's gown for washing. "Always hard on him, though in truth the master was at fault, too. Mistress had birthed easy before and so the master did not send for the midwife until things began to go badly. Mind, have you seen the knack Master Hugh has with creatures? There is something devilish there, I warrant."

Joanna, who had also been called a devil in her time, said nothing.

That evening, when Hugh came, she did not goad him quite so much, did not remind him that he had snatched her from her home, or that he was an ungentle knight for trampling Sir Tancred like a broken doll.

The following day she was aggrieved with herself. Hugh was her captor; she owed him no courtesy. That day she asked for and was given permission to leave her work and join Sir Yves for lunch. She was even allowed to sit close to him, on the high table. There she flaunted all the courtly manners she could recall from seeing embassies at the bishop's palace and let it be known she was indeed the mistress of Lord Thomas. In the evening, Hugh's face was dark with suppressed anger.

"I say nothing and then you tell the world you are that man's whore!" He stabbed at a pair of small bellows as if they had attacked him. "Have you no decency?"

"A mistress is no whore!" Joanna retorted, seething at the suggestion but also glad that he was so put out. Yet when Hugh left early, storming off with a curse and Beowulf following with his tail between his legs, Joanna soon stopped work. She felt out of sorts all evening, and her dreams that night were evil.

Now that she was awake again, Joanna admitted she was ashamed. To be a noble lord's mistress was not unworthy, but for her to broadcast that she was leman to a man like Thomas? Was it seemly? Yes, she enjoyed goading Hugh, working out the frustration of her captivity on him, but did that help her work?

"It does not," Joanna admitted softly, staring down at her bare legs. They looked ghostly and insubstantial, not at all lean or tanned, and she was naked in bed, as was the custom. She thought of Hugh—Where did he bed down? In the corridor outside? She had no way of knowing: the castle walls were thick and icy cold, even with the wall hangings. Although it was spring, she was glad of the small new furnace in her room and glad it remained warm as she "baked" and dried off some newly washed bandages, a trick of healing she had learned and tried from an Arab text on alchemy and medicine. She cautiously touched its domed surface, wondering from where Yves had acquired it. For now, Sir Yves remained amiable, but if he turned against her, would Hugh protect her?

Thinking of Hugh, she rubbed her bare legs, guessing that he too would be naked. What would he look like? Long and lean? Would he be long and lean all over?

Why are you interested? What are you to him, apart from a means to an end?

"He likes me," she said aloud. "I think."

But that was before she had confessed to the world that she was the mistress of the bishop. Now, in the fastness and quiet of the night, Joanna admitted that she loathed the idea of being Thomas's leman, especially where Hugh was concerned. Or was he sleeping soundly with another woman?

If he is, why do you care? Gathering the blanket he had

handled earlier, she draped it across her back and sat on the edge of her bed. The rough warmth of Hugh's cloak was a comfort and, when she sniffed, she thought she caught his scent: musky, intensely masculine.

What would it be like to be Hugh's leman?

She leaped off the bed as if her mattress was on fire and strove to dress as rapidly as possible. Looking out through the window, she saw the bright star Venus, the sign for female and all that was mutable, a signal for growth. The work must save her and her father. Nothing else mattered.

And she must charm Hugh back.

Later that same day, around midday, Sir Yves appeared with a page who handed her a bucket containing three dirty-looking lumps of ore. "Can you assay this for gold?" Yves asked.

"I can," Joanna replied. "Do you wish me to try for gold and silver, or purely gold?"

"Oh, purely gold, I think." He gave her a broad smile that he probably thought was charming.

"I can do that, too."

"Good! I shall leave the task in your capable hands."

He hurried off, no doubt to his lunchtime table, but the page lingered. He was a lanky, curly-headed, curious boy whom Joanna had seen before, loitering in the corridor outside.

"Do you wish to stay and watch me?" she asked. The work was no secret and simple enough.

The lad nodded, the freckles on his forehead and chin showing up like blisters as he colored with excitement. Joanna smiled: she, too, had once been this keen.

"Very well—"

"Peter," the lad supplied.

"Peter. If you pay heed to all I say we shall see wonders together. But you must stay back when I tell you. Substances that are undergoing transformation can be very volatile and dangerous."

"I know. I have watched smiths at work."

There was something about his glib answer that she did not like, but then she decided she was being overprotective. When she began her studies in the art, she had been far younger than the page.

"This is a process called cupelation," she explained, showing Peter the small clay vessels or cupels which she would use. "It draws the impurities from the lead, leaving any pure gold behind."

"I know," Peter said.

"You have seen it done?"

"I have heard of it already. Where do you keep your unicorns?" Peter prodded one of the flasks with his dagger, his bottom lip jutting in disappointment as the flask refused to emit a unicorn or any other magical creature.

"I do not study that branch of the art," Joanna answered, torn between amusement and exasperation. "Careful," she warned when he hung over the furnace as she opened its door to stoke it. "You must stay back. Vessels can explode."

"Only if they are faulty," Peter replied.

She debated then whether to ask him to leave, but he took up a place by the end of the table, far from the furnace, and she decided to give him another chance.

"Look, ask, but do not touch," she warned again.

"I know."

Peter did not speak again, or move, and soon Joanna was lost in the assay, adding salt and barley husks to drive off any silver and using bellows to blow air over the molten metal. Intent for any sounds of cracking or scents that would warn the assay was not going well, she watching the walls of the cupel discolor as the impurities were oxidized and burned off.

"This is dull stuff," said Peter, yawning and rubbing his belly. "I am bored with it."

Joanna did not remind him that it had been his choice to stay. "It will not be long now," she said, pointing to the cupel and explaining the significance of the discoloration, "but you must stay where you are when I fully open the furnace door."

Moving carefully in her bulky leather apron and heavy gloves, she heard the chamber door open. To her surprise, for he was not usually so early, she sensed Hugh entering, knowing him by that peculiar thrill low in her belly that she always felt whenever he was nearby. Sometimes when she looked at him she expected the very air between them to crackle, so loaded did it seem with expectant possibilities. This noon, busy with her task, she merely nodded and kept her eyes on the cupel as she lifted it clear of the furnace.

The page was not so restrained. "We are making gold—look, look!" He flung his arms wide and lunged toward the furnace, forgetting Joanna's instructions and ignoring her shout of alarm.

Hampered with gloves and tongs, she could do nothing as the lad lurched closer to the scorching, dangerous sizzle of the furnace, but Hugh seized the lad's collar and yanked him back, clear of the fire.

"You want to be burned, or worse?" he demanded, giving the page a rough shake. "Stay where your mistress bids you!"

"You can both look now," Joanna said, glad that her voice was steady as she turned the blackened cupel on its side to reveal the small bright pearl of gold lying at its base.

* * *

"Thank you, Hugh," Joanna said later. Unscathed and a little more thoughtful than he had been in the morning, Peter the page had gone to report to Sir Yves, and she wanted to say something while she and Hugh were alone. "I realize you are here early today and I am glad you came when you did. I had told him to take care. I am most grateful. You saved him."

"Only from his own idiocy," Hugh growled, sitting on the bed with his back against the wall. "But then that bold young fool takes no notice of anyone." He raised his cup of sage tisane to her. "I am glad to have been of service, my lady."

Joanna raised hers in turn—it had become a custom of theirs to drink a cup together while mulling over the day, and this midafternoon was no different—"And I thank you again, my lord."

A new look of challenge burst into Hugh's handsome, saturnine face. "May I claim a kiss, in fellowship and peace?"

"Of course, my knight." Chaste embraces and kisses were part of the courtly game that she had instigated. And she could, after all, tease him: an added bonus.

A single kiss, she thought, kissing her fingers and extending her hand. "Here is your kiss. You need but claim it."

"Before Beowulf does? Away, hound!" Hugh clicked his fingers and the dog approaching her padded back and jumped onto the bed, sprawling as his master rose. Joanna's heartbeat accelerated as Hugh closed on her, her hand raising in a half-gesture of defense.

"Fear not." He smiled down at her, touching the tips of his hand lightly against hers, trailing his fingers into the soft shadowed hollow of her palm. "A single kiss, 'tis all, and from you, Lady, enough."

His large, battle-hardened hand drew up and down her

narrow fingers, smoothing and caressing, his touch tingling her from her hands to her feet. He was smiling, his mouth curved and generous, his blue eyes soft as the down of ducklings. His fingers swept over hers again, swirling, tickling, making her whole spine prickle with delight.

"All this from a kiss?" he said softly, as she swayed a little on her feet. "How would we be if you allowed more, eh?"

Still smiling at her, he lifted his hand away from hers, leaving it hanging in the air between them like the sacred promise of a saint, painted on a church wall. He withdrew as deftly as a herald, backing from the chamber without colliding once with chest or stools or earthenware vessels, his eyes never leaving hers.

Chapter 13

The following day the messenger returned to the castle. Bishop Thomas had gone to Oxford on church matters and the messenger had missed him. Now more horses must be found for the messenger to try again, to trail after the bishop's party and, pray God, catch them soon.

Joanna heard this news from the castle laundress, listening in appalled horror as the woman recounted how Sir Yves had hurled a mutton bone at the hapless messenger in the castle great hall.

"Dislikes his dinner being interrupted by bad news," the laundress concluded. "Shall I take this headscarf? It is stained along the edge."

"Thank you." Joanna waited until the slim, dark woman had sped from the room and then she began her work afresh, grinding, testing, burning, mixing. The air in the chamber became thick with smog and still she worked, first by daylight and then by star- and candlelight.

I must find something.

She labored on through the night. The white powder, a mixture of chalk and other mineral compounds, was ready in its presentation box: an elixir to cure the ills of the stomach and head. Joanna knew she should find a better title than this but she could not think: she was too fretful and weary. Sir Yves and Bishop Thomas would be pleased with her elixir, yes, but they wanted gold. They wanted that most rare, most precious, most perfect of forms and she had only a few scant pieces from Orri's hoard, the nugget from her assay of the previous day, and odd grains from the river.

She tried a new experiment, with the blackened cupel left from her assay from the lead and silver ore. Perhaps if she heated this to white heat, the purifying element of fire would grow her more gold from the dross of the silver and lead. She set to using the bellows with a will, pumping furiously into the furnace until her arms ached like the toothache and the very walls of the castle chamber seemed to be sweating . . .

"Hey, hey, you will tear yourself to shreds."

Hugh took the bellows from her and she tottered, scrabbling after them. "Give those back! I am no puffer!"

She snatched for them, just as the table and furnace seemed to turn over and slide away. Feeling as if she was falling off the edge of the world, Joanna tumbled down. She yelled and struggled to surface through a haze of blackness, tasted soot and then wine.

"Taste the wine again. It will restore you."

Hugh was holding her somehow, and they were outside— not merely of the chamber but of the castle.

"Where are we?" she croaked.

"The garden. I returned from West Sarum this evening to find you huddled over your furnace like a fighter with his last lance. What is going on? The servants tell me you have not eaten or slept all of yesterday or today."

Joanna took another sip of wine and tried to recollect. "Have I been so long?"

"It would seem so."

"And you have been away?"

Hugh smiled. "So much for asking if you missed me. I never knew so intent a maid, once you are lost in your work."

"Do you stop when you are in mid-joust?"

He laughed and waved a chunk of cheese before her eyes. "Eat. Do not talk for a space. Feed yourself and I will tell you of West Sarum, although in truth, there is little to say." Frowning, he took a drink of wine himself. "I trawled the town for news of David and found none. No one would talk, not even for coins. There were guards around—not many, but enough, and their presence quelled all gossip. And before you ask, I was not stopped or questioned because I was disguised as a herbalist."

"But—but what wares did you have?" Joanna stammered, trying and failing to imagine Hugh as a herbalist.

"None!" came back the cheerful answer. "I knew I would sell nothing; the West Sarum folk are careful with their chattels. Though I did tell many a goodwife and carpenter about your sage tisane."

He had remembered that. Joanna felt a rush of tender feeling unbuckle her body. To her horror, her eyes blurred with tears. "Stupid woman!" she muttered, smearing a hand across her face.

"Hey, I know that you like David, but you need not fret. No news means no change." Hugh dangled a piece of white bread before her. "Agreed?"

Joanna opened her mouth to say that no news meant nothing of the kind, but she felt too dispirited to argue. "You do not need to tempt me like an ailing horse, Hugh."

"That would make you a nag, eh? Now I know you are not yourself; you would never have left such an easy opening for me, else." He nodded as she took the bread and began chewing. "So are we agreed?"

"David is not alone in the donjon."

At her quiet observation Hugh put down the cup of

wine. "You do not mean that French fellow, do you, but the older man who is with them. Is he your father? And why, if you are the bishop's woman, is he in prison? What did he do that was so terrible?"

"He is innocent and has done nothing! We have never done anything, yet we are harried and hunted—" She was so furious that she could no longer speak: the very words seemed to be choking her.

A wall came about her, warm and steady, with a living, beating heart: Hugh, drawing his arms around her waist and easing her so that she rested with her head tucked comfortably into his shoulder. She was on his lap, she realized—how had she simply accepted this before? She had not even struggled!

She thought of squirming now, decided it would be absurd, and wondered again how she had noticed but not noticed her position. Comfort, she thought. She felt comfort and a tingling safety in Hugh's arms, which was a powerful contradiction. She was his captive, yet she felt safe with him. More than safe. It was pleasing to sit on him, to feel his muscled thighs beneath hers, to sense, by his powerful tension, that he was attracted to her.

After peace, a reckless sense of goading, of pricking him, overcame her. "Are you jealous of the bishop?" she breathed.

He stiffened further and she almost cheered. "I was before," he said.

It happened between them. Joanna lifted her head and Hugh lowered his and their lips touched.

Volatile yet permanent, Joanna thought, sighing as she closed her eyes and kissed him. For a wild instant she imagined a whole heavenload of stars, shining gold and silver above them. Her eyelids fluttered and she glimpsed Hugh's eyes, also closed, his lashes dark and lustrous as rare black silk. It was twilight, and the sky was the color of Hugh's eyes, and the herbs about them were as fragrant as his breath.

"Lovely," Hugh whispered, tracing her eyebrows, nose, and the gentle curve of her face with his thumb. "A grace of God in truth, and a worker of wonders, besides. I can only destroy, but you—" He kissed her eyes and nose and mouth. "You make, you heal, you read—"

"My father, too," Joanna prompted, smiling as Hugh smiled at her. The world between them was so all-embracing she wanted to float in it forever, but she must not forget Solomon and he must not forget David.

"Tell me about him," Hugh said, but now Joanna heard Sir Yves's heavy tread on the path behind them. She skimmed down from Hugh's knee onto the bench and they were sitting modestly side by side when Hugh's father hailed them.

"Hello! Taking in the fresh air? How are you, Joanna? Have you grown more gold?"

"I am in hopes of doing so," Joanna answered, the reply she had often given the bishop. "I have your elixir ready, my lord." Seeking to escape before Yves could ask more searching questions, she stepped away from the bench. "I will bring it to you directly."

"A page can surely do that," Hugh said, glowering at his father. So far, the two men had not greeted each other.

"I will be quicker." Joanna moved off, though not before she heard Hugh saying to Yves, "Why must you be always so impatient? Is Joanna not doing enough that you must harry her?"

"Pah! You cannot recognize work when you see it! Not everyone has your lazy streak—"

"I am no more idle than you are a cowardly glutton, Father."

"How dare you, sir?"

"Say that with our combined forces we might storm the bishop's palace? Why not? It is the truth."

"And where are the Templars in this grand plan of yours? Why do you not ask them and hear their answer? You know what it will be because it is madness and cannot be done, yet still you berate me, as you have always done. . . ."

"I berate you? I berate you, Father, when you have filled my days with a thousand, thousand complaints?"

Alarmed that she was the cause of this quarrel, Joanna wove back along the garden path toward the castle, flinching as a moth flew straight out of a lavender bush and fluttered past her head. Above her the sky was now the black of night, sprinkled with stars, and a slender moon.

The moon was new, but it was there now, and it was rising and growing. And when it was full, Lord Thomas would cast her father into the prison pit.

God help me!

Chapter 14

Rushing past the beds of springtime flowers, all silver in the moonlight, Joanna spotted Peter, hiding from sight of the castle and kitchen windows. He was crouched behind a stand of hyssop and thyme, playing a solitary game of dice.

Seeing him, Joanna recalled Hugh's previous comment and greeted him at once. "Peter, well met! Will you fetch a box of white powder from my chamber and deliver it here to Sir Yves? He has asked for it most urgently."

"Unnn—" Peter assented, coming slowly to his feet, his face a beacon of shame at being discovered.

"And hurry," Joanna pressed, keen for the lad to be away.

As Peter slouched off to do her bidding in some fashion, she scanned the high walls of the castle garden. If there was a gate, or a tree close to the wall she could climb, she might escape the keep. She had her own pitiful share of Orri's gold with her—she always had her gold on her—so she would have something to give the bishop. Pray God it would placate him for a space, and win her more time.

Why not wait to see what the messenger says? her reason argued, but her feelings were all urging her to flee.

The truth was, she did not trust Bishop Thomas. Hugh had taken her as a valued hostage, but what if she was not? What if the bishop did not care? He could get other women to share his bed, and other alchemists to try to grow him gold. At least back at West Sarum she could be useful in many ways: making rose water, elixirs, sweets, helping in the kitchen. Now she was away from him, Thomas might forget her altogether and her father would be left to rot in the donjon, or worse.

"Let me find a gate," Joanna panted as she traced another high wall without any opening.

Her prayer was answered at once. No gate, but a wild crab apple that must have seeded itself from the woodland outside and was now growing beside the wall. Its sturdy branches reached beyond the huge, smooth stones and a wide canopy of blossom gleamed as beautiful as stars in the deepening twilight.

"Thanks be to God," Joanna murmured, stretching her arms up to the tree. Its bark was grainy under her hands and a piece flaked down into her face, but she was too jubilant to care.

"Are you not old to be climbing trees?"

Hugh's question startled her and she lost her grip, scrabbling for a hold as she plummeted toward the swaths of violets, pinks and black-looking speedwell.

Hugh caught her and silenced his dog's howling abruptly. "Enough, Beo! She is not hurt." He gripped her more tightly, his arms as firm as a ship's ribs beneath her trembling legs and shoulders. "She is safe."

He touched her face, lightly brushing away the scrap of bark from her lips. "You are as light as a moth." His blue eyes gleamed with a mixture of amusement and exasperation. "And as treacherous."

Joanna found her voice again in her raw, dry throat. "I was merely examining the blossom."

"That is an idea, but I have a better one. I will assay you for cuts—have I the word right?—and examine you to ensure you are not bruised."

He was enjoying this, the devil, but even as he spoke, Joanna found herself imagining Hugh studying her. It was the kind of game she had never played with a man, but how might it be with him? To be touched and touch in return . . .

Joanna wrung her mind from a disturbing mêlée of images, desperate to fob him off somehow. "I must—I must use the garderobe," she whispered.

"I am not surprised, after such excitement. I shall escort you there and thence to your chamber."

It seemed he meant to carry her to both places.

"We shall be quicker if I walk," Joanna said.

"But not if you run. You may run too far." Hugh allowed that none-too-subtle hint to hit home and then changed the subject. "My men speak highly of your white powder. It soothes their aches better than any other tincture they know. I have found the same."

He raised his arms slightly, to lift her smoothly over a rosebush.

"I am most intrigued as to what it is. Can you speak of its basics? How did you make it? How did you choose its parts?"

Had she not been trapped by him and the bishop's deadline, she would have been glad of, even a little flattered by his interest. As it was, feeling aggrieved with all men and their power games, she answered sharply, "All my work is secret."

"A way to keep control. I understand."

His soothing reply exasperated her more. "Do you tell other jousters how to win? It is the same for me."

"Competitive alchemy?"

"We all have exacting patrons."

He shrugged. "Find some other labor if you dislike it so much."

His smug, overweening, ignorant superiority made her burn with rage.

"As you would, if you did not spend your days dashing out your opponents' brains? And what new labor would that—?" Joanna began, then snapped her teeth together. She would not give him the satisfaction of a waspish answer. Besides, they had passed the outer stair of the keep and were heading rapidly for the inner staircase and she was anxious as to what Hugh might do next, faced with the tight narrow spiral.

"I can walk ahead of you upstairs," she said quickly.

"No, you are plainly overset. We will keep as we are."

"Do not put me over your shoulder!" Joanna warned, shaking a finger at him.

"To carry such a wee bag of bones as you? I think not." He lowered his head, kissed her finger, and now bore her in one brawny arm up the spiral, shielding her head against the stones with his shoulder. The smooth, steady rush would have been exhilarating, had she not been so irritated.

"There."

Finally he set her down, outside the door of the garderobe. She knew he would be lurking when she came out again, and so he was.

"Stay with her, Beowulf," he told the wolfhound. "Guard."

Instantly the dog began to pace to and fro, exactly like a human guard, and Joanna realized what would happen if she attempted to move along the narrow corridor. Staring out from an arrow slit at the dark garden, she relieved some of her feelings by cursing Hugh, Sir Yves, Bishop Thomas, and even David.

"I wish I were a unicorn," she grumbled. "Too magical to hold."

"I would have had you for a lioness," said Hugh behind her. "Valiant as a queen."

"And you would be the lion?" she asked archly.

"A phoenix," came back the prompt, unexpected reply. "Then I could burn away to ash and be reborn with no hurt to anyone."

Joanna thought of Hugh's mother, dead in childbirth, bearing him, and said nothing. She had heard of fathers blaming offspring for the deaths of their spouses but had not witnessed its raw pain until encountering Hugh and Yves. A memory of her mother, more precious than gold, shimmered a moment before her eyes. Miriam had been small and dark as she was, merry and chattering and with hands softer than silk. She had loved to comb and dress people's hair, even her husband's own sparse locks.

"What are you thinking?" Hugh asked softly. "You seem far away."

Joanna shook her head. To speak of her mother when he had never known his was unkind. To talk of Miriam was to invite questions, and she was not ready yet to answer the worst one—how her mother had died.

"Do you have no other captives to pester?" she demanded.

"No," he said, without apology. Instead of drawing back as she wanted, he stayed where he was, absently rubbing his lower back.

"Long hours in the saddle," he remarked, catching her look. "How are your legs now?"

"Better. Why do you ask? Are you thinking of riding me into the ground tonight? Riding with me?" she amended, horrified by what she had just said. A picture of her and Hugh, rolling together on the soft earth, slammed into her head and stayed there.

"You need not fear me, you know."

What did he mean? Had he noticed her mistake? Joanna did not hit back with the obvious answer, that she did not fear him. She lifted her head and looked at him directly, spearing her eyes at him, facing down him and her own imagination. So she had daydreamed of his touching her, of him embracing her as a husband does a wife. Could she not enjoy that notion?

Even as she admitted to herself that she did, Joanna knew she was torn between wanting to touch Hugh and wanting to escape him. She made a mummer's show of a yawn, hoping he would take the hint and leave her on the corridor. Then she would try again to weave her way out of this castle keep.

"If your legs are well now," Hugh went on, seemingly oblivious to her inner turmoil, "then I can help you."

"To do what?" Joanna asked.

He knew she was as jumpy as a caged wren and divided in herself. How she must have hated letting slip that remark on riding! It made him wonder even more sharply what her true relationship was with Bishop Thomas. And what were her true feelings for him?

She liked him, yet not. She was drawn to him, yet constantly pulled away.

You hold her against her will. What do you expect?

"Were it not for David I would take you wherever you wish to go," he said.

Surprise glittered in her eyes, bright as unshed tears, and in truth he was startled and ashamed himself. He had not meant to admit anything.

"But we are in this world, not heaven," he added, feeling hotter and more squalid than ever. He was unused to thinking on matters of fault or conscience—in the joust there was one winner and no blame. Joanna was forcing him to question his assumptions, and it made his head ache as if he had toothache. Was this how monks felt, all the time? "I am sorry."

The glitter in her face had been replaced by flat suspicion. "That is easy to say."

"I can teach you how to evade capture. Then, when you are freed, you will remain so."

She glowered, seeing through his feint at once. "You look for an excuse to handle me!"

In the joust he would have charged and grappled, but this was a girl.

"Come then," she goaded. "Am I not your father's servant? All maids are fair game, to men such as you."

He backed away. "Not me." As a squire at tourneys he had seen wenches thrust weeping and terrified into the pre-dawn when they were hauled out of the tents by the grooms and guards of the lords who had idly bedded them for the night. He had vowed then to leave servant lasses alone. "It is no sport to—"

He was going to add "bully" but she swung at him.

"Oof!" He had avoided her fists, but she did not miss with her flailing feet. As she blazed in afresh to batter his shins he lunged low, hooking her off balance. She yelled and began to pummel his back as he hoisted her over his shoulder.

"Watch your head," he warned as she reared up, and then he jolted with her down the corridor, his knives and keys clashing, calling out to a startled page, "The lady has twisted her ankle."

He carried her to her chamber and let her down. "I am no bully," he said, spreading his arms to prevent her escape.

She said nothing, merely stared at his arms.

"Yes, yes!" He dropped them down to his sides. "But how else will you stay to listen?"

"By your talking sense!"

He laughed, amused by the aptness of her complaint, and after a moment she joined him. He sat down on the stone floor, patting his knee, delighted for an instant when she sat down his legs and then a moment later wondering how he could move her off his calves onto his thighs.

But aching legs or not, this was progress and he was determined to make the most of it.

"I am trying to win David's freedom by other means than hostage exchange. I have sent a messenger to the Templars, reminding them he is their man. I hope to have an answer from them soon, one where they agree to help."

Hugh thought he sounded too apologetic but Joanna had not moved yet. Did she know that, sitting on him like that, she was making his calves burn? She could, most easily, for she had a hefty streak of mischief. But then, watching her by the torchlight, he admitted that she made other parts burn, too, parts that were more personal and distracting.

And you considered her too sallow and drab, his conscience goaded in the voice of his father, but he knew better now. Her skin always glowed with health, and in summer she would be as glossy as a beech nut. He imagined unlacing her gown, revealing that slim, vibrant figure and small, softly peaked breasts. Would her nipples be as dark and luscious as her lips?

"I know my hands are stained, you need not stare."

Hugh hastily withdrew his gaze from her bosom and directed his attention to her face. She looked thinner, he thought, his guts feeling to shrivel inward with shame.

"Do you have brothers or sisters?" he asked for something to ask, wishing afresh that she was not his hostage.

She shook her head. "There is only me and my father now. My mother died when I was ten."

He heard the ache in her voice, saw it in her dark eyes, and wished he could bring her mother back for her. He had always thought himself lost, having no mother, but to have known a mother's love and lost it when still a child must be worse.

"It must be good to have a brother."

Joanna had the faraway look he often saw on her face when she was working. Swiftly he agreed: "It has its moments."

"Are David and Nigel your only close kin?"

Hugh nodded. He thought of Nigel, the eldest of the Manhill clan, the one blessed by birthright and fate, the handsome, golden boy, the rich, everything-falls-into-my-lap Nigel. He did not want to sour his mouth by speaking of him.

"Your father . . . is he the same with David and Nigel as he is with you?"

He knew what she meant but did not want to talk about his old estrangement with Sir Yves, either. Yet, because he was her knight and he did not wish to be accused of discourtesy on top of keeping her against her will, he said carefully, "Father and I cannot be peaceful together. It may be we are too alike. He and Nigel are close."

"And David? Sir Yves has not quarreled with David, has he?"

"More that my father does not think of him at all."

Because that was bleak and pitiful and he wanted to distract her, tempt her to eat, and see her smile—*and how will she do that as your captive?*—Hugh held out his hands and shifted sideways, rolling her gently off his legs. She caught his fingers and allowed him to help her to her feet.

Hugh called to a passing page, "Bring us some bread and soft cheese, any pottage that is heated, and a jug of ale, if you please.

"We shall eat in your workshop," he said to Joanna,

guessing she was too hungry still to refuse. "And then I will show you how to wrestle out here. I know your work and bed space is no place to roughhouse," he added, pointing to the furnace and the many basins, jars, and glasses in the room.

"Roughhouse," Joanna murmured, as if she was tasting the term. She raised her brows. "Should we not do that before food?"

"Of course, you are right," Hugh said quickly, happy to agree.

They ate a little first, anyway, while standing outside in the corridor. Hugh as a further delaying tactic had asked for more torches to be brought to light the space and, as these were placed in the wall sconces, he encouraged Joanna to taste each of the dishes the maids and pages had carried up to the chamber. As she was eating, he dragged her pallet out into the narrow landing between her room and the stairs.

"Somewhere for you to fall, my knight?" Joanna queried from the doorway, pointing with her slice of "poor knights"—toasted white bread loaded with honey, pine nuts, cinnamon, and pepper.

In answer, Hugh teasingly threatened to bite off part of her "pokerounce," chuckling as she rapidly devoured it instead.

"I am surprised your teeth are not rotten to the gums, given your love of sweets," he observed. "And as for the pallet, I would not have you bruised, my lady."

With her mouth full, Joanna could not answer at once, but then she swallowed. "Nor would I have you required to make an account of your hurts to your squires, my knight."

Hugh noted her smile and took another sip of ale. "You are very confident, my lady."

"I have every reason to be so. You are trained in arms, my knight." She folded her arms across herself. "Without a lance or sword you are no different from anyone."

"Perhaps not from any *man,* my lady."

"If you think me so disadvantaged, then you should wrestle as a one-armed *man.*" Still smiling, she leaned forward on her toes. "You should also pay me a forfeit each time I win."

"What manner of forfeit?"

"A chain or coin from Orri's hoard."

"You drive a keen bargain," Hugh replied, momentarily disconcerted by such a practical, mercenary answer. "It is custom for a lady to pay by kisses, and accept the same in return."

"Oh, I will pay and receive those, too. I always honor my debts."

Disquiet coiled in his mind. Was she so eager for gold?

No. She seeks gold as the symbol of wisdom and healing.

Then why did she want it?

A face hovered in his memory: a man's face, dark, with bright eyes. David had spoken of him, though he had not paid heed at the time and could not recall what his brother had said. But he knew that he had seen the fellow in the bishop's donjon. Joanna's kindred. Was he, too, like David, imprisoned and dependent on the whim and favor of Thomas? Would Thomas do such a thing to his own mistress?

No sooner thought than answered. . . .

"You may have the hoard," he said. "All of it."

He took another drink of ale to avoid looking at her, ashamed now of how he had glibly assumed that she needed no wealth save trinkets.

"I will bring it to you," he said, still without meeting her eyes. "And then I will return your bed to its proper place. It is too late now for any match between us."

He left before she could answer, wishing again that he could achieve his brother's freedom by some other way.

I will send another message to the Templars and offer all my prizes to the order, if they will but intervene on behalf of David and the other prisoners.

He could only hope and pray it would be enough.

Chapter 15

Days passed. Joanna worked, missing her father, anxious about him, wondering how he was. Hugh spent time with her every evening, bringing food up from the kitchen himself and coaxing her to eat. She no longer spied on him when he practiced in the bailey yard. She had no time.

He had brought her Orri's hoard, leaving it on her workbench wrapped in a rough cloak. He brought her colored stones in the hope that they would contain rare ores. When a traveling artist came to Sir Yves and offered to repaint the keep's great hall with a frieze of running stags, Joanna helped the man to make his paint and Hugh, who had a good eye for an amateur and would gladly have wielded the paintbrush himself, was persuaded to take his father hunting so they could work undisturbed.

He cares for me, Joanna told herself at night, watching the rising, fattening moon and loathing its bland, silvery face. But still she knew he would not release her.

Then a messenger returned to Castle Manhill, along with one of the bishop's men, a priest Bishop Thomas sometimes used as a clerk. Joanna knew nothing of this until Hugh brought the man to her chamber.

"You will know each other," he said as the grizzled,

bearded priest wheezed in the muggy atmosphere of the room. "Why not go out on the battlements and talk in the fresher air? It is a very bright and sunny day today. If you come with me—"

The priest, wary of Beowulf sniffing at his crotch, was already backing away, but Joanna was determined to speak to him. She caught up with his burly figure as he stepped after Hugh onto the battlements and tugged at his travel-stained cloak.

He turned to her, a protest forming on his lips, but glad enough to pause in the relative shelter of the keep while he gathered his breath to complain.

Swiftly, Joanna spoke first. "Father Paul, have you news of Solomon, please? Does he still enjoy *'Ego Sum Lae-dunum'*?" She switched seamlessly to Latin, chanting her words as if repeating the lines of a song. "I will soon have much gold for my lord and am progressing well with my greater work," she sang in Latin. "I will be most glad to return to my lord's household, especially if I know that my father is in good health—he and the other guests," she finished, thinking of David and Mercury.

Hugh, who had been watching a flock of rooks rising from a nearby woodland rookery, baiting and playing on the rising breeze like black balls of fluff, now turned to regard her with a mild, quizzical expression, as if he knew exactly what she was doing.

Father Paul stared at her, then Hugh, and answered stiffly, in English, "Solomon the alchemist is living and working at present within the palace of West Sarum. He sends his good wishes."

"And were you going to tell Joanna that?" Hugh asked, still mild, but with extra grit in his tone that had the priest swinging round and glancing with longing at the narrow door off the battlements. Beside Hugh, clamped as close as a burr, the wolfhound Beowulf growled softly.

"That, and also that her lord is most eager for her return."

"And the gold?" Hugh prompted.

Before Hugh could admit that she had gold now—and then the priest would demand to take it, the one thing she dared not allow to happen—Joanna pointed over the crenellations. "See! My lord's standard!" She clapped her hands, allowing the priest to think she was in bliss merely at the sight of the flapping pieces of flag-cloth displayed below them in the bailey yard, where even now the horses of the priest, messenger, and guards were being tended.

"I will tell our lord that you are looking forward to returning to his service. And that you, sir"—the priest bowed stiffly to Hugh—"are ready to go ahead with the hostage exchange for your brother."

"Most ready," said Hugh, touching his sword belt. "But I see my father waving—we should go down to the hall." He glanced at Joanna. "Will you come?"

She shook her head. She had no time for a formal greeting and meeting and now, as they walked back along the narrow walkway, the priest muttered in Latin, "You have until the full moon, Joanna. Our lord told me to remind you of that."

"I have it always in my heart," said Joanna, feeling sick again as her stomach rolled with anxiety and her mind tumbled with dread.

Afterward, Hugh returned to her chamber earlier than usual, a few hours after lunch but before sunset. He leaned against the wall, watching her using her small bellows to tease the furnace into a steady, baking heat.

"I am no fool, even if I cannot read," he said. "I would not have told that priest about the hoard. He would have then taken it and you gained no advantage. What did he say to you on leaving? And do not give me the name of a song."

"He told me again that my father is well," Joanna lied. She laid aside the bellows, ashamed of her deception but feeling she had little choice. Her first concern had to be for her father, just as Hugh's must be for David. At times those desires worked in tandem, but there might be an occasion when they were in conflict. However much she longed to share with Hugh, she dared not.

She sighed, rubbing at her aching head.

"Come out with me today," Hugh said. "At Manhill-de-Couchy, over the hill, the villagers have sent word to me asking for help. Why not leave this for a space and take a Sabbath?"

Joanna flinched at the word, wondering if he had guessed that aspect of her past, but his face was thoughtful and still. "The break will do you good," he said, inhaling deeply and frowning.

She breathed in, too, and almost choked: the fume here was so dense.

"I have just readied the furnace," she murmured. "It would be a sin to waste it."

"Do what you can, so it can be left, then bar the door. I will set a guard and we can go. It is not far to ride," he added.

I shall be riding with him, pillion. My arms around his waist or his around mine.

Joanna nodded and so it was agreed.

"What is this quest they want from you?" she asked later as they rode out of the keep's long gatehouse and longer shadow, pillion as she had hoped, with her sitting on the saddle before Hugh.

"The lad would not say before my father, for fear of his

demanding payment, or wary of his ridicule, but I know. It is the season for it."

Ridicule Joanna understood, and Sir Yves was a master of it. Yesterday, going to the kitchen for a pail of water, she had found Sir Yves berating the cook, scolding the bald, harassed, skinny man for scorching a curd flan.

"Can you not even do a simple dish?" Sir Yves had asked, hooking his fingers into his belt as he hitched it over his bulging belly. "Is it a new fashion now? Will you be frying my pottage next?"

Joanna had interrupted the tirade by deliberately stumbling across the flagstones, but she had remembered it, and now she thought of Hugh, of his having to endure such scorn when he was a child.

Spare your pity, he is grown up, she reminded herself, but she could not help touching his hand, a silent comfort that he would not even know was such. "What is it, then?" she asked.

He squeezed her waist. "You will be surprised."

"A wolf, raiding stock? A wild boar? A deer in the wheat? What?"

She sensed him smiling.

"You will see."

He hugged her again—any excuse—and reluctantly spurred Lucifer on. The village lad had been pale and in a hurry, even refusing a bite to eat in the kitchen in his haste to return to tell the elders of Manhill-de-Couchy that help was coming.

And if it was what he suspected, he would need his wits about him, not be distracted by Joanna's warmth, the scent of her hair, the dazzling rush of inner light and weightlessness that exploded in him each time her thighs brushed slightly against his. He tried to gather himself.

She is your lady and you are her knight. Treat her with all courtesy.

He asked after her health. Was she warm enough? Too hot? Would she like a drink of mead from his flask? Did she have any questions for him? Would she like him to do anything for her?

"Tell me the local name of that flower," she answered, swinging about and fixing him with a steady look, as if she knew very well what he was about.

He stared at the thistle she was pointing at, growing out of a cart rut like a spear from a fallen warrior, and gave a grunt of laughter. "Shall I pick it for you, my lady?"

"Only if you wear a glove."

"When are you going to stop mentioning gloves?"

She shrugged. "When I am free."

This territory was too dark. Hugh whistled to Beowulf and Lucifer and cantered on, giving the horse his head as they drove through a mess of oak and lime saplings growing as weeds in the middle of the track. He heard Joanna coughing at the raised dust and checked Lucifer, standing up on his stirrups to check where on the winding, sunken road they were.

"There is the church. Not far." He settled back in the saddle without mentioning that the village had set out trestles by the churchyard and laid out a dancing area. She would see it soon enough for herself.

"Do you give your word, my lady, that you will stay with me today? No wandering off?"

She studied her fingers hooked tightly into Lucifer's thick mane. They were pale and a little chafed in places: she must have scrubbed them. He wanted to tell her that the stains were a badge of her calling, but she was answering his question and he needed to listen closely.

"I swear that I will not wander off, my knight."

That was not the same as a vow to remain by him. She could swear that and then still try to flee for West Sarum, not *wandering off* but making straight for the palace.

He did not fault her for it—he would have done the same in her place.

"Soon you will meet the villagers. They are good people. Very observant."

"I am sure," she answered primly, but he guessed the game was on between them.

He would need to watch her closely—and hope the villagers did the same.

The village of Manhill-de-Couchy was a scrap of houses clustered on a low hill, with water meadows and grazing lands about and woodland bordering all. In high summer the meadows would be bright with butterflies and dragonflies, Joanna guessed, and for now her heart lifted as the musky perfume of the churchyard orchids stole through the more basic scent of pig. One tawny piglet squealed at Lucifer, then turned tail, darting back into a thatched homestead where a flour-covered matron wielding a cloth chased it out again.

The woman stopped, her bright color fading, and bobbed a rapid curtsy at Hugh, who nodded. "Fine day for your maying, Agnes," he called out, and slipped down from the saddle to stroll beside his horse.

"Why is she anxious?" Joanna whispered, swaying a little as she leaned down in the saddle and glad of Hugh's steadying hand against her flank.

"She fears I will tell my father's steward that she is grinding her own wheat, not using my father's mill or paying my father's mill tax."

"Will you?" Joanna asked, hearing a child crying within the hut.

"My father is rich enough already."

She heard the anger in his terse reply and recalled an earlier cryptic comment of Hugh's.

"What did you mean, the lad did not want to admit much in your father's hall for fear of him demanding payment?"

"Look ahead at the church porch."

Joanna glanced along the thatch of the simple wooden church to its tiny triangular-roofed porch and understood. Hanging from the inside of the porch, almost hidden by shadow, was a long dark ellipse, shaped somewhere between a funnel and a sphere. Even as she realized what it was, she also understood why the village was so silent; why no one had rushed up to greet them. "Bees!"

She could hear them now: a muted low buzzing that might leap an octave any moment in a frenzy of attack.

"An early swarm."

She looked at Hugh, inconsequentially realizing that his eyes were bluer than the sky about them. "That is important?"

"Early swarms have a spark and mettle in them. They are much prized."

"And they sent for you to retrieve them."

"They know I can help—and I will help." He winked at her. "Takes one ill-tempered brute to understand many little ill-tempered brutes, does it not?" He offered his hand. "May I help you down?"

He took her silence as consent, lifting her from the saddle onto a narrow path running along the fronts of the houses. At ground level again, Joanna could see the villagers, crowded into their cottage doorways, their faces tense and expectant. From this viewpoint, the settled swarm looked bigger than ever, thrusting down into the church porch like some deadly unlit lantern.

"How came it here?"

"Bees like a calm, dark spot. And now that most churches must be closed because our pope and king are in dispute, this porch will be quiet."

Joanna thought of the excommunicated King John and shivered. Even in West Sarum the story was well known: how the whole of his kingdom suffered under the pope's interdict so that almost all churches were closed. Folk could not marry in church now and must be buried in ditches and fields, not in holy ground. She shivered a second time.

"Can I help?" It seemed right to her to whisper.

He nodded. "I am going to fetch a sheet from my pannier. We can work together." His face was solemn. "You will need that still patience of yours, not your quickness. Bees do not like bright light or loud noises. Come. We should use this daylight."

He was checking the position of the sun as he unfurled the sheet and Joanna sensed that that too was important. She followed on behind Hugh, skipping almost in her haste to keep up and all the while feeling the eyes of the villagers on her back.

"How did you know what it would be? Really?" she hissed.

"The lad they sent had pollen stains and a dozen bee stings on his tunic."

"You have good eyes," she marveled. "Had I been in the hall, I would not have been able to see that."

Ahead, he rolled his large shoulders. "I can claim no virtue: 'tis my good fortune, or fate, but no more than that. In the tourney I need them."

He held up a warning hand. "Wait." He stalked off to the left, crouching to enter a cottage, retrieving or being handed something and then returning. "We shall need this."

He showed her a wicker beehive, shrouded over in dark cloth. Hugh studied this a moment and then repinned the cloth. "They have forgotten to leave an opening," he muttered. "The little beasts must flee somewhere."

When he had finished the beehive was closed off apart from a narrow opening on its side. He patted his belt, seemingly checking the pouch that was there, and looked round at her.

"Will you bring me a basin of hot water, please? The elder's house will doubtless have one ready. That's the house with the biggest garden."

"Elder? Not Sir Yves's man?"

"He died last year. My father and his officers have forgotten this place for now: it never brought in much goods or money to him."

Would Hugh be any different, if he was their lord? Joanna found herself hoping that he would be fairer as she sped around the rows of beans and peas in a well-tended vegetable plot, aiming for another open door. There she discovered a wooden basin of steaming water already waiting for her on the threshold. She squinted but could see nothing except the central fire in the elder's house: whatever folk were inside, they were hidden under the low eaves.

She nursed the basin into her hands, whispered, "Thank you!" and returned by a different way, climbing through a patch of sage and rosemary toward a small gate that marked an entrance to the churchyard. Moving steadily so as not to slop the water, she walked to the porch.

Hugh was there already, spreading the sheet directly beneath the swarm, weighting it with pebbles. He gave her a swift smile, his eyes glowing, and the lean chiseled planes of his face seeming to soften a moment as he took the basin from her. Setting it on the beaten earth floor beside the sheet, he dropped several pieces of a dark, thick, heavy-looking substance into the hot water, stirring it vigorously with a twig.

"That is sugar, is it not?" Joanna knelt for a closer look.

Rare sugar, more costly than pepper, was a thing she had heard of, but not seen.

"I filched it from my father's private store. He will not notice."

Joanna rather thought Sir Yves would but said nothing: she was too interested in what Hugh was about.

"The sugar will tempt them. Out of their hive and safety, they will be hungry." He added some clear water from a flask, to cool it, then began flicking the swarm with the sugar water, spraying the mass all over.

The humming increased and the swarm seemed to flex itself like a dark fist, but it remained whole. A few solitary bees broke away but Hugh motioned Joanna to stay down and he himself kept still, allowing one bee to crawl along his arm and another to meander across his forehead. For herself, Joanna was full of horrors, imagining him stung in the eyes, but he remained quiet and motionless and the bees whisked off him.

"Now it begins," he whispered. "If you stay in the shadow by the church door behind the swarm, they will not see or trouble you. The sun is nicely bright and shining where I would have it, on the sheet, so we are ready."

"But what can I do?" Joanna asked as Hugh stretched up, very slowly, toward the narrow timber bisecting the porch roof that the swarm had settled on.

"Watch that the sheet does not flap—if it does, weigh it down more. And pray for us, Joanna: me and the bees. Whisper out when you see one greater in size; that is the leader, the one we need to lure into the new hive."

The shroud-covered wicker hive was laid on its side with its opening facing upward, toward the swarm. In a moment of inspiration, Joanna scattered some sugar water about its shady entrance.

"Good, good!" Hugh gripped one of the two upright beams of the porch and swarmed up it as if it were a rope, kicking a hole in the wattle by mistake as he climbed. With his long legs wrapped tight about the upright and his upper body blending with the thatch, he leaned out over the narrow roof space like an avenging god, above the pulsing swarm.

"Let it go well," Joanna prayed, chanting an ancient alchemical saying in her mind as she spotted a ripple in the sheet and rapidly pinned it down.

Above her she heard the roof creaking and complaining as Hugh vigorously shook the narrow beam from which the swarm hung like some giant, rotting fruit. She looked up to see the whole mass tumble down onto the white dazzle of the cloth, the angry song of the bees now drilling into her ears. Her neck bones crunched as she jerked her head back farther and saw Hugh alive with bees. They rippled over his arms and torso like some terrible necklace, and the sound they made in the closed-in porch seemed deafening.

Yet, astonishingly, they were not stinging him. They clung to him and moved over him as if he were another branch; a place of safety. Then when he gave the lightest of shakes, as if he were a branch tossing in the breeze, they too spiraled off, downward toward the sheet.

"There!" Joanna hissed, amazed, as she saw the long, slow-moving leader of the bees, its entourage tight about as the great bee, seeking new shelter, flew magisterially down the inviting opening of the new hive. After it, obedient as courtiers, the other bees followed in flowing procession.

Soon, amazingly quickly it seemed to Joanna, the whole swarm was snug in their new home and Hugh was carefully righting the wicker hive. He turned to her then, still kneeling, his face peaceful, as if in sleep.

"Hugh?" She was reluctant to disturb his calm, but he shook his head, seeming to return to himself as he rubbed his fingers through his fine black hair, sending it this way and that.

"Thank you," he told her.

"I did nothing."

"You stayed with me, you helped, you did not break away in panic. I have known warriors who would not have done as much; not when faced by bees."

Without thinking, she reached across and touched his forehead where the bees had wandered. "Pollen," she said, as an excuse, brushing aimlessly.

He took her hand in his and kissed her fingers. "Shall we meet the village?"

Chapter 16

The villagers were shy of her at first but not wary of Hugh at all. The men stalked up and shook his hand. The women egged on a stout matron in a checked head-rail to thread her way from the back of the small gaggles standing in the churchyard and plant a kiss on his bristly cheek. Everyone nodded at her when Hugh introduced her as "my lady Joanna," but swiftly returned their attention to him, the hero of the hour.

The new wicker hive and its bees were slowly carried off by two men on an old door, with Hugh strolling beside them, his fingers clasping hers. Joanna knew that to onlookers it would seem a gesture of courtesy and perhaps it was, but it also ensured she did not wander off.

Hand in hand they walked the length of the churchyard, the children straggling along behind in mock procession, seeming to play a game of king, queen, and court. Most of the village remained in the grassy yard and were soon busy erecting trestles and bringing out benches and stools from their homes.

"Is it a holy day here, for your local saint?" Joanna asked Hugh, glancing over her shoulder at the activity behind them. Although churches throughout England were said to be closed, such festivals still went on.

"May-time, when we dance, when there is time to dance," Hugh said. He gave her a warm, admiring look that brought fresh heat to her face. "I look forward to your dance, my lady."

"I will dance with every man in the village," Joanna warned provocatively.

Hugh's smile broadened. "Even old Henri, with his two walking sticks?"

"Yes, if he—"

Joanna broke off as the men in front of them stumbled slightly on the track leading to the hives standing in a garden enclosed by a low stone wall. The bees in the new wicker hive thrummed like the strings of an out-of-tune harp and a few flew out.

Hugh made the sign of the cross above the hive and murmured something to the bees. The low throbbing died away at once and the men were able to slide the wicker hive carefully off their carrying platform and onto a stand of turf. The two villagers remained a moment, standing alongside the hive, as Hugh slowly circled it, chanting softly under his breath.

"What were you saying?" Joanna asked as the villagers left, bearing away the door.

Hugh pointed to the other hives. "I was telling all the bees that here was their new home and here were their neighbors. Bees are all as curious as cats and want to know what is happening, like women."

Joanna ignored the jibe. She watched the few scout bees return to the hive.

"Sit with me." Hugh spread his cloak upon the beaten earth of the stone pen. "It is warm and snug here and the folk will be a while yet, fetching their drink and victuals."

She wanted to sit with him in this sunlight spot, listening

to the distant sport of children and cheerful clatter of preparation, but there was always her deadline. "Should we not be returning to the castle?"

"You will need to try the ale here," Hugh remarked, as if she had not spoken. "It is potent stuff."

Drink and a festival. People happy, people carefree; Hugh careless: Joanna saw the chances in a flash. She had the gold from Orri's hoard with her, sewn into the hems of her long oversleeves with the laundress's needle and thread. She might escape.

And if you do, what happens to Hugh's brother?

"Have you any word from the Templars?" she asked, hoping he would say yes.

Hugh shook his head. He sat down on the ground beside the cloak.

After a moment, Joanna joined him, sitting on the cloak. It was something of Hugh's and she was glad to have use of it. She rubbed her hand along the fur collar and absently brought her fingers up to her lips, inhaling his scent.

"Bees are said to be chaste creatures, but I do not think so."

Joanna's eyes flew open. Hugh was watching the hive, not her, and for an instant she was disappointed. "Why not?" she asked. She could not escape now, she thought, and there was no harm in being civil. Indeed, she and Hugh had gone much further in each other's company than mere civility. She felt she was beginning to know him, the real Hugh beneath the grim knight, and he was a man she liked. He dealt with the villagers here not as slaves, as Bishop Thomas would have done, but as people worthy of respect. He was kind, and that was a virtue worthy of admiration.

"You cannot say why not," she added. He would stand being teased, too.

"Is that a challenge, my lady?"

"If you would make it so," she quipped, feeling her heartbeat quicken.

"Then I would answer you that bees are lovers of sun and sweet flowers and live in great noisy colonies. I think they are seekers after pleasure."

"Scholars would not agree." Joanna smiled as Beowulf flopped beside her and dropped his large head into her lap. She was used to him now, too.

"The hound likes you."

"I like him." She ran her hand over the wolfhound's coat, treacherously imagining it was Hugh's hard, long body. "Will you tell me more of bees?"

She was interested, she told herself. All lore was useful. It had nothing to do with talking with Hugh and definitely nothing to do with sitting here, in this quiet, private spot, their backs resting comfortably against sun-baked stones.

He told her of bees, of collecting bees by "moving" their homes—if they had swarmed into a log, say—out of the forest and into a garden. How they looked like gold, dusted with pollen, flying back to their hives in the midday sun. How they were as loyal as warriors. How, if you allowed them to walk over you, they tickled.

"Only one such as you would allow that, I think," Joanna observed, leaning back and stretching.

Hugh fought not to stare at her breasts. She was a bee herself: a hard worker, seeking the heart of things, and when she smiled that way she made all his senses fly.

"I think it is time for the dance," he said. "I can hear the piper and drummer starting up."

In truth he could hear neither yet, but if need be he would get the folk clapping their hands and whistling, so that he could dance with her.

He rose and held out his hands, gladdened when she took them without hesitation. "Their honey is a kind of gold," he went on, deliberately intriguing.

He loved it when she tilted her head up to peep at him through those long, dark lashes. He loved the interest and keenness in her eyes.

"How so, my knight?"

Ah, my knight. He felt a bee himself, drenched in honeydew. She was as potent as mead, and far sweeter. How had he ever thought her otherwise?

He squeezed her finger slightly, yearning to touch more of her.

"Let us dance first," he said, praying she would agree.

She nodded and the blood hummed merrily in his ears, louder than the bee swarm. This intensity was new to him—was it also for her? Did she feel the same?

She was swishing along beside him, her long skirts rustling like fallen leaves. She was in red again, with blue sleeves, gaudy as a kingfisher. She was studying the village: the tidy garden plots, the small, neat thatched houses, the sturdy church. Seeking a way to escape, he guessed. Why did she have to be his hostage? Why had his idiot brother fallen into the clutches of his unholiness, the bishop of West Sarum? *Her lover.*

Hugh fought down the black anger that swirled in his chest, piercing him through, as hard a crossbow bolt. Suddenly he wanted to be away, fighting, smashing his lance into helmed knights who fought for Thomas.

"Would you ever wish to live in a place like this?"

Her question doused the black rage. He heard the slight catch in her voice—regret? desire?—and answered truthfully, "When I was a lad I would hang around the farriers, helping them with the horses. I often thought then that had I not been a knight, I would have been a smith, perhaps in a village like this one."

"I can see you as one," Joanna replied. "For sure you are hearty enough. How would I fare in this place, you think?"

He heard a faint clicking noise and realized she was clenching her teeth: perhaps she felt she had given away too much, or asked too much? Did she fear his mockery?

"Well, you are not yet a crone, so you could not be a wise-woman," he began, grinning as she glowered. "But as a cook, why not?"

"A cook?"

"A baker. You are used to furnaces."

She smiled, unconsciously swinging her hand in his. "Would we do well?"

Relishing the "we" Hugh said, "In certain seasons, yes. The winters would be hard, but then the dark and cold of the year is hard for everyone."

"My mother loved the snows. Did you and David play snowballs when you were boys?"

Be wary here. Hugh sensed a past that was less than happy. Two months ago, before he had met Joanna, he might have asked her directly about her mother, but now he appreciated subtlety and tact. Joanna would tell him when she was ready.

"Every moment we could. And throwing stones, like the young ones here."

"Older ones, too." Joanna raised their clasped hands, pointing her fingers at the churchyard. A row of men were throwing rocks the size of a man's fist into the road beyond, while the women arranged trenchers of cheese, salad, and dried fish on the tables.

Hugh decided he would join in the rock throwers but, as he and Joanna strolled into the churchyard, he heard the distinctive wail of pipes. The drummers and pipers had finally brought out their instruments, and the dance would soon be beginning.

* * *

She had never danced but she would. If Hugh faced down warriors without flinching, she would master this slippery maze of steps. Joanna held her head high and stepped out as his lady, their hands scarcely touching as they weaved and circled.

It was a carol dance, round and round with the women and men of the village, all laughing and gasping and in their brightest holiday clothes, sometimes linking hands with those beside them, sometimes breaking from the circle and weaving through the other dancers like a shuttle. Hugh clasped her hand throughout, going with her on her swaying progress, not releasing her fingers even when the other men slapped their thighs in time to the beat of the drum. He was the tallest and best made of the company, with the blackest hair, the bluest eyes.

"You like?" he called as the dance became a spiral, winding down to a single point where all became huddled in a tight embrace.

She laughed at him in answer, flicking her skirts and kicking up her heels. At the rim of her eye-line she noticed the village priest standing in the church porch, arms folded and frowning, but then he too was drawn into the festival by an old man giving him a tall beaker of beer. The other villagers were like herself: wide-eyed and smiling, sneaking little glances at Hugh.

Then the dance flung her against him, to a thumping of drumbeats and her pounding heart. He was a tower, a donjon, but living, with his own racing heart that she could feel as her hand came to rest against his chest.

"Up we go!" He lifted her out of the tight mass into his arms and high into the air, above the heads of the smirking villagers. Avoiding the children who had slammed into the group to join the fun, he carried her away from the dance.

"I wish to go on!" she protested, but not too loudly and she did not struggle. Not with others watching; that would be unseemly.

"I saw you licking your lips, my lady. I thought a mug of ale." His eyes challenged her to contradict him, so naturally she did not.

"That will be welcome. Thank you." She inclined her head and, because it was more comfortable and she did not wish to see the knowing looks of the village matrons, she rested her flushed cheek against his shoulder, closing her eyes as she breathed in his scent.

The day slipped away in music and dance. Sometimes she and Hugh rested and he would serve her with ale or small pieces of fish and cheese, whatever she fancied. He introduced her to the elders of the village and the richest widow of the village, who patted Joanna's cheek and called her a lucky girl. As the afternoon drew on, the ale became beer, then mead. The priest was scowling again and she had no doubt that if his church had been open, he would have preached a fearsome sermon the following Sunday. She said as much to Hugh, who grinned.

"No matter, even if our king and pope make peace, for we shall be away from here by then. Ah—they are bringing the sweet things. Will you have something?"

It amused her to discover that he had so sweet a tooth. "Surprise me," she said, sitting for a moment on one of the stools ranged round the churchyard for just that purpose and listening to the drone of chatter and bees as the musicians also took a rest. It was only when Hugh was returning from the newly laden trestle table with a tray of tiny sweet flans, stewed cherries, and other delicacies that she realized she had lost a chance to slip away.

She had forgotten to escape.

* * *

Hugh drank from another cup of mead, seeing the sunset reflected in its golden depths. He passed the cup to Joanna, who took a sip. "I thought the villagers would be abed by now," she remarked.

"Not at May-time. They will dance past moonrise and beyond."

"Not all."

Hugh too had noted the steady exodus of couples from the dancing floor and could hear the whisperings in the nearby houses and hedges. "Do you wish to leave? If we do not go now, we will be best to wait for sunrise: the road is unfit to travel at night."

She did not contradict his lie about the road but shook her head. "May I see the bees again? I wish to see how they bed down." Her eyes sparkled with more than the mead. "You did promise to tell me more of bee lore, and I think we have time."

The dance had stopped again, while one of the drummers had gone off to be sick in a garden—all the musicians were by now very drunk.

He nodded—he did not want to speak lest he say something that made her change her mind. As couples had done earlier, they left the churchyard by the small wicker gate, stepping out in the direction of the setting sun.

They strolled hand in hand, then arm in arm, Hugh feeling the whole of his right side tingling because that side was closest to Joanna. She remarked on a primrose growing out of the side of a stone wall and he encouraged her to touch the moss and lichen garlanding the wall top, imagining her fingers gliding through his body hair as teasingly as they did over the mosses. From far off, he heard the piper start up again, a straggling series of notes, more wail than tune, and knew from her small smile that Joanna had heard it, too.

He looked at her hands, noticing for the first time that they were ringless and glad that they were.

"Have you ever seen bees dance?" he asked.

"They do not!"

"Yes, they do. Look into a hive on a sunny day and you will see."

"Only you could do that without being stung."

"Perhaps." Hugh neglected to mention that the old bee-keeper had been with him when he saw this, and Edward had opened the wicker hive so skillfully that none of the bees had been disturbed. He wanted to intrigue Joanna and entice her a little, not discuss bee stings. "I could mime their dance for you."

"Sway your hips for me? Would that not dent your dignity with your people?"

"Do you see me undermined today, Joanna?"

She waved his question aside as he held open the gate for her through to the bee hives. "Where is Beowulf? And the horse?"

He smiled, knowing her nervousness over horses. "Both safe in the care of the priest, so you need not fret." He did not ask if she wanted to know so that she might better plot her escape: the subject was a raw grief to them both, so why speak of it?

"Has your father blamed you all your life?"

So much for not speaking, Hugh thought, but then Joanna must still be on edge, still choosing how this encounter would go. He knew now that it was vital he gave her the choice, and he went along with the abrupt change of subject. "I did kill his lady wife, my mother."

"And your father faults you, instead of himself."

He was sure his puzzlement showed on his face and indeed she went on quickly, "A birth is no small thing, Hugh, and for your mother to have no midwife by her bedside from the start was unwise. But then it is easy to look back and see what might have been."

"As you say." He had known nothing of this. Realization was a shock and then a swift wave of anguish swept through him in a cold, numbing tide. After sorrow burst a blaze of anger: he found himself wishing that his father was here in the bee garden. He wanted to berate Sir Yves; he wanted to strike him to the ground and go on hitting. . . .

Tasting black bile, Hugh turned his head so that Joanna would not think him furious with her.

Why did you raise the matter of his mother? Where are your wits? Joanna scolded herself, astonished at her own folly. But then she had wanted to say something to Hugh for days, ever since she had learned the sorry circumstances of his birth. She did not want him to blame himself anymore.

In truth, she was finding it hard to blame Hugh for anything, including her captivity. She could understand it. Was she not also striving to free her father by whatever means she could?

Seduce Hugh, then, tonight. Escape while he sleeps.

Solomon's wry, bony, trusting face lodged in her mind, so clear she could count the number of his teeth. Not to do her utmost for him would be a betrayal. Why should she not use the looks God had gifted her? Hugh thought her pretty, so why not exploit it?

Guilt is a luxury: indulge it later, when you are free, she warned herself, wishing, as she smiled, that there was some other way. To lie with a man again, even Hugh, was no easy matter.

She looked back at the towerless, tiny church, memories of the last occasion a man had been with her bleeding out into her mind from her memory, wounding her afresh. What if this time was the same?

"Joanna, what is it? You sounded then as if you were suffocating."

Hugh had stopped and taken her in his arms.

Tell him the whole truth about your father! Tell him what happened to your mother! Tell him you are useless in a man's bed!

She opened her mouth, but Hugh spoke first.

"You are all pink and bright in the sunset."

His lips brushed against her forehead. His tongue flicked the tip of her nose and he lifted her slightly in his arms.

"Quicksilver little squirrel."

He kissed her left cheek. His left hand brushed the side of her neck: a thrill of lightning in her veins. He kissed her right cheek. His right hand circled her back and she stood straighter and on the tips of her toes so she could meet his dancing fingers.

"Precious as salt."

He kissed her mouth. Joanna felt as if she were dissolving into his kiss: only their lips seemed real.

"Sweeter than honey."

He kissed her mouth a second time and she wrapped her arms about his neck, drawing him closer still.

"Dance me this bee dance," she breathed. "Dance it on me." Her senses hummed as they trembled together, she amazed that so strong a warrior could shake like gold leaf.

"I dread to harm you, sweeting," he murmured. "So small and trim."

He lowered his head and tongued her nipples through the cloth of her gown. "Do I do right?" he whispered, nuzzling between the shallow curve of her breasts.

In answer she touched him *there,* in the core of his manhood, tracing him through his jutting tunic. The knives and

keys on his belt jangled as his hips jerked toward her hand.
As his head jerked up, she caught and nipped his earlobe between her teeth, whispering, "You are my champion. You."

They bore each other down to the ground, scrambling
backward on their hips and heels to be in the shadow and
shelter of a stone wall. The night was warm, or it seemed
warm to Joanna: when Hugh muttered of the need to make
a fire she shook her head. "Our cloaks will be enough,"
she said, draping hers across his legs, ignoring his snort of
laughter when he saw how little of him her cloak covered.

"We will need to bundle close later," he warned.

"Show me this dance, my knight," Joanna reminded
him. She knew what would happen between them and she
wanted to go on now, before she lost her nerve.

"What is it?" she stammered, as he seemed to hesitate.
Was he listening? The villagers all seemed busy with dancing again. Did he fear being spied on? This place was private, surrounded by walls, bordered by bee hives—an
onlooker would need to see through stone and wicker to
see them. There were no trees overhead where a child
could climb and stare.

"We have no haste, my lady." He kissed her deeply. "We
have the night. None will disturb us here." He touched
the lacings of her sleeves. "I will give you an array of
sleeves to wear. What colors will you have? Gold, of
course."

"Blue, please," Joanna whispered, staring into his eyes.
Even his light caress on her shoulders made her almost
forget the grassless, dusty patch of ground they were settled on.

"Red, too. You favor rich, deep shades. Tasseled belts."
He flicked the long ends of her belt, his hand resting between her thighs. He ran his fingers up, over her loins and
belly and breasts; a light, sweet touch.

"There are wicker stands by the wall behind the hives. They will be easier to rest on than bare earth."

He rolled her away from him, lightly smacked her rump, and walked—in an awkward crouch—to the row of wicker hurdles. In moments he had made them a rough couch, topped with his cloak and a blanket.

Joanna squeezed a corner of it between her hands, sending a look of silent inquiry to Hugh.

"Saddlecloth," he said, freely admitting, "I carried it here with me. Did you not notice?"

"I was watching the sunset," Joanna lied, conscious that she had been watching him and flustered by her lack of attention. How had she missed such a ploy, such presumption? Why was she not angry now?

"It is for comfort, no more," Hugh said gently. "You are queen tonight."

I am safe, Joanna thought, and a tension relaxed within her. She settled onto the wicker "cradle," finding it surprisingly springy, and beckoned to Hugh. "Will you unlace my shoes? They pinch a little after our dancing."

Chapter 17

She was nervous. Not afraid as she had been—tension no longer strung her up like a bow close to snapping point—but she was still wary. Hugh moved very slowly and spoke in a low, slow voice, as if she were a mare to be gentled.

She has known no pleasure in her mating with the bishop, he thought, and he was sorry for that, but relieved, too. Bishop Thomas was no seductive rival for him to worry about.

"Bees are fluffy, did you know?"

The question diverted her: her fingers stopped clawing at the saddlecloth. "How do you know that?"

"They must be, to collect pollen on their legs as they do. And they love the sun."

She smiled. "Who does not?" She lay down on top of the blanket, rolling onto her stomach and propping her chin on her hands. He saw the dark, inviting hollow of her breasts and felt his manhood twitch afresh. "What else, my knight? This is ancient news on bees."

She was a naughty tease. For two finger snaps he was tempted to straddle her, hoick up her skirts, and spank her, but instead he laughed.

"New, eh?" He sat cross-legged beside her, walking his fingers up and down her spine. "Bees flavor their honey."

"How so?"

"They love the red and white clover and love to gather from those; the honey they make is sweet but not over-flavored. They take from borage and the honey they make is clear and pale. If they fly to dandelions, their honey is yellow."

"How do you know so much?"

Hugh smiled. "I have a liking for sweet things, remember?" He felt about his belt and found the small flask he had been given earlier that day by the village elder. "I have some honey here, the liquid, and honeycomb, too." Unless it had melted into his linen undershirt, which was quite possible, given the heat he was feeling. "Will you taste?"

She nodded and held out her hand but he shook his head. "Allow me." He leaned closer, his heartbeat racing as she did not draw back. "Close your eyes."

He almost whooped with triumph when she did so but fought it back down his throat and dribbled a small portion of honey onto his personal eating spoon. As he held it up, the setting sun flared along its metal edge in a burst of light: a lucky sign, he hoped.

"Mmm, it tastes quite smoky. Is this the dandelion honey?"

"Yes," Hugh said, though in truth he neither knew nor cared. She still had her eyes closed and he could stare at her without restraint. Her tongue was small and pink and she lapped like a little cat. He wanted her tongue to lap him, to taste and suck and kiss, and his tongue do the same to her in return.

"Bees feed each other honey," he said, and now he lied, quite shamelessly. "They smear it on their bodies and let their hive fellows taste. Look you now: like this."

He unlaced his tunic drawstrings, tugged off his tunic

and undershirt. Her eyes were open again and as wide as milk pails as he took a generous dab of the bronze, fragrant honey and drew the sign of the cross on his breastbone.

For an instant he lay still, feeling the wicker pricking through the blanket and cloak, listening to a cheeping of sparrows and a low buzz of bees. *What do you expect her to do, fool!* his conscience goaded, but then she lowered her head and her body and kissed him lightly, over his heart. A spasm of delight jerked through him, threatening to undo him altogether.

She smiled, the little evil elf, and licked his chest, first one nipple and then, passing a finger over the drizzle of honey in the middle of his torso, brushing the honey drop onto his left nipple and gently sucking.

"You taste of sweetness and salt." Gently she nipped his swirl of chest hair between her teeth. "You are hairier than a bear, Hugo."

"More randy, too," Hugh growled under his breath, praying then she did not hear. She could drown him in honey if she kept on kissing.

Lower her tongue worked, tasting and licking. When she reached his navel, Hugh raised his hips slightly, wishing he was naked and at the same time longing for Joanna to strip off and for him to do the same to her.

Back she came, her hands now joining in the caresses; up and across his belly, over his ribs, up to his shoulders. With his eyes still closed he sensed her hovering above him, sensed her shy and tender anxiety. He smoothed his own hands down her narrow face and along the slender column of her throat, cupping her small, perfect breasts, then gliding to her softly flaring hips.

He heard her breath catch and opened his eyes.

"You are grinning at me!" she protested.

"Smiling, my lady." Surely he was smiling? His whole body was a smile. "Eager to serve." He kissed her on the mouth, slipping his hands about her flanks and rolling so she was beneath him. "Joanna." Her name was sweeter to him than the honey. "Truly you are a grace of God."

She colored but did not look away, her eyes calm and trusting, with specks of fire in their depths that he would kindle more, if he could.

"I did not know you were so glib with words, Hugo."

He let the jibe go: it was a feint, nothing more.

"I have used honey on grazes," she added, now cooperating with him, the contrary madam. "Have you?"

"Many times." He dipped his finger into the small jar and touched the corner of her mouth. "You have a small cut here."

Her face glowed at the contact and she turned her head and sucked his finger. Looking at him, she looked above him and now she raised her arm. "How lovely."

A little aggrieved she did not mean him, Hugh turned and saw the low brilliant star, winking in the southwest above the dark blue twilight, textured as a starling's wing.

"What star is it?" he asked, although he thought he knew.

"Venus," she confirmed. "The goddess of honey and copper." She rubbed at her elbow. "I think I have a graze here."

Hugh kept his face straight. "Let me see."

He dabbed her flawless elbow and then tugged at his leggings, exposing a small, scabbing wound on his calf. At once she bent to it, her hair spilling from its golden net as he "accidentally" pushed the net free of its pins.

"Forgive me," he said quickly, but she only smiled and pooled a drop of honey on his leg, smoothing it slowly, as if it was the rarest and most costly of unguents.

"By all that is holy—!" He craved more of her touch, her scent, her skin. In moments they were tearing off their clothes and pitching into each other's arms, fitting together as close and tight as a key into a lock.

"You are burning!" she exclaimed, and he laughed, kissing her naked breasts, glorying in their dark, pert nipples.

"Grace, such grace," he murmured, shivering as her hands skimmed down his back. He brushed her dark bush between her sleek, taut thighs, delighted, as she ran her hands over his buttocks. She moaned and opened her thighs and he fingered her intimate softness, her own sweet honey-spot.

"Come to me, come!" she urged, clawing at his shoulders, but he wanted her to have pleasure first, see the rapture on her pretty face. He kissed her mouth and breasts again, all the while tickling and stroking her, running his fingers through her dark intimate curls and her glossy fleshy folds, hearing her breath quicken and watching her begin to soar.

He quickened his fingering, darting his hand across her womanhood, placing one finger and then two within her, turning her so he could have her lie on his thigh and he might caress her bottom.

She began to plunge and rear like a frisking filly and then she stiffened and shuddered, a word he did not know breaking from her lips, a cry of exultation. He cuddled her, reveling in her open responsiveness, sensing the moment was new to her, seeing the wonder on her face.

"I—I . . ." A tear spilled from her eye and he kissed it away.

"Be at peace, we have all night," he whispered, ignoring the urgent ache in his loins. He was no callow youth, to grab what he wanted: women were gentle, soft creatures, his Joanna most of all.

But she opened her thighs again and now drew him inside her, hissing in his ear, "Come now, please: I am lonely without you."

She was snug in his arms and snug about him, and her heat and sweetness and passion were too much. He pounded into her, losing himself in a great rush of blazing feeling, knowing a desire and need he had never known before and a roaring sea of pleasure he had never experienced.

She nipped his earlobe, and the taut, tingling pain sent him over the edge. Rearing, he bucked and gave himself, shouting out his release.

Chapter 18

Joanna stirred, finding Hugh draped over her like a heavy flag, an arm wound like a huge adder about her middle and a massive leg threaded through both of hers. She felt replete in a way she had not known before, but then she had not known making love could be like this. She touched herself, remembering, wondering when she and Hugh might make love again. She was tempted to wake him, tease him, beguile him, but he was so boyish, so peaceful in sleep. She kissed his ear and murmured, "Roll over, Hugo," hugging herself when he grunted and did as she asked, thrusting his hips back toward her so that they might cuddle together.

She snuggled against him, tracing old scars on his arms and a deeper, old wound on his right flank. For a warrior he was almost unmarked, but then she knew he was a skilled fighter. When she recalled the joust he had taken her to, she felt only pride, recalling the wary men and avid-eyed women.

Happy and content as she had not been since a child, she dozed again, then came awake in the darkness, blinking up into the night sky and spotting the waxing moon, half hidden behind gray clouds.

The moon!

Joanna's spine cracked as she snapped up into a sitting position and found herself unable to stop her forward momentum, rolling out of their makeshift bed onto the hard-packed earth. Ignoring her dirt-encrusted knees, she stumbled to her feet, her breath coming in sharp, shallow bursts as she fought down a searing rush of panic and shame.

How had she forgotten her deadline, even for a day? And here surely was her chance: she must steal away while Hugh was sleeping, while the villagers were sleeping.

She dressed with fumbling fingers, putting her shoes on the wrong feet and having to change them about. She kept glancing at Hugh, telling herself she was ensuring he was still deep in slumber. She replaced the net on her hair, taking pains with the pins. She brushed down her skirts, making them hiss. Still he slept, his arms now raised above his head. It pierced her to think of leaving him without saying good-bye. He would never know how much he had touched her.

She was sniveling again. Swiftly, before her tears became sobs, she turned and ran softly out of the enclosure, leaving Hugh with the sleeping bees.

Hugh yawned, stretched, and reached for his woman. Finding her gone, he leaped up with a curse.

But no, she had not left him. She was standing with the village elder and two lanky young men by the gate to the bee enclosure. As Hugh scrabbled for his leggings and cloak under the rough horse blanket and began to dress, Joanna raised her hand to the three and started walking toward him.

"I lost my way in the dark and these gentlemen found me wandering and guided me back," she said.

"That was kind of them," Hugh answered, not believing a shred of it. He was glad, though, that these fellows had been more wakeful than himself, or his disruptive little hostage would have escaped his custody.

Well, he was wakeful enough now, and when he saw the trace of tears on her pallid face and marked her drooping shoulders, he said nothing. He knew what it was like to be scolded and berated when already heartsore and weary. He raised an arm in greeting and farewell to the men, then turned his full attention to Joanna.

"Are you hungry? I am."

She chewed at her lip, a rare gesture of nerves. "We have the honey . . ." Her voice trailed into silence, as if she did not know what to say, how to interpret his mood.

Sweeting, I am not going to scold, Hugh thought, producing the honeycomb, together with some cheese and rather hard bread—a day's travel in a cloth had done little to keep it fresh.

"I did not know if the villagers would have anything for us to eat, so I brought some provisions," he said, spreading the meager offerings on their bed. "'Tis well the bees are asleep or they would be after this." He broke off a piece of comb and stretched out his hand to her.

She took it with a precision that reminded him he was still naked and she was still nervous. He wanted to prove to her that she need not fear him; that he would save her and her father and David.

He sat again on their couch and lifted the blanket. "Get in. No, do not trouble with your shoes; you are shivering like a wren in a gale." He gulped down his piece of honeycomb and folded her firmly into his arms, holding her until her trembling stopped.

"Eat. You will feel better."

"Are you a healer now?" she asked, between mouthfuls of cheese and honey.

"If my lady requires me to be so." He watched her trying not to wriggle with pleasure at the sweet comb. "They work well together, do they not? Cheese and comb? Will you have more mead, too?"

"Thank you."

He rejoiced at the thanks. "Are you warm enough?"

"Can we . . . ? Can we make love again?"

He was delighted at her blushing directness. "For sure, if you are sure!" He did not want her offering herself as a peace offering, but could think of no elegant way to say as much. "If it pleases you, Joanna."

"It does," she said quietly. "Unless it is now too late? You were sleeping . . ."

He wondered why she felt it needful to give him a means to refuse her and again wanted to strangle Bishop Thomas. He put down the flask and wrapped his arms tightly about her, knowing she would feel his desire.

"You are my pretty lady, my hazel-willow woman, brown as the hazel and slender as the willow." He touched her hair and waist and kissed her. "I have ached and lusted for you for weeks! I would love you for a week and not be sated."

She ran both hands over his chest. "Only a week?"

Two can tease, squirrel. He turned her onto her stomach and fondled her beautifully plump backside and pert breasts, alive to her squeaks and gasps, lifting her skirts and caressing afresh as her whispered, "What if someone comes?" became a moan of "Oh, yes!"

"You have a saucy tongue, lady." He patted her bottom and, as she raised her haunches higher, slipped his hand between her legs.

When Joanna stirred it was still dark, but this time Hugh was up and dressed. He gave her a flask of ale and nodded to the clear skies.

"We can ride now by the moon, and I think it is time we left. The village elder knows we are going and we can leave with his blessing." He shrugged. "It saves them having to find us more food for a breakfast."

"May I thank the elder?" she asked.

Hugh gave her a very knowing look. "The villagers here have welcomed you in ways far better than others have elsewhere, I warrant. Yes, I think he will be delighted by your thanks. I have to gather our things and collect Beowulf and Lucifer, so you have time." He pointed back to the village. "If you follow the track you will see him sitting under the church porch, feeding scraps to a young pig."

He paused. "You will not rush ahead?"

"You have my word," Joanna answered firmly. "I will not stray."

They both knew what that meant.

Chapter 19

Joanna stared at the bishop's messenger, a man unknown to her. She and Hugh had scarcely returned to Castle Manhill when the messenger appeared. Joanna was still trying to understand what had happened to her; how she could respond so completely to Hugh. She was his hostage and he was her captor. How was it that, riding with him, she was so at ease in his company? So glad of his touch? So happy?

The messenger, Sir John Woodvine, clad in the blue and purple of the bishop's entourage, woke her out of her girlish daydream. She was inside again, trapped within stone walls again, and with work to do. Hugh might speak of loving her for a week, but he was not soft enough to release her to Sir John.

Not that Sir John was asking for anything so overt, merely to "have words" with her in private. A dapper, older man with smooth fair hair and a baby-fine complexion, he reminded Joanne of a ferret: sleek and dangerous. She would not want to meet him in any street in West Sarum alone: not with the burning looks of interest he kept giving her. Standing in Sir Yves's private solar behind the great hall, straddling a wolf-skin rug and occasionally touching the coat of arms emblazoned on the front of his surcoat,

Sir John seemed all courtesy. But each time he glanced at her, sitting on a stool beside the fireplace with a scrap of another woman's embroidery on her lap—provided by Sir Yves, who thought it made her look "aptly feminine"—Sir John stripped her with his eyes.

Standing at the other end of the fireplace, fanning his long tunic by the flames, Sir Yves looked bored and embarrassed. Hugh meanwhile prowled around the solar, asking if she needed a drink, or a cushion, or a maid: any question to claim her attention and make it clear to Sir John that if he so much as breathed on her, Hugh would rip out his heart and roast it on a spit. The tension crackled between the pair as much as the roaring fire in the grate, an opulent, showy fire that Joanna longed to escape. Her left side felt to be scorched and at one point she was certain she could smell her own hair singeing.

"I see from your sword belt and its repair that you have fought in Outremer," Hugh was saying, pacing relentless beside the couch on which his father sat and threw scraps of old bread to his dogs. "Did you go on crusade?"

"I am with a military order," Sir John replied, glancing at Joanna as she tried to lean away from the fire. "Are you too hot, my lady?" Somehow the tone of his question suggested she would be cool if she allowed him to peel off her gown, and his sharp brown eyes were a fire in themselves.

Before Joanna could answer Hugh was beside her, lifting the stool off the floor timbers and moving her and her seat away from the blaze. He touched her hand and then confronted the messenger afresh.

"Templars or Hospitallers?"

"The Templars, Hugh Manhill. And before you ask"— Sir John held up a narrow hand on which his third finger was missing—"I am here as friend and herald of my lord Bishop Thomas, not as the emissary of my order."

There was an astonished silence, but only for a moment.

"By all the teeth in hell!" Hugh smacked his thigh in frustration. "David is in your order, man! You will have known him in Outremer! You will have fought beside him! He is your brother-in-arms!"

Sir John stiffened. "I did not know him. I never saw him or met him anywhere and I have not seen him in West Sarum. All I do know is that the charges against him are heavy—"

"False!" Hugh spat.

"—and as such, reflect badly on my order. Sir David is obdurate," he went on. "My lord bishop had ordered him placed in the lowest prison of the donjon but he has lately allowed Sir David back into the first-floor chamber. Still your brother refuses to deny these charges."

"Hell's teeth! He put David into that hellhole!"

"He is out of it now, Sir Hugh, so save your protestations."

Joanna clutched the scrap of embroidery in her lap and willed herself not to be sick. David trapped in that foul lower prison, beneath the trapdoor, in the darkness . . . She gagged and swallowed a bitter mouthful of bile.

Sir Yves raised his eyebrows at this exchange but said nothing. He seemed unconcerned at the fate of his middle son and the pain of his youngest son. "State your terms, Sir John," he remarked, motioning to a thin, limping page— not the lanky, curly-haired Peter, this time—to refill his wine cup.

Sir John glanced at his own empty cup, deposited by him on one of two great chests, but when no wine was forthcoming, he sighed and spoke. "My lord bishop shall, as a gesture of his goodwill, release his prisoner into the care of the Manhills."

On what terms? Joanna wanted to yell at him, but Hugh was already asking that vital question.

Sir John appeared surprised. "Why, that my lord may

see this lady for himself, on neutral ground. That, and some other minor issues."

He meant the gold, Joanna knew. She had spoken of it eloquently in her previous messages and the bishop was interested. But she would not hand it to a messenger.

"That is between my lord and me," she said quickly.

Sir Yves frowned at her interjection: in his eyes, her function at this meeting was supposed to be decorative, nothing more.

Hugh nodded. "Agreed. So when will this exchange take place?"

Sir John looked at them one by one, a ghost of a smile suggested on his narrow lips. "Today at sunset, if it please you all. My lord Thomas is returning to West Sarum this very day and can break his journey here to resolve this matter."

"Do you trust him?" Joanna asked Hugh later. They had remained in the solar by the ruse of Hugh offering her a game of chess. She had accepted, though she did not know how to play it, and now they were bent over the chessboard on one of the chests, their heads close together. A maid was sweeping a twig broom slowly round the chamber: Sir Yves's idea of a chaperone.

"What now?" Joanna whispered, pointing to the maze of pieces.

"Move your queen, to the fourth square. There!" Hugh whispered. He was playing both sides, and to Joanna's amusement *she* was winning.

Hugh rubbed at his chin as if deep in thought and lowered his head still more, as if studying the board. "I do not trust the bishop for a moment," he admitted. "And now, after hearing that news of David spending time in the oubliette, I understand why you do not trust him, either.

Hell's teeth! It makes me livid to think of it! Such filthy behavior is against all forms of honor."

Joanna waited, not daring to ask Hugh what he meant by her not trusting Bishop Thomas. Memories of their night together swept through her, making it impossible for her to think. She had to know one thing, however. Half-knowledge would drive her mad.

"Do you blame me?" she asked. "For last night? Do you see how I was—acted—as a betrayal of the bishop?"

He stared as if her question surprised him, his ready color fading from his lean features, and then he shook his head at her. "No, Joanna. You have betrayed no one."

Hope flared in her. "Truly?"

"Truly, wench! But now we must play what we have. If Bishop Thomas is at all honorable, if the meeting goes well, then there will be an exchange: you for David."

Unless the prisoner was her father, Solomon, Joanna thought, wishing with all her heart and will that it would be. Her father was older than David: he would fare less well in the donjon or worse, the oubliette. She was very sorry for David, appalled that he had been treated so, but her wish remained the same.

Hugh picked up his own queen and cradled it in his large hand, tracing the rough-hewn features of the figure with a thumb. "We shall all be back in our own worlds: my brother with the Templars, should he care to trouble with them, you with your elixirs, me with the joust."

He replaced the queen on the board with a small snap. "If you ever wish for a change, send me another of those golden tassels and I will bear you off to a tourney. The life is interesting, though I do not think you could practice your arts, which would be a pity. I think in the end you would miss it too much."

Joanna gave him a sharp look, wondering if he meant as the bishop's leman, but his face was solemn.

"Send me word when you find gold, eh?" He looked deeply into her eyes. "I will be glad to know you have attained your heart's desire, my lady alchemist."

Say more, please! Joanna felt the passion in her heart brimming as tears in her eyes. But what could Hugh say? He was a landless knight with less treasure than he had begun with at the beginning of the year: he could support her but not give her a home. She was as he termed her: an alchemist. For her to continue her work she must have a constant place, not a traveling tent.

He took her cold hand in his and warmed her fingers. "This is a maze, but we may yet find our way out."

"I pray so," Joanna said, stopping before she broke down and wept.

Chapter 20

Hugh braced his shield before Joanna, amused that it hid most of her except for her eyes and forehead.

"Metal modesty," he chuckled, humor sparkling through him as she winked at him over her iron "veil," but in truth this was a serious matter. He was wary of archers, even here in the stout wooden watchertower of the bailey, scanning down over the woodland and water meadows surrounding Castle Manhill. He had hung a dark pelt across the entrance to the tower so that he and Joanna would not be nicely framed by the doorway and ensured she was standing next to the thickest beam on the walkway.

Beside him Joanna was as still as ice—a trick he had seen her do before, in her work. She had been with him here for hours, long before sunset, without shelter from the steady drizzle or drink to warm her, but she did not complain. She knew it was vital they look out for the bishop's party, be prepared as much as they could be.

"Here they come," he whispered, aware that she did not see as far or as clearly as he did. In this gray, wet murk the galloping figures were drab and indistinct, only the pennants of their standards showing any color. He scanned the troop of men, counting two score guards, and felt a twinge

of disquiet. Was treachery afoot here? He must ensure his
father asked for many hostages before he and Joanna ventured out beyond the bailey walls; ensure too that his men
were positioned on the walkway, armed with their bows.

Let Bishop Thomas feel some threat, also. . . .

"Where is the hostage?" Joanna asked, her breath fog-
ging his shield. "I cannot see in this rain."

Hugh studied the horses, not the cloaked, bedraggled
men. Picking out a spirited, very handsome piebald palfrey
in the middle of the mass of horses and riders, he knew
he had found the bishop. His was clearly the best horse, although he was far from the best rider.

Alongside him, not really flowing with his black mount,
was a hunched figure, tall and slender enough to be David.

"There, just off to your left." He gently guided Joanna's
head. "That man is galloping along with ropes tied about
his middle; that is why he moves so poorly."

"I cannot see his face," Joanna lamented, standing up on
tiptoe as she tried to see more.

Hugh swept the landscape for archers, glad that the rain
was increasing. In this cloudy, muddy day it would be
harder for a bowman to sight a single target, though there
were always knives, spears, and maces, not forgetting
long swords.

"I am useful to the bishop," Joanna reminded him. "He
has no reason to cut me down, least of all before witnesses."

Her voice was breathy, as if she was trying to convince
herself. If she was the bishop's mistress, the cleric must
have been with her only rarely—that, or the fellow was a
brute. She had been unused to pleasure, that much was
plain to Hugh. He felt no shame in what they had done last
night. Joanna might think she had betrayed her loathsome
master, but Hugh now knew she had been no volunteer in

Thomas's bed. When he thought of the man pawing her he went cold with rage.

"You cannot go back to him!" he burst out. He had been aching to say it for weeks.

"He has my father. He has David. I must."

"But the donjon is not so terrible."

It was not the wisest thing to say and his clumsy attempt to comfort failed as she turned her face to the timber column and shuddered.

"The oubliette is," she whispered.

Ashamed that he had actually forgotten David's brief stay in that prison, Hugh tried to clasp her shoulder, but she flung him off.

"Joanna." He hated the hopeless bleaching of her face, the rain clinging to her eyelashes like tears.

"The prisoner could be your father," he said, betraying his own brother by wishing, in that moment, that it was.

Another brief shudder ran through her, then she straightened. "How will this negotiation work?"

"We shall go down when my men are ready. Then we shall see."

She was studying the prisoner. "I have not seen my father ride for many years. It could be him, though why should my lord bishop bring him here? It makes no sense. The man looks tall in the saddle, as your brother would look."

It amazed and humbled him that she was offering *him* hope.

"Unless it is another altogether. That fool Frenchman."

He watched calculation slide across her pretty face. "Why should Mercury be brought forth from the donjon? It is clear he is rich: once he recovers his wits he will bring a huge ransom."

"But your lord bishop is not a patient man."

She nodded once, then started forward, almost breaking

past Hugh's shield. "See, see! That man there, that prisoner! He is hooded!"

Hugh had seen it already. The sight sickened him but, even as his mouth filled with foul bile, he swallowed it, and curses, in silence. Was Joanna not his hostage, too? He had no right to berate Bishop Thomas for any treatment of his captive, not when he had seduced Joanna. And, at the very beginning, gagged her with a glove.

I am perverted, he thought, as he took Joanna into his arms again and held her, trying to reassure her when nothing he did or said would make any difference. *I am no better than Thomas.*

With that bleak thought he guided her back through the doorway, under the wolf-skin pelt, and down the steps, taking care that she did not slip on the narrow wooden treads of the walkway staircase. He gestured to his men and walked her to his horse.

"We shall ride pillion, as always," he told her. "But first we must get you ready."

He did not trust the bishop. Whoever was beneath that black hood, be it David, the Frenchman, or a crazed assassin, he did not trust Lord Thomas.

Joanna sat before Hugh on Lucifer, feeling hopelessly conspicuous. He had assured her that the padding made no difference to her shape but he had not seen page Peter's knowing smirk in the bailey yard, when she had been helped into the quilted coats.

"This is what knights wear under their mail," Hugh remarked cheerfully. "These two little quilted jerkins belonged to a young squire, so they should fit."

Joanna suspected that he had been the young squire, but could think of no tart response. The reunion with her lord loomed in her mind. She could dwell only on their forthcoming meeting and the poor prisoner. To ride bound and hooded—the idea and indignity of it, swaying about helplessly on a huge horse, not knowing where one was being led—was the stuff of nightmares. She did not think the wretch was her father, but whoever it was, she pitied him with all her heart.

Hugh squeezed her round her middle. "When we meet them, do not lean forward even if he whispers," he warned.

"No, Hugh." He had said this earlier. They were canter-ing now toward the mass of riders on the open meadows, Hugh's own men flanking them in a huge defensive arc, and she was feeling increasingly hot in her extra clothes: two padded quilts and a heavy cloak over them.

"Keep your hands on Lucifer's mane."

"Yes, Hugh." If she pointed, she could be vulnerable to a sword or spear thrust, coming up at her from a soldier on the ground and jabbing into her side. Hugh had spoken at length on her need to be steady and safe on the horse.

"I am no knight!" she protested, to which Hugh replied, "And if it were up to me, you would not be taking part in this. It is your bishop who insisted you be present."

Joanna touched a hand to her forehead, feeling the cap of mail digging heavily into her skull. Hugh had insisted she wear this hat of chain mail, too; another piece of squire armor that made her head and neck ache like the devil.

"How do you stand this weight, Hugo?" she had whis-pered, when he "crowned" her with the cap and began ar-ranging her veil about the hideous headpiece.

He had shrugged. "In time and with practice they seem as light as spiders' webs."

"To you, maybe."

That remark had won her a brief smile then, but, as they rode, one end of her blue veil had become unpinned from the heavy metal links, flapping against her cheek and Hugh's chest. Briefly she wished she were the silk, as she longed to smack Hugh for placing her in this position, Hugh and Lord Thomas between them.

The bag of gold hanging visibly amidst her skirts bounced against her thigh where, if she survived until tomorrow, she would have a bruise.

She had left some gold behind in her chamber for Sir Yves. "Always pay your debts," Solomon had taught her and, whatever happened, she wanted Hugh's father to respect her, and her skill.

The rest of the gold, the river gold and Orri's hoard, was divided into two bags. One was hung about her middle. The other lay along her lower spine, padded and disguised with a shawl under her skirts. If she was searched, this second bag would be swiftly discovered, but she had done the best she could. She had to keep some gold back. If she gave Lord Thomas the bag on her thigh, she wanted to be able to promise more and, if need be, produce more gold later.

Hugh, if he suspected anything, was saying nothing. She did not know whether to be relieved or indignant. Did he truly think her as broad-hipped as this? But then, why did she care? She might be riding to West Sarum tonight, with the bishop.

It worried her that, quite apart from the gold, the mail cap and quilted jerkins were valuable. She was carrying a goodly ransom on her back, but it belonged to Hugh, not her.

"This mail," she began, but Hugh understood without her saying more.

"Think no more of it. If you leave with the bishop tonight and the mail goes with you, 'tis no grief to me."

He had not used that expression for a while, Joanna thought, wondering why his comment now should trouble her. Indeed, why was she fretting at all? If the prisoner was David and she returned to West Sarum, she would be with her father again. Once she was back with Solomon, she could work to free him from the donjon.

And for how long? How long before your bishop decides you have not provided enough elixirs, enough gold? What then?

Chapter 21

The rain had increased. It dripped in a steady stream off Hugh's hair and trickled down the back of his neck. Lucifer snorted and pranced below him, delighting in the mud. Beneath knit and knotted brows, his men scanned the gray skies for signs of a storm—everyone knew lightning and armor was no good mix. Looking at their mail and helms, Hugh saw them furtively glance at his bare head and simple shield. Though none would dare say it to his face, he knew they thought his lack of armor madness.

Perhaps it was, but if treachery was afoot he wanted himself to be a big, juicy target, an obvious one, and not Joanna.

Damn you to hell and damnation, Father, for not giving me more men! Another two score soldiers and some good archers, and he would have settled this mess without Joanna needing to set foot out of the castle. Yes, a fight on these water meadows would have been risky, but more for the bishop's men than his own, who knew the lay of the land. Yes, the hostage would be at risk in a skirmish, but he could have been snatched away, too. Besides, it was a man, and a man should expect conflict and danger in his life.

But his father had not budged on the matter of men, and Joanna had begged him not to change what had been agreed between him and the bishop's messenger. "Would you have it said you are forsworn?" she asked. "Please, Hugh. I must speak to my lord. If there is news of my father, I must know it."

Her pleas, even her tears, he could withstand, but not the likely horror and disgust that he would see in her face if he ignored her, went his own path, and then saw his attack on Bishop Thomas go amiss. In such a case, and in pure spite, the bishop might even order his hostage to be killed before the castle walls, in Joanna's sight.

So, because he wanted to spare her such a deathly vision, because his father would take no chances except in the meat he would eat at dinner, they were all dancing to Thomas's tune.

Here he was, waiting on a small rise in the sodden water meadows with his men encircled around him. Hugh could spot no weapons beneath the long capes and gloves and cloaks, but that meant nothing: he had his sword and daggers and a visible shield.

Here he was, unholy man of the church, prince of the grasping, of the venial and the accursed. Hugh wanted heaven to strike him down, but the rain continued to fall without thunderclaps, and the bishop, clothed in a cloak of sable and wearing a hat with a brim as broad as an ancient shield, was as pale and sleek as ever. Under his hat his face was dry and his voice seemed coated in the dust of old, unopened chambers.

"Manhill and his men. Disgustingly hearty as ever. We should conclude this business as swiftly as possible, then I can complete my journey."

Hearing her lord's voice for the first time in weeks, Joanna did not move. Hugh felt her pressed back tight against him, as snugly as when their bodies had been coiled together in bed. The memory steadied him, reminded him again what was at stake: her and David's safety. He squeezed his thighs gently about her stiffened figure, trying to offer what support he could.

"Before we go on, I need to see the face of your hostage. I want to know who I may be getting."

He watched the hooded and roped figure slumped in the saddle. It could be David. The man was the same height, weight, and lean shape as his brother. At the sound of his voice, the man had swiftly raised his hooded face as if he knew him. The man's clothes he was less sure of, having little interest in what men wore, only in how they fought. He could not even remember the color of the tunic or cloak David had been wearing the last time he had seen him.

He scanned the hostage's empty sword belt, his shoes, his neck. David had a red scar on his neck . . . but no, the hood obscured too much.

"I am waiting," he said, glancing at the man's hands. They were gloved, but he wore a silver ring on his smallest finger, a ring Hugh knew well. It had been his, his "lucky" tournament ring, his first gift from a lady. He had given it to David for luck, before his brother went off to Outremer.

Hugh felt his breath gush from his body. He felt as if he had been poleaxed by emotion: a strange mingling of relief, happiness, and sorrow. If this was David, he would have to let Joanna go.

But I do not want to!

"My lord bishop?" he queried. "I would see the face of your captive. Is such a request beyond the ken of your guards?"

Behind him he heard swords scraping in their scabbards as the soldiers went for their blades, but Bishop Thomas merely smiled.

"You are a godless man, Hugh Manhill. Did I not promise

a prisoner as a sign of my good faith? Will you honor your side of the bargain and allow me to speak to my alchemist?"

Joanna tried to leap down from Lucifer but Hugh clamped his thighs more tightly about her and hoisted his shield before them. He trusted his men to watch their backs. "So talk. That is, as you say, what we agreed: a prisoner in exchange for you seeing your alchemist and speaking with her. I have kept my side of the bargain, but you will get nothing else from this meeting unless you show the prisoner's face." Even if it was David, he would not give Joanna up; not without his brother being de-hooded first so he could be sure he was David, and hale and hearty.

"That I will not do, Manhill!"

Hugh lifted his shield still higher. "Then you must make do with talk, and in my presence."

The bishop's pale fish eyes narrowed but Joanna was not confounded. She began to speak in a fast spate of words. It was Latin, Hugh realized, a language he dozed through in church.

Smiling again, Bishop Thomas replied and the two continued their exchange. Hugh said nothing. Although she was his hostage, he trusted Joanna not to betray him to his or his men's deaths. Such evil was not in her.

Still, he wondered what was being agreed, especially when she unclipped the purse at her belt and threw it underarm to the bishop. Thomas caught it, exclaiming a word that Hugh guessed was the Latin for "Done!" and then rubbed his mouth and chin with the bag, as if he was tasting what was inside. Beside him, the knight clutching the ropes tied to the hooded hostage let them fall into the mud.

It was a signal for the party to depart and they did so with speed, Bishop Thomas wheeling his horse around without a single further word of farewell or anything else.

He and his men galloped off into the murk, leaving their hooded prisoner stranded on his horse in the pouring rain.

Again Joanna tried to leave Lucifer's back, but Hugh whispered urgently, "Let us see who it is first."

She nodded and sagged against him, while he debated whether to ask her what she and Bishop Thomas had talked about. Since she did not seem in a mood to say much, he gestured to two of his men, who briskly rode alongside the abandoned prisoner.

"You are safe now," Hugh said, repeating the same in French and German, the two other languages he knew smatterings of. At his signal his men began to untie the strings surrounding the hood.

He braced himself. "Now we shall see."

The rough hood fell away and Joanna gasped.

The prisoner was Mercury.

Chapter 22

The Frenchman smiled and continued to smile as Hugh cursed steadily. Joanna could feel the heat of anger pounding off him and heard the words rumbling in his massive chest before they spilled out above her head in clouds of fury.

"That damnable, treacherous, misbegotten, lying, thieving, devious bastard! No brother, no father, no hostage worth having, only this grinning ape! I wager he has not got back his wits, either!"

He barked out a question to the hapless Mercury, who nodded and tapped his forehead. Joanna saw that the Frenchman was hale and well fed, with a high, good color. His mimed claim that he still had no memory seemed highly unlikely, but she was not about to share that thought with anyone, least of all Hugh, who was dark-faced with anger.

"All those fine words of negotiation and he meant none of them! And you gave him gold!"

"Not all of it," Joanna said hurriedly. She did not want Hugh venting his fury on her, but he swung down from his horse to berate her face-to-face.

"Ah! So you do not trust him fully! This your great lord

and master! How can you serve him? Why did you speak in Latin to him? What were you plotting with him?"

She heard the hurt beneath the anger and kept tight rein on her own temper. "There is no plot. I spoke in Latin so my lord would know I spoke freely. I gave him part of the gold as a sign of my continued good faith."

"Faith? Pah! Your bishop has none. He would have taken you back if I had allowed it and left me with this idiot! He even put David's ring on the fellow, so I might be the more convinced! Teeth of the devil! I will have the ring back, for sure!"

Joanna went cold, wondering if Hugh had imagined the worst: that David might be dead.

"That sly bastard!" Hugh raged on. "Mercury, or whatever you call him, is the same height as David, the same build. I did not dare to hope too much, but I so wanted to *believe*."

"So did I," said Joanna, thinking of her father.

"And you!" Hugh swung a pointing finger at her as if it was a deadly sling. "Would you have gone along with this deception? If I had agreed to your leaving in exchange of this lump of French turf, would you have said anything? Or said nothing and tripped back into your bishop's meaty arms?"

"I did not know."

"Then why were you speaking in Latin?" Hugh kicked the ground before Lucifer, raising a huge divot of mud. "If you had nothing to hide, why not use English?"

"I have told you why already," Joanna began, but Hugh cut across her.

"He is an oath breaker of the vilest kind!"

"Here." Joanna was sick of being harangued. She tore off her veil and the skull-crushing mail cap and flung both at Hugh. Dropping off Lucifer's back so the massive horse was between them, she began to blunder back to the castle through ranks of riders who were suddenly intent on the rain clouds or their saddles. Only Mercury continued to watch, as bland and seemingly as unconcerned as a hermit in a cave.

"Joanna, wait."

She plodded on a few more paces, her shoes sinking ankle-deep in mud when Hugh raced up behind her and scooped her into his arms.

"What of Mercury? Lucifer? Beowulf? What of David's ring?" she demanded, staring at the waterlogged ground. She did not want to look at his handsome, grim face.

"I have the ring already, you may be sure! As for the rest, my men will take them in. Beowulf may come with us, but that is no grief to me."

"Let me down, Hugh."

"You would sink nose-deep in this."

She felt too dispirited to fight him. "Do you think you are the only one who has lost by today's exchange?"

He acknowledged her point by a small nod, but would not let the matter go. "I know you have your father to worry about, but you are both part of that creature's household. David is accused of sorcery. He has already spent time in that damnable oubliette!"

Do you think alchemists immune to such a charge? Joanna bit down on the retort and swallowed it. Bishop Thomas had told her in Latin that her father was well and safe, working at alchemy again and outside the donjon. If true, that knowledge was as precious as gold to her, but how could she share it with Hugh? It would bring home the loss of his brother more keenly. Unwilling to flaunt her small good fortune, she said nothing.

"He never looked back at you when he rode away."

"I know." Desperate to put a stop to their quarrel, Joanna rested her head against his shoulder and closed her eyes. She wished they were still in the village, where loyalties were straightforward. "Since I am still here, what plans have you for me?"

"I suppose you think I should set you up tomorrow with horses and guards and send you back to West Sarum."

"How can I answer that, honestly, Hugo? I know you feel ashamed that I am your hostage, but you must do what you think is best for your family."

"Family! A fine breed, with a father who gives no help, an elder brother who never asks, and David, who dreams his way through life."

"A Templar, and yet a dreamer?"

"You did not know him as a boy." Hugh touched her cheek. "You are cold, as well as sodden. Time to bear you indoors." He brushed beads of water off her forehead, as if oblivious to the fact that the rain was still falling. "I like it when you call me Hugo."

The name, a half-endearment, had slipped out without Joanna realizing it. "I am cold," she agreed quickly, aware that she would not get away tonight, from Hugh or the castle.

And truly, did she want to anymore?

I am a womanish fool. I have fallen in love with my own hostage taker.

Why?

Because Hugh Manhill Destroyer is also Hugo the bee-charmer.

Because he cares and burns so greatly.

Because he laughs with me, and makes me laugh.

Because he is stupidly, abundantly jealous of Bishop Thomas.

Because he accepts me as an alchemist.

She counted the reasons, all logic and sense, while her body was enclosed in the solid, baking furnace of his arms and her mouth yearned to kiss him all over.

* * *

Where do we go now? Hugh was thinking as he strode toward his father's keep. Joanna was quiet in his arms, no longer shaking, but for how long would their truce last? For how long could he, in conscience, hold her?

If she were a man, would he be troubled? Probably not. But he would have left a man to wade through the grime. As for what had happened in the village between them . . .

Hugh grunted as a rush of memory and desire burned through him. Even in the midst of his fury against the bishop, a small, treacherous part of his mind, and all of his heart, was glad. Because Thomas had played false, he had been given a legitimate reason not to release Joanna.

Had the hostage been David instead of Mercury, would he have given up Joanna?

I do not know. It is no grief to me that I did not have to find out.

He was within the bailey, passing the stables. His men trudged a few paces behind, soaked through to their skins and doubtless eager to steam in the comfortable heat of the fires in the hall and kitchen. He went into the largest stable, where the warhorses would be bedded down for the night.

"Lads, to me!" he called, giving each a small coin as the grooms appeared from shadows and corners and hay piles. "Off you go to the kitchen tonight."

He let Joanna down onto the beaten earth floor, saying to the final three grooms, "Bring towels, blankets and a brazier, plenty of food and wine, and there will be another penny in it for each of you."

The lads hurtled into the pouring rain and he set Beowulf to watching the horses, knowing the hound would alert him to any trouble. As his men entered the stable, the great chargers soon were settled for the day and, after a few snorts and kicks of the wooden partitions, lowered their glossy heads into their food buckets.

"Let my father know that the lady Joanna and I are in the chapel, praying for my brother's safe return," Hugh told his captain. The man saluted and left with the rest of the troop, his footsteps fading into the drilling rain.

"He will not come seeking you?" Joanna had already guessed where he wanted them to sleep tonight. As she had not protested, he took that as a good sign that their truce was holding.

"Not in this weather." He avoided the stable lads' straw pallets at the darkest, narrowest end of the stable and drew together a fresh bed of straw behind the doorway. He sensed Joanna watching and glanced at her. "When the food comes, we can eat and I will escort you to your chamber if you wish. Or you can stay here. The day is very wet."

"It is," she agreed.

"The horses will help with warmth." He decided to give her another chance. "Though if your prefer somewhere with a fire?"

Joanna looked from him to Lucifer and back. "I am becoming more accustomed to horses."

"It comes with use," Hugh agreed, praying that he did not look smug.

The lads had done him proud, he thought some time later, when it was full dark outside and the rain hissed in the black bailey yard. Joanna was sitting on a sweet-smelling mass of hay, warming her bare feet by the brazier. Beside her was a comfortable bundle of blankets, and he had taken possession of the flagon of spiced mulled wine.

"More leek porry?" He nudged the small cauldron with his knee. It was a meatless day but they had eaten handsomely. For once, Sir Yves's greed had served him and Joanna well.

Joanna shook her head. "I have eaten too much already. Those cheese tarts were delicious."

"You have a crumb," he lied, and swiftly brushed away an imaginary speck on her chin. He felt her tremble and knew it was with desire, not fear.

"Quicksilver darling." He loved her speed, the shimmer of her when she was relaxed and happy.

She gave him a look. "I meant to say this before. Quicksilver is Mercury, and that is male."

He leaned across and hugged her, amused by her teasing, but Joanna's face clouded.

"Who is Mercury? Why did my lord give him up?"

Hugh thought of the Frenchman, a hostage he did not want. Resentment bit into him afresh. "Who would want to trouble with him?" he growled. "Without his memory he can tell us nothing of his kin. He is an empty cup that has to be filled and housed. As your lord knew well."

Joanna sat up straighter, accidentally spilling her drink into the straw. "Hugh, I am sorry. Mentioning such a matter was a mistake."

Because you were hoping we would make love? Hugh stood up and strode into the darkness of the stable. To say that would be crass, crude, and unkind, but his tongue seemed to burn with the unsaid words. He looked back and saw her standing up, poised ready to face him, and wished anew that she was his, wholly his.

He wanted to say something caring to her, but what his mouth actually said was, "Your lord! How can you call him that? A greedy, lustful, pig! How could you lie with such a leper?"

The dreadful accusation fell into the darkness between them, a black cave of silence and despair.

"And you are perfect?" she spat in return, her eyes bright and pooling with unshed tears. "What are you, if not a brutal man who earns his bread by war? What are you, if not a kidnapper!"

Anger at his cloddish stupidity at hurting her afresh merged with rage at her constant defense of the loathsome Thomas. Why could she not admit the fellow was a running sore in the world of men? He strode back toward her. "You defend him! Him! Bishop of West Hell!"

"He is a man of spirit."

"But I am a man of flesh." Hugh reached her and wrapped his arms about her. "And you a woman of copper and flesh. You are mine."

"What I meant to say—"

Determined to love her—*really* love her; have her admit to him, in sobbing, panting breaths, that he was the greatest lover, the champion, the first and last—Hugh did not let her finish. He began to kiss her deeply, savoring the sweetness of her mouth. Her tongue skimmed his lips and teeth as she kissed him in return, her fingers pulling at his clothes. "Hugo!" she moaned, writhing against him like a spiraling flame.

To slow her down, lest she please him so much he could not restrain himself, he took both her wrists in one hand. Kissing her again he unlaced her gown, freeing her breasts.

Call me lover, greatest, champion, he wanted to say, as he lowered his head and lifted her, caressing her breasts with his tongue. *Tell me you want me all day, each day, every way. Ride me, have me lance you, give me your breasts and mouth and hair and arse.*

He wound a brawny arm about her thighs to keep her raised and off her feet and cupped her budding petals of breasts, their silken warmth stoking his own desire. Her dark nipples stood out, proud and taunting. He licked and kissed them again, her fierce upward arching to his tongue making his own loins leap in answer.

He wanted to put her on hands and knees in the stable,

flip up her skirts, and go into her like a stallion. Instead he dropped her softly into the hay and, still fondling those sweet little breasts, he drew her onto his lap, running his free hand up and down her legs. She gasped and ground her hips against him.

"You are as dark and wanton as a girl from the harem," he said against her ear, nipping her lobe softly between his teeth, distracting her as his hands drew up her skirts. "I may not read but I have heard of such women: girls in silks, smelling of ginger and honey, with jewels in their hair. Girls who dance."

"I cannot dance."

"No?" He fluttered his fingers up and between her thighs, dipping into her most delicate softness, delighted at how pliant and honeyed she was. She closed her eyes, her fingers clutching his shoulders, her hips bouncing and dancing in response to his caress.

"Alchemist by day and dancer by night, eh?"

Joanna was almost beyond speech. Hugh's fingers seemed to be trailing everywhere, elevating her body and freeing her mind. A fragment from the Song of Solomon drifted into her mouth and out of her lips, "'I am my beloved's and my beloved is mine.'"

He laughed and she was pleased with his laughter, but she wanted to touch him and he would not let her. Each time she tried to reach him with her hands—even so far as caressing his chest—he would block her with his hands.

"But you are lovely!" she burst out, kicking her feet against him in sheer frustration.

He grinned, his eyes bluer than any sapphires she had seen. "You are a naughty, wicked little harem girl. If I were a groom in an eastern lord's palace and caught you out-of-doors, I would use you thus."

He tossed her lightly back into the hay and, as she reared toward him, caught her round the middle and lifted her hips and legs. Head down, she tried to stretch to sweep her fingers across Hugh's back, but then he began to touch her again and she was helpless with pleasure.

"You smell delicious." Hugh lightly spanked her bottom and stroked her dark intimate curls. Soon he was patting between her legs and slapping her buttocks, alternating his attentions swiftly between each sweet place, and she was a growing rush of heat and delight. He lifted her higher and higher, patting and slapping, and the whole stables seemed to be glowing and she was as hot as the brazier and Hugh was glowing, too, and when he flicked her breasts with the tips of his fingers the rush of sweetness poured through her in a golden haze.

Hugh knew from her face she had known rapture and now he rolled her onto her side and entered her, adoring the way she was so tight yet so embracing. Dizzy with his own release, he tried to hold on, keep rearing and plunging, but she was too sweet, too comely, too much a harem girl dancer. He roared and flew with her, a pure masculine, primitive part of him howling like a wolf.

"The horses are restive," he said, an uncounted, unknown time later.

"I have no doubt," Joanna answered. Both of them were snug in the golden, prickly bed of hay, and she lay quiet in his arms, held hostage by his embrace.

And by her own desire, she admitted, as Hugh gave her a sleepy kiss and rolled his cloak into a ball for a pillow. She had not known such abandoned passion was real. But how could she? How could she feel so alive while her father was still under threat?

I should be trying to escape from Hugo, not snuggling with him.

Every day, that task seemed more impossible, as her feelings for Hugh became deeper. She did not want to hurt him. She wanted to please him.

Although not at the expense of my father.

While Hugh snored beside her, she lay awake, thinking.

Chapter 23

The Frenchman Mercury was outside her chamber when Joanna, accompanied by Hugh and Hugh's squire Henri, returned to it at daybreak.

"I have a message from your father," Mercury said in southern French, nodding to Hugh.

"What did he say to you?" Hugh demanded, stepping between her and Mercury.

Joanna repeated what the Frenchman had said, careful to translate it exactly. A tiresome three-way conversation ensued, with Mercury talking to Joanna and her translating to Hugh.

It seemed her father was well and the "red work" was going very well. Joanna took comfort in the thought that Solomon was back to pursuing his goal of finding the perfect elixir, the secret of life and all things, symbolized by gold.

"He thinks of you and prays for you every day," Mercury added. "He may have added more, I forget." He lowered his head, as if in penitence. "Do you forgive me?"

When Joanna did not instantly say, "I do," Mercury dropped to his knees on the flagstones. "Sweet lady, let me know I am pardoned, or I die!"

"Of course." Waving him to his feet, Joanna wondered how she had ever found Mercury charming. "How is David?"

Mercury's blankly handsome face grew still more blank.

"The man imprisoned in the donjon with you."

"Ah, the Templar! Good!"

"Is he in health? I heard he had been taken elsewhere."

"As to that, I know nothing. He is back with me. More quiet than before, more moody."

"Is he allowed out at all? Have any of his order visited West Sarum?"

Her urgent questions earned her another blank look. "He plays chess quite nimbly," Mercury said at length, as if he was imparting a major secret.

And that was all Joanna could discover. Mercury did not claim loss of memory or ignorance: he did not say anything. Joanna wanted to shake him.

Clearly she was not alone in her feelings, for Hugh suddenly slapped the nearest wall with a hand and said bluntly, "I'm for the garderobe. Watch him, Henri."

He stalked away, Beowulf padding along by his heels, and Joanna knew her chance had come. "I must get back to my father," she said in the French of Languedoc, confident that Henri knew nothing of what she was saying. "I do not know how I can do it, do you?"

Faced with a direct appeal, Mercury took her hand and kissed it.

"My lady, you must not distress yourself. If I may help in any way, I swear to you I will. Smile now, so this fat youth thinks we are flirting."

Joanna attempted a smile that she was sure was a grimace.

"Good! Now your father thrives and he is a good man: he was always kind to me."

"But I do not know what is happening!"

"Smile, my dear. We are all in that state, are we not? I

have no memory, but see? I trust in God and his saints. I have an amulet, a luck charm." Mercury deftly tucked at the small purse on his belt and dropped a small green- and blue-striped stone onto her palm. "Take this from me. It brings good fortune."

The stone was bright in her hand, and strangely, Joanna found herself touched. It was not much, but Mercury was trying. "Thank you," she said.

"That is better! A lady as pretty as you should not despair: it pains your looks. All will be resolved."

Joanna lifted the stone and held it up, as if admiring it in the light from the arrow slit. "I have to escape," she said in Languedoc. "My lord has given me another month to work, but I cannot work properly here and I have to see for myself that Solomon is safe."

"As is natural. You are a good child, and I will help you, if I can." Mercury looked beyond her. "The man returns. Say no more for now."

"Agreed," Joanna said quickly, her spirits lifting as Hugh strode back toward them. Yes, he was a lightweight, but Mercury would want to escape as much as she did, so they were natural allies. It was not much but perhaps it was a start.

Before she could make any kind of plan, however, the page Peter came with a message that Sir Yves was waiting for them in the great hall.

The lord of Castle Manhill was happy: it showed in his gleaming eyes and the way he swept from side to side on the dais, waving his arms as Joanna, Mercury, and Hugh filed into the hall.

"Join us!" he called, beckoning to his youngest son, and now Joanna saw the others, standing beside the benches and trestles that were drawn to the walls of the hall. It seemed every servant in the castle, from the lowest spit boy and laundress to the grandest steward, had been summoned.

Hugh gripped his sword hilt. "What is this? What has happened?"

"Is it David?" cried Joanna. "Is there news?"

At once Hugh shook his head: he had less faith in his father than she.

"Has King John died? No? Then has he been readmitted to the church again?"

Hugh pointed discreetly with the smallest finger on his left hand to a man folded into a stool on the dais beside the lord's central chair. When he stood up from the stool, Joanna guessed the stranger would be the tallest man she had seen: he was certainly the thinnest and most bald. The top of his high, domed head shone like a ram's skull. Dressed in mud-stained cloak and drab brown leggings, he wore no badge, no rings, yet it was clear Sir Yves knew him.

"Here is Capet, come fresh from your eldest brother's," Sir Yves announced, while Hugh said in an undertone to Joanna, "That explains it. Nigel treats his messengers like the meanest of serfs: none stay with him for long. This Capet is new to me."

Joanna looked at Capet more closely but could read nothing from the man's smooth, skinny face. He must not have brought bad news; at least nothing bad for Sir Yves.

"How is my elder brother?" Hugh asked, but Sir Yves spoke before the messenger.

"Nigel is well, he is always well. He has sent me a fine pair of gloves and a fine leather belt, a brooch, very finely wrought . . ."

"Is there another word coming, I wonder?" whispered Hugh to Joanna, who kicked him softly with her foot.

". . . and such excellent provisions! Rock samphire and

pepper, the finest salt. Fresh morel mushrooms and spring black truffles from his wife's family estates in Perigord. Even your strange fellow, who speaks only the language of the south of France, will know of such truffles. They are famous throughout Aquitaine!"

In an appalling, horror-struck flash, Joanna understood. Sir Yves had no news of David or of any great event: he had summoned them to the great hall in order to brag.

A squire was holding up each of the gifts as his lord spoke: first the embroidered gloves, then the bags of pepper and salt. He knelt by the fireplace to undo a small bag and the rich scent of truffles swept through the hall.

The servants standing by the trestles and wall hangings glanced at each other and began a pitter-patter of applause as the squire rose to display the truffles. The dogs were yapping in excitement, held back from mobbing the squire by Hugh's curt command. Hugh's face was thunderous.

Mercury, meanwhile, the "strange fellow," strolled up to the squire and put his face into the bag containing the small, dirty-looking spheres: the scent of the truffles was amazing but their appearance was a disappointment.

Mercury, his long nose still in the bag, inhaled deeply, then surfaced. "Good," he said, in the language of the south. "Not as exquisite as some I have known but very good."

"What does he say?" Sir Yves asked, his face reddened with pleasure.

"That they are exquisite," Joanna said quickly.

Hugh folded his arms across his chest and tapped a booted foot. "How does he know?"

But before Joanna could ask Mercury that very pertinent question, the Frenchman flung an arm around a startled Sir Yves and tried to do the same with Hugh, who struck aside his reaching hand. Mercury shrugged and whispered in Sir Yves's ear, who first looked startled and who then began nodding.

"The fellow does speak our French! He says he has just remembered it! That is as may be, but I think you should hear this, Hugh."

Hugh looked at Joanna as he stepped toward his father and in that instant, glimpsing Mercury's sanguine face, she knew.

Mercury, smiling, boyishly handsome, carefree Mercury, was betraying her confidences. He had suddenly and conveniently "remembered" how to speak Norman French and now he was telling Sir Yves and Hugh that she could not work properly at Castle Manhill, that she was still determined to escape. The man was only interested in himself and what he might win from such tale-bearing: he was not the least concerned what his "news" would mean for her.

I knew that he was charmingly selfish—why did I not consider how far that selfishness would go? Just because I would never tell a secret, why did I assume that all men are the same? Especially a man like Mercury?

Her heart felt as if it had dropped down within her body and the scent of the truffles seemed to clog her breath. She wanted to run from the great hall and keep on going. She felt people staring at her, marking her as different, strange, dangerous. She had not felt this way for years but she knew the dread too well: the stark yet creeping fear she and Solomon had struggled with, on and off, for all their lives.

On and on Mercury whispered, first in Yves's listening ear and then in Hugh's. Would he never be done?

Soon she would have to face her captors and give her own account.

Soon she would have to face Hugh.

Chapter 24

"Where are we going?" Joanna asked, as Hugh lifted her onto Lucifer and swung up behind her.

In truth she was glad to be getting out of the castle. Sir Yves had not spoken to her and would hardly look at her. Mercury had met her stricken look, smiled, and also said nothing. Hugh had hustled them from the great hall as if he had a pan of acid scorching somewhere that he must extinguish before it exploded. So far, he had not spoken either, except to warn her to watch her footing on the outside stone steps, still slick with rainwater.

As Hugh snapped on riding gloves she repeated her question.

"A place I know," came back the scarcely informative answer. "It is some way away, so we must hurry."

He snapped the reins and they were off at a smart gallop, Joanna hugging the horse's mane as they burst through the standing puddles of the bailey yard. Their speed was such that she had no breath to speak: she was too busy hanging on.

The day was bright and cloudy about them, rainbow weather, where all the new bright leaves and grasses were silvered with rain. Hugh checked Lucifer into a steady canter and tapped her on the shoulder—a sign of fellowship, she hoped—pointing to a small spinney lush with bluebells. She mouthed "pretty" but still was surprised when he drew rein directly alongside the woods.

"You said we had a way to go," she stammered as he unwound himself from Lucifer's back to lead the horse to the gap in the banked enclosure surrounding the spinney.

"Changed my mind. Besides, stopping now will save your thighs. Here will do us just as well."

"I do not mind," Joanna said quickly. "We can ride on."

Hugh shook his head and unlatched the hurdle gate, closing it behind them as they pressed deeper into the wood. Twisting round, Joanna could no longer see the track they had just left as the tall oaks, beech, and hornbeam loomed about her. In this dense grouping of trees the ground was bone dry despite the previous rain: Hugh's feet cracked on dry old leaves and Lucifer stamped on dry branches riddled with fungus.

"Do truffles grow here?" Joanna asked, for something to say.

"No." Hugh stopped by a fallen birch and tethered Lucifer to one of its prone branches. "Forgive me, I am a bear today. Nigel's gifts have that effect on me: I loathe the way he flaunts his lands and wealth."

Joanna knew she must have looked startled, for he smiled. "I suppose you want to talk about Mercury's very selective recovery of his memory this morning?"

I would rather pitch off this huge charger, bear you to these dry leaves, and love you, again and again. Joanna said nothing. Women were supposed to receive and serve but not initiate.

Hugh rested his hand against her thigh. An idle touch, perhaps an accident, perhaps a more deliberate taunt. She felt her body tingle and tighten in response.

"Would you move your hand a little?" She was pleased with how she sounded: courteous, as a lady to her knight.

He brushed her leg lightly with his fingers, trailing his hand from her thigh to her hip. "Is that better?"

She managed to nod. "I did not know he could speak Norman French."

"He will know that and English, too, when it is useful for him to recall it. When it serves him." He squeezed her thigh. "I should think your bishop has made a guess as to who Mercury might be and so has passed him on before the fellow claims to have recovered all his wits. That way Thomas can say later that he did not know who he was holding, and made a genuine mistake."

"He can say he meant no insult or disrespect," Joanna said, understanding what Hugh meant. She was vividly aware of his hand on her leg: his touch made her thigh throb and the blood prickle in the tips of her toes.

"And if I or my father later mistreat the fellow, that will also work in Thomas's favor."

How could he speak so calmly when she felt as if her head was boiling? "Perhaps my lord thought Mercury worthless. A lowborn knight without—"

Too late she stopped, but Hugh finished for her. "Without lands or riches, like me? Perhaps. The Frenchman is certainly sly enough to play it that way, if he thought it would win him an advantage. He made a mistake with the truffles, though: admitting the kind of knowledge that only comes through wealth."

"Unless he does not care anymore."

"Or perhaps he thinks my father's castle an easier place to escape from than the bishop's new donjon. As it seems do you."

They had come to it at last. Joanna straightened her spine and looked straight ahead into the lush canopy of trees. The sun flashed on the bright new beech leaves and her eyes pricked with tears in response. But she would not apologize. "You do what you feel you must. As do I."

"Even though we are lovers now?"

His question twisted in the space beneath her heart but she refused to cry. She flung the challenge of emotion back at him. "We are lovers, yes. But you do not release me."

Hugh sighed. He was still not angry, she realized, more disappointed. The sense of a blade being twisted just beneath her ribs increased. "You are disillusioned with me."

"Never!" Hugh snagged her by the waist, tugged her to him, and kissed her hard on the mouth. "Never."

He wrapped his arms about her and she her arms about him. She was hugging him and he was embracing her fiercely, whispering, "Never, never," and kissing her over and over.

She was swept off Lucifer into Hugh's powerful arms, tossed up into the air like a flapped blanket, and caught again. "Never," he said firmly. "I would scour hell for you."

"Yet you will not let me go!"

"Do you not know why? Have you not understood it?" Hugh sat down into a heap of leaves with her in his arms and now on his lap. He traced the line of her cheek with a finger. "Clever yet blind."

Joanna caught her breath. "What do you mean?"

"Ask yourself. What kind of lover is Bishop Thomas if he does not truly release your father? Promise you his release and keep his word? What manner of lover is he if he does not strive for your freedom? He rode away without looking back! If I keep you, it is to keep you safe."

He did not understand, the dolt. He was a man, and big and able, and he did not understand. "That should be my choice, Hugo."

"In a world that is like heaven, yes, I agree. It should be

your choice." He nipped her ear with his teeth. "This is not heaven."

He leaned back against the beech tree under which they sat while Beowulf yapped softly at Lucifer, making as if to leap at the horse. "Stay," said Hugh to both, and they were still.

"If I could do what you can with beasts, folk would call me witch." Joanna tapped Hugh's sword scabbard with her heel. "They would not dare call you such."

"As I say. We do not live in heaven." Hugh moved her foot away from his sword. "But I would still scour hell for you."

He wrapped his cloak about her. "You are so pale now. Too pale. You should be as brown as this beech mast." He knotted the cloak strings for her.

"What is it, Hugh? What are you working yourself up to say?"

"I have treasure. Not a vast amount, but some. I hoped Thomas would bargain with me for David, but to tell truth, your bishop will not let David go so long as he suspects my brother has relics hidden away somewhere. I think he may be happy to trade for your father."

He took her hands in his. "Let us get one of our kin out of there."

He would do this for her. Joanna felt a great wave of feeling rising in her chest and up her throat. She bunched her hands into fists, trying not to cry. He would do this for her. No one had ever offered so much.

"I—I—"

Now the wretched, blistering tears were coming, tearing out of her eyes. She could no longer hold anything back— the memories, the vileness was all rising in her mind again. She sat on his knee and sobbed, weeping with a passion she had never dared to show before.

"Sweetheart! Please, do not cry. We can do much, there is no need to cry." Hugh cradled and rocked her, horrified at what he had provoked. If he could, he would wrap her into his own heart to soothe her. "Do not cry, please do not cry."

She was talking, the words bursting out of her. It made him think of the bee swarm; a dark mass, hurtling through the air, faster than the flight of birds. She was incoherent: between the speed of her speech and her sobbing he could make out nothing. He waited until she had stopped shivering, and brought out his flask of mead.

"Drink."

She did so.

"I have a pie in a cloth: I filched it for breakfast this morning from the kitchens and only ate half. You have the rest."

She did so.

He clasped her, stroking her limbs as he might do a startled horse. He whispered a charm to calm her. When she sighed, he said, "Will you tell me?"

She shook her head. "It is a maze. All things, all together. My mother and the bishop and my father and our life."

Her mother, who had died. Not easily, he guessed. "For how long have you and your father—Solomon? How long have you and Solomon been on the run? That is what it is. There is something different about you both, quite apart from the alchemy."

She looked at his hands and then his face and said nothing. He sensed a long habit of silence and of flight.

"What is a puffer?" he asked, to break the silence. If she answered this, she might begin. "You told me once that you were no puffer."

"Someone who plays at alchemy. Or worse, who fakes it."

"Were you ever accused of being such?"

"There were other accusations."

She lapsed into silence. Hugh waited, recalling a doctor

he had encountered once at a tourney, one who was dark
like Joanna and sallow like Solomon. The doctor had been
highly skilled, setting limbs himself instead of reading
from a text and leaving the work to others. His nickname
round the camp was "Hands-Washer" but he was much
sought after. His patients survived. Hugh's own Jewish
healer, Simon, was much the same.

He said the word Joanna had spoken in the moment of
her rapture. "That is a Jewish word, I think. A Hebrew
word."

He saw her blush. "It is a holy word and I should not
have said it," she replied.

"You are Jewish?" Hugh asked. He wondered why he
had not seen it before, her likeness to Simon. But Simon
was off in France and he had always thought of folk as
from somewhere: from London, from Winchester, from
West Sarum. He had never thought of race.

"I think my family was. Father does not speak of it
much, it upsets him too much. I think his grandfather was
forced to convert. I know some prayers, some words. Not
enough." She put her head in her hands. "Father and I are
part of the lost."

The poignancy of the phrase brought tears to Hugh's
eyes. He felt ashamed of his own unthinking faith. The
Jews had killed Christ: that was all he had been taught, by
a priest. A priest in the same church as Bishop Thomas.

"And your mother?"

"She was small, like me, but very handsome. Dark hair.
Blue eyes. A strong face. She could sing. She knew many
songs, many Hebrew songs. I hear them in my dreams but
I cannot remember them properly by day."

"What happened to her?"

"We were living in York. My father sold herbs and
cures, my mother sold books." A small smile tugged at

the corners of Joanna's mouth. "She taught me to read. She once showed me the name of God."

Without thinking, Hugh crossed himself, then wished he had not. Joanna, deep in the past, did not notice the gesture.

"One day a priest came to our lodgings and wanted a book. He would not pay for it. He said we were people who should give everything, because of what we had done to Christ. Father and Mother talked after that and packed their things, everything we could carry. Even as a child I knew it was time we moved on.

"We went out of the city before curfew but the priest came back. He was on horseback and he rode ahead of his congregation. He wanted all my mother's books. He pursued us.

"It was evening. A bloodred sunset. The trees were bare, I think. No, that cannot be right: there were burning haystacks. I cannot remember. I remember my mother running, Father running, me running. I do not know where we ran. I only knew we must not let the mob catch us.

"We came to a village where a troop of men drank at a tavern. They joined in the chase, and more: they burned parts of the village and sacked the bigger houses and burned their haystacks. Those people lost everything, because of us, and we were still running."

Hugh could picture it too well. With shame he thought of his own men firing crops in Picardy, simply in high spirits. *Why had I never thought of the farmers?*

"In the end my mother dropped her sack of books and we finally escaped the troop and the raging priest, although our clothes were black with fire smuts. But on the road south of York she collapsed and died. Father said later that her heart must have burst with the effort."

Joanna closed her eyes. "That priest must have all her books."

She leaned her head on Hugh's shoulder, turning her

face toward him. He held her, breathing very slowly, very carefully. He wanted to smash that priest and even more smash himself, for being so thoughtless in his own past, and so blind to hers.

They sat together in silence, while birdsong returned to the woodland.

Chapter 25

Later Joanna stirred. "Love me," she whispered. "Love me, Hugo. I did not know what loving was, until I was with you."

Pity and desire warred in him, the one dampening the other, but then she began to kiss him and burrow her fingers into his tunic.

"Teach me, Hugo." She was coiling her fingers over his flanks, tugging his body hair. "Show me more." She giggled. "Show me your lance."

He raised his eyebrows at that and she laughed afresh.

"Please, Hugo?"

He heard the tension in her voice, and the inexperience. How had he ever thought her a mistress of any man? She was a babe in such matters.

Still, it was gratifying to have her asking him to teach her, and he was glad to go along with her game. "I would see you first," he countered.

Instantly she blushed a fiery red and her hands flew between her legs.

"My lady is not going first?"

She shook her head, adorable in her confusion. *All*

that intellect, squirrel, and you know less than a young tavern lass.

"Then you must pay a forfeit of my choosing."

He clasped her wrists. "Perhaps I should tie you up in ribbons, harem girl, and then release you at my pleasure."

He meant it as a jest, no more, but she stiffened in his arms and suddenly he had a girl as unyielding as a log in his lap. Instantly he released her. "Did I hurt you?"

She was breathing quickly, her color fading. He brushed her arm and found it cold, her face the same. "Whatever it is, I do not blame you," he said urgently, keen to reach out to her through whatever hell she was now reliving. "Whatever was done to you, whatever act you were forced to do, I do not blame you. Tell me or not. Whatever brings you ease."

Joanna looked into his anxious, loving face and was ashamed. She had told no one. But she wanted Hugh to understand.

She closed her eyes. "He forced me. One night he summoned me. I was so naive then! I thought I was going to him to answer questions about the movement of the stars. I never expected what I found." Joanna lowered her head. "My father never knew. Why give him grief over what he could not stop?"

Bishop Thomas had ordered her into his bed. He had bound her wrists and gagged her—not to stop her from struggling or crying out, because she would have dared do neither, but because in some way seeing her tied thus had excited him. He had used her in that way for a month, then cast her off.

"He called me cold." She had almost believed it. How could she do otherwise? Until she had met Hugh, Bishop Thomas had been the only man she had known in an intimate way. "Cold and useless in a man's bed."

"You are none such."

"I know that now." Joanna opened her eyes and looked at him. "I was never his true lover."

"Nor was he yours." Hugh kissed her hands, one after the other. "If he were, he would not keep you, or your father, in doubt of your safety."

"It is worse than that," Joanna admitted. "The reason I have been so keen to work, the reason I have tried to—to leave, has been because of this."

Hugh said nothing but waited patiently.

Joanna took another deep breath and told him of the dreadful sentence she and Solomon were under. "I know I am your hostage, but I am in truth also the bishop's. My father is out of the bishop's donjon for the moment, but my lord made it clear that if I do not give him gold or the elixir to everlasting life within this month, then he will take Solomon away from his work and cast him into the prison pit, the oubliette."

Hugh's brows drew together in a frown. "Where is this pit again?"

"It is under the donjon floor. There is a trapdoor—"

"Truly, then, an oubliette," Hugh muttered. "The worst kind of prison. And he cast David into it for a time."

Joanna said nothing. She was thinking of her father and of the month. How many days now did she have left? How much longer had Thomas allowed her? She could not remember.

"This pit. How many are in there?"

She shook herself. "I do not know. I try to pass them water, bread, when the guards allow me to. The guards think it a great jest to open the trapdoor to a hand-span and have me drop things down into the dark."

"Hell's teeth! And David was down there. My dreamer of a brother, cast into that dark."

"Yes. It must be a kind of hell."

"We must stop this. There must be a way."

"How?" asked Joanna. "How? I can use my skill to unlock the doors of the donjon, if need be, but I do not have the strength to fight the bishop's guards. I could drug them, but they will be wary of my potions and perhaps ordered by my lord not to drink them."

"Leave that to me," Hugh said, and his mouth set into a grim line.

Chapter 26

The following day, Hugh gathered his men, put Joanna's things onto a cart, and told his father they would be leaving.

"Excellent!" Sir Yves made no attempt to disguise his relief. He patted his large stomach, his pale blue eyes already looking past Hugh to the kitchen. "Thank Joanna for her excellent cordials and gold and such."

"You could thank her yourself."

"I think not. She might cry. I cannot cope with a weeping woman."

That evasive answer was no more than Hugh had expected.

"You will take care of the Frenchman?" He distrusted Mercury and did not want the man with him and Joanna on their risky mission, but he seemed too lazy to do much harm at the castle. Ever since he had come here he had spent his days lolling in the solar, in Sir Yves's private chamber, flirting with the maids and playing chess with the pages. Mercury spoke of fine wine and good food and, to Hugh's private disappointment, Sir Yves was much taken with him.

"Oh, he is no trouble. Did you know he told me yesterday

of a wine that aids the digestion? He is a fascinating fellow."

"That is good," Hugh answered, stroking the top of Beowulf's shaggy head. He felt an old pain stir deep in his gut but ignored it: Sir Yves would never change.

"Are you leaving soon, then?" Sir Yves asked, looking over Hugh's men and the cart. "You have not purloined anything of mine?"

"You ask each time, but you should know by now I do not do such things."

"It is a jest, boy! Only a joke."

Hugh moved toward him to embrace his father but Sir Yves backed off, his stocky frame radiating alarm. "You should be off. It is a long ride to where you are going."

"It is," Hugh agreed, as the feeling of a rusty knife in his gut increased. His father had not asked where they were going; he never did. "Give Nigel my good wishes, when his next messenger comes."

"I will." Sir Yves was smiling now that his younger son's departure was close. "I will."

"Does he always do that?" Joanna asked, when they were on their way. "Let you ride off without waving goodbye or giving you a blessing?"

"He has never done that for me, or for David. Only for Nigel."

Joanna touched Hugh's arm, wishing she could hug him. "Where are we going?" she asked. "You did not like to talk before."

"My father's castle has ears," Hugh replied tersely. "I wanted no sermons on my foolhardiness. But I thought— well, Thomas can hardly hurl your father anywhere if he cannot have you. He would be an alchemist short."

Joanna smiled, touched by his practicality. "There is more, though, is there not?" she persisted.

She felt him tug at her sleeves, then her skirts.

"Are these your grandest clothes?"

Joanna glanced at herself. She had dressed as she always did, in clean fresh under-linen and whatever gown was handy. Today, to her own private pleasure, it was the red gown that Hugh's maid Mary had passed to her.

"You gave this to me, or leastways the younger Mary did. Are you saying it is poor?"

"Not to me, but it is not *grand*."

"Fine gowns and sulphurs do not blend, Hugo. What is amiss?"

"Naught for me! But Templars are rich, and those at the Somerset house very rich, so we need to make a show. Before we reach Templecombe, we must change."

"Where you sent messengers and have had no reply?" Joanna craned about to look at him. "Is that wise?"

"Let them refuse to my face to help their brother monk," Hugh said, spurring on Lucifer.

At midday, when the troop stopped at a river ford to water the horses, Hugh's squire Henri raised the question of her clothing for a second time.

"Sir, your good lady will not do, dressed as she is." Henri spoke bluntly, man to man, his round face radiating honesty. "The Templars act as though they are higher than God."

"I know, and 'tis no grief to me," said Hugh.

"But our lady is too plain!"

"I know, and I have the remedy."

"Might I speak?" Mortified, Joanna tried to break in to the exchange, but Henri, legs akimbo and hands on hips, was fixed upon Hugh, who was checking Lucifer's hooves. Neither noticed her.

"Lady Elspeth is Joanna's height. We are less than three leagues from her manor," Hugh went on as Joanna fought to keep her temper. "She will give us a gown and stuff."

"Then let Elspeth wear it!" snapped Joanna, scandalized afresh as knight and squire looked at each other and smiled. "And if you would dress something, let it be a partridge!"

"Oh, lady, lady!" Laughing, Henri sat down in the river, grinning more as the men-at-arms erupted in mirth.

Hugh grabbed her by the waist, half tugging her off Lucifer as he smacked a kiss onto her mouth. "Enough complaint, squirrel. We go to Elspeth's and she can dress you in her finest."

Joanna was still seething two hours past noon, although she hid it, especially from the lady Elspeth. She told herself grimly it was necessary, that Hugh and Henri were right, that she should not fret while their main goal was in sight. But afterward, she decided, and once her father and David were secure, then Hugh would have a severe reckoning with a pail of cold water.

"Joanna? Do you like this gown?"

Too late, she realized she had been frowning and tried to show her genuine gratitude to Elspeth, who had welcomed her into her manor as if she were a prodigal daughter.

"It is beautiful," she said automatically, then looked truly and gasped.

The gown laid over the plain wooden chest in Elspeth's modest solar was a sunburst. A rich deep color, it shone back into Elspeth's thin, freckled face, turning her golden and her narrow braids of red hair a luscious red-gold. It had sleeves as wide as sails, each sleeve trimmed with ribbon of the brightest blue, and a scooped neckline edged in blue. It shimmered like mercury, a thing of eastern glamour in this English, butter, cheese, wattle and roses house.

"It was gifted to my grandmother by her husband, Sir Thomas." Elspeth sat on the chest beside the gown. "There is a story in the family that he brought the cloth back with him from Outremer, intending it as a gift for a bride."

"What was his full name?" Hugh asked, speaking for the first time in an age. He was standing by the window shutters with a hand half-raised, as if dazzled by the gown.

"Sir Thomas of Beresford. He returned from the Holy Land much scarred, it is said, and in doubt that any woman would agree to wed him."

"But your grandmother did."

"She did, Joanna, although in truth the match was a scandal of the district." Elspeth looked at her steadily. "She was a widowed smith's wife, claimed by some to be a serf, by others that she was a Jewess."

"I have heard of Thomas of Beresford," Hugh said, parsing his thoughts. "A doughty fighter in his time. The Jews, too: they had Joshua and David. She must have been lovely, your grandma," he added, surprising Joanna.

Elspeth, twice widowed herself, returned his smile. "My boys say my red hair comes from her, and my temper."

"You? Temper?" Hugh said, but Elspeth waved aside his flirting with a crisp "Go back to your mead cup: this is your lady's choice. I have a veil, also, Joanna, if you would wear it. Pink as my roses. You must have a rose for your hair: it would look well against your dark tresses and skin."

"But but your rose is so unusual: I marked it when we came in. To bloom so early is rare indeed!" Joanna was confused by this generosity, and to her horror, she was prattling on with inanities: now she even felt the prickle of water in her eyes. "Do you not want every bud for yourself?"

Elspeth continued to look at her steadily. "Hugh," she said, without breaking eye contact, "your wolfhound needs a walk and so does my spaniel."

At once, Hugh detached himself from the wooden wall paneling and whistled to Beowulf, scooping a shaggy, loose-limbed dog off a stool. "This creature does need something," he mumbled. "He is all fat and hair."

"Away!" Elspeth pointed to the door. She waited until Hugh and dogs were out of the chamber and closed it after them, waving to Henri kicking his heels in the great hall before turning back.

"Hugh heeds me because I am the age his mother would be," she said, "but what can I do for you, my dear?"

"Forgive me for asking," Joanna said bluntly, throwing caution to the wind, "but why do you want to help? I am a stranger."

"Ah! You are another one like Hugh, unused to it! Wary of others, too. I saw that at the tourney."

Joanna put her hands behind her back so Elspeth would not see her shaking fingers. "Where was this? I did not see you."

Elspeth strolled to a couch beside a piece of weaving and picked up a spindle from the couch. She teased out the spindle wool between finger and thumb, then began to twirl her spindle weight as she spun more thread.

"I took care to stay away from those foolish girls in the wagon," she said, spinning more thread. "Berengaria and Matilde and their kind are not for me. But to answer you fully, Joanna, I owe Hugh the life of my middle son. Hugh saved Gerald at a mêlée in Picardy and brought him home to me. Since then Hugh knows he is always welcome here; he and any one of his."

"I am not his, not in the way you believe. Our paths run together for a space, that is all."

"I see. Still my question remains. What may I do for you?"

Joanna glanced at her fingers. They were stained with potions again. The answer, *Make me beautiful for Hugh,* hovered in her mind but instead she said, "How did you guess? My grandfather was forced to convert."

Elspeth sighed and spun more thread. "The teaching of our church is not generous to Jews, any more than it is generous to women." She wound the thread about her spindle. "What else?"

"Lady Elspeth?"

"What else has happened to you? I see much, I dream truly of the future and I see the shadows in your eyes."

Thoroughly disconcerted by the older woman's uncanny directness, Joanna looked away to the window. An earthenware pot of those pink early roses shone on the deep sill and for a foolish instant she had a sense of another time, another woman, carrying a similar jug and posy to stand there.

"What was it? A lifetime of being discovered? Hunted? Moving on under cover of dark?"

Joanna felt herself sway as the memories assailed her. Before she fell, she sat down on the stone floor, making a play of studying the golden robe.

"How much does Hugh know?" Elspeth asked softly.

"The death of my mother." The gold cloth shimmered before her eyes. "When we reached West Sarum and Bishop Thomas became our patron, my father hoped we were safe."

She heard the snap as Elspeth placed her spindle on the floor.

"But Thomas is a greedy man who wants more and so he threatens, I presume."

Joanna said nothing. She felt Elspeth's hands on her shoulders.

"I will help all I can. I will help *you*, Joanna. For the sake of Hugh, for my grandmother who was once hunted like you, for my grandfather Thomas, who saved her, and for myself."

Confused, Joanna raised her head.

"There is a fable that goes with this gown." Elspeth sat down beside her. "It is said in my family that grandmother Gila put a charm on the silk: that great good fortune should come to the womenfolk in our house if we loaned or gifted the gown to another, a woman who was in greatest need herself."

She smiled, showing a chipped front tooth. "I have a mind for some good luck, so I will gift the gown to you. I know you have need, for I can see it. Forgive me for being blunt, but I sense, too, that you have little time to waste."

She rose to her feet and clapped her hands. At once two pages almost fell into the solar in their haste to obey.

"The lady will bathe here. Tell my maids to come in and the menfolk to keep out."

"Including Hugh?" Joanna asked as the lads hurried off, bright in their tunics of blue and red, like a pair of hungry kingfishers.

"Hugh will wait with the rest, or answer to me."

The lady Elspeth held open the door for her maids to carry the bathtub out into the great hall, for anyone else to use it if they wished. She nodded to Hugh and Henri, playing dice on the high table. "You may go in now."

"Find the others and tell them to be ready," Hugh told Henri. He was tired of loitering about like a courtier at King John's court. He wanted them to be away to Templecombe, to gird the warrior knights at their own tilting ground.

"Softly, Hugh," Elspeth warned as he strode toward her. "The lady is as balanced as an angel on a pin, but without an angel's wings."

"Hmm." Sometimes Hugh thought Elspeth spoke the greatest nonsense, but she glowered at him, so he tried. "I will do my best."

She stood aside and he stalked into the solar.

Joanna has done it. She has turned herself into gold, was his first thought. She shimmered in gold, in a gown that scooped low over her bosom, flared over her hips, nipped about her waist. She held out her hand to him and her arm spilled gold in a rustling whisper. She was the beautiful still point in a river of gold, her face and eyes gleaming.

"My lady." Never had he meant it more profoundly.

"I am still your alchemist," said the glittering figure. "See? I wear my belt with tassels. Lady Elspeth found me a replacement tassel."

Somehow that absurd human detail was enough to make it possible for him to touch her. He kissed her fingertips, bowing low over her hand. "Unstained for once," he remarked, knowing this would irk her.

"As you say." She was calm: he wondered for a wild instant if she were laced so tight that she had to keep her cool. He missed the golden net for her hair: he liked the contrast; the bright threads against the dark. But the billowing long veil, pink as sunset, was pretty. He was torn between wishing to set her on a dais and adore her, and tug her into his arms.

"Should we not be going? I heard you ordering Henri."

"We have time."

She looked as puzzled as a bewildered angel and he pounced, catching her against him. She felt softer than flower petals and both warm and cool; a trick of the woman and the silk.

"Harem girl," he whispered, and kissed her, grinning as she lanced her tongue into his mouth, jousting with him for a delicious moment, until it seemed she came to her wits.

"We cannot do this here!" she hissed, squirming to pull back from him.

"We can if we are quick," he whispered in return, gathering her still more snugly. "Henri has gone for the men, and the lady to her kitchen."

She stared at him, and then a fierce, determined expression came over her slim face. Next instance, she was dragging him away from the window, whispering as they both tripped on a wolf-skin rug, "Here, then, stand here, by the door. It opens inward, so we shall have warning." She kicked the rug aside.

He was now blocking the door and she was unbuckling his belt. He seized her silken skirts and billowed them upward, his fingers entering her an instant later and then himself.

"Ooof!" She closed her eyes, her face flushing with fresh pleasure.

"Harem girl, harem girl." He kissed her as he thrust deep within her, laughing as the door creaked behind them. Grabbing her hips he pounded harder, feeling the pleasure explosion building steeply in his loins.

"Hugo!" In her bliss she bucked in his arms, her feet leaving the stone flags as he rode her, her cries becoming sharper, higher. Driving his tongue into her mouth, he tasted her orgasm as she yielded utterly, her throbbing parts more lush and luxurious than any silk.

"Mine!" His own force rushed through him, speeding into her. The door shuddered and the world rocked about them and he did not care. He was master of all and Joanna was his, his own harem girl, overwhelmed in his arms.

"Are you well?" he asked later, brushing down her skirts.

She gave him a sweet, dreamy smile. "I am, lord. Very."

She looked better than well: she was a placid, languid angel with crumpled golden wings, and, madly, he found his desire stirring again.

Which was impossible. They were just in time as it was, for as he guided her back from the door, Henri pounded back into the great hall, shouting, "We are ready, sir! All done!"

Chapter 27

Joanna rode with Hugh pillion behind her. She tried to think of the Templars, of their meeting with the order, but was distracted and undone by pure sensation. The silk dress seemed to have stimulated her to more passion. All she could think of was when she and Hugh would join again in love.

Perhaps the gown is bewitched, she thought, her hips and the space between her thighs tingling as the silk slid against her like Hugo's tongue and the galloping of Lucifer jolted deep inside her.

What if we are making children by this lovemaking? she asked herself, but then all she could think of were youngsters with black hair and blue eyes; strong sons and clever daughters. She would teach them to read. She must teach Hugo to read and reward his progress with kisses.

"Is the sun too hot for you, Joanna? We can stop."

She could hear the need in his voice and feel it, hard as a saddle pommel, against her buttocks. A daydream of lust flared through her but she managed to croak, "We have no more time. We must reach Templecombe today."

Hugh kissed the top of her head. "We are already within

sight of the combe, as you would know if your eyes were as strong as your heart."

She jabbed at his rock-hard thigh with her fingers. "Instead of taunting, my knight, why not send your men ahead as messengers?"

Then they would be alone, she was about to add, but Hugh was already shouting orders and the road was suddenly filled with dust and flying stones as the troop galloped away. She felt the ground shuddering and then all became still, a thread of birdsong the only break in the silence.

"There." Hugh pointed to a small wicker enclosure off the road; a place where herdsmen kept animals in times of winter flooding. Leaning down from his horse, he untied the hurdle gate and urged Lucifer inside. The stallion whickered softly, then bent his head to a mound of windfall crab apples, clearly left in the pen as fodder.

"Eat all those, boy, and you will be ill," Hugh warned, sliding off the horse's back and leading him away from the tempting pile. He tethered Lucifer by a hawthorn bush and swiftly gathered the horse a few apples and more grass and hay from the surrounding hedgerow.

Joanna looked about. They were in a hollow of landscape and the spring sun was very warm. Above her the sky was as blue as a sparrow's egg, threaded through with a latticework of branches from a stand of wild cherries, apples, and black poplars.

The pen, bordered by sturdy wicker hurdles, was filled with packed-down sheep dung, but there was a smooth round oval of stone beneath an old, cracked apple tree whose blossoms were just starting to wilt. Hugh swept his cloak over the boulder.

"We are hidden by the tree," he said as she alighted from

the horse. "You are becoming more nimble at that. Soon you will be riding alone."

Joanna shook her head. "Truly, have we time? Will the Templar Knights not be looking for us, as soon as your men tell them we are coming?"

Hugh shrugged. "No grief to me. I will say Lucifer cast a shoe."

"But to lie to men in holy orders!"

His blue eyes flashed black for an instant. "Why not? They do naught for David, though they are but a two-day journey or less from West Sarum! I think to lie is no sin."

Her previous desire was giving way to scruples and hesitation. "We are on a road."

"We are off a road and under a tree." He caught her round the middle and drew her close, unwinding her from her travel cloak. "It is too warm for this when you are not riding, and I wish to see you in your pretty gown by sunlight."

She knew by the glint in his eye he meant more than looking. "Hugh, someone may come."

"At this hour, so close to noon? I think not. All folk will be at their board and dining tables." He let her go, stepped back, and motioned with his fingers. "Do a curtsy for me, sweet. I like the way you rustle as you move."

"You are wild," she remonstrated, although in truth it was balm to her, to be admired and yes, to be, lusted over. Thomas had lost interest in her almost as soon as he had plundered her virginity. Hugh seemed to want her still, as urgently as she desired him.

Flattered, she spread her golden skirts and swept as low as if he was King John.

"Hey, hey, you will get dirt on your gown." Hugh clasped her elbows and drew her up to his lips for a swift, tickling kiss. "A lady never bows so far, 'tis her knight that should be grateful."

He cupped her bottom in one of his large hands and tongued her ear close to where her veil was pinned. His act pulsed through her like a shower of sparks.

"I am always grateful."

He traced the length of her thigh with his fingers and the furnace between her thighs glowed hot in answer. She touched him in return, running a hand across his flanks, wishing she could undo his clothes as easily as he always seemed to undo hers.

"My lady."

He kissed the side of her neck.

"Always my lady." Abruptly, he moved sideways and she lost her footing as he coiled a muscular arm about her waist. Before he could guess what he was about, he plucked her from the churned-up earth and sheep dung.

"Hugo!" Her arms flailing, she tried to beat his legs, but he ignored her protests, upending her further so her bottom was raised and her head down.

"Such a juicy little rump, tilted at me. I have a mind to enjoy you this way. A lush pleasure for both of us, I warrant."

His other hand dived under her gown and his fingers kneaded her bottom. Dizzy with sensation, she closed her eyes and now she felt the boulder warm beneath her belly. She was draped over the round stone, her face nestled in Hugh's cloak. He had put his cloak over the boulder, she realized, as his fingers pleasured her still more intimately, skimming gently through her folds as a bee might rumple through the heart of a flower. He had planned this.

"Ravisher!" she managed to spit at him, but he chuckled, fingering her more until she mewed with pleasure.

"No other lady but you, Joanna. You give my fancy flight. Hell's teeth, but you are delectable! Such a pink, round—"

He came into her then, fiercely and strongly, and her last scruple, of being seen, was gone. The golden gown seemed to pillow them both and for an instant she had again a sense of a different time: another knight and his lady had joined in this way, blessed by silk and sunshine.

Chapter 28

She was quiet now, his lady alchemist. Going at a slow canter across a low, wide valley filled with scattered trees, meadowlands, and sheep, he suspected that she dozed in his arms and was pleased, feeling very proud of himself.

"I can see smoke," Joanna announced, checking the pinning of her veil with one hand while the other gripped Lucifer's black mane with a vengeance. "What can I hear?"

They were riding toward the main road along a track boarded by an blooming apple orchard on one side and a vast plot of vines on the other. The rows of vines on sunlit slope were being tended by two crouching figures in drab homespun. These gardeners made no sound but the ground thundered like a struck drum.

"Knights, practicing gallops and charges," Hugh explained, his blood stirring at the familiar sounds. This was a male world, a world of charge and thrust, a world he understood.

He almost rumpled Joanna's hair but thought better of it. "When we pass this hedge and turn onto the road, you will see them."

"More horses," said Joanna, in tones of such disgust he almost laughed, but scraped the lees of his memory instead, recalling the dregs of a single visit here, years ago with David.

He must never forget that David was imprisoned, when by rights his brother should be here, riding with his brother knights.

"There is a handsome church," he added, choking back the useless, black anger that smothered him whenever he thought of David at West Sarum. "And an abbey across the valley and stream."

Mother of God, I sound like a doting father or husband, pointing out what I know will please her.

He spurred Lucifer and the great horse responded, pricking back his ears and swinging round the corner onto the main road, almost colliding with a great iron-wheeled cart, dragged by mules, that lumbered up the slope toward the middle of the settlement. Smoothly speeding past the cart, Hugh heard the curses of the mule driver as he was struck by a shower of muddy clods from the churned-up road.

He grinned. "One back for the traveler. Those iron carts are a devil."

"At West Sarum they keep me awake at night with their endless clanking. Oh!"

"The warhorses grow very weary quickly and must build their strength as their knights do," Hugh explained, thinking she had spotted the grooms busy tending lathered, steaming mounts close to the road, but she was pointing to a small, round building off to the side of the road, close to a blacksmith's forge and then a farrier's forge. Made of wood and thatch, the place that was neither church nor house was topped by a cross.

"The Templars' presbytery, and I would not point too long," Hugh warned. "David told me nothing, but 'tis said they have strange rites in those small chapels."

"As it is said that Jews eat babies?" Joanna answered

quietly, twisting in his arms to give him a steely look beneath her pink veil.

"There are my men." Hugh was relieved to change the subject, though he acknowledged her hit with a small grunt and a nod. "By the alehouse! I should have guessed."

His men, sitting outside a low-roofed hovel with a bush on a pole hanging over its dark open door, stood up from their bench, raised their cups and gave him a ragged cheer.

"These knights have no hostelery for guests?" Joanna queried.

"They will have somewhere," Hugh replied, raising his voice to cover another thundering charge from the common lands running beside the length of the village. "The last time I came here, I did not stay."

She moved again, her backside snug aside him, reminding him of sweeter times. Now she looked over the common fields, although no pigs browsed these meadows. Instead a troop of men on horseback pitched and wove round wicker poles and pens, hacking clumsily at man-shaped targets with their swords. Mud flew like rain over the field, and dust and grit made a dirty cloud over the whole common.

He felt her flinch and gripped her with his thighs a little more snugly. "Better a clean stroke," he said softly.

"Or none, Hugo."

"Perhaps." He noticed one of the hunting dogs creeping toward a young groom playing with a spinning top on a cleaner part of the road and shouted at it. The dog whined and fell back.

The smell of fresh bread overcame the stink of sweat, horses, and dogs and, like Joanna, he followed his nose, turning his head to check where the cookhouse was.

"Something to eat?" he asked her, but a new cry bellowed out from the common field.

"Destroyer comes! The Destroyer is here!"

Joanna's knuckles whitened in Lucifer's black mane. "How do they know you? You wear no armor, or badge."

"They have been told of our coming, and no doubt some recognize my horse," Hugh said grimly, aware, as Joanna was not, that their privacy was over. "Now they will all want free lessons."

"In jousting? But if you do that, surely they will owe you in return?"

The Templars are ever poor payers, Hugh thought, but he did not have time to speak. Already the troop were stampeding toward them in a swirling mass. Some fools had even couched their lances as if they expected him to fight.

"That red-beard has his lance too low, besides," he growled.

"You can show him."

She sounded calm, but her limbs were as cold and stiff as metal. He sensed her terror, though she showed nothing. *My lady? She is my queen!*

"Stop!" he roared, standing up in his stirrups, folding his arms crosswise across Joanna, to shield her. "Are you blind? My lady is upon my horse!"

Joanna clamped her eyes shut, repeating a fragment of an ancient prayer in her mind: all she could remember at that moment. The road seemed to shift beneath her as the world about her shrank to horses galloping; warhorses galloping in a dark storm.

Because Hugh was a warrior and she did not want him to think her cowardly, she straightened her shoulders and let go of Lucifer's mane. That simple act made her feel as if she was letting go of a safety rope on a high tower.

She opened her eyes. Hugh's long, strong arms and large, sinewy hands filled her vision. Surrounding his spreading fingers like a nimbus was a cloud of standing dust and the ground about them shook like an old dog scratching for fleas. "Sit, or you will fall!" she hissed, but he shook his head.

"I have no buckler, so I shield you how I can.

"Hold there!" he roared out again. "Any who touches my lady will answer to me!"

She heard horses snorting and skidding and one blood-chilling crunch and a scream as some of the great beasts must have collided. What shrieked out in pain, whether man or beast, she could not tell: as quickly as it sounded the cry was over and a heavy, breathing quiet hung like a miasma over the meadow. A faint bleating of lambs in a hidden valley came to her and a man calling a toast to "Our fair lord Hugh." The rest of the common was silent.

Hugh jumped down from Lucifer and drew his sword.

"Come at me who will," he challenged, keeping his blade lowered but his arm tense. "Only let a squire guide my lady in comfort to your hostelery."

"No need, Hugh de Manhill. You are both our guests."

The man who spoke rode out from the middle of the messy column of men and horses and swung down from his richly arrayed mount. He had removed his helm but he was in full armor and he clanked a little as he strode across the field and into the road. Joanna bit her lip to stop herself from smiling: this was a vital encounter, and much rode on this meeting.

Closer the man strode, stumbling over a dropped mace that jutted from the mud. His leggings were caked in mud and his chain mail up to his waist was thick with the stuff. She saw a look of longing cross Hugh's face and was astonished at the brutish ways of men.

"I am Sir Gaston de Marcey," the half-mud figure said. "Late of Outremer and head of this preceptory."

His face was burned by years of hotter suns than she had known, Joanna acknowledged, as his smooth, beech-brown features clarified from the murk and dust. He wore a golden earring in his right ear and his nose had once been broken and had mended somewhat amiss. Beside him, Hugh was taller, leaner, and more handsome. She loved the way the breeze tousled his rich black hair, something she promised she would do herself later. His hair had grown a great deal, she thought inconsequentially.

But now here was serious business, and she prayed that Hugh would not charge into it at once.

He began well. "I thank you for your welcome, Sir Gaston. I know your family has won great renown as warriors in the East."

Sir Gaston took the compliment without any sign of pleasure. "That is so."

He was very high and mighty, Joanna decided. Beside her, Hugh's face darkened as Sir Gaston added, "I am surprised that you do not join in this holy crusade. To destroy the infidel and the Jew"—and he looked directly at her—"is the right ambition for any Christian knight."

"My brother, Sir David Manhill, is already one of your order."

Let him recognize David as one of theirs, Joanna thought, still smarting after the Templar's insult, but Sir Gaston merely remarked, "That is so. Allow me to escort you to our hostelery, where you may refresh yourself."

Self, not selves, Joanna noted, feeling more dismissed. She found herself gripping the silk of her gown and unclenched her fingers. She was determined to balance elegantly in the saddle as Hugh slapped Lucifer's haunches and he and the horse started after the grubby but haughty Sir Gaston.

Let him speak now of David, she prayed. *Let this proud Templar say that the order will help Hugh secure David's freedom.*

"Good horse," said Sir Gaston, marching along the road, tossing his gloves to a scampering page.

"Sir Raymond thought so," Hugh replied, giving Beowulf a pat as the wolfhound padded at his heels. "He was sorry to let him go after the tourney where I took him and his brother prisoner."

"Such tourneys are frowned on by our holy church," said Gaston severely, ignoring the reference to any brother. He stepped off the road and approached a small thatched building Joanna took to be a barn.

"Yet you know my jousting name."

"I could not fail to mark it, with your men bawling to you like market women. Now, Sir Raymond is of a good family."

Sir Gaston pushed open a low, warped door. "Our next holy service is at terce, should you wish to join us in our chapel. A groom will tend your horse."

Hugh thrust his head into the gloomy barn and backed out rapidly. "Scarcely a place for a lady."

Sir Gaston remained unperturbed. "That is our guest-house. A squire will bring you a brazier and food, should you wish to eat in private."

He does not invite us to dine with the order, Joanna observed. *Is that because of me?* For a moment she was ashamed, guilty of her family and her past, but then Hugh spoke.

"This *sty* is not sufficient for my lady." He hit the daub wall and a huge flake came away with his fist. "Find us a better place."

Sir Gaston shook himself like a fighting cock. "It is our guest chamber!"

"Do you know where your brother knight rests today? The brother whom your order has betrayed?"

The Templar stiffened at Hugh's mention of David. "We are a poor company here."

"Armed to the eyebrows and beyond! You are rich as Croesus, man!"

Sir Gaston's beech-tanned face was now as red as fire. "Not so! All is for God! A Christ that woman knows no part of! She is a Jewess!"

He choked on the rest as Hugh slammed him against the door, causing a hinge to snap with an explosion that sounded like a crossbow strike. Impossible as it seemed, he paled as Hugh bent his dark head closer, his handsome face now a gargoyle snarl.

"She is also a skilled and subtle alchemist and if she wants to pour a flagon of boiling mercury down your scraggy throat, I will help her! For shame, man! Jew or Christian, or Muslim, we are all people of the Holy Land, and you should well know it. How did you miss that lesson?"

Sir Gaston struggled limply in Hugh's grip. Seeing him thinking of yowling to his men, Joanna entered the fray.

"Sir Gaston!" She pitched her voice so he had to look at her. "I have spoken with David. I know what he has carried with him from Outremer. I can help him escape from the bishop of West Sarum, but we ask your help. A few men, 'tis all."

"You cannot know what he has: he vowed secrecy before God!"

Hugh did not know that her words were a lucky guess but he backed her to the hilt. "That is neither here nor there. Think of the sacred relic that will enrich Temple-combe when David is free to return here."

"I cannot be seen to go against the Bishop of West Sarum. He has the ear of the king. And you!" He jabbed a finger at Joanna. "You are his leman! His sorceress! A foul spawn of Jewish alchemists. Ach!"

"You keep a gracious tongue before my wife," Hugh said grimly. "More, and you and your knights will answer to me in personal combat. I will take you hostage and your order can pay me for ransom."

He calls me wife!

Sir Gaston was stammering an answer but Joanna could not hear it. She had never dared to hope to be anyone's wife. After the bishop, she had never thought she would be anyone's lover. To be lover and called wife was better than gold; suddenly she had a new and lovely word to play with.

"My husband treats his captives better than Bishop Thomas deals with his." Joanna paused to let the threat sink in, then added, "It may be, husband, that my lord bishop will exchange Sir Gaston for your brother."

Sir Gaston stared at her, then Hugh. "You would not dare."

Hugh tightened his grip some more. "You will not help us willingly, why should we not?"

Suddenly, he pitched the smaller man into the guest chamber, coming out an instant later. "He is sleeping."

Joanna's heart plummeted. "Not forever?"

Hugh shook his head. "We should leave, though." He sighed. "Hell's teeth! I cannot trust the bishop, but I have no stomach to take that arrogant fool of a Templar with us."

"I do not blame you."

Hugh straightened a little as she said this. Glancing about to ensure that none of the Templars had noticed that Sir Gaston was no longer with them, he scowled at the page holding Sir Gaston's gloves. "I truly hoped they would help. Face-to-face, I thought David's brother monks would not refuse me."

"I know." It pained her to see his hopes so dashed.

"What are these relics you mentioned? Has David told you something?"

Joanna shook her head. "He has told me nothing. I spoke of what I hoped would catch Sir Gaston's interest."

"Pity it could not have kindled his courage, also." Hugh swung back into the saddle behind her. "This may be a rough ride. My men will know to follow: we have fled such traps before."

Joanna nodded. The prospect of the wild gallop did not alarm her as it should have done: her head was busy with other matters.

He called me wife. Hugh called me his wife.

Chapter 29

Lady Elspeth greeted them in her small orchard. Though she was in truth very surprised to see them, dirty and disheveled with travel and Hugh's men glowering at anything that moved, she took care not to show it.

"Not a success, I take it?" she remarked, waiting for a scowling Hugh or a pale Joanna to answer.

Hugh cursed long and heartily, several of his men joining in as they all sat slumped on their horses, steaming with tiredness and ill temper. She allowed them to rant and put down her basket of apple blossom to study Hugh's girl more closely.

Joanna, sitting before Hugh, was proud and straight in the saddle, although to Elspeth's experienced eyes she looked ready to fall off Lucifer.

"No one died," she said now.

"No grief to me if they had." Hugh launched into another spate of baleful language, which Elspeth ignored. Something more important had happened than Hugh and his troop having to outrun more armed men: Joanna was weary and triumphant together. She looked as Elspeth's daughter had looked just after giving birth to a healthy boy.

"What has happened?" Elspeth asked.

She listened to a garbled tale of Hugh's. The Templars had refused to help. He had told them Joanna was an alchemist and instead of being impressed and asking her for gold, the head of the preceptory had called her a sorceress. The Templars were ungrateful, idle pigs.

"We left after I had knocked de Marcey unconscious. The others scarcely gave chase," he finished, in deep disgust.

"Terrible indeed," said Elspeth, marking how Joanna had not interrupted or corrected this account. Her eyes were very bright and her cheeks flushed with color.

She looks loved and in love, Elspeth thought. She was glad, and for a brief, selfish moment, envious, but mostly she was happy for this handsome young couple. She wished them both very well.

"You and your people rest here tonight, Hugh," she said, mentally checking through her stores and deciding she had sufficient bread and leeks for Hugh and his men. She had a good venison tart, too, and she and Joanna would have a taste of that in her own private solar. Out of the way of men, Joanna would be happy to talk, she guessed.

Elspeth smiled, anticipating a gossipy, girlish evening.

"What did you talk about with Elspeth for so long?" Hugh asked later. He stretched out like a great cat on the sheepskin rug before the fire.

"Our own private room." He looked about, his eyes lingering on her, sitting on a stool with a small psalter in her hands. "Very fine indeed. Elspeth has not let me in here before, nor anywhere near her precious books. The last time I stayed, I was out in the hall with my men."

"Good," Joanna said honestly, before she realized she had spoken her thought aloud. "We chatted on women's matters." Elspeth had urged her to tell Hugh more of her past. She rose from the stool and carefully put down the psalter. "Will you have more mead?" She plucked a flagon of Hugh's favorite drink off the floor.

"You will need to come closer than that to pour it." Hugh tugged off his tunic and tossed it down as a pillow for his elbow as he lounged on his side. "The fire feels good."

"When I first saw you, I thought you a salamander, a true lover of fire," Joanna confessed, edging closer with the flagon and knowing she was hesitating.

"Still shy with me, sweet? Is it because this is our first real bed?" Hugh's blue eyes lightened as he smiled. "Should I sleep on this rug?"

"Do you want to?"

He stretched his arms above his head. "Pour me my mead, wench, and stop fussing with nonsense."

There was a knock at their door. "Enter!" Hugh called.

Henri pushed open the door but remained on the threshold. "Sir, I am sorry." His round, shiny face was puce with embarrassment.

"Out with it, lad." Hugh was already rising to his feet.

"James and Malcolm are playing dice in the great hall. You said I should tell you, sir, if they were gaming."

"You did right." Hugh kicked aside the rug as he strode for the door, calling over his shoulder, "Take your ease, Joanna. I may be a while with these fools: they dice and quarrel in equal measure. Hell's teeth! They are already at it!"

He stormed out, Henri stumbling after him, as there was a crash from the great hall, and the cry of a maidservant, and the breaking of pottery.

Joanna took her cup of mead to the fire and sat on the

rug where Hugh had been. Staring into the twisting flames, she thought of her father. How was he faring? Was he safe? Did Bishop Thomas know she had left Castle Manhill? How could she find out about Solomon? Could she and Hugh somehow bring her father and David out of their captivity? How could they do it?

The walls of the manor fell away. It was no longer spring but winter and she was no longer snug and safe inside a house but out on the road. Limping and cold, she labored on alone, wondering where she was.

The wolves came out of the freezing winter fog and raced toward her, teeth barred and tails aloft like war banners. As she backed against a tree with no head-holds to climb, the wolves changed into men.

"Filthy Jew!" the leader shouted as they closed in on her, pawing her with hot, greedy hands.

"Joanna!"

Hugh was holding her, smoothing her hair. "You are safe, Joanna. It is a dream. You are safe."

The wolf-men vanished as she opened her eyes and looked into Hugh's calm face. He waggled his ears at her, a trick she had never seen before from him and which, in another mood, would have delighted her.

"Finally a smile." Hugh swung her onto the bed and covered her with a blanket. "I have sent for some tisane. You are chilled to the bone. You need soft bedding and care."

"I let the fire go out." Her tongue felt stiff and she was too ashamed to look directly at Hugh. "Did I make a lot of noise?"

"Enough to arm the guards. No, love—" He pressed her back onto the bed. "I jest. You were sleeping by the fire grate when I returned. You were moaning, so I came to you at once."

"You have just got back?"

"This moment. And I am glad I did." He took her hand in his. "What were you dreaming? Do you remember?"

The denial flew to her lips but she recalled what Elspeth had said: that she should tell Hugh the whole.

"It may have been a memory," she admitted. "Before we came to West Sarum, we moved many times." She paused, taking faith in Hugh's acceptance of the Jewish Joshua as a warrior. "My grandfather had converted to Christianity and we kept the faith most carefully, but still we were persecuted."

Hugh lay beside her on the bed, on top of the covers. He put an arm across her, to comfort and warm her while a burning brand was brought to them from the kitchen to relight their own fire. In the darkness of the room she could only just make out his face, not his expression.

"How many times did you move?" he asked.

"One year, we fled to sixteen different places. That was when my mother was alive. It was hard on her, not to have a proper home of her own." She rolled onto her stomach, remembering too much. "I learned the signs. Whenever people questioned me on my family name, or asked me about Christ, or remarked on my coloring, I knew it was time to leave again."

Hugh felt helpless in the face of such grief. He wanted to say something, but words failed. He wanted to cuddle her, but she might despise such comfort as being too earthy, not fine enough.

I cannot read and she is so learned. What can I say to her?

There was a knock at the door and he jumped from the bed to let in the maids with a drink of hot strawberry tisane and a shovel of burning brands for the fire.

He goes from me. The bishop did the same. Perhaps now

he knows for sure what I am, the stock I came from, he no longer wishes to touch me.

Joanna curled into a ball. She wanted to flee again, rush from the room. The maids were leaving now and Hugh was looming above her. The relit fire glinted on a copper goblet.

"Drink while it is warm." He took a sip and the smell of strawberries seemed to fill the chamber. "Try it."

He was willing to share with her. Heartened, Joanna sat up in bed and Hugh fussed the cushions behind her. The copper goblet was almost too warm to hold.

"Here."

A shadow dropped onto her lap. A glove, she realized, picking it from her thighs. She put it on and the palm dwarfed hers but she was glad to wear it, because Hugh was happy that she did.

They sat together, sharing the tisane and staring at the fire.

"This is not the same glove you left with me first," she said, seeking to tease him a little. She waited for an answer, her nerves taut like Beowulf straining after a scent.

"It fits you ill. I will give you better."

They sat quietly again and Joanna fretted over his answer. What did he mean? Was he sad? Distracted? Bored?

Her mind conjured Bishop Thomas's face out of the shadows in the corner of the chamber, and his scorn struck her like a fist. "Your bed bores me, Joanna. You have as much wit in a man's arms as a tavern whore."

Hugh cleared his throat and the memory exploded like a puff of smoke. Her fingers clenched in the huge glove and she almost spilled the tisane.

"You are my first love to last longer than a day and a night," he said. "The women I knew before you never wanted more than hectic bed-sport, as if I was an itch to them that must be scratched. After they had scratched their fill, they wanted no more of me or my company."

He touched her cheek. "I am so happy you do. I like being with you and I want you all the time." His black brows drew together. "You do feel the same, do you not?"

Joanna nodded, then dreaded he could not see. "Yes," she whispered.

"Thank Christ!" Hugh took the goblet from her hand and put it down into the dark. He lifted the bedcovers and reached for her, caressing her everywhere.

She woke the following morning, naked and warm. The golden gown was draped over a chest. The rest of her and Hugh's clothes were coiled in a heap at the bottom of the bed. She closed her eyes again, smiling as she remembered how he had kissed and praised her breasts, her flanks, her belly. More still, for he had kissed her *down there.* She had been horrified at first but he had pinned her close and ignored her squeals of protest, kissing and tonguing her until she did not know truly where she stopped and he began.

It was a heady feeling, to know she was truly desired. In so many lovely ways, Hugh was no Bishop Thomas. He reveled in her and in her company: in every touch he seemed to discover a new wonder. It was the same for her: an unending journey of delight.

She touched Hugh's back. "I love you," she whispered. She wanted to say the words but did not want to wake him, not when he was sleeping so peacefully.

"Marry me," he growled. Rolling over, he trapped her between his powerful thighs. "I will not let you go until you say yes, so say it. Marry me, Joanna."

He saw emotions skid across her face, complete surprise

and then joy. She blazed like a ruby, her dark eyes glowing as she brought both hands up to hug her face, then his.

"Oh, Hugo!"

"Say yes." He tried to sound threatening. He clutched her more tightly, then released her in case he hurt her.

She jumped out of bed and sped round the room.

"What are you doing?"

"Looking for my shoes."

Amused, he held up the pair, small and neat and so tiny he wanted to kiss them, both heaped at the bottom of the turmoil of clothes that was now their bedding. "Joanna?"

He knew when she turned from profile to full face and dropped a shoe what her answer would be.

"Hugo." She dropped to her knees as if she were the one who had proposed. "Hugo, that is lovely. A lovely idea, but it is impossible." She tried to tug at something, then seemed to recall she wore nothing and pulled at her hair instead. "You should marry a beautiful"—her voice cracked—"a beautiful, fair lady with a castle and rich lands, not a female alchemist who is ever under suspicion by the church."

"Then what of us?" he demanded, deliberately blunt, perhaps even a little cruel to force the question. For her to think he would be interested in some insipid blonde annoyed him.

The glow in her face became a furnace as she blushed right down to her throat. "I could be your mistress?"

He saw that if they spoke more on the matter she would break down utterly, so he did the unexpected. He poured himself the last of the mead and sat up comfortably in bed. "Very well, young mistress mine. We will speak no more of it. What is the day like? Is it dry? Can you peep through the shutters?"

The scorching glance she gave him then would have

been like Medusa's and turned him to stone had he not another plan already up his sleeve.

No, not his sleeve, for he too was naked. This plan was held in the depths of his heart, where Joanna was.

"If the day is bright I shall wear red," he announced, his heart thumping wildly as he began to work out a new strategy.

Chapter 30

"You do not know how many guards there are?" Hugh kicked at the base of an apple tree. "Are you blind?"

Elspeth looked up from the spinning. "It is hardly Joanna's province."

Joanna, quelling a desire to tell Hugh not to take his temper out on the tree, looked up from the flower bed and said sharply, "How is it you do not know? You entered the bishop's palace."

"Hell's teeth!" Hugh flung both his hands in the air. "How can I plan with no facts?"

"You are both concerned about your people," Elspeth said quickly.

The poor lady was trying, Joanna recognized, but she wanted Hugh to placate her. She folded her arms and tapped a foot, a pose she dimly recalled her mother adopting with her father.

"This wastes time," Hugh growled.

"Bickering always does. We can agree on that," Joanna answered.

"Little wretch," he mumbled in Latin, a phrase she had taught him.

Elspeth twirled her spindle again. "Careful where you

weed," she warned Joanna. "I have some marigolds amongst those roses."

"I will," Joanna promised.

She hoed away in silence for a time, hearing the sheep in the fields outside and the cawing of a crow. Hugh's men practiced swordcraft in those fields but their clash of arms had fallen silent: they must be taking a break. In the yard beside the enclosed garden, a laundress was singing as she washed clothes.

Hugh swung on one of the apple branches. He was the only one without a task, which irked Joanna. He said he needed his head clear for thinking, but she had not seen much evidence of that so far.

"I do not have the men for a direct assault," he said now. "I knew that from the beginning. Even a smaller force is risky: it means more men to sneak in and out again."

"But what if my father or David cannot run?" Joanna whispered, stopping in her hoeing and leaning on the hoe for support as the world about her seemed to darken. "What if they cannot walk?"

"If we return to my father's, would that fellow Mercury help?"

Joanna shook her head.

"I agree. Chatting with my father about truffles seems about his mark. And the Templars will do nothing." He almost kicked the tree a second time, but spied Elspeth watching and kicked the turf instead. "I can carry both, if needs must. I have carried two men before. But we need to get inside the donjon first. I could disguise myself."

He broke off and looked at Joanna. "If you returned to West Sarum and told Bishop Thomas you had escaped, would he believe you?"

"I think so, yes."

"What must we do to make your tale convincing?"

"Leave the yellow gown behind, for one," Elspeth said

calmly. "But no matter. I will keep it for you, for your return. You can return here with your people," she added. "Your men can stay here, too, while you are away in West Sarum."

"We could be many days, possibly longer," Joanna felt compelled to warn, but Elspeth was not disconcerted.

"I like to hear the cheerful row and racket about the place; it reminds me of when my sons were in training for arms." She smiled at their astonished faces. "See? That is one problem solved."

"No, no!" cried Joanna later, in the great hall. The day had darkened and turned to rain, so they had retired indoors. She and Elspeth and Hugh's men were sitting on the small dais, watching Hugh's "performance."

"You are too hunched and stagger too much," she said urgently, as Hugh glared at her and straightened.

"How do you know?" he demanded, sober in a flash.

"I have seen it! Drunks are more careful."

She mimed walking on the dais, stepping along the edge and around Hugh's men with exaggerated caution while they cheered her on. A maid brushing out old floor rushes leaned on her broom and applauded.

"But I am a belligerent, drunken fellow," Hugh protested, windmilling with his arms to prove his point.

"You are when crossed," Joanna said quickly. "We do not want you to be so drunk that you do not get through the palace gates!"

In a swirling blur of motion, Hugh pelted across the hall and hoisted her into his arms. "What I wish to learn, mistress," he said, as his men roared their approval, "is how you know so much about drunks."

"How can you jest!" Joanna hissed against his chest, wishing she did not feel so warm and safe there: a dangerous illusion of safety. "Even in disguise you will be in danger! We do not know how the guards will react! What if they put a knife in you when you pretend to be drunk? What if they put you in the prison under the floor and not the donjon? What if someone recognizes you?"

"Peace, squirrel, all plans have risks." He tipped up her face and kissed her. A be-silent-before-my-men kiss. Joanna complied but only because she was plotting herself. There should be more to Hugh's "disguise" than an eye-patch and a baggy hat. She would ensure there was more.

"What is that?" Hugh lifted the wooden spoon and trick-led a potion of the muddy liquid back into the bowl.

Joanna tugged at her skirts. She was once more in her plain brown gown, and very drab it seemed after the glo-rious golden silks. She and Hugh were once more in "their" chamber, while Elspeth found more clothes for Hugh, no easy task when he was so tall and sinewy. The clothes of her own sons were too short in the leg, which had made Joanna giggle, but mostly with nerves. What they were planning was still a dangerous undertaking.

"It will dye your hair from dark to chestnut," she an-swered, making a swift sign of the cross behind her back for luck. The dye she had devised months ago, as a des-perate "amusement" for Bishop Thomas, and it had worked well enough on her own hair. She could only pray it would not make Hugh's hair fall out. Or that the bishop would not remember her hair dye when he saw the tall, strapping man.

Hugh stirred the tincture with the spoon, frowning. "It is a woman's trick."

"It has saffron in it," Joanna said, feeling a twinge of guilt at using this most expensive spice. "And if women alone do it, who will suspect?"

"Folk who remember me as a dark man will not recognize me as a red one? I see that, Joanna, but what of my beard? My stubble is black and I would not stay to wait while it grows for you to dye it."

"I have the answer for that, too." Joanna held up a small flask. "This contains a potion that will irritate and redden your skin. That, and if you wear pads of cloth in the sides of your face to bulge out your cheeks a little and alter the shape of your profile. Only for a day or so," she added quickly.

"A plump, red idiot." Hugh nodded. "So be it."

"You need not put it on now," she warned, as she handed him the flask. "In truth, I would use it only if you think the guards are noticing you too much. It will make your skin itch as if there are a thousand devils fighting in your face."

Hugh moved closer. "I have other parts that itch. Have you a salve for them?"

"If we are to reach anywhere close to West Sarum today, we must make haste. I should make myself more disheveled," Joanna replied.

She knew she was right, but even so she was disconcerted when Hugh stepped back, crouching to tug at the hem of her gown.

"You need to tear this and muddy your shoes. You have walked for hours in your past, yes? You know how really weary folk limp along?"

"I do." She had done it herself, too many times.

"Can you make your hands red? Spill sulphurs and mud on your gown? Then you can claim I forced you to work all hours and that you escaped as soon as you could. Your have your gold to dazzle our lord bishop?"

Joanna nodded. She felt numb in the face of this planning, although she knew she ought to feel excitement. If it worked, they would free Solomon and David.

But why did he break away from me? Why did he not want to kiss me? One kiss, just for us.

She heard Hugh humming and felt more downcast, agreeing to his every suggestion.

Lady Elspeth sank onto her chair in the great hall and absently touched the great salt server in the middle of the high table, as if to convince herself that it at least was real.

"Both of you look so different," she said faintly. "Are you taller, Hugh, as well as a redhead?"

"I packed cloths into those boots you found me," Hugh agreed. "I wear three padded jerkins, too."

He did look even more huge, Joanna agreed, dressed in a gaudy blue, gold, and red—rich fabric to show status—but the most startling change was his hair, a bright, fiery red, shot through with strands of dark. With his blue eyes, the result was astonishing.

"Are you not too conspicuous?" Elspeth ventured.

"I want to be noticed." Hugh folded his arms, his red hair glinting like fire as he shifted slightly.

"You are always noticed, my dear, but this? And Joanna?"

"It is an old gown," Joanna said quickly. She knew she was ragged and untidy, her hair feeling dreadful; messed and uncombed.

"You look like a hedge-woman," said Elspeth.

"Or a pedlar," called one of Hugh's men. They were ranged round the great hall, watching with careful interest.

Joanna knew she looked worse than that. From her waist down she was daubed in a mixture of mud, cobwebs, and strands of bramble, artfully placed there by Hugh, who had a good eye for color and shape. Her fingers were heavily stained again and her sleeves torn and shredded.

"Grubby girl," said Hugh, giving her a wink.

"Copper-headed mountebank," she retorted, feeling more heartened for the nickname and the wink.

Around them the hall thundered with stamping feet and nervous laughter and Hugh had to pitch his voice to be heard. "Hey, we shall be riding together. And on a different horse."

"Not Lucifer?" Joanna understood why, but she had grown used to the big black stallion.

"A good horse, for sure, for then Thomas's men will treat me well, but different."

"I wish you Godspeed," said Elspeth, rising to her feet to see them off.

"Lord Thomas is still staying at West Sarum?" Joanna asked when they were on their way.

"So my spies tell me." Hugh had assumed he would find her less distracting in her drab gown. How wrong he was! He rode with memories and associations rising fast and urgent in his mind and loins; all he could pray was that she had not noticed. "How do you find the bay gelding?" he asked, resisting a desire to tug on her familiar golden hair net.

"At this rate I shall be very convincing as someone who has run over twenty miles by the time we reach the town!"

Hugh chuckled, relieved to hear her spiky indignation. He loathed the whole idea of her return to Thomas, the loathsome.

"The bishop will be delighted with the gold I am bringing."

"It was generous of Elspeth to find us more."

"It was indeed. Bishop Thomas will be happy."

She no longer calls him her lord. I wonder if she even knows?

Joanna flinched, saying quickly, "It is nothing. Nay, you need not hug me, Hugo—it was only a lad scaring crows off the seed corn. I saw the movement in the fields. Where do you think we should part? And what will you do?"

"I will set you down a mile from the city walls and follow at a bowshot distance, leading my horse and keeping you in my sight."

This was a promise he had made to himself. He did not want her troubled or abused on the last part of her journey. There was danger enough, without that.

"Then, when I have seen you within the palace gates, I shall visit every tavern in the town, and end at the public bathhouse and stew, spending money, giving beggars alms and looking every part a braying, rich redhead, come to the city from the country for the day. Then I shall lace my tongue with cider and act the drunken sot, and curse the bishop in good hearing of Thomas's men."

Hugh looked over the low green hills and flat water meadows, seeing no threats, but no answers, either. The plain truth was he did not want Joanna in the palace.

"Stay at the best tavern. I can rent you a room and you can wait for me there."

She answered without looking at him. "You know it will take two to break in and out of the donjon. Even two might be too few. Only I have the skill to undo the locks and fetters, and the sleeping potion to drug the guards."

"By use of acids and draughts. I could do that."

"You would not know which."

"You could mark the vessels for me."

"And what if they are broken in some mishap? What if more needs to be made?"

"Then I would ask your father." Hugh drew rein and stopped the bay gelding on the track. "I do not want you at the palace."

She sighed. "But we agreed, Hugo, that this way rouses least suspicion. I return to the palace, having escaped my own captor, and you are flung into the donjon the next day or the day after, with no connection between us. We talked all this through."

"I disliked it then and I hate it now. Why can it not be me and a man of mine?"

"Because Hugh, neither you nor any knight of yours knows enough alchemy!"

"Your father can help us."

"Only if he is outside the donjon. What if he is not?"

"Hell's teeth!" He wanted to jump off the horse, fling her over the saddle, and smack some sense into her, except that she was damnably right.

"I do not think we should do this," he announced. David had been a fool to get himself captured, so let him make his own way.

Joanna was shaking her head. He felt her gold net scrape against his chest and knew he was trapped again when she said softly, "I cannot leave my father in the palace, subject to the whims of the bishop. Nor can you, Hugo. You cannot leave your brother. What if he is cast into the prison pit again?"

"I know." When he had him safe, he was going to punch David.

But Joanna and her father would be safe, too.

Hugh gritted his teeth and spurred the horse on again.

Chapter 31

Her father was no longer with Bishop Thomas in the palace. No sooner had news of her desperate "escape" flown about West Sarum than Solomon had been taken back to the prison chamber in the donjon.

"Solomon swore to me that he had made a potion that would seduce the Templar into speech. He promised me that once Manhill has drunk it of his own free will, he will tell me anything I want to know.

"I must have those relics." Thomas paused to run his fingers through the gold Joanna had brought with her. "Do you think that possible?"

"Only if Manhill drinks it of his own free will," Joanna answered carefully. She was relieved that her father, who had a habit of promising marvels in his enthusiasm for alchemy, had been prudent enough to add that small clause. "Does my father know I am here, safe?"

"That is what I thought." Thomas waved aside her question. "I have returned Solomon to the donjon, to keep the Templar company. So far, Manhill refuses to drink anything but ale."

You hateful man! Quickly, Joanna lowered her eyes. The ache in her limbs, after sprinting through the outskirts of the city and up the long, steep high street to the palace, vanished in a hot wave of distaste. It was, now she thought of it, no more than she would have expected. Always, by one means or another, Thomas kept people in doubt and fear. Only this time, by placing her father back with David, he had made their rescue easier.

Hard on the heels of her dislike followed hope. Hugh at this moment was already in West Sarum, carousing and calling, acting the part of the rich, drunken redheaded fool.

As for herself—Joanna flicked her mud-stained gown and scowled.

"May I go to bathe, please?" she asked, playing the role of escapee to the hilt. "I long to wash him off my skin. He was vile."

"Hugh Manhill gave you the means to practice alchemy."

"That was his father." About to add that Sir Yves loved gold, Joanna stopped herself in time. With Bishop Thomas sitting at a huge desk in his private solar, running his hands through the heap of chains, coins, and nuggets that she had spread before him, she did not think it wise. "I thought of flight all the time. Every day, each night, I waited for my chance to get away, to return to you."

I should have called him "my lord." What is wrong with me?

"You seized the moment. Well done, Joanna."

There was a dryness to Thomas's tone that she did not like. He had not questioned her about her escape. He had not asked after Mercury, the hostage he had "gifted" to the Manhills by a ruse. He had not asked if she was injured, or thirsty, or hungry. He did not even inquire if she had walked all the way.

"You will be able to resume Solomon's work? Pick up where he has left it?"

She gave a small bow, avoiding his avid eyes, hoping to

hide the revulsion that welled in her. "If I am allowed to see him. If I can ask my father what assays he has already performed, my own work will go quicker."

Thomas yawned, a sign he was no longer listening. "Why is some of this gold marked with the heads of kings? Kings from long past?"

"It is how it grew. May I see my father?"

"Later, perhaps."

"Thank you." At least Thomas was no longer asking after the provenance of Orri's hoard. "It is good to be home."

Thomas stroked the cool, gleaming gold. He was mildly hungry, although not certain what he fancied. Perhaps it was merely the girl. She had returned dusty and care-worn, quite broken down and untidy, and yet at the same time, different. He recalled how she had walked into his solar, glancing at the guards, smiling at them. There was a brighter color in her face, a merry glitter in her eyes. She was desirable again.

"You may bathe," he conceded, anticipating her transformation. "I will send maids to attend you. Come to me at supper. You can tell me then how yours and Solomon's work progresses."

She bowed out of his presence. Dimly, he was aware of a clerk at the other end of the long table, staring after her over bundles of scrolls and parchments. He cracked his knuckles together, smirking at the scribe's discomfort.

The girl was back, with gold. He had her, and her Jewbred father, exactly where he wanted them. Soon he would have a potion to get the truth out of the Templar and then he would have the relics, too.

Life was good to him.

* * *

Counting guards, checking who was armed as she mounted the donjon staircase, Joanna knew that Bishop Thomas expected to bed her that night.

Then I must take the ancient story of Penelope as my guide. Thomas is my unwanted suitor. Like Penelope with her unlooked-for suitors, I must delay the bishop without him realizing what I am about.

She quailed at the task ahead of her, her feet slowing as she climbed the narrow spiral of the donjon. How could she delay? How many days and nights would she have to delay?

I may have to lie with him. What if there is a child? I will not know if he or Hugh is the father.

You know potions and elixirs. Use them!

Because she knew the guards would report it, she did not pause on the first floor but kept going. She did not glance at the iron-studded door and gave no sign of having heard a muffled cough from within the chamber.

"Be calm and easy," she told herself under her breath. The bishop ruled by spite and fear. If she asked the guards beside the door about Solomon, Thomas would know her question within the hour. She must appear content to be at "home" inside the palace and keen to resume work.

Stifling a sigh, she stepped into her old alchemical chamber, seeing at once that her father had left his favorite cup on top of her leather apron. The pit of her stomach felt to drop by another hand-span. She touched the earthenware beaker, hoping against all sense that it would be still warm; that some essence of her father lingered. Guilt dropped onto her like a moldy cloak. Yesterday, Solomon had been free, drinking his fruit tisanes, pottering about this workplace, studying the star charts. Today he was in the donjon. Did he know she was back in the chamber above his? Had he been told anything?

Joanna closed the door on the lingering guard, crouched in a corner with her father's cup, and wept.

On the first night, at supper, she drank a loving cup with the bishop that had him snoring as soon as his head rested on his bed. She had eaten charcoal and bread beforehand, so the sleeping draught did not affect her. She dozed on a chair and slipped out of his chamber in the pre-dawn chill. The guards and servants, accustomed to such behavior from the bishop's latest leman, did not stop her.

On the second afternoon, she sped to the kitchens for a fresh manchet loaf. More than ever, she was glad that as an alchemist the guards and castle servants were wary of questioning her, and even the haughty steward Richard Parvus would not condescend to ask her anything on a subject in which he knew nothing. No one troubled her as to why she needed the bread, or noticed when she stuffed part of the loaf, now soaked with a sweet sleeping potion, into the body cavity of a partridge. Later, she saw the bird being glazed and decorated for the bishop's own trencher and knew she would be undisturbed that night.

On the third morning he went hunting water fowl and was gone all day and most of the night.

By day four, Joanna sent word by a page that she had reached a stage of vital sublimations and the work could not be left.

The following day, a delegation from the Abbot of Glastonbury arrived at West Sarum. At their coming, Bishop Thomas became an instant model of piety. Less than twenty years earlier, the monks of Glastonbury had spectacularly recovered the bodies of the great King Arthur and his queen, Guinevere. Thomas was eager to acquire a sacred relic from the body, bones, or clothes of the pair.

"For how long do they stay?" Joanna asked the maid who brought her a leek pie in her tower chamber.

"Four nights. So no meat or treats till they are gone." The maid blew out her cheeks in disgust. "A pity!"

"It is indeed," Joanna agreed, her spirits soaring as she thanked the maid for the ale and pie. *Four more nights of peace.*

While the bishop and the party from Glastonbury Abbey were busy at high table with the grandest of ceremonial lunches, she took two copper cups and filled both with ale, adding a pinch of volatile salts to each to make them bubble and foam. This would be her chance to speak to her father and to David, and for that she would play the role of alchemical wizard to the highest order, until the guards believed her very robes breathed smoke and gold. Her head high and the blood storming in her ears, she sped down the staircase to the first floor and knocked on the iron-studded door with her foot. The two guards playing chess outside the door hurried to unlock the door.

"For Sir David Manhill and my father," she announced, as she swept into the chamber. "I bring them the gift of a restoring elixir from my lord."

My lord. The face that flashed before her as she spoke was not the sleek, pale features of Thomas but the lean, tanned face and bright blue eyes of Hugh. How did he fare? Where was he?

Hugh leaned against the pillory right outside the bishop's palace and took a slow drink from a flask. A young vendor of old clothes, carrying a large bundle of robes under one arm, glanced his way, spotted the flask, and veered off in the direction of the fish market.

"Not good enough for you, am I?" Hugh bellowed after the scurrying youth. Slipping on imaginary pig dung, he smacked down onto his backside on the cobbles. An old woman gripping a basket of fish heads crossed the street to avoid him. He leered at her, then drank again.

He had already been put out of five alehouses in as many days. He was renowned as West Sarum's worst "rich" drunk, generous in his ale buying but deep into his cups by midday.

He was not as drunk as he pretended to be, but he was still drunk. Thinking was hard and his feet hurt. Not his haunches, which was strange. He peered at his toes, thinking them a long way off, and tried to consider his position.

It was the quiet time of day in the city, when most decent folk were at their meat. The motley crowd of hangers-on who clustered round him in the grimier alehouses were begging for scraps at the houses of the rich. It was a good time, he decided. What it was a good time for, he could not quite remember.

He must—make a show. A show for the guards.

There were no guards about, although there had been plenty of men at the brewster's house, where he had kicked the legs off a table. Three gold coins had kept him out of prison then: he aimed for no common jail. He wanted the bishop's prison, and for that he needed the bishop's men.

"Come on, you," he growled to no one, fisting the pillory.

Do not be taken too soon, Joanna had warned. *There must be no connection between us that any can guess at. I must be known as the girl who escaped her captor. You have to be the drunk, rich sot.*

It had been amusing at first, a falling back into a mis-spent youth that, in truth, he had never known, being too busy fighting and winning. Now he was bored. The taste and smell of ale bored him. Tottering along the cobbles bored him. His face ached, where he had smeared the stuff Joanna had given him—he had not heeded her warnings about it smarting and now he regretted using so much:

his cheeks felt to be burning and popping like roasted chestnuts. The screeching of a metal-wheeled cart lumbering up the high street further set his teeth on edge and his head pounding.

"How are you, friend?" asked the carter as Hugh walked deliberately toward him and his devil's cart.

"Stop," said Hugh to the mules drawing the cart. They did so at once and he allowed them to nuzzle him, stroking their heads and necks.

"Hey!" The carter strode up to him. "You are in the middle of the road, friend. Stand aside and let me pass."

Hugh planted his feet more firmly, feeling the stones beneath his heels. "Your beasts are taking a rest with me," he said.

"Yes, I see that, but we can rest in the bishop's bailey yard, so why do you not release the mules' bridles and let us go on?"

"Friends should talk." Hugh heard the carter mutter about a "big brute, could turn ugly," and knew he could start his show soon.

He turned, ran to the corner of the high street, and plucked a long pile of entrails from the bloody slop under a butcher's table.

"Oi!" bawled the butcher's lad, trying to menace him with a cleaver, then standing like a statue as Hugh tapped his wrist and knocked the blade from his hand. Hugh grinned, wrapped the entrails like a scarf about his neck, and strolled back to the carter, who was busy urging and failing to persuade his beasts to stir.

"Master, master!" cried the butcher's boy behind him. "A fellow is making off with our offal!"

"Move, will you?" roared the carter, gripping the mules' bridles and tugging on them.

"Shall we dance the May in, friend?" Hugh cavorted toward him, watching the man's face change from a bewildered smile to horror as he grabbed the carter by his tunic. From the high walkway around the bishop's palace he heard the first shouts and drumming of rushing feet.

Soon, soon, he told himself, dropping the carter back onto the road and spiraling about to face the oncoming assault.

"Your bishop is the devil!" he roared. "Devil and spawn of the devil!"

Here they came, the bishop's little guards, eager to prove their loyalty.

Hugh laughed and burst into song. He was still singing the refrain when six guards smashed him to the cobbles and planted a boot on his face.

Chapter 32

She was hurried into the chamber by the two bored-looking, scarred guards she did not know. The smaller of the two knew Joanna, though, or thought he did.

"You have a visitor," he told David and Solomon, as soon as the door was bolted. "The lady of my lord bishop. You will conduct yourselves accordingly. None of your odd, Eastern manners!"

To her, he said, "If you will but sit on the bench before the fire, my lady, I will bring the men to you."

David and her father might have been half a league away, not a few paces. So simple and tempting it was, to cross the dusty floor tiles and ancient strewing herbs to where Solomon was, in his favored place, standing beneath the arrow slit and torch. He had been reading a text by torchlight, but now he rolled up his parchment and smiled.

Shalom, he mouthed as the guard turned to beckon David, a greeting that wrung tears of longing to her eyes. Eagerly she marked the tiny changes in him. His beard had a few more gray hairs. His fingers were stained with sulphurs and his own favorite herb, alkanet. His face was more fleshed out. His dark eyes twinkled at her.

That he was hale and whole and in possession of his wits was better than she had dared to hope. She had been so afraid for him, so terrorized at the thought of the malice of Bishop Thomas against him, especially when she was held hostage by Hugh. For so long this slight, stooping father of hers was all she had.

To stop herself doing something foolish or giving herself away—for this new guard did not seem to know that one of the prisoners was her own father—Joanna forced herself to step to the fireplace.

She could sense David and her father watching. Solomon was still smiling.

Does he not recognize the danger we are now in? The thought made her annoyed, then ashamed. Her father was otherworldly, with his mind on the starry heavens. Perhaps it was a blessing he was as he was—he could cope with imprisonment as he had coped with the many blows life had dealt him: with a mild, sanguine heart.

David was different. With the grace she remembered in him, he strolled to the bench with the guard. As he paused, awaiting further orders, his face remained impassive, no longer open and boyish. He had, she realized with a pang, some new gray hairs amidst his fair hair. A legacy of his time in the prison pit? Was he pleased to see her? She did not know.

"I bring news from your brother!" she wanted to burst out. "We are striving to free you!" Their previous ease, when she and David had spoken of Jerusalem and the great Arab scholars, seemed impossible to recover.

"You, sit here," said the smaller guard to David, pointing to one end of the bench. "You, there." He pointed to the other end of the bench.

The two men settled where indicated and she was perched between them, all three of them staring at the two cups in her hand and then at the small fire in the grate.

"Sir, have you another two cups, please?" Joanna asked. "Then we might all partake of the bishop's bounty."

Panic crawled over the guard's face. The ale had stopped foaming, but it was clear he believed it a lethal brew. He stared at the copper cups with hesitant fascination.

"I will see if there is another cup for you," he said, stepping away from the fire with alacrity.

"You escaped my brother," David whispered in Latin. "Pray God that you do not fall into his hands again."

The harshness of his voice chilled Joanna.

"I am here because of Hugh!" she began, desperate to explain.

David shook his head, his thin mouth a wire of disapproval. "Not on my account," he replied, misunderstanding her. "You do nothing for others, my lady."

"That is not true!" To her horror, she realized that she and Hugh had erred. They had not thought of any message or token that she could deliver to David to show her true intent. *How could we forget,* she berated herself, but knew the answer all too well. For the last mile of their journey she had been consumed with dread for Hugh.

"We are striving together in this," she said, but David turned away from her on the bench, as if he blamed her for his imprisonment in both donjon and prison pit.

"It is good you are home safe, daughter." Solomon spoke for the first time, holding out a hand to receive one of the cups.

Joanna leaned toward him. When their hands touched, she wanted to kneel at his feet and wail forgiveness for having been away and now, with her return, for being the reason he was back in the donjon. All she could think to say was the bald truth. "I am truly sorry you are here."

"No matter. You will continue the work." Solomon drank from the cup, giving a sigh of pleasure. "When he is ready to speak to me again, David and I will continue our disputations."

The guard was returning from turning out the contents of a chest, carrying a pewter cup.

"That will not do," Joanna said at once. "I am sorry, but the bishop said that for this potion to work, the cup must be the color of the sun, either gold or copper."

Together, the two guards glanced at the scatter of objects beside the chest. "There are none such here," said the smaller one.

Joanna, her heart hammering afresh as she told lie upon lie, spread the fingers of her free hand. "I am very sorry. The bishop was most insistent on the point."

The guard looked ready to kick her and the useless contents of the chest about the room.

"I have two more copper cups within my chamber." Joanna rose from the bench. "If you allow it, sir, it is the work of moments for me to fetch them. I am sorry, indeed, that I did not think."

"Go, then," the guard interrupted, mollified by her apology.

Before he or his companion changed their minds, Joanna moved to the door.

Running upstairs, she found the cups and wrote a hasty note for her father. Returning to the first-floor chamber, she fretted outside the door until the guards readmitted her.

"Here we are." She displayed the copper goblets and hurried to the fire to pour the contents of the remaining cup between three. As she did so, she skimmed the slip of parchment along the bench to her father.

Quick as a waterfall, David fell upon the note and hefted it aloft, his eyes glinting with triumph.

"The lady is passing messages." His accusation echoed round the stone walls.

"David," said Solomon, mildly, as if all the Templar had done was to point out a mistake in her pouring.

"What is this?" The smaller guard had the paper now and was squinting at it furiously.

"You are mistaken." Joanna was so furious, so hurt, she wanted to lash out at the man she once thought of as a friend, but she could do far more than that. "I heard a blackbird call this morning and have written down the song in the language of birds. My lord bishop said that Solomon had a delight in such matters."

"I do indeed." Her father understood at once. The language of birds was a veiled reference to alchemy, of which, pray God, David had no knowledge. "Blackbirds and wrens and eagles."

She appealed directly to the guard, who, between shooting dark looks between her, David, and Solomon, had laid out the slip of parchment on the palm of his hand. "Does that appear as any writing you know, sir?"

"It does not," the guard said, peering again at the alchemical symbols, "although it may be code." He showed it to his fellow guard, who nodded.

"Then take it to my lord," said Joanna at once. "It is no grief to me." She sensed David's baleful glare at her use of one of his brother's phrases but ignored him. Her breath kept stopping in her throat as she willed the guard to pass the note to her father.

Solomon spoke directly to David. "You should try the fortified ale. It is most agreeable."

David folded his arms and kicked at a fallen log in the fireplace.

"Then I shall drink yours." Still appalled by his malicious attempt to make trouble, Joanna drained the second cup and offered one of the other copper goblets to the nearest guard. She smiled in a winning way, pretending in that moment that she was giving the cup to Hugh. "For your patience and courtesy, sir."

Stepping forward, the guard reached his decision. He flung the note on the fire and took the cup.

"To your health, my lady. Next time, you must sing the song of the blackbird to us, so we might all enjoy it." He sipped the drink and nodded, possibly in approval. "I will keep the cups."

It was a dismissal. Fearing that there would be no "next time," Joanna rose to her feet. She did not know, now, what the guards might say to the steward, or to Bishop Thomas. She did not know when she might be allowed to visit again. Close to tears of frustration, her reunion with her father shattered before it had even begun, she had no choice but to walk around the bench to the door.

She could have avoided passing David but she deliberately brushed past him, allowing her long skirts to slap against his legs.

Chapter 33

Hugh woke with a sore, throbbing head. It was no worse than he had endured after a night of strong ale, so he counted himself as fortunate. Better yet, the bishop's guards had filched his gold and brooches, and his dagger with the fine hilt, but they had reckoned him a drunk of quality. He had been brought to the donjon.

Had Joanna seen him brought in? Was she safe? Had he been hauled before Bishop Thomas and then dragged up the tower staircase? His back and knees ached as if the devil himself had thrust long spikes into him. He could feel huge bruises on his arms and legs. His captors had not troubled to carry him much. He checked his teeth with his tongue: all there, which was a pity. He fancied having Joanna fuss over him with a gap-toothed mouth. He was still wearing the stacked boots, and his dyed chestnut hair must still be just as red; with that and his mazed head, he felt a stranger to himself.

But he was in!

He was inside the bailey of the bishop and inside the stone tower. A new hostage for Thomas, someone rich and foolish, for whom a noble family would pay handsomely.

The plan was working: he had not been recognized as Hugh Manhill.

If only Thomas knew.

Hugh smirked, then regretted moving any part of his face as the thunderstorm in his brain shot lightning bolts up and down his body.

"Lie quiet," said a voice he knew, close to his ear. "The guard is yet within the chamber and he thinks you still dead to this world."

Hugh half opened his eyes and the dim light clawed at him. He was sprawled on a rough heap of bedding. Yes, the guards certainly thought him quality: they would have dropped a poor man onto the floor timbers in a corner. David, the brother who did not know him yet, was sitting on a stool beside his pallet, playing dice on top of another stool. Where was Joanna's father? And Joanna herself?

He tried to open his eyes a little more and decided it was easier for the moment to keep them closed.

"Davey." He whispered the name he had called his brother when they were boys. He could hear the faint rattle of the dice. "Davey."

David dropped the dice into the rushes between them. Scrabbling there gave him the chance to come closer.

"How do you know my name? Are you a brother?"

Hugh sensed his wary interest, but it pierced him that David should think him a fellow Templar, rather than a brother in true blood.

"As a boy, you feared the moon would fall on your head. Nigel told you the moon was white because it needed blood and it was looking for a boy with golden curls to crush for blood. We both had light hair then."

He forced himself to open his eyes. "I am your other brother."

David looked as moon-crushed as any gold-haired lad. He looked as flattened as a beetle under a boot. With widening eyes and a gaping mouth, he pointed at Hugh's hair, his padded cheeks, and reddened face.

"My brother is not so tall, either!"

"I have pads in my boots and Joanna changed the rest. Good, eh?"

David swore some oath in Arabic and lurched to his feet. Hugh could feel the anger and despair of his brother pouring from him like smoke from a fire. He braced himself for more blows, hissing urgently, "'Tis no grief to me, what you cannot understand, Davey, but what of Joanna? How is she?"

"Oh God." David put his head in his hands. "God forgive me."

"What have you done?" Hugh demanded. His head pounded, feeling as if it was about to explode like an old cracked pot. His brother had done something: he had that closed-in, guilty look from boyhood. "David?"

David lurched away, tottering as if he were the one who had been beaten. Sweating with alarm, trembling in every limb, Hugh forced his legs off the pallet, forced his body to rise, and promptly lost all sense again.

Chapter 34

In the chamber directly above the donjon hostage room and "prison" Joanna worked to produce *aqua fortis,* the "strong water" made from saltpeter and used in alchemy to dissolve all metals except gold. She needed the *aqua fortis* to break the door locks and, if needed, iron fetters.

The sleeping potion and its antidote were ready. She would have to make certain that she and her father had the antidote, and Hugh, too, when he came. David she was less sure of, but if Hugh said she should give David the antidote, she would.

Was Hugh here in the donjon? She did not know. Yesterday she had heard a commotion as a new prisoner was hauled up the stairs, but Richard Parvus happened to be with her, prowling and prodding everything he could stick his fat finger into without being burned. He had barred her chamber door with his broad body, silently daring her to ask him to move. Because she knew his response, she did not ask.

Was the new prisoner Hugh? Hugh in disguise?

She heard no news. Since she had tried to pass the note to her father—and thank nature she had used signs of alchemy in it, instead of words!—the guards had changed toward her. No one had said anything directly to her, but worse, they did not speak to her at all. The maids, too, must have been instructed not to gossip with her and now delivered her lukewarm meals in silence.

"You should labor hard," Richard Parvus told her, his round face shining with amusement. "Our lord grows weary of your lack of results." He left soon after that, firmly closing the door after him.

"David, you fool!" she roared into the unlit furnace. She longed to smash something, anything, but all was too valuable and she had no time to waste. Grimly, her hands still shaking with frustration, she set to her work again.

"You stupid bastard!" Hugh was raging inside. His insides were molten and his temper roared. If Beowulf had been there, or one of the bishop's alaunts, he would have cheerfully set the dogs on David. His wolfhound would be pining—he was pining for the good beast—and he was terrified at the thought of Joanna, pacing the floor above him, not knowing he was here, not sure now if she could trust the Manhills. "You utter, stupid, bastard, bastard idiot!"

"The guards will hear you," David said, hunched over the chess set.

"They are outside, fool!"

"And they will still hear you, with the rage you are making." David had changed from his session in the prison pit, and not for the better. Where he had been easy in manner he was now surly and laconic, determined to be right in his mistake. "I thought Joanna returned to West Sarum for her father. I thought she had evaded you. I assumed she had forgotten me."

"Me, me—it is ever *you,* David. You are as bad as Nigel." Hugh slapped his queen onto the next square. "Your king is dead," he snarled. "I win."

"What if I am right?" David persisted, smug as only a Templar could be. "What if she has indeed changed sides?"

"And if she has, brother, whose fault is that?"

But now the door was opening and a guard approached: it was time to be the rich fool again. "Will you give me a match, sir?" Hugh asked, as if he had no care in the world. "Shall we wager on it?"

"You have no money," the guard answered, with a faint sneer.

"My family will pay," Hugh said, meaning it in quite a different way.

Today was the final day that the Abbot of Glastonbury and his party were staying at the bishop's palace. Close to the cages where the low-born or those deemed worthless were imprisoned, the abbot's carts were being loaded. The bailey yard was filled with shouting youths and men, hurrying to put chests and clothes and church plate under cover before nightfall.

Tomorrow the party of monks would lumber out of West Sarum and the bishop might remember her again. Worse, he could want her in his bed. Worst of all, he could demand she turn all base metal into gold at once.

The *aqua fortis* needed to dissolve the iron locks was condensing into a glass flask. Soon she would have enough.

She checked over her supplies. Gloves, so she did not handle the acid. The "strong water" in its glass flask. Her pot of sleeping potion. Her pot of antidote. If she could somehow draw the guards into the chamber and give them the sleeping draught there, the *aqua fortis* might not be needed. She could perhaps filch the keys off the sleeping

guards, unlock the door, then lock the guards inside—
a nice revenge.

Or should she wait until the guards were changing?
Sometimes the new guards were slow to come to the
donjon and there were no guards outside the chamber
door, sometimes for as much as an hour. If that happened,
she and her father could work on the locks and both of
them be away—

*That will not work. You have thought this way months
earlier and decided it would not work. There are too many
other guards. If you should meet the new ones on the stairs
or in the bailey yard, what then? You, a girl, and one old
man cannot fight your way out.*

And what if David raised the alarm again? In that case,
they might not even reach the ground floor of the donjon.

There were now three guards, not two, a sign that a new
prisoner was within the first-floor chamber. Was it Hugh?

"I have to know," Joanna said to herself, pulling her
cloak over her shoulders and hiding the precious flasks in
the unlit furnace. "Until I know that Hugh is indeed inside
this prison, I dare not set our plan in motion. I cannot do
this alone."

It was a bitter thing to admit, but it was the truth.

"We need Joanna's help," Hugh told David. "I cannot
work our flight alone." It humbled him to acknowledge
this, but it was no more than the truth. "I cannot ram my
way through the door. Once she gets us out of this chamber, things will change."

He would get swords for him and David, for one, and if
any guards were drugged, so much the better. "But we
shall need to be fast. Surprise must do most of it. Can you
still run?"

"I am not yet in my dotage," David replied. "What of the girl and her father?"

"Use her name, David." Hugh stalked about the chamber between the arrow slits. He was unused to being confined within one room and by now felt like a capon in a pot. "Are you going to introduce me? I wish at the very least to exchange names and good wishes with the man, before we break out of here together."

They were speaking in their local dialect for the sake of privacy, and Hugh was careful not to look at Solomon as he spoke, but the older man stepped away from the torchlight and tucked the roll of parchment he had been reading into his tunic.

"I know the speech of the West Country," he said. "Your words hold no mystery to me. Yet you"—he nodded to Hugh—"you speak as if you know my daughter well. How is this? And do I know you? I cannot recall having seen you before, but you seem familiar to me."

Hugh walked over to Solomon. He saw Joanna's bright, compassionate eyes and her small determined chin, translated into a masculine form. He had expected to be tongued-tied before the man from whom he wanted so much, but the words came easily, perhaps because he already felt he knew the father through his daughter.

"You know me as David's younger brother, Hugh Manhill. I know I am much changed, thanks largely to your Joanna. Yes, I am the thief who stole away your daughter, who kept her hostage, but now she and I have joined forces to free you. My being here, in this prison, is proof of my intent. My words to you now are proof of my good fellowship, for, if it pleases you, should you wish it, you can denounce me to the bishop."

Behind him he heard David's hissed intake of breath and knew his brother despised him for a heart-ransomed fool. But for all his former easy ways, David was ever more careful and grudging than himself in matters of the heart.

"I have a place of safety where we may go," he went on. "A place of quiet, where you can continue your red work."

I sound like an anxious house steward with an angry prince. Solomon is not my father—be not so desperate.

He could heard David tutting in disapproval as the silence drew on.

Then Solomon said, "Raise your hands."

Puzzled, Hugh did so.

"I always make a study of hands." Solomon circled him, giving his arms and hands quick, darting looks. Hugh felt he was being pricked all over, tested in some way.

"Faces can be trained to lie. Even the eyes can be made to look wide and guileless." Solomon stopped his stroll directly in front of him. "A man's hands are true."

Solomon leaned forward, closer to his upraised palms. "Square-tipped fingers, big thumbs, calluses everywhere. A scar on the left palm. I have seen these hands before, Hugh Manhill." He snapped his own hands on his thighs and looked directly into Hugh's eyes. "You have a gentle touch for choice. Your dog has no fear of you. How does your good beast?"

"Beowulf is well," Hugh replied, thinking the man quite as exotic as his daughter. He breathed out slowly, finding himself relieved to have been accepted. "Joanna helped me change this, and this." He tugged at his red hair and tapped his raised boots.

"Quite so. Does my daughter know you are here now? Is that what she was trying to tell me, with her message?"

David cleared his throat. "I acknowledge I was mistaken in her intent."

"It is for mankind to make mistakes. Do you not agree, Hugh?"

Hugh snorted, not yet ready to kiss and make peace with his brother. "Have you seen her? She is well, unharmed, untroubled?"

Solomon nodded, his narrow face calm, without expression.

"Do you know when she may come here again?" Hugh went on. "Or has my fool brother frightened her off?"

"Joanna will come."

He longed for such confidence. "Soon, you think?" The question escaped before he could stop it.

Solomon was unrolling his scroll of parchment but now he raised his head. "Ah."

What did he mean by that?

Unwilling to know the answer, Hugh tried to focus on the practical. "Can you leave your things?"

"Things can always be replaced."

"So are you ready to leave? Willing to leave?"

"Most gladly." Solomon touched the nearest stone wall with the tips of his fingers. "I believe my daughter and I have long outstayed the welcome of the bishop. I doubt if he will even chase us, or not so far. We were a fancy for him, which I think he will not miss. Alchemists grow more common every year, even in West Sarum." He smiled and Hugh saw Joanna again, a sight that threatened to melt his heart.

"Your brother on the other hand, with his promise of relics . . ."

"I have none nor know of any," David said hurriedly.

"Can you run, if need be?" Hugh asked, still thinking on Joanna, remembering how she ran.

"For my life and freedom? Assuredly." Solomon held out his hand.

Hugh took it and as they shook hands and he sensed Solomon's easy goodwill, he felt a fine beginning had been made.

Now if only Joanna would come to deliver them—

You are to be rescued by a girl, a dark, unyielding scrap of his mind mocked. *By a woman!*

"So be it," Hugh said aloud, his words a promise and a hope.

Chapter 35

Within the vast, high-ceilinged, smoke-filled palace kitchen, Joanna avoided the steward by stepping behind a burly spit boy. When Parvus strutted into the buttery to bully the cellar man, she hurried to a kitchen maid she knew well. Madge was slicing stale bread into trenchers, ready to use as plates for the midday meal. Her formerly acne-ridden skin glowed with health, thanks to Joanna's unguents and suggestion of more daily fruit in her diet.

Plucking a wrinkled water pourer from its peg on one of the kitchen beams, Joanna shook it beside Madge.

"I need your help."

"Anna!" Madge was the only one who called her that. Instants later, Joanna was enfolded into a close hug, the maid exclaiming at how well she looked. "And see the pastry cook over at that far bench? We are betrothed!"

Joanna congratulated the pair and genuinely wished them well, aware at the same time that if Parvus spotted her in the kitchens he would send her back to her chamber. "Please, Madge." She was sorry to interrupt the maid's wedding chatter but this next step was vital. "Can you bring me some of the best wine? I know the cellar man likes you."

"Likes me! Tries to grope me each time we meet in the kitchen corridor, if truth be told. My Gregory says that will stop now, or he will bake Master Fletcher in a pie."

Joanna feared to interrupt or remind her again but Madge, enlivened by this contest between admirers, thrust her knife into the rest of the loaf and said, "The best wine, you say? I may have to let him kiss me for that."

Joanna blushed, recalling the kissing games between Hugh and herself. "Do you know who the latest prisoner is, in the donjon?"

"That creepy Frenchman who has lost his memory?"

"I thought it was another."

"There may be, you know how these hostages change." Madge glanced across the kitchen, flounced her skirts at Gregory the baker, and bustled round the table, mouthing, "Need the midden."

As soon as she disappeared into the clouds of smoke that wreathed the kitchen close to the buttery doorway, Joanna realized she was still gripping the wrinkled water bag. She had forgotten to hand it over.

She leaned against the table, feeling light-headed with shame and anxiety. If she had missed such a simple thing, what else might go wrong?

Madge was already coming back. Had she been unable to kiss the cellar man with sufficient zeal? No, she was carrying a good-sized jug in both hands.

"Madge, you are a wonder!" Joanna felt herself sag with sheer relief but Madge took her by the shoulder and whipped her about like a spinning top.

"Go, that evil Parvus is shuffling over. We do not want his pestering questions. Go!"

Desperate not to drop the jug, Joanna fled from the kitchen, worrying with every hasty step that she would be called back, hauled off to make an account with the bishop himself. Instead she emerged blinking, with smoke-filled lungs and eyes, into the bailey yard.

She would have to pass the man-cages again. Was Hugh perhaps languishing in there, with the other common criminals? It was against her every instinct to walk slowly by the cages but she made herself do it, enduring the taunts and the lewd gestures.

"Hey, sweetheart, let me give you something!"

"Whore-bait!"

"Help me—"

She hurried past that section of cage, away from the blind, ruined eyes and clawing fingers. The sight of the filthy, pale prisoners shamed her, as it always did. Dared she use the *aqua fortis* on the locks to the cages? Their breakout would keep the guards busy, but what if she was caught by those reaching hands?

I cannot be a hostage again. I will not be.

She backed farther away from the cages and sped on, almost colliding with a monk carrying a book with golden clasps in her keenness to be away. His angry shouts followed her as she stepped into the black shadow of the donjon and braced herself for a possible encounter with guards.

The wine was very fine. Back in her chamber, Joanna was sorry to have to adulterate it but knew she must.

Meanwhile the mystery of the new prisoner remained. There had been no guards within the donjon when she had entered, but two had appeared as if summoned by a charm and then followed her up the stairs. She had longed to call out or sing as she reached the first-floor landing, but one guard was the man who had burned her note and he was already suspicious. She climbed the stairs in silence.

Still she did not know if the third prisoner was Hugh. What if he languished in the open-air cages, too stunned to call out? What if he, like Mercury, had lost his memory or wits in his capture?

Joanna gave the wine one last stir and tasted it. The sleeping draught had tempered its sweetness, but only slightly. "If Mercury has no memory, then I am the Queen of Sheba," she said aloud, tapping her spoon on the jug.

"Is that why none of your potions to recover his wits would work?" asked a neat, cloaked figure from the threshold. "I had assumed as such. I passed him on because I want no blame, whenever our Mercury decides his memory is whole again. Whoever he is, when he chooses to reveal it, I think we shall all hold our breaths and bow our knees. I had not the men to guard him, else I would have kept him, but I want no earl's army appearing outside my palace, demanding his release and determined to have vengeance."

He pursed his lips. "A pity no one could say who he was, but sometimes a hostage is too dangerous to keep."

"My lord." Joanna hurriedly lifted some books off a stool and polished the stool with her skirts for Bishop Thomas to be seated. Inside her guts were churning as a prickle of wild terror swept over her body. "My lord, you grant me abundant honor by coming here."

"The abbot and his party are at prayer. Tomorrow I am for Oxford again, so it must be today."

Joanna dared not ask what must be today: she knew it would be nothing good. She allowed the spoon to slide back into the jug, wondering if she should give an account of why she had such fine wine in her chamber.

"This works better than ale at hiding the taste of other things," she said quickly, deciding on a version of the truth.

He had not seen her sleight of hand with the wine but what was he doing, scanning her chamber, picking any bottles within reach off the workbench and shaking them? Swiftly she palmed the glass flask of the dangerous *aqua fortis*, spreading her fingers to hide as much of it as she could. Why was he visiting now? He had not stepped foot in the donjon for months.

Thomas pointed a ringed, gloved hand at the jug. He was robed in scarlet and blue silk again, and his ermine cloak was bright in the room. "You have the means in there to get that stubborn wretch downstairs to tell where he has hidden my relics?"

The elixir for truth—she had done nothing to make it, but now she knew there was only once answer to give. "Yes, my lord."

"And it will work?"

"Within the half hour, or less." The sleeping draught would certainly take hold by then. "It needs but one addition to make it complete: it is but ordinary wine without it. I chose to make it in this way so the Templar would drink with us. If he thinks we are all drinking the same." She stopped, nervous of her tongue saying too much, and hid the *aqua fortis* behind an earthenware crock.

Her lies were met in silence. Bishop Thomas held out a hand and she placed the jug before him, praying he would not smell or recognize the sleeping draught.

"Do I smell Malmsey? That is good wine indeed. You were going to use this without telling me?"

Did he mean the wine or the potion? Joanna chose to believe he meant the latter. "I thought that if I drank with David Manhill and the guards today, and asked him one or two questions to which I know the true answers, I may establish trust with him, and know for certain that the potion is effective, my lord. Then, the next time, with your leave, I may ask more."

"A plan of sorts." Bishop Thomas appeared mollified. He tasted the wine and smacked his lips. "Will this also work on that new fellow in my prison, a gangling red-headed fool who claims kinship with the lords of Exeter? I have sent messengers hence to verify his claims, but though his clothes are fine, I like him not for a lord. He has no retinue and kept no state. He does not have a good horse, much less a splendid horse. A jumped-up merchant, perhaps, whose family I can squeeze for coins, but no noble."

"Yes, my lord." Joanna fought to cling to her composure as this blessing of news fell on her like a shower of gold.

He does not recognize Hugh. He has his enemy in his grasp and he does not know it.

Unless the bishop was deceiving her? Joanna became clammy at the thought. She dared not look too closely at Thomas, lest he sense her concern.

But why should he suspect? Who would expect a knight of the realm to submit to changes in his appearance even so far as the color of his hair and wads of padding in the cheeks of his face; to allow himself to be made a figure of ridicule?

Thomas would never do such an act, so he cannot conceive of it. Pray good nature I am right in this. Please let me not be dazzled by my own relief, and hope.

"Let us go down, then. My guards will join us there presently."

Within the chamber? That will be too many to drug or dupe.

"My lord, if the guards remain outside and you enter to speak with my father and take wine with him, will that not be more natural? Will David Manhill not then partake of the wine more easily, he and the stranger together? Then you shall know the truth of both."

"You are right," said Thomas at once. "Bring the wine and cups."

"Yes, my lord." On her way around the workbench to collect more cups, Joanna saw the bishop distracted by her star charts and astrolabe. While he peered at both, she seized the chance to slip the flask of *aqua fortis* and the smaller bottles of her sleeping potion and its antidote into the inner pockets of her work robe. She tried to tell herself to be ready, in case the new hostage was not Hugh, but inside she already felt to be floating, light-headed with anticipation. Soon she and Hugh would be reunited.

Unless Hugh had changed toward her, like David?

She took a deep breath and tried to steady herself. "I am ready."

Bishop Thomas surprised her then by going to the door and opening it himself. "I shall summon the guards and my dogs." He smiled broadly at the alarm he must have spotted in her face. "My alaunts also have a nose for the truth, Joanna; they can come in with us. Now I will lead the way."

Still smiling, he did so.

Chapter 36

Hugh heard the bishop speaking to a guard on the first-floor landing. He could not hear the words, but a few moments later he heard the barking of dogs and the rushing of heavy bodies up the spiral staircase.

"They are coming here," he said, wondering for an instant if Thomas would try to set the dogs on them, then dismissed the idea. Those rowdy alaunts would obey him as before, as all dogs and good beasts heeded him, so Thomas's ploy, if ploy it was, would be in vain.

David, who had not yet left his bed, groaned and pulled the covers over his head.

"He dislikes my lord bishop and so would feign sleep," said Solomon. "He has done so before, especially since his return from the prison pit."

He spoke as if David was a substance, Hugh thought, rather than a man. Indeed, since David had accused Joanna of betraying the Manhills, her father had not uttered one direct word to his brother. Such a habit was good kinship, perhaps, but Hugh was frustrated by the silence between them. "You are worse than women!" he had roared at both yesterday, but it had made no difference.

"Will you not meet the fellow on your feet, man to

man?" He appealed to the lump that was his brother and
to Solomon, who, though sitting up, was also still abed.
For what would they rise? Their food was not due for another hour.

Hugh, not yet resigned to imprisonment, had been up
and pacing for hours. Resuming what he done every day,
he had tried the locked door and rattled the lock and
kicked at the doorjamb until his feet, even in their stacked
boots, were sore. He had tried to thread his bedding
through a window slit before admitting it was folly. He had
peered at his jowls in his washing water, wondering if the
dark stubble was showing yet through the reddened skin.
He was weary of his disguise, of pretense.

*Give me a sword and I will clear this place from top to
bottom!*

"You should rise," he said, irritated with his despairing
companions. "I have told you—we need to be ready to
leave at a finger-snap's notice."

David rolled down his bedding to show his scowling
face beneath his fair hair. "No one is coming for us. She is
not coming."

"Should the dogs not be leashed, sir?" asked Joanna outside the chamber, proving David's assertion a lie. Solomon
turned his back on David and began feeling beside his
rough heap of bedding for his shoes.

*Good, old man. Do it for your daughter, if not for
yourself.*

Hugh heard the great key clank in the lock. He stood
back, too wily to make a rush and be battered afresh by the
cluster of guards. Yipping with excitement, the alaunts
launched into the chamber and instantly rushed to David's
bed to worry at his bedding, and David yelled.

"Stop that!" Hugh snapped his fingers and the alaunts
fell back, coming to sniff his fingers and receive a friendly
pat. And now Joanna was in the room beside three guards.

She carried a jug and cups and stared at him as if she would know all of him afresh.

Their eyes met. How open and sultry and yearning she was: his harem girl in another master's drab garb. He longed to strip her there and then on the spot, tear off the bishop's proofs of ownership, and make her truly his.

Bishop Thomas, sleek as a weasel, was also staring. "You are the second man to charm my dogs. Are you a warlock, redhead?"

"Eh?" Hugh strove to think straight. What did the fellow mean? Had he seen through the disguise, or remembered Hugh Manhill's skill with beasts? He had made a stupid mistake, there, quelling the alaunts.

"It is written that witches have red hair," Solomon remarked, coming to his rescue. He rose and bowed to the bishop. "My lord."

"A word." Thomas beckoned Solomon as casually as if he were the least page, but his ill grace gave Hugh the chance to give David's bed another kick, further rouse the despairing idiot. As Solomon stepped warily past the dogs, Hugh nodded to Joanna.

"Is that our breakfast wine, girl?"

"Yes, sir." Her voice was as pretty, and as dry, as the substance of mercury. It gave him no clue to her feelings.

"Will you serve me, then?" He sat on a stool beside the chess table. Off to one side, Thomas was hissing in Solomon's ear, while David aped slumber. He was tempted to fling his brother out of bed, but then heard the loud click in the lock.

Joanna, having placed the cups on the chessboard and now pouring something—*is that wine drugged?*—glanced at the door. "My lord, we are locked in!"

Is her panic real or false?

"As I instructed, I would have no interruptions." Bishop Thomas waved off her alarm. "Do you doubt these sturdy fellows?" He glanced at the alaunts, haunting meekly by Hugh's heels, and said nothing of them. "Pour the wine for us, girl. You." He pointed at the shorter of the three guards. "Rouse that prisoner. I would have us all drink a toast to our good king, John."

David wallowed half-upright on his pallet and Thomas was on him, snatching a goblet from the chessboard and thrusting it toward him.

"Drink, man, drink! Even Templars pledge allegiance to kings! Drink!" Thomas swung round, spilling part of a second cup. "You drink, too, Red-face!"

Do I trust Joanna now?

Hugh did not hesitate. He took the cup and gulped it down.

"Drink, drink!" Thomas instructed his own men in a frenzy of excitement. "I would know all, so drink!"

David had not taken the cup, so Thomas flung the contents in his face while the guards hastily swallowed and drank.

"More!" Thomas snapped his fingers at Joanna. "More for the Templar, and *you* hold his head and *you* make him drink!"

"Please, my lord—"

"Silence!" Thomas bawled, overriding Joanna's protest. "I will have those relics now! They are mine, for the Almighty brought the Templar to me! What are they, man? A part of the true cross? A lock of our savior's hair? Tell me now, while you still have a tongue!"

David, the lees of wine dripping from his face, shook his head. The guards put down their empty cups and nodded to each other.

"Seize him! Hold him! I would know."

Two guards stepped closer to David and then one rubbed at his eyes while the other clutched at his belly. They tottered another pace and then sank to the floor, the third guard slumping down with them but falling across Hugh's pallet.

Thomas opened his mouth to scream and Hugh punched him hard in the face. The bishop of West Sarum crumpled in a gaudy heap on the floor and lay as still as his guards.

"Fine wine, that," said Hugh. "What was in theirs?"

"Treble-strength sleeping potion in the bottom of their cups. I had no means to stir it properly, but I knew it would work. I have the antidote here, but had no means to give it you, so I had to know which goblet to give you, without the sleeping draught."

Answering, Joanna was already hurrying for the door.

"That was risky," David said, wiping his face on a bed-sheet. "What if Thomas had seen the potion in the goblets?"

"I walked behind Thomas on the stairs and added it then," Joanna said, kneeling by the lock and pulling a flask out of her baggy work gown. "We must hurry, David, or are you still in doubt of me?"

"I never doubted." Hugh was eager to establish this point, even at the expense of some exaggeration.

"Never?" Her voice was very soft. "Had it been me, in your place—" She stopped, looking down at the flask in her hand as if she did not know what it was, and then glancing everywhere but at him.

"Come, David, let us tie up these guards and the bishop." Solomon dragged at the Templar, compelling him to stir.

Hugh stepped over the prone figure of Bishop Thomas and knelt beside Joanna. Padding beside him, the alaunts whined.

"What must I do to help?" he asked, making his voice and manner gentle. "I know we have little time here."

She stared despairingly at her hands. "I must feed this into the lock and let it burn, little by little. There will be foul smoke, so you must cover your nose and mouth, and I must be steady."

She lifted her hands to him and he could seem them trembling. "Hugo, I do not know if I can do this."

He lifted the flask from her, set it on the flags, and gathered her close. "Easy, there." He trailed his thumb across her dark brows and lashes, feeling the cheekbone beneath her pale skin, feeling how she had lost weight in the time she had been back here. He stroked her hair, his wish to comfort warring with his desire. "I will be your surgeon here. Tell me what to do."

"Make haste, Hugh, before more guards come." David was changing his clothes with those of the taller guard. "A pity none of these have keys."

That was the first comment of sense his brother had made, Hugh thought, and now he answered, "Search them in case they have something we can use. No rough stuff," he added. For himself, he might have dispatched all three, but he knew Joanna would disapprove.

He tore a sleeve from the bishop's robe and wrapped it about his head, picking up the flask again. Reunions were sweet and Joanna his girl with wide and dreaming eyes, but they could not woo like lord and lady in a French romance: they must get out of the donjon first. "Tell me what to do," he said again, shaking the flask before her eyes.

"Do not do that, Hugo!"

His ploy worked: Joanna's attention snapped back into focus and her face blazed with concentration. "Never shake or tip *aqua fortis,* 'tis too dangerous! Here, give it to me!"

She shoved him aside and took the flask, tipping it to allow the liquid to slip into the door lock. A loud hissing and sizzling broke from the metal and a cloud of acrid smoke bloomed from the lock. Joanna leaned sideways, coughing, her eyes streaming, and Hugh tore a length from David's bedsheet and wound it across her mouth and nose.

She tipped the flask a second time and more sizzling ensued. Hugh saw a trickle of something—waste metal?—weep from the lock.

"It works, keep going!" He gagged on the foul acid smoke but ignored it, pressing his shoulder to the door and pushing with all his strength. "David, help me!"

It was Solomon who came, pounding at the door with narrow fists while he shoved and Joanna poured.

With a final groan and sizzle the lock broke and their way was open. Hugh snatched the sword David had taken from the taller guard and whistled to the alaunts. "I go first," he said. "Upend those pallets and get behind them now. There may be archers coming. I go out first and you follow only when I say. Agreed?"

David and Solomon grunted something. Joanna said only, "I have never seen a man wear a veil before. You look well in it."

Behind his "veil" Hugh grinned, and grabbed a stool as a shield, ready for the next.

Chapter 37

I am a lovesick fool, Joanna thought as she crouched behind the pallet. *Is that the wittiest thing I could say, after we have been apart so long?*

Hugh rushed out onto the landing like a dark storm cloud, the alaunts flashing round him like bolts of lightning. After a few moments he returned, plucking the flask containing the *aqua fortis* from the floor.

"Hurry!" he said, throwing a second sword to David.

Joanna rose and sped to the door. She must make an effort. "I would have a blade, too," she said, running round in front of him like one of the dogs. David slipped past to scour the stairs: she would not speak to him.

Hugh stared down at her from his huge, extended height, strapping as an oak tree and twice as dark in his rich borrowed clothes, only his keen, bright eyes showing behind his rough "turban." Again, her heart raced at the sight: he looked so mysterious, so full of vigor and pith. She wanted to fling her arms about him and have him carry her off, as in those stories she had heard of Saladin.

Tales she had heard from David.

That woke her from her daydream as nothing else could

have done. She seized Hugh's wrist and shook it. "Give me a blade."

"Take this instead." He thrust the flask at her, dragged the cloth away from his lips, and before she knew what he was about, dragged his "turban" off his head and smacked a kiss on her mouth. "Haste, wretch, we have scant time."

Her father—where was he? Joanna scanned the chamber and then heard the unbelievable: Solomon padding upstairs.

"He wants some stuff. I told him to go." Hugh grabbed her arm and scooped her along, half dragging her over the floor.

"Are you mad? He will be there for an age, choosing, selecting . . ."

"I told him to take no longer than he can run a hundred paces."

"Have you seen my father run?"

Hugh laughed—by good nature, she had missed his hearty laugh!—and smacked her lightly on her rump. "Off with you."

She was not supposed to be speeding onto the landing with her loins tingling, thinking of lovemaking. As her eyes grew accustomed to the shadowy tower and the narrow stair, she knew this was the moment. If they were spotted now, it would go hard for them. The bishop had not yet been missed, but he must be soon, and though David now wore the chain mail of one guard, there was no disguising Hugh.

"I go first," Hugh said again. "Then you, David, then you, Joanna. Solomon—" He broke off and bawled up the stairs, "Solomon! Come now!"

"That will bring the guards, little brother," said David, ever joyful these days.

"They will be busy enough, soon," replied Hugh, and he

set off for the stairs, hurling the stool down first and saying to the dogs, "Fly, lads, go down, go on!"

Barking a frenzy, the great white hounds barged forward to do his bidding and in a swirl of teeth and tails careered down the steps. Joanna, gripping the flask, desperate not to drop it or shake it too violently, found herself half tumbling down the narrow stair, striking her shoulders against the wall and central pillar. Conscious of her father coming down slowly behind her, one step at a time, she found herself pressed at one point against David as he stopped suddenly on the stairs.

"Get on!" she hissed, disliking having to touch him.

"Do not order me."

"Peace, both of you," called Hugh. "Solomon, are you with us yet?"

"I have quite caught up," replied her father, as serene as if he was strolling by the river.

"A wonder this, but no one in the bailey has yet noticed," Hugh whispered back up the stairs.

"The folk here are used to screams from the donjon," Solomon remarked.

Joanna shivered, thinking again of the oubliette. She studied the flask in her hand: was there enough?

"Our luck may yet hold and we come through sweetly. Maybe we simply walk through the gate. No grief to me to fight, but I'd rather go easy."

"There is a small postern on the eastern side of the bailey," Joanna reminded him, feeling her face glow as Hugh said, "Good, good!"

"Can you two not keep silent till we are through this?" grumbled David. He squawked as Joanna moved past him, elbowing him in the ribs.

"What are you about?" Hugh barred her progress with an arm.

"The trapdoor. If I can break the lock there, those poor creatures may have a chance, too."

She expected Hugh to object but he was already shifting the heavy weights on top of the door. "You pour and I'll pull," he said. "Just be sure you have sufficient left for those outside cages. It will make a fine distraction if those prisoners break loose."

Joanna nodded. "We are of the same thought, Hugo."

"Hugo! God in heaven!" David sneered, but he subsided when Hugh glared at him.

"You can work, too, brother. Watch by the outer door."

David stepped across the trapdoor to do as he was bid, muttering to Joanna as he strode by, "You will not last."

His spite, though startling, did not touch her. Speed, she knew, was vital: she had no moments to waste on the Templar's change of heart toward her.

Calling out a warning, she poured more of the "strong water" onto the trapdoor lock, ducking her head out of the way of the stifling, acrid fumes. It was best not to think about those trapped in the oubliette, what it would be like to have that scalding, choking liquid cast about head and face. . . .

Hugh was laboring, too, dragging at the huge iron ring on top of the trapdoor, cursing as he struggled. "Solomon, get a ladder! There will be one somewhere close!" he bawled at one point, gulping in a massive breath and straining again, wrestling with the ring as if it was alive.

"Keep back!" he warned as Joanna tried to also seize the ring. The whole door shivered like a dog shaking itself and came free. It groaned open, Hugh red-faced and sweating as he hauled on a door designed to be lifted by two men, and then swung back onto its hinges as he jammed it open with the stool.

He took the short ladder Solomon had found in the debris of tools and fetters by the door and slid it down into the dark. Dropping his water flask into the hole, he called down, "You are free, come out!" and shooed the dogs back.

Joanna tried to see into the tar-black chamber, coughing on the acid fumes and the fouler, older stench of human filth and ordure. Hugh caught her round the waist and lifted her, wriggling, away from the open trapdoor.

"They have their chance."

"But they may be fettered!"

"A guard," David said, and they froze, Joanna then gathering her wits and singing a chorus of "King John went a-hunting," as if she had no cares in the world.

"Gone off to the kitchen," David reported, and they all sagged a little, in relief.

Hugh clasped Joanna by the shoulders. "We must leave now, sweeting," he said gently. "Let us free the prisoners in the yard and get out while we may. My men are waiting for us in the city with horses. They will be here by now."

This was the plan as they had agreed and all she need do was walk out of the donjon to the cages and stop as if to stare at the prisoners while she broke the locks. She picked up the flask again but Hugh took it from her. "I will do that. I will not have you taken hostage again. Go to the eastern postern and wait for me there."

What he said made sense, but it was hard to leave the tower and leave behind the open, gaping oubliette. As she looked back a final time before slipping through the outer door, Hugh murmured, "Some things we cannot know. Trust to God, girl, and leave it to him."

Even his provoking use of "girl" could not shift her sense of shame, but at least it made her move. She took one of her father's rough bundles and slung it over her shoulder, picking up her skirts and preparing to run.

Chapter 38

Hugh strode into the yard, dogs trailing him, ears pricked for his orders. Strolling like a prince in his kingdom, he made for the cage closest to the main gate. Two monks, carrying a chest between them, paused on their way to a cart in order to let him pass. A guard hailed him and Hugh waved in return but kept on walking. In a moment of inspiration, he took the sword and ran it along the bars of the cage, hearing the guard who had previously stepped over to the kitchen laugh and call out, "Good jest!"

Few of these men know each other, he thought, but that did not surprise him. Bishop Thomas commanded by fear: there would be little loyalty at the palace and much changing of guards, many new faces amidst those who through age or family ties must stay on here.

Yet even guards as slack as these would eventually wonder where their lord was, so he must hurry. He poured the rest of the flask over the lock. A hand grabbed at him. He grabbed back and smashed it to the bars.

"I am helping, friend, so do not interrupt." A whimper told him he had been understood.

He turned, leaving the cage smoking gently, a yellow

vapor issuing from its lock, and paid no heed to the gasps and curses from the prisoners.

"Go, lads!" he encouraged the dogs, and the great hounds, gladdened by his voice and sweeping finger, shot off in the direction he pointed to and crashed into the approaching guards.

"Hey!"

"Down! Down, I say!"

"You, soldier! Wait!"

He ignored the turmoil and the command and turned his back. Listening to his heart, hearing his boots striking the cobbles like a ram at a castle wall, he stalked to the postern gate. A swirl of midden and cooking smells hit him, then another whiff of acid. Surely the lock must soon break on the cage? He walked on.

There were no archers but his shoulders pricked as he lengthened his stride, striving not to break into a run. A running man attracts attention, and so far these guards were bewildered. They had not marked that their bishop was missing, nor that his prize hostage of months was out in the bailey.

Doing what? What exactly was David about? He could see Joanna moving in the shadows like the clever wench she was, carrying a bag over her shoulder as she guided her father smoothly to the postern. David was standing by one of the abbey carts, looking up at the cloudless blue sky as if the arch of heaven was new-made for him.

"Give a Templar a nail and he will try to use it as an astrolabe," Hugh muttered. Exasperated, he moved out of the palace wall shadow to recover his errant relative for the second time.

"David." He had reached the cart.

"I had forgotten how blue." David lowered his head and looked at him, his wide eyes puzzled. "Are you sure we should leave?"

Are you gone mad? Six months ago, Hugh would have said it, but being with Joanna had taught him to consider words. He took David's arm. "We have only a little way to go now. Joanna and Solomon are there already."

They were, too. Joanna was speaking to the postern guard, pointing to the distant glitter of the river, and did not seem to be making much headway. The guard was shaking his head and motioning her back.

"Come," he said to David, wanting to be with Joanna. He had other, quicker methods of persuasion.

David rubbed at his eyes and yawned. "I am for my bed at this time; a sleep before midday. She will leave you, once she is free of here. Why should she stay with you? No other woman has."

"That is in God's arms, now go." Hugh gave his brother a mighty shove, possibly harder than was needed, but he had no stomach for their father's old complaints. "Move or I cut you," he growled, and that threat stirred David into a lumbering run.

Finally—

And behind him, now, at last, he heard a sudden crash as the lock on the first cage shattered. Twisting round, he saw ragged prisoners pouring into the yard. Some made for the main gate, others were struggling with the monks to seize goods off the carts, a few made straight for the guards, swearing vengeance.

"Stop them!" shouted a new voice. "No, you fools! *Them!* Hold them!"

It was the fat steward. He had appeared by the postern, returning to the palace from the town, and was now blocking the narrow gate. Even as Hugh sprinted for the fellow, barging through knots of straggling, blinking men, the steward snatched a bow from the postern guard and notched an arrow.

He is aiming at Joanna!

Hugh plucked a book from one of the carts and threw it. "Not her!" he roared, charging for the man.

The heavy volume struck the steward in the middle of the chest. He tottered, but did not release the bow.

"No!" Joanna dropped her sack and launched herself at him.

"Stop!" Hugh's desperate warning came too late. The world about him seemed to slow down, turn to dust and stone, as he strained and strained to reach the enemy first, as he dropped the sword to avoid striking Joanna, as he reached, arms outstretched, to seize the man's throat.

The steward was yelling something he could not hear, his mouth jerking into an ugly scowl, and then he fell like a cast stone slingshot. He hit the postern cobbles and sprawled in the gateway, silent and still. The guard had already chosen his path and was gone.

"I hit him with this," Solomon remarked, staring down at the unconscious steward with an expression of mingled delight and dread. He looked to Hugh like a small boy caught eating an apple in an orchard. "When I saw you throw the book, it gave me an idea." He shook the sack. "I hit him with these," he said. "Pestle and mortar and a crucible. Did I do right?"

"You dropped this," said a voice behind them. Hugh turned to find David with the sword. He looked less abstracted than he had earlier, and seemed to have more sense, which was a start. "What?" he asked now, glancing round as one of the monastery carts crackled into flames. A group of prisoners was dancing round the blazing cart, buffeting the monks aside.

"Keep that for the moment and keep moving." Hugh picked up the sack in one hand and plucked Joanna off her feet with the other. Ignoring her protests—"I can walk as well as you!"—he stepped over the sleeping steward and walked out of the palace into the town.

"Let me go!" Joanna tried to nip at his ear with her teeth. He tightened his grip about her middle until she gasped. "Unfair!"

"Yield, then, wife. Wife-to-be," he amended. In the victory of the moment, delighted to have Joanna snug in his arms again and determined to keep her there, he turned to Solomon. "If that is acceptable, sir?"

This was not how he had planned to ask, but the question thundered out of his mouth with the force of a warhorse charge. He could not stop it and now he could only wait with stopped breath and sweating palms for the answer.

Say yes, say yes, say yes. . . .

"You have my blessing," Solomon said at once.

Thanks be to God and all the saints of Christendom! Hugh kissed Joanna lightly on her round, astonished "O" of a mouth, swung her higher into his arms, and kept on walking.

Chapter 39

"I cannot marry him," Joanna said a third time to Elspeth. They were at Elspeth's manor, kneeling in the bright warmth of the walled garden, pounding and preparing powdered chalk and water to make whitewash. It was a beautiful, sunny day, perfect drying weather. Elspeth wanted her wall pictures in the great hall and solar repainted, and Hugh had volunteered them all as helpers.

Joanna guessed the real reasons why he had done so, and it was not for the sake of friendship, or generosity. David was still strange, shutting himself whenever he could into the privy, as if still imprisoned. He would scarcely talk to anyone.

"Then help me paint flowers," Hugh said. He had David in the great hall with him now, washing brushes and muttering to the faded paintings on the newly dusted walls.

"He can draw, as I can," Hugh explained, when Joanna questioned him. "If he cannot speak of his time as hostage, maybe he will paint it out."

She was impressed by his logic, but she knew there was more to their staying than that, or even care for his withdrawn sibling, changed so profoundly by his time in the oubliette.

"He keeps us here to persuade me," she admitted. "I am a guest-hostage."

"A most useful one," Elspeth remarked, puffing a wisp of auburn hair away from her sun-reddened forehead. "And Hugh! I did not know he had it in him."

Joanna dare not ask if her companion meant his enthusiasm with brushes and paint, or his proposal to her. Or was she turning on this point because it was all she could think on?

"How can I say yes?" she burst out, startling a blackbird in the nearest flower bed. "I have no lands, no title, nothing a rising knight requires. To the church I will always be suspect for what I am. If we stay as we are, he may marry an heiress."

That thought shot a pillar of ice through her heart, but she persisted.

"I can be his mistress. Better that, than we marry and he comes to resent me as a woman without lands."

"You are an alchemist!"

"Gold is not land. For a knight, land is what matters."

Elspeth gave the whitewash another stir with a stick and tapped it on the bucket before looking up into Joanna's face. They were kneeling very close together, stirring and pounding the dusty chalk in one bucket, and her freckles were all obscured by white. She looked as pale as a ghost. She looked as she felt, thought Joanna.

Elspeth reached away from the bucket and took a drink of ale to clear her mouth. "You have said as much to Hugh?"

Joanna nodded as a sick heat of shame rose in her throat. "For a woman like me, to be Hugh's mistress is, is . . ." She faltered. Her eyes smarted and the nodding cowslips in the border blurred, doubtless due to the clouds of chalk dust.

"As much as you should expect? That puts you very low, Joanna! How does Hugh answer this?"

Joanna closed her eyes. How had he answered? She could not remember. She gripped the narrow brush until her hand hurt but still no clear thought came.

"But then I am surprised you have had time to talk. He scrubs and sketches and you busy yourself about the manor with me, and your nights together in the solar are busy in other ways, are they not?" Elspeth smiled at Joanna's startled stare. "You are lusty enough for newly-weds."

In her mind Joanna returned to the solar, in the warm dark, with Hugh making love to her. He called her his harem girl, his squirrel, his own. Last night, before pulling her back into his fierce embrace to sleep, he had tongued over her breasts and murmured, "I love these. I love you."

He had fallen asleep before she had time to answer, but she had lain awake for many hours.

"He loves you, Joanna."

"I know. He told me so."

"And asked you to marry him."

"David says he is not constant."

Elspeth sat back on his heels, wafting impatiently at a passing fly. "I would not trust David to lace my shoes. Are you gone mad, too?"

Joanna gawped at this forthright speech, but Elspeth was not finished. "What if there is a child by all these vigorous unions? Would you have a son or daughter as a bastard? Have you entirely lost your wits?"

Joanna tossed her brush into the whitewash and jumped to her feet. The sudden movement caused her breasts to brush almost painfully against her gown, but she ignored the discomfort. "How can I work, though? If Hugh is at joust after joust, winning and fighting, what do I do?"

She paced up and down beneath the fruit trees, the

mellow cooing of pigeons in the nearby dovecote an accompaniment to her every anxious step. "How can I assay gold in a tent full of chattering gossips? How can I investigate the secrets of the cosmos and the stars when I am forever slumped on a horse's back, jogging from place to place?"

"How will being Hugh's mistress instead of his wife change any of that?"

"I—" Joanna had not thought so far. She realized, with a jolt, that she had been thinking as a wife, of wifely duties, of being with her man and caring for him and putting his needs ahead of hers. *And I have been reluctant to do so, although I love Hugo with all my heart.*

"I know not," she said dully. "The whitewash is ready."

"Only when you remove that stick," said Elspeth, also rising to her feet. "Talk to Hugh," she said. "Tell him you need a place, a settled place. How many months are you prepared to travel with him? Half the year?"

"More, to be with him," admitted Joanna, relieved to discover that to be the utter truth. "I need a place, for me to work, for my father."

"I agree. Solomon is getting too old to be jaunting with you round England and France," Elspeth said tartly. "So this is what I propose."

She paused as a crash and cursing came from the great hall. "Hugh, dropping his brush again," she remarked. "He will come hurtling out here in a moment to find something to scold you for: it is ever a husband's way, so you may as well accustom yourself."

She took hold of Joanna's hand. "I will grant you a parcel of land, for you and your father. I know the very place. In return, you will give me the rent of a posy of cowslips each spring; a flask of that useful *aqua fortis;* a cupful of your white powder for when my head aches, and some fine red dye and blue dye to dye my cloth. You may live and work there in the winter months, when tournaments are nothing but mud and blood, and have a place for Hugh to return to each Michaelmas, to take his ease and feast and count his blessings."

"I do not know how to cook," Joanna stammered and then stopped her mouth with her hands. In the face of El-speth's miraculous offer, what was she saying?

Her companion laughed. "For a woman who bakes gold, all other cooking will be easy. I will teach you. But look, here is Hugh, and I am leaving now. I have no wish to be mauled."

She strolled away, shaking the chalk dust from her skirts, and vanished between the fruit bushes and trees, chattering to the pigeons in the dovecote.

Hugh knew he was in a mood to rip heads off and he did not care. "Elspeth! Come you back. I want you to hear this!" he yelled, not caring if the gardener stopped his weeding to back out of his way. "Do you know what my fool brother has done? Only gone and sent a message to our father! We are here, quiet, no one knows, the bishop and his creatures know nothing, and David sends a single squire to our father with a *written* message!"

Joanna dropped the bucket of whitewash she had been bending to pick up, a splash landing down the front of her gown in a spreading stain as the bucket rolled away into a mat of speedwells. "Written?" she whispered. "But what if he is stopped?"

"I have sent swift riders after the lad," Hugh went on grimly. "They will fetch him back."

"Your brother was perhaps fulfilling his filial duties?" Elspeth remarked. She had returned, in that quiet way of hers, but Hugh was not listening.

"We will set forth tomorrow, for Castle Manhill. David

wishes to greet our father and fulfill his duties as his son, and so he may, in person. My father can do his part for a change and give us shelter if the bishop's men come calling. I have left David grinding up the paint now and he knows he is to finish it. Solomon is with him, to help, and my hound." *To keep watch,* he almost added, but did not say it.

"Good!" Elspeth smiled at him and whispered something in Joanna's ear. "Now go with your lady. I have told her the way, and I do not want either of you back before sunset. Go. It is a lovely day. Go on!"

Chapter 40

"David is ever sour and asserts himself most when he knows that he is wrong."

Although Joanna knew the way, it was Hugh who pounded ahead up a steep track, kicking up clouds of pebbles and dust. He had been grumbling ever since they had left Elspeth's garden.

"Not a single word of thanks have I had from him, not one word! He moans like an old woman: he complains to you that I change my womenfolk more often than my breeches, to Solomon that I loathe all those who are foreign born or bred, and to me that you will leave me!"

Hugh halted so abruptly that Joanna smashed into him. It was like striking an angry, living wall.

"Why should he say such things?"

Joanna tried to clasp his hand but he was off again, his long, rangy strides devouring the chalk path.

"He is foul."

"Your brother is in pain," Joanna panted. Her feet hurt from rushing and kicking through the stony path, trying to keep pace. "He is abandoned by his father."

"Not by me!"

"And by his own order. Listen to me, Hugo—"

Her voice cracked across the hillside and now he did turn and wait for her to catch up, but not to embrace, as she had hoped.

"How can you defend him?"

His face was blank with hurt, his blue eyes dark with bewilderment. Seeing him so, Joanna bit down on her own furious retort. "I was angry with him at first, too, but then I realized. He is released from a long imprisonment when his very life was in danger. He was for a time in a very place of hell—do you remember the foul stench from the oubliette? It sickened us both and we were above it. David was down there for who knows how long, in the dark. Now he is confused. He has no clear place anymore in the world. Who wants him? David is to be pitied."

"Pitied." Hugh folded his arms across himself and tapped a foot. "You pity him but will not say yes to me."

Joanna, already breathless from the relentless climb, now felt her jaw sag but Hugh was still speaking.

"What is it? Am I too rough for you? Unlettered, uncouth? I know I cannot read yet, but you could teach me. I know some alchemy now and I could help. I want to help. You say you love me, yet you will not marry me! Why not?"

She gasped at this spate of questions and accusations, promises and hope, love and rage. Trying to conceive a reply, she did not watch where she was going, brought her heel down hard on an unyielding flint, and slipped on the hillside. Falling hard, she bit her tongue with her teeth and her heart felt to be jarred right through her ribs. Though she tried to stop it, a high, sharp cry broke from her.

"Eow!"

Hugh knelt beside her. "Let me see."

Joanna spat out a bit of blood and shook her head.

"At least come here, squirrel." He lifted her off the

tough grassland, gesturing with his eyes. "You were perched on an anthill."

Twisting, Joanna saw that he spoke the truth and promptly burst into tears.

"Hey, there, I did not mean to make you weep, Joanna. I am not angry with you, I swear it. There." He was patting her arms and head, rocking her. Joanna luxuriated in his baking warmth and strength and wept harder.

"What? What is it, sweeting?"

"I do not know. Truly. So much noise. So much pain." She pressed her breasts, which for these past few days had felt overlarge and overtender, she now admitted to herself. "Perhaps it is my monthly time." She blushed, to be confessing such a thing to a man, horrified, too, at her overreaction. What was amiss with her? A little tumble in the grass should not have her crying like this. "We have so little time together, just for us. I wanted it to be perfect." She tried to stifle her sobbing, disgusted with herself. "I can do nothing right!"

"Why perfect?" he breathed into her ear. "Have you something to tell me?" He swung her down lightly onto her feet, looking always into her eyes. "Something perfect? A little sweet?"

He thinks I am with child, and that thought delights him. Joanna's aches and her sore breasts were forgotten in a giddy rush of joy. "You are pleased, truly pleased," she said, astonished and grateful that he should be so. She had known for a long time that Hugh respected her and her father, and that although her grandfather had been raised in the Jewish faith, he thought no less of her. This was more, though: this was blood and sinews and heart; this might be a baby, their baby.

"Pleased, happy, and proud." He grinned, the sun glinting on his dyed hair. "Now you will have to marry me. It would be sin, else."

"Since when were you so concerned with sin?" She caught a lock of his hair and tugged at it. "I cannot marry you—"

With your hair that shade of red, she meant to say but was forestalled. Hugh stepped in front of her. "Horseman, over there, breaking cover from the woods. A Templar."

Joanna's mouth went dry with fear. "David sent out two messages?"

"Or someone has asked some clever questions in West Sarum and has tracked us."

Joanna tried to start down the hillside but found herself blocked by Hugh. His arm was as strong and unyielding as his sword.

"He has seen us. I will speak." He checked his dagger, testing its edge with his thumb. "That will serve. Remember, you say nothing."

If nothing else, his unconscious arrogance irked her so much she felt too aggrieved to be afraid of the closing knight.

"You do not prefer me to snivel behind that hawthorn, my lord?" she asked. "Or perhaps await his coming and let you use me as a footstool?"

Hugh laughed. "I think I preferred you weeping."

"You will not kill him?" she persisted, no longer fearful but still worried at this uncertain meeting, worried that Hugh had misunderstood her, and most worried at this moment for the stranger himself.

"Have no fear, mistress sour. I would not bring that trouble to Elspeth. Listen now, he is shouting something." He held up a hand and frowned. "No, the wind takes it." He glanced at her. "Still stubborn to be free, eh?" He lowered his arm and ran his fingers across her flank, a half-smile playing on his lips as she leaned into his caress. "We shall see."

Somehow, with that swiftness of movement, he had come alongside her and continued to touch her even as he waved to the closing horseman. The Templar would see nothing; he would merely think them standing close, side by side. He would not see Hugh's large hand skimming the small of her back and then dipping lower.

"Hugo! The knight!"

He cupped one cheek of her bottom, lifting her slightly so she was almost on the tips of her toes, and she had to widen her stance to keep her balance.

"We are hostage to each other," he said, still waving.

His other hand slipped between her thighs. Even with her long skirts between her and his smoothing, questing fingers, Joanna found her sight becoming hazy, clouded by a sweet mesh of desire.

"Stop it!" she hissed, but she did not move away. Her heart leapt and hammered and the ache in her breasts was replaced by a delicious tingling. "I cannot reason!" she protested, as he lowered his waving arm and "accidentally" brushed her flank. At once her whole side flamed. "Don't!"

This time she broke away, stumbling forward, promising herself to pay Hugh back in kind when they were alone.

"Stay back!" Hugh hollered, and for an instant she thought he meant her. Careless of the courtesies, she sank onto the hillside, putting her backside out of reach of his devious honey and bee-sting hands.

"I will attend to you later, madam," he remarked, but she knew that he was not as calm as he sounded. She flicked a speedwell at him and made herself pay attention to the approaching stranger.

She stiffened but Hugh remained relaxed, save for the jutting front of his tunic. "Yes, he brings dogs. Did you not hear them earlier, or spot them? Or were you busy?"

Refusing to add to his conceit by replying, Joanna pushed down on the turf with her fists.

"Stay down. I swear they will not touch you." To emphasize this point, Hugh strode forward. "To me, lads!"

He whistled and the three pounding wolfhounds yipped and flew to him, gray whirling arrows, their tails a blur of wagging. They danced about him in a tight spiral, reminding Joanna of the honeybees. She smiled at the memory, her face warming, and not only with the bright morning sun.

"Manhill!" The Templar charged, his bay horse galloping up the rolling curve of the hill like a kite tugged on a string. Whatever curse he was chanting was lost in the breeze and the harsh, high cry of a buzzard.

Joanna grabbed a fistful of flints and scrambled to her feet, but the duel was already over. Hugh ignored the dogs, ducked under the Templar's flailing sword, and punched the horse's head. It screamed, rearing and plunging, and Hugh yanked the man off its back. In a welter of dust he smacked the stranger to the turf and stones, stamping on his sword arm and dropping on him. As Joanna ran closer she realized he had his dagger to the man's throat.

"And now I would know your name, sir."

"Let me up, damn you!"

Hugh rammed a knee onto the man's belly, leaving him to writhe and choke. "Joanna, is the horse standing?"

She did not know what to make of the question but answered at once. "It is."

Hugh nodded and spoke to the stricken Templar. "Yours is a good bay, a fine palfrey, but no destrier. You do not wage war on a untrained horse, and you do the beast no service by using it so. Do you yield?"

"Yes, damn—"

Hugh put more of his weight onto the knight. "Do you yield, man?"

"Yes, yes!" The Templar wheezed and clutched at his chest, going very red, then pale. "Truly, your brother was right, you are the very devil in arms."

Joanna felt no sympathy for the man. He had come and tried to attack Hugh: he deserved what he had. She peered about the grassy hill and lush water meadow below but could see no more movement. Above, only the buzzard flew and cried again, its shrill note piercing against the stranger's gasping breaths.

"Why are you here alone?" she said. "Where are the rest of your order from Templecombe?"

The man gargled, and she said quickly to Hugh, "I pray you, my lord, to let him up, if he gives his word to be still."

The Templar nodded, turning red in the face again. Hugh released him and stepped back, glancing into Joanna's face and mouthing, *All well?*

Yes, she whispered back, and they turned as one to the stranger, who had rolled onto his side and was touching his jaw and then his shoulders and arms.

"I broke no bones of yours, man," Hugh said, sitting cross-legged on the turf. He tilted his head to Joanna, smiling at her with his eyes while his mouth remained still. She was glad of his notice and concern, and more glad that he did not pull her down with him. She wanted no distractions now.

Sprawled on the turf as if it were a bed, the stranger broke the silence between them. "How did you know I am of Templecombe?"

"I did not," answered Hugh, seemingly as blithe as a soaring lark, though Joanna saw the lines of tension in his neck and shoulders. "You must direct yourself to my lady."

The knight was in no position to protest, but made his displeasure known by refusing to look at her. Addressing her with his eyes tightly closed, like a child about to count down a game of hide-and-seek, he repeated his question.

"My lord understands horses and weapons and men," Joanna replied, wondering if she should be as peevish as this middle-aged, florid knight and lean in to give him a pinch. "He saw you riding without warhorse, helm, or armor, and he made what he would of such matters. I see writing and symbols. Your cloak is embroidered with a cross standing in a dark, low valley. The combe or valley where your order has its preceptory. Why did you attack my lord?"

That made him open his eyes. Beside her Hugh chuckled. "She is ever to the core of the matter, and you must accustom yourself." He flipped his dagger and caught it, stroking a hound under its gray throat. "Your reason interests me, too, and your name."

The knight looked from one to the other of them and sagged, shaking his head. When Joanna spotted his lips moving in prayer, she thought she understood.

"Did David send you a message saying his brother was bewitched?" she asked, smiling as the knight stared at her. "Nothing else would account for your folly."

"And how do you know me?" Hugh put in. "We have never met."

"David spoke of your skill with animals," the knight replied, in a heavy, despairing way. "I recognized you from that."

He said nothing more and did not give his name. Understanding him and his fear more than these latest actions of Hugh's brother, Joanna now leaned in and touched the cross on his cloak. Gently she recited the creed, and when the knight began to echo her, she knew he had accepted her.

"I am no witch," she said then.

"No, you are not," said the knight. "But when I saw you at our preceptory, and later, received David's message, I was in dread." He sat up and extended his hand to Hugh. "I charged to draw you away, as I thought, though in truth I was not thinking clear at all. Your brother also spoke of your battle prowess. I am Sir Brian of Templecombe and Outremer. I knew David in the Holy Land."

He and Hugh shook hands and Sir Brian went on, "A lad came to Templecombe this morning and sought me out. He did not know the message he carried: David had put it in writing on a scrap of old parchment."

"I thought he had taken that to use in the privy." Hugh kicked his heels into the hillside and muttered a curse Joanna had not heard from him before.

"There is more," she said quickly. "Why did you come alone, Sir Brian? Was the message strange?"

Sir Brian nodded. He rolled his heavy head and stretched his arms above his head, seemingly glad to relax, to talk.

"I knew David in Outremer. A quiet, steady man, courteous and learned, even-tempered. I recognized the writing as his but not what was written." He sighed. "Demons and witches. Hostages to a demon. Ancient evil clad in a loving shape. I do not recall the rest. I burned the note. But I knew I must do something, so I came to see for myself."

"David has excelled himself this time," Hugh muttered.

Joanna said nothing. She too had known David as learned and polite, even a little jesting in a good-natured way. When had he changed? When had imprisonment changed him? After he had been in the pit, or earlier? When had she become his enemy?

It hurt, to think of Hugh's brother so distrustful. Had she not talked to him in the donjon, brought him news, tried to lift his spirits? Had she not given him books to read? It seemed David had forgotten all this.

Like Mercury, he is a man out only for himself. She had not thought David was like that, although she knew Mercury was. And it had been a long time since she had considered the mystery Frenchman. Was he still at Sir Yves's castle? Did he still claim to have no memory?

"As long as he is being well fed and entertained, why not?" she muttered.

"What now?" Hugh was asking. "Do you wish to see David? You can for me—and take him back with you." *For all I care,* ran the unspoken but obvious conclusion. If she had been surprised and aggrieved by David's seeming change of heart, how much worse for Hugh, who had striven so mightily for his brother.

But Sir Brian was stretching again and slapping his legs, possibly to stir the blood, and missing all of Hugh's bewildered hurt.

"I would see him, Sir Hugh," he said. "He wrote word to me; he remembers me, and kindly, I hope. We could talk of our time in Outremer."

"I think David would like that," Joanna observed, recalling the comfort she and her father had from speaking of old times, of times when her mother was alive.

"I want to tell him, too, that not all Templars think only of gold, or of relics." Sir Brian's cheeks became more red: he looked as bright as a red kite. "There is also good fellowship, true companionship in arms."

"He is fortunate to have you as his friend," Joanna said, feeling that needed to be voiced, while Hugh jumped to his feet and whistled to the hounds as if they were his own.

"Elspeth will be surprised." He winked at her in passing and strode off down the hill to catch the horse, leaving nothing settled between them.

Chapter 41

So he was returning to his father's castle, with his brother. That thought, which should have been a victory, brought Hugh no pleasure. He was estranged from David, who was as remote and unfathomable as the moon these days. His father would give them no welcome, and he mistrusted Sir Brian, too. The fellow seemed honest enough, but when was that a guide? Before David turned against him and Joanna, Hugh would have said that his brother was as true as steel.

Most of all, he disliked this traveling out on the open road. Elspeth had heard nothing from West Sarum. His own men, also, had no news, but that meant nothing. It could be that the bishop was playing a new and more subtle game, one that involved the Templars. What if Bishop Thomas and that smooth bastard Sir Gaston de Marcey of Templecombe had joined forces? His own men, though seasoned, were a small, tight force. If the Templars and the bishop's men came at them on the road, it might go hard.

Worse, Joanna was with them. He had left the other maids at Elspeth's, and Solomon, ever sanguine, had taken over the painting of her hall, but Joanna would come. She had wished to come and in truth he wanted her with him. He wanted this nonsense of her being his mistress resolved. He wanted to kiss the top of her head as she rode before him, in her now accustomed place, but David was watching.

No grief to me, Hugh thought defiantly, and kissed her, squeezing her lightly with his legs. She briefly released her iron grip on Lucifer's name to pat his hand and he smiled at her forced daring. She was a brave little wench: they would have doughty youngsters.

Soon, soon, I will get you alone and then I will know the truth. I have seen enough mares in foal, I will know. Once I have you stripped, I will know.

He could think no more of plots or counterplots. Daydreaming of Joanna, he let the miles slip by.

Arriving unannounced with Hugh at Castle Manhill just after midday, Joanna found Sir Yves at his dining table. Sitting beside him, in the place of honor, was a slim, handsome, dark-haired man she knew well, even though neither she, nor any other, could put a true name to him.

She tugged on Hugh's sleeve but he had already leaned down to whisper, "Look who it is: Master Mercury. Looks well, does he not, for a man with no memory?"

He did indeed, Joanna agreed. Sprawling on his chair with a pale hand draped languidly about a pretty serving maid, he sported new clothes and a broad new smile: a possessive, contented smile, all dimples and teeth. He looked cared for and in control. He ordered the servers as if they were his and not Sir Yves's.

With a pang and a certain exasperation, Joanna saw that Mercury's fine black hair shone and waved, as Hugh's had once done, before he daubed it with red dye.

"What is this?" demanded Sir Brian, who had entered

the great hall and taken up a space beside her. On her other side was Hugh, waiting for his father to notice him. David, meanwhile, detached himself from them and sank to his knees in the herbs strewn on the floor. Snatching up a handful of rushes and meadowsweet, he buried his face amidst the heady white blossoms.

"David, attend me here," Hugh commanded in a low growl, but Joanna doubted if his brother had even heard. She sensed that for the first time since returning from Outremer, David felt to be truly at home.

Which was a pity when his own father did not seem to recognize him. Sir Yves was peering at Joanna through the steam from a dish of stewed fruit of some kind, and seemed puzzled by her sudden appearance. She watched his eyes pass over her, then Hugh, then look very quickly away from David. He clicked his fingers at a page and the lad approached, clearly about to ask them who they were.

"He has very bad sight at long distance," Hugh said, "and with my hair changed, he will doubtless not know me. And he has not seen David for two years or more."

"Yes," said Joanna. She understood Hugh's need to make excuses and truly she could think of nothing else to say. "Yes, Hugh, I understand."

"Well, I do not." Sir Brian rocked on his feet as if he wished to hurl himself at the seated diners. "That is David's father? Hugh's, too?"

Joanna felt a rush of indulgence for the older knight. His clear indignation at Sir Yves's casual treatment made her want to laugh—it was that, or weep. "Hugh's also," she said softly, to make him turn to her. The page had not yet reached them through the milling servers and she thought it would be more seemly for all if the lad could whisper to the lord here that two of his sons were before him. Perhaps then Sir Yves would make a semblance of welcome.

"But I know him." Sir Brian flicked his eyes at Mercury:

for him a most discreet gesture. He looked at David, still
kneeling in the rushes, and obviously decided it was better
to whisper urgently to Hugh. "My lord, why did you not
say that you are connected to the king?"

"King John? What mean you?" hissed Hugh.

But Joanna hushed them both. Mercury was rising from
the table. He had deigned to glance at the latest supplicants
to Sir Yves's justice and charity and now his pale face was
a little less smooth.

"Sir Brian!" he called out, strong and clear. "God's
bones, this is a blessed day! You restore me to myself! You
are Sir Brian de Falaise, late of Outremer. In recognizing
you, I know myself!"

"Truly, Mercury?" Sir Yves had finally risen. Clasping
Mercury's outstretched arm, he regarded him as fondly as
any father might a favored son. "Your memory has at last
returned?"

"It has indeed," said Joanna and Mercury together.
Joanna could almost predict his every word and gesture:
the surprise, wonder, and delight. As a performance, she
thought it as good as any dance.

"Finally, we come to it," remarked Hugh, grimly. "Will
he remember you and David, I wonder?"

Joanna shrugged: she thought it unlikely that Mercury
would trouble to recall her, but she was mistaken. He
leaped right over the dining table, almost knocking a basin
of washing water flying, and ran straight to her.

"My lady Joanna! My sweet lady!" He fell on his knees
before her. "My dearest dreams and wishes have come
true, now you are returned!"

"The alchemist woman who was with Hugh?" Sir Yves
was slowly walking round the table, his earlier pleasure
fading quickly. "She is here? What is happening?"

"And your sons, Sir Hugh and Sir David!" Mercury
winked at Joanna, jumped to his feet, gripped Hugh's arm,

and brought David off his knees. "My former comrade in captivity!"

He made it sound a great adventure, Joanna thought, as Sir Yves stared at Hugh.

"You are a mess, sir!" he barked, his mouth a rigid line of distaste.

"Nothing changes," said David, speaking for the first time in an age. "I am home and nothing changes."

"But the kin that is true stays true," said Hugh, and now David finally stretched out a hand to him and shook Hugh's: a silent compact of reconciliation, Joanna guessed, and one she was glad to witness.

Still, she wanted more and wanted to know more. "What should we call you?" she asked Mercury directly.

Mercury again dropped to his knees before her and kissed the hem of her gown. "You, lady, may call me your slave."

"And to the rest of the world?" Joanna asked, determined not to smile.

"I am Lord Roger-Henri Angevin of Aquitaine, a son of King John of this proud country."

The whisper, *"The king's son!"* rustled through the great hall like a flood of water. Joanna's own heart was racing again. She had guessed him to be noble, but a son of the king, even a bastard son of the king, as surely Lord Roger-Henri was, changed everything.

"How came you into the bishop's tender care?" Hugh asked. Of all of them, he seemed the least alarmed by this revelation.

Lord Roger-Henri snapped his fingers for wine and only replied when he had taken a sip. "My main estates, you understand, are in France."

Which perhaps accounted for why Sir Brian de Falaise knew him, Joanna thought.

"The journey to my English holdings is not one I wish to make: I do not like the sea." Lord Roger-Henri sighed.

"But then I thought in good conscience that I should come, and so I ventured from the places I knew best."

There was doubtless more to this pretty tale, Joanna thought, but they would never know it. She listened intently as the prince explained a little more.

"I chose to come with a modest escort. I wished to travel discreetly, you understand."

Everyone in the hall nodded and no one dared ask why.

"Coming into the barbarous west, we were set upon by bandits. These ruffians wished to take me hostage for gold and coins, but then I and they were swept up together by the bishop's men, and I was deposited in the bishop's donjon as a likely hostage."

Where it was prudent for him to lose his memory, Joanna thought, and where he was content to remain unknown, at least until Bishop Thomas decided that this noble stranger might be too dangerous to keep.

"But my lord," stammered Sir Yves, coming late to the threat that he was now under, "you have never been a hostage here! You have been my guest!"

"I know that and I thank you for it," said Lord Roger-Henri. "You and yours have ever treated me with kindness and respect. And you will be rewarded."

He smiled, and the whole hall, including Hugh, thought it best to applaud and kneel to him. Joanna would have also knelt, but the prince stopped her. "I do not forget your care for me, my lady," he said in a low voice, as the men and women in the hall tried to outdo themselves in clapping. "I will help you in return."

"Thank you, my lord." She inclined her head so he would not read her face, or her rebellious eyes. Over and over, a question beat in her mind.

If Sir Brian had not come with them, for long how would this prince have kept up the pretense of his lost memory? And what of his men, still languishing in the bishop's cages? Or were they free now? Whichever, it was clear that Lord Roger-Henri did not care. If he was in comfort and safety, then the world could go to the brink of hell, that much was plain.

He will do nothing for Hugh or me. Nothing.

Chapter 42

"Are we right to come here?" Joanna asked. They had ridden through the night from Castle Manhill, but she was not weary. Too much was going on for her to be tired.

First Lord Roger-Henri had sent out messages. Then he ordered a feast. Next he embraced David and Sir Brian, calling them "my dearest brothers-in-arms" and praised Hugh lavishly, calling him "a true champion, better than William the Marshal."

Under this Sir Yves had merely observed that he should send word to his eldest son, Nigel, so he might come to show honor to his great guest. He had seemed dazed throughout the feast and scarcely spoke a dozen words to either of his sons.

"No grief to me," David had said, using Hugh's words as he tossed a candied fruit at his brother with a little show of his former lightheartedness.

Late on in the feast Lord Roger-Henri called for musicians and dancing. At that point, Hugh lifted his eyebrows and caught Joanna's eye.

They had slipped out of the hall at different times and met on the stairs.

"Will you come with me?" Hugh had asked her.

"I will."

So they had gone to the stables and taken Lucifer and left Castle Manhill. Joanna's mood lifted more as they rode away without looking back. Where they were heading, she did not greatly care, so long as they were together. It was not a cold night, but Hugh asked if she wanted his cloak to wear and she said yes, because it was his.

On the road they did not speak much, although Joanna did ask once, "Are you and David friends now?"

She felt Hugh kiss the top of her head and sensed him smiling.

"We are, and more: he admits he was a fool over you. I think David will do well enough now, especially as Sir Brian has offered to be with him when he returns to the Templar house at Templecombe."

"Good!" Joanna snuggled more deeply into Hugh's cloak. She and David would have years to make peace between each other, so for now no more needed to be said.

"Should I guess where we are going?" she said later, as the full moon winked at them through gray clouds.

"If you like."

"The village of the bees."

Hugh tapped her thigh lightly with a finger. "Almost."

"There is more to tell?" She twisted round and almost fell off Lucifer. Hugh grabbed her back and steadied her till she had caught her gasping breath.

"You are a half-wit on a horse." He was chuckling: she could feel his laughter roll against her ribs.

Joanna agreed but she was not about to admit it. "I think I should teach you to read. Then I can look down my nose at you for a change."

"I am a bad pupil." Hugh lifted her hair and kissed the back of her neck. "My old teachers could tell you much."

Joanna wriggled her hips against his thighs to distract him. They rode past a darkened hut, then an orchard, then a field of some crop too dark to see.

"Enough," Hugh said then, and he rode Lucifer off the track into the field. In another moment they had stopped, Lucifer was grazing the crop, and Hugh had pulled her, and his saddle, off the stallion's broad back.

Before she could speak, Hugh had dropped the saddle off into the darkness and was kissing her.

"You will marry me, or I will tie you over this saddle and use you thus until you beg that we are wed." He cupped her backside as he had earlier that day and lifted her off her feet. "I know your passion, harem girl, and I will use it in my favor."

His hands were where she most liked them, caressing, scooping, lifting, tickling. His manhood rose like a standing stone between them and all Joanna could think of was of ripping back his clothes. "Use me, Hugo," she moaned, barely aware that she had spoken aloud.

He had bared her breasts but now he paused. "Say yes."

The night air peaked her nipples but she felt as warm as the summer. "Yes?" she whispered, tonguing his chest through his tunic.

"To our marriage. Yes?" He lowered his head and sensation flooded her as he kissed her breasts, first quick and darting, then slowly.

Her legs buckled but he had her safe. Caught in his arms he floated her safely down amidst the sweet-smelling crop of hay.

"The priest will marry us at his house. The churches may be closed by the will of the pope and King John, but he will see us truly wed."

He was drawing off his cloak and lifting her skirts and

she was saying nothing. When he dragged the saddle out of a nearby ditch and rolled her onto it, facedown with her rump in the air and her head cushioned in his arm, she said nothing.

He did not enter her, as she hoped, but stroked her flanks and her bottom, kissing down the length of her spine.

"You are a little more plump, my lady," he drawled. "A little rounder here and here. I think you are in lamb."

"You are the expert when it is we women who bear?" Joanna gasped, not as keenly as she would have liked, for Hugh was caressing her more intimately. Even as a nightingale burst into midnight song from the nearby hedge, she was singing and soaring herself, in her head.

"I have seen mares in foal." Hugh drew her more over the saddle, wrapping an arm about her middle. "You are in foal to me, and I will have your answer: Do you say yes?"

"But my father—"

"I spoke to him at the start of that never-ending feast. He is happy we wed and says I must do as I will. I will this."

His stroking hand had quickened, his fingers questing more deeply. Joanna clenched her teeth and tried to ignore the building pleasure within her. She wanted to tell him first of Elspeth's generous gift.

"I have a dowry!" she gasped out.

"From the lady Elspeth? I guessed as much. And when were you going to tell me that, eh? Wicked wench." He smacked her lightly and said in a more urgent tone, "Good girl, rise yourself to me. Come now."

The moon broke through another bank of clouds and Joanna raised her hips, feeling the delicious reward of Hugh's fingers exploring, fondling, playing between her thighs. With her face half smothered by the cloak and half on hands and knees over the saddle, she raised herself again to follow Hugh's caressing hand.

"Yes!" she cried, as the silver moonlight seemed to

change to rose about her and the sweetness of her yielding was richer than gold.

"Marry me, Joanna." Hugh had turned her again and now they were face-to-face and he was in her, deep within her. "Say you will."

"Yes."

"Say you will." He began to move.

"I will."

"Say it!" He was kissing her and staring at her, his eyes fierce with possessive tenderness.

"Yes, yes, yes!"

He caught her rhythm and moved with her, their joining suddenly urgent yet luscious, honey of the body and spirit. As he reached his climax he roared her name; as she crested her second she was beyond speech, but that no longer mattered. In this they had their own language, their private language, one they were constantly learning and re-shaping.

As one they flew into slumber, rocked and locked tight into each other's arms. When the new day dawned, it was only the alarm call of a blackbird and Beowulf's baleful howling that roused them reluctantly from sleep.

"To the priest's house?" Hugh asked.

"To the priest's house," Joanna agreed, privately hoping that the holy father might give them breakfast, too.

Epilogue

Late September rolled out like cloth of gold, rich and mellow and warmer than midsummer. Hugh had lately returned from a joust in Picardy, loaded with money, and at once addressed himself to the challenge of their orchard.

"How long has he been picking apples?" David asked.

Joanna looked up from her furnace and frowned. She was counting down in her head and did not want to break off. It was Solomon who answered.

"My son-in-law has been battling with crabs and pearmains since first light," he remarked. "I believe the lady Elspeth and your father are now with him."

"My father was fussing, was he?" David asked.

Solomon glanced at Joanna and nodded. It was common knowledge in both households that Hugh's father was besotted by the thought of his first grandchild. As Hugh had observed, he and Joanna between them had finally beaten his eldest brother, Nigel, to a claim for Sir Yves's attention.

Joanna worked the bellows and closed the door to the small furnace. She rubbed at the small of her back.

"I will see to the rest, daughter," said Solomon. "You must walk now."

She nodded and eased her way past the delicate glassware on the workbench, smiling at her father as she passed him.

"I am glad I have no stairs to climb here." She stepped out of the small workshop directly into the yard. "Father loves it here, too. He can stargaze as much as he wishes with clear views of the whole sky."

"It is a very pretty place," David agreed, falling into slow step with her. "This was a gift of the lady Elspeth's, I believe?"

"It was. Her parcel of land. The old shepherd's hut was already here and Hugh and Father built the workshop. It was the first thing Hugh did, before he went off to tourney."

"You do not mind his coming and going?"

"It is his trade." She laughed at David's startled expression. "Forgive me. That is how I think of it. He has his trade and I, when he is away, have mine. 'Tis true that he has cut down on the number of jousts he attends. He says he no longer has the taste for it and he thinks the time is coming when King John and his barons may wage war against each other here in England."

David offered her his arm as they crossed over a ditch and out into the narrow track leading to the fields and orchards. "You are comfortable walking?"

Joanna glanced down at her own wide midriff and nodded. In truth she had felt well throughout her pregnancy, although standing tired her.

"Are you comfortable now, David?" she ventured.

"I am accepted back within my order. They accept I have no relics from the Holy Land."

"Truly?" Joanna still was uncertain about David and the relics, but again he was adamant.

"I have no relics with me."

He did not say he never had, Joanna noted. The mystery

remained, although she found that she did not greatly care. "But are you content?"

"I do well enough at Templecombe." He turned and walked backward for several paces, watching her rather waddling gait. "I paint when I can. That brings me peace. I finished a new painting yesterday evening: the head of Christ. The head of the preceptory is to install it in his house."

"He gave you leave to visit today?" Of late David had begun to call on her and Hugh: the entire Manhill family seemed utterly fascinated by her burgeoning pregnancy.

David coughed and shifted to stride forward again. "Sir Brian knows I am here," he said evasively. "But Joanna—" He stopped her with an arm. "Why are you and my brother on this little small holding? You have a full, rich household and lands."

"A new stone castle with well-stocked kitchen and buttery, and lands bordering these here," Joanna agreed. "Lord Roger-Henri delivered most generously on his promises." *To Hugh's delight and astonishment.* "But for my own work, this place is best."

"Secret, certainly," remarked David. "I cannot see the homestead now, surrounded as it is by trees and the curve of the hillside."

"Discreet," said Joanna firmly, and now she decided to sharpen their conversation. "Why are you here, David? You came but two days ago!"

"I have news. News Hugh will enjoy." He smirked, suddenly shedding twenty years and looking almost a lad again. "Bishop Thomas of West Sarum is under investigation by his archbishop. The chatter at Templecombe last evening was that he may face charges of heresy, and questions as to his treatment of prisoners."

"Not so!"

"Indeed."

"Lord Roger-Henri again?"

"Who knows? Does it matter?"

"Not to me," Joanna admitted. Nor, she suspected, would Hugh care greatly. She stepped up to a wattle gate and ditch, the boundary of their orchard, and stood aside for David to go first. "If you will tell Hugh I am here, he will fetch me in."

"I can lift you over the ditch and move that gate," David offered, but she shook her head. "I have had this already with Sir Yves. Hugh is most determined it should be him and no other."

"I would be the same," David remarked. Surprising her then, he kissed her softly on the cheek and touched her forehead, as if he blessed her.

As he hurried away, Joanna thought of how matters had resolved and sublimated of late. Thomas under investigation, David reconciled within himself, Sir Yves closer to Hugh than he had been for years.

And Hugh, her powerful, wonderful Hugh, her new husband, running to her through the orchard, the sunlight honey on his restored, midnight-dark hair. She waited his coming, secure in the knowledge of his love.

"Dear heart!" He reached her and swept her up, big and heavy as she was, circling with her slowly, so she would not feel sick. "You do well, little one?"

"Very well, Hugo." It amused her vastly that he still called her little. "And you?"

"How can you ask? You are here. The keeper of our child. My beloved."

She kissed him. "Are you sorry now you took me hostage?" she asked, to tease him a little.

"How can I be?" His blue eyes shone with love and trust as he kissed her in return. "You hold my heart hostage. We are quit in debt. We are equal, love."

"And safe," she said. Finally, after years of wandering, she and her father were safe.

"Rich, too, which always helps!"

Laughing, Hugh lifted her again, over the ditch and into the orchard, where she readied herself for many tales of his battling with the apples.

Thrilling Suspense from
Beverly Barton

__Every Move She Makes   0-8217-6838-7 $6.50US/$8.99CAN

__What She Doesn't Know   0-8217-7214-7 $6.50US/$8.99CAN

__After Dark   0-8217-7666-5 $6.50US/$8.99CAN

__The Fifth Victim   0-8217-7215-5 $6.50US/$8.99CAN

__The Last to Die   0-8217-7216-3 $6.50US/$8.99CAN

__As Good As Dead   0-8217-7219-8 $6.99US/$9.99CAN

__Killing Her Softly   0-8217-7687-8 $6.99US/$9.99CAN

__Close Enough to Kill   0-8217-7688-6 $6.99US/$9.99CAN

__The Dying Game   0-8217-7689-4 $6.99US/$9.99CAN

Available Wherever Books Are Sold!

Visit our website at **www.kensingtonbooks.com**

Nail-Biting Romantic Suspense
from Your Favorite Authors

__Project Eve   0-8217-7632-0 $6.50US/$8.99CAN
   by Lauren Bach

__Klling Her Softly   0-8217-7687-8 $6.99US/$9.99CAN
   by Beverly Barton

__Final Scream   0-8217-7712-2 $7.99US/$10.99CAN
   by Lisa Jackson

__Watching Amanda   0-8217-7890-0 $6.99US/$9.99CAN
   by Janelle Taylor

__Over Her Dead Body   0-8217-7752-1 $5.99US/$7.99CAN
   by E. C. Sheedy

__Fatal Burn   0-8217-7577-4 $7.99US/$10.99CAN
   by Lisa Jackson

__Unspoken Fear   0-8217-7946-X $6.99US/$9.99CAN
   by Hunter Morgan

Available Wherever Books Are Sold!

Visit our Website at **www.kensingtonbooks.com**